More Than a Game

Fayroll
Book One

Andrey Vasilyev

Copyright © 2017 LitWorld Ltd. (http://litworld.info)
All rights reserved.

ISBN: 9781520952741

With special thanks to:

This books is dedicated to all those people who spent their youth in the online world, but now because of work and family can only visit the online world through our books. Also to the wonderful readers in Russia and the CIS who made my work popular so that new readers can discover Fayroll.

I would also like to show my special thanks to Jared Firth who has done such a wonderful job translating my work and also Marat Gabdrakhmanov for his wonderful illustrations.

And finally the team at Litworld who have been so supportive and helpful during the process.

Table of Contents

Chapter One 5
Chapter Two 15
Chapter Three 26
Chapter Four 38
Chapter Five 47
Chapter Six 66
Chapter Seven 86
Chapter Eight 104
Chapter Nine 116
Chapter Ten 128
Chapter Eleven 138
Chapter Twelve 150
Chapter Thirteen 170
Chapter Fourteen 180
Chapter Fifteen 190
Chapter Sixteen 201
Chapter Seventeen 217
Chapter Eighteen 229
Chapter Nineteen 240
Chapter Twenty 252
Chapter Twenty-One 268
Chapter Twenty-Two 284
Chapter Twenty-Three 295
Chapter Twenty-Four 307
About the Author 326

Chapter One

A Frolicking Mammoth

Our head editor, Mammoth, knew how to surprise everyone in the office. His real name was Semyon Ilyich, of course, but behind his back, the only thing anyone ever called him was Mammoth. He was imposingly tall, had a powerful build, was hairy as a bush, and spoke with a booming voice. Sometimes, he'd curse up such a storm that even correspondents accustomed to war zones and other hot spots were impressed by the variety and intricacy of his language. At others, you'd find him in the editorial office chatting with the Koreans in their native tongue. Once in a while, he'd even drop some breakdance moves at corporate parties.

And every time, the wide-eyed expressions of everyone else in the office (and we'd seen just about everything there was to see) would elicit the same response, "What are you so surprised about? Back in the day, I..." That would be followed by, "...served on a submarine," "...acted in a movie," "...spent a year in Seoul." The list goes on. And it didn't matter when it looked like there might be a discrepancy in his timeline; if Mammoth said it, it was true.

And that brings us to this particular day, as I picked up my phone to hear his voice, "Nikiforov, is that you? Sober?" *You've got to be kidding me.* Only once had I ever shown up to work drunk, and that was after a long party more than a year before. Needless to say, it was an occasion he refused to forget, enjoying every chance he had to throw it in my face.

"Come over to my office."

When the boss asked you to come to his office, it meant somebody needed something—and I was never that somebody. I could do without those little taunts, but what could I do? I stepped through the door to see that something was wrong; he was sitting at his desk with a thundercloud expression on his face that Genghis Khan, himself, would have been proud of.

This can't be good.

"Nikiforov, it's about time you did some work around here."

I was right; it looked like I was the day's sacrifice to our fearless leader. He really was a vampire—couldn't go to sleep until he'd gorged himself on someone's blood.

"You call this journalism? I call it crap. And everyone else does fabulous work! Take Petrova. She got a job as a bank teller, worked for a month, and got an inside scoop on their HR problems. They hire country bumpkins, leave them on probation, and pay them so little they're jealous of bums on the street outside. They enjoy these young little bodies and then fire them the day before their contract is up."

He waved his hand. "Hell, Sevastyanov worked with the police to uncover an underground casino. So maybe he just wanted to write an article about a casino he had found, and maybe he got drunk and blabbed to an old friend, and maybe that friend worked for the police. But they figured it out. He got an official award from the cops, and that same night, the casino cracked his skull with a pipe—a bonus, I guess. That may have landed him in the hospital, but our numbers are up, and that's the important thing. And what about you?"

"What about me?" *The defense is ready, your honor.* "Petrova has her 'Give it a Try' column, and Sevastyanov is on the crime beat. If you care to remember, all I have is the society column. It's one long string of nothing. What is there to write about? Who's fighting with whom; who cursed who; which men are sleeping with which other men; how we're all just drinking our lives away? It's the same people traipsing from one club to another, doing the same thing day after day." I paused as at thought struck me. "Well, sometimes they throw in a little cocaine or heroin for good measure, to spice things up a bit."

Mammoth grunted and said, "I'll give you that. People aren't who they used to be… Just take you, for instance, showing up for work straight off a bender." He saw the glare on my face and waved it away. "Okay, okay, I'm just kidding. But really, your articles lately have been rough. No, let's call a spade a spade; they're terrible, and that's why I'm giving you a story."

I wilted on the spot. Mammoth had decided to give me a story? Himself? Of his own free will? Up was down, black was white, and hell had frozen over. After all, he might as well have had a sign over his door that read, "Let your imagination run wild, you parasites, and don't forget to liven up the facts. And if that's not what you're about, then don't let the door hit you in the ass on the way out." And here he was giving me a story? I looked at him warily...

"Okay," Mammoth said unfazed. "Do you happen to know what the most popular form of entertainment is right now?" Again, he waved any answer away. "Eh, don't answer that—you'll just mutter something about booze. Virtual worlds are currently at the top of the list—the latest generation, I mean, with full immersion. You know, where there's a capsule you get into, and they attach some kind of electrodes to your skull. Then voilà, you're transported into another reality where you're covered in iron with a club in your hand...or a sword. Whatever.

"They say your real life is *there*, and you come back here just to wolf down some food and go to the bathroom. It's ridiculous, obviously, but there must be something to it if so many people are doing it. I want you to try it, see what it's like, do some fighting, and write an article..., actually, six or seven feature-length stories with follow-ups."

"Semyon," I quickly whined. "I don't play games! You should really have Petrova do it; she's the one who should 'Give it a Try.' But no, she gets to be an animator in Turkey or work for someone on Rublevka.[1] I'm the one stuck climbing into capsules. And you know what—"

"Oh, stop it!" roared Mammoth, shaking his disheveled, uncut, gray mane. "All Petrova knows are the letters on her computer, and sometimes she has problems with those. Just recently, she was looking for the 'any' key on her keyboard. She couldn't find it and spent the whole morning crying. And don't give me that crap about how you don't play games. Do you think I don't know about those office LAN battles you started a few years back? You obviously know something about games."

"Where would I even get a capsule?" I broke out the big guns, playing on his stinginess. "I know how much they cost. And subscriptions cost an arm and a leg. You think I'm paying for all that myself?"

"You don't have to pay for it." Mammoth grunted. "Remember the people in suits who came by the other week? No? It doesn't matter. They were from Raidion, the company that designs the capsules—and the game, of course. Naturally, they gave me a capsule and a game certificate. And that got me thinking about how I don't do any of that stuff…"

Then, it all made sense, the old fart. Jeans—it had to be jeans—advertisements, usually paid for in cash, that masquerade as part of an article or movie. So he was getting a cut under the table. *What do you know?*

"…and a VIP account for a whole six months. I don't think people like that would give us just any old crap, and whatever they made, can't be that bad. So, I want you to walk around in there, check it out, and write an objective, good—let me emphasize, GOOD—article. And if it isn't good, we'll have another talk about your alcohol problems. Or maybe I'll just fire you for betraying the level of trust we've placed in you. Anyway, tomorrow the capsule will be delivered, so make sure you're at home starting at around two. As soon as they set it up, get in there. You have two weeks…no, make that a month. Just so long as I have a six- or seven-part series on my desk at the end of it. And write something about Raidion—the capsule is comfortable; your back doesn't hurt afterward; it's easy on the ass; something like that…"

If I was logical about it, Mammoth's stream of consciousness should have sent me off to drink my sorrows away with a drooping head—if only to maintain my reputation. *Hey, if you say I'm an alcoholic, that's what I'll be.* But I wasn't in the mood for booze. Instead, I quickly gathered the papers on my desk, stuffed them into a drawer, and announced to my officemates, "Ciao, suckers. Mammoth sent me on a work trip for a month, so you all are welcome to turn green with envy."

"I hope you're on your way to Chechnya or Antarctica," Kaleria Georgievna chimed in sarcastically. She wrote the "Our Little Friends" column about pets. We all called her the Rat, thanks to her toothy face, gray hair, and gnawing personality.

"The perfect place for you!" she declared.

"Nope." I shook my head. "It's Sochi for a month to write about life on the beach. The velvet season[2] is coming up, so everyone who's anyone is there!"

"Son of a bi-i-itch!" groaned half the office, and I ran out with a wave of my briefcase. Everyone was about to go jump down Mammoth's throat about how he paid the annoying kid to spend the month of June in Sochi instead of someone better or more decorated, and I wasn't about to stick around for him to make life miserable for me. *But really, what business did he have bringing up my drunken adventure or giving me jeans assignments? And without offering me even a tiny cut!*

On my way out of the building, I contemplated my profession. The work of a journalist is something like that of a detective. First, you collect information, then you mull it over for a while, and then... Well, then you finish the job. Detectives use the information they gain secretly against a specific person or group of people, so long as they had an agreement ahead of time. For journalists, the opposite is true. We put the information before the public, and in so doing, earn ourselves a reputation and enough money to put food on the table.

Although, hold on a second, I thought, maybe "reputation" wasn't the right word. From then on, I'd talk about the "experience" or "XP" I got from beating quests, killing monsters, or going through whatever else there was to do in the game.

I'm a gamer now. Phew boy! Although, maybe you have a reputation in the game, too? That doesn't matter now. Time to collect information.

On my way home, my mind wandered back to the RPGs and MMORPGs I'd played umpteen years before. I hadn't been hardcore or anything. I had been a normal kid growing up in the age of computers, so I spent plenty of time browsing social networks, paging through forums, and sometimes even looking up porn. (And don't give me that "only perverts look up porn" nonsense—everyone does...it's just that not everyone admits it.) And, of course, I played games. Shooters had taken up most of my time, though I played enough RPGs to know my way around them. Everything was different now: capsules and virtual reality that felt, well, real.

Incidentally, let me take a moment to introduce myself. I haven't told you anything, which isn't right, though there isn't much to tell... I'm 36 years old from Moscow. I'm divorced and don't have any kids. I live alone, and I've spent my 36 years much as anyone else my age has. I'm a typical big-city guy, who grew up in a typical home, and I have a typical life ahead of me. I was born, went to school, went to college, and enlisted in the army. (Okay, so it's a little out of the ordinary to enroll in the army after getting a degree...) I served out my contract, found a job, got married, got divorced, and here we are.

I joined the army because I had nothing better to do. You know, sometimes that's how it goes. You're living a full, satisfying life, and then one day, something happens, and you're left with nothing. That's how it was for me. I had a degree, a girl, KVN[3], a sweet ride (it may not have been new, but at least it was a Chrysler), and a best friend. Then I graduated, my KVN fell apart, the chassis broke on the Chrysler, and it would have been cheaper just to buy a new car. Then I caught my girlfriend with the guy I thought was my best friend. So that's how it went, almost like in a movie—one minute I was on top of the world, and the next I had nothing.

Then I did something I'd never done before: I unloaded the whole mess to my dad, who downed a shot of rum and said, "Go join the army. That'll clear your head. When you spend all your time hungry, people yell at you all day long, and you wonder if you'll be given a rag or your toothbrush when it comes time to clean the toilet, you stop caring about everything else. It's just in the movies that soldiers think about their girlfriend back home. There, you just care about finding more food and getting out of extra work. Well, and you try to get hit as little as possible. Or you could join the navy—they'll make your life look like a fairytale. It's brutal."

So, I headed over to our local recruiting office, where the shocked blockhead of a recruiter almost signed me up for the psychology division. *From Moscow? With a degree? Wants to join the army? Came and volunteered because he wanted to learn something useful?* The poor guy's head almost exploded.

Off I went for a year and a half. Marines? Paratroopers? Nope. I went for the military engineers. And wouldn't you know, my old man was right; when you're always hungry, your most valued possession is a roll of toilet paper (newspapers make your butt itch), and your ribs are sore from the punch Sergeant Poletaev gave you the day before (those hillbillies sure do love city people, and especially Muscovites...they love them straight into the hospital sometimes), everything else takes on a different perspective. My KVN fell apart—no problem, we were never all that close to begin with. The car broke down—no worries, the subway was built to weather a nuclear war, so it would be there until the end of days. Your girl ran off with your ex-friend—is that really that big a loss? Ah, though a helping of mom's borscht and a few of her tiny cupcakes...

Still, six months in, it got a lot easier, and nothing lasts forever; everyone's contract is up sooner or later. Eventually, I was back home, bedecked in ribbons, commendations, and a shiny service record. My dad took one look at me, told me I was a man now, and handed me the key to the apartment he had gotten from my grandfather. I celebrated with a healthy helping of vodka, made the night better for a healthy helping of girls, and heard the good news that my ex-friend had already had time to both marry and divorce my ex-girlfriend three months after the wedding when he caught her under a neighbor.

I spent some time wondering if she was then passed on to the neighbor like just another hand-me-down. Then, I dug up my old journalism diploma, blew the dust off it, looked for a job, and found one at a newspaper called the Capital Herald. And so, there I was, waiting for the capsule. Actually, I did more than just sit there; I also collected information. The day before, after I left work, I had decided to just grab some food and hit the sack, but today, I dove into the game forums.

So there it was: Fayroll. It had a ton of players, swords, magic, and a bunch of races, specializations, and crafting. There were four enormous—absolutely gigantic—player zones with lots of locations on a single-player continent. A newly discovered second continent was still being developed and wasn't as densely populated. There were extensive quests, a fully nonlinear process, and myriad NPCs (non-player characters) built into the game to give players quests, help them, hurt them, or simply create a fully immersive atmosphere and ambiance. The main thing that had changed since my gaming days was that, instead of a monitor (and later a neuro-helmet) and third-person view (or sometimes first-person), the game featured 100 percent immersion. In other words, the only difference between it and the real world was that it wasn't real.

I glanced at the clock and shook my head. Already three o'clock, and still nobody. *Maybe they won't come?* I thought. *What then? Maybe everything had changed, the certificate had been canceled, and I was off the hook?* And, of course, just when I started to hope for the best, the doorbell rang. I opened the door, and two glowering, uniformed men tramped into my apartment, one older than the other.

"Is something wrong?" I asked gloomily. They didn't cheer me up.

"Of course there is," answered the older one. "You live on the seventh floor, and your elevator doesn't work. We had to carry this monster up here ourselves, and it's a beast."

And with that, they carried in a box about five feet tall in which, it appeared, a fairy-tale steed waited to rush me off into a magical world of swords, magic, fatal beauties, and daring adventure. My only comfort was that it wouldn't be for long.

An hour later, the furniture had been moved around (it turns out that the capsule had to be set up just so in a certain area), swear words had flowed freely, and the capsule was in place. My new friends left, and I circled the novel object that had taken over my apartment.

A few turns, and I had a grasp of what, from the outside, looked something like a bathtub and something like a small boat with wires and other attachments sticking out of it.

"Well, waiting won't change anything. Let's see what this guy can do."

And I sat down at my computer.

Before the installers left, they explained what I needed to do and press. According to them, during the first launch, the machine read your subcortex, aligning the equipment to maximize player comfort. I asked them if it was possible to get overly engrossed in the game, and they told me it had a feature that disabled player activity when the system detected that the player's brain was at its limit. The player was forced into a dream state where his vision was blurry and he lacked coordination. Basically, it made it impossible to play the game. I thought that was a smart way to do things. I remembered friends back when I used to play games who would get so involved that they went for 12 to 16 hours without eating or drinking. I've seen junkies who looked better...

The whole monstrosity (the installers called it a "neural bath," though I stuck with "capsule") was hooked up to my computer, where I first registered and created an account. My first surprise was that I could only play one character. Back in the good old days, I could have five accounts per server, and many more characters, and there were almost unlimited servers.

But not here. *Pick something and play. Level-up; develop skills; and accumulate things, friends, and enemies.* And if I didn't like the result or got tired of it, I could delete it—with everything I had accumulated and my entire backstory—and get a new one. Those were my only choices.

Here we go.

The first thing the program asked was if I wanted to select a name. I could either pick one from the list or think up a new one myself, though I was too lazy for the latter.

I knew finding a good name was important. It's something I needed to be smart about. And what was funny was that, while you could take all the time you needed for the game, when you were born, you had no choice but to accept what you were given. Sometimes, as in my case, that left you with a less than ideal moniker. I have no idea if it was alcohol, atmospheric pressure, shock and happiness that I was born, or what, but my father named me Harriton. He named me and never gave it a second thought; I was the one who had to live with it. All through school, college, and especially the army, I was just happy when people called me Harry (which means ugly enforcer in Russian). The alternatives were much worse.

I entered the first letter of my real name, and the program pulled up a list of prepared usernames. One, in particular, caught my eye:

Hagen. There was something about it that I liked, and as someone who tends to trust his intuition, I decided to go with it. Much better than my real name, anyway.

Race: human. I had decided that back when I was a young gamer before anyone had ever heard of Fayroll. Elves were too watery, dwarves were ugly, and halflings had hairy legs. And forget about orcs, trolls, and goblins—they were just evil. I mean, sure, lots of people enjoyed playing them, and that's fine; some people like lollipops and others prefer pickles. But I stuck with humans, seeing as how that's what I was most used to.

And that was pretty much it. Fayroll was different from the games I'd played since you picked your class and specialization after the tutorial—a starting location without aggressive monsters, where players can't kill each other. This area was called Noobland (some developers have a sense of humor).

Now, I had to decide who I wanted to be by choosing an instructor and getting a class quest from him. For instance, if I wanted to be a mage, I had to find the mage instructor and get a quest. If I wanted to be a thief, I would have gotten my assignment, and head off to steal something, grab a drink, and land in prison. *Want to be a hero? Go for it!*

Attribute points were assigned more or less how they always were: players distributed them themselves with each new level. One important difference was that Fayroll didn't have any multiclasses; everyone picked a specialization for themselves, and that was it. That specialization would be the only one you'd work on. No archetypes like mage/thieves or warrior/clerics.

I agreed to let the program base my physical appearance on my actual appearance and decided not to read all the digital garbage they threw at me. And with that, I was treated to solemnly drawn-out music reminiscent of a drunken bagpipe band. I grunted. On the screen, a message let me know that the character Hagen had been created.

"Thank God. We'll start with a prayer," I said as I lay down in the bathtub/capsule, manipulated what the installers told me to manipulate, and saw a light at the end of a tunnel that led my new character into a whole new world.

Chapter Two
A Brave New World

"Ha! It's Beloomut!"

That was my first reaction to the Fayroll world. The light spat me out onto a fairly narrow street lined with stumpy wooden houses that reminded me of Beloomut, a small provincial town where I spent many happy summer vacations as a child. Even the newest buildings there looked exactly like what was on either side of me. For a split second, I could smell the fields of my childhood, the bonfires we lit in the evenings, baked potatoes, and the dust under my bike tires.

Turning around, I looked at where I had come from. It was a carved arch surrounding a pearly film. The childhood aromas wafting around in my head were quickly blown away when some guy dressed in something markedly exotic tumbled out of the arch, glared at me ferociously, and announced, "Geez, dude, why are you standing in the way like that?"

And off he ran. I turned to look down at myself and realized I wasn't dressed any better. Thinking about it now, the word "dressed" doesn't begin to describe the picturesque rags I wore. *Maybe you've seen those old kalikas*[4] *in movies set in Vladimirian Rus? It's the same thing, only I don't have a harp.* A tattered shirt made out of canvas...or hemp, I have no idea, pants made out of the same thing, and a bag fit for a beggar, with a wooden cup and a few clumps of bread inside. Oh, and the smell—again, fit for a beggar.

And that brought up an interesting point: the Fayroll press release said players could play as anyone. What about a bum on the street? What skills would they have to develop? "Begging," "tin-can scavenging," and "stink," a passive ability that weakens opponents for five minutes? I'm kidding, of course. Although to be fair, one popular internet portal I read mentioned that beggars made the best RPG players because they were used to poking around all the nooks and crannies they could find in a relentless search for anything people left lying around.

And that's exactly what the game was about—picking up the loot you got from monsters, crates, pitchers, and anywhere else some sick developer dreamed up. Ultimately, bums on the street spend their time looking for anything interesting lying around, trying it on, and eventually just keeping the best trash they can find. *So what's the difference between a gamer and a bum? Okay, forget it. None of that matters. We don't need a beggar; I am a warrior, a powerfully built tank of a man; a pillar of the band; and the hope of orphans, the wretched, and the destitute. A barbarian or a paladin, although it doesn't look like there are any paladins here.*

So, I started walking down the street.

"Hey, man, want to join our group? We're going to take a look around Noobland, do some quests, jump up a few levels."

I turned to see a stocky dwarf with a ragged beard and leather clothes that were actually kind of decent. Next to him, was a pair dressed the same as I was.

"Come on," said the little guy, whose name, judging by the label above him, was Frori. "We'll find one more and get going. I know where to find some good quests, so it'll be great. Then we'll head over to Aegan."

Aegan, Aegan. I mentally paged through the guides I'd read briefly. *A-a-ah, Aegan—the city players go to after Noobland. The gate to the big world.*

"Sounds good," I told the little guy. "Send me the group. Though I should tell you ahead of time that I'm going to be a warrior."

"No problem," he answered. "Be whoever you want. Here's the group."

A window popped up that read:

Frori is inviting you to join his group.
Accept?

Needless to say, I clicked "Accept."

You joined a group! Leader: Frori.

"So, Frori, can we go now, or what?" I asked my new leader.

"No, we're going to find one more first," the dwarf answered as he attentively scanned the players walking and running by. And the stream of players entering the game was still going strong, lending credence to the traffic numbers I hadn't really believed.

"All right, cool. Then I'll be over in that corner looking through the settings."

I walked over to a fence in front of a building, crouched down to lean against it, and pulled up the attribute menu.

Basic attributes:
Strength: 1
Intellect: 1
Agility: 1
Stamina: 1
Wisdom: 1

Well, I thought. *Not great. Whatever. I'll go do some fighting with that dwarf, unlock a few levels, and that will help. He obviously isn't just trying to help people—there's something in it for him, too. Every operator has his weak spot, though. You just have to find it.*

While I was there mulling things over and waxing eloquent on the meaning of life, life wasn't just standing there waiting for me. The same misfits kept marching by like a rag parade, though the rags differed in color, the number of holes they had, and how they were patched. Admin certainly spared no expense when it came to design. Oh, and one of the tramps had been snagged by our fearless leader Frori. Noticing me watching him, he beckoned me over with his shovel-like hand:

"Hey, warrior, get over here. The group's ready, so let's head off to see Auntie Doris and start our first quest. Some lake goblins are bothering her during the day and keeping her up all night with their noise. And you know Auntie Doris—she's the kind of woman you respect and appreciate. So let's go find those goblins their own little corner of hell."

"That sounds fine," I started. "But what are we going to use to kill them? Our bare hands?"

"Oh, right." Frori seemed taken aback. "You don't have anything. No money either. Right? Nobody has anything? Yep, thought so. Okay, let's do this: I'll buy you each a club from the NPC in the store over there. He'll give me a good deal. And in return, you'll give me all the loot you collect today."

And there we have it! A smooth talker, that one. So, that's how they did business around there. Let's see: five shmucks, 6-7 hours of fighting to get through 2-3 levels…that was a lot of marketable loot, even if it was cheap. Farm that for a couple weeks by plowing money back into gear that costs next to nothing, and you had your start-up capital. And you even got some experience to boot. Plus, there was no risk whatsoever, and it wasn't as if we had a choice. If we said no, there was always someone else lining up to take our places.

But I wagered, later, right before it was time to leave Noobland, he would say, "Sorry, guys, there's something I really, really have to go take care of." And he would go create a new group. If someone he helped along ever made it big, he could even sidle up to them later with a small reminder, "Hey, you don't remember when I bought you your first club, do you…?"

And wipe away a tear…

Two of our groupmates gleefully shouted that they were in, even if the little man was a dwarf, while an elf named Oygolinn (the one Frori recruited last) stood there weighing the decision. Soon, he too acquiesced and nodded. Well, as long as everyone else was down for it, so was I. *Life's more interesting in a group.*

After we all decided to make a go of it together, giving up our loot to the entrepreneuring dwarf in the process, he quickly took us to the local supermarket and bought us the simplest clubs he could find. There was a lot in the store, though it was all kind of plain. On the other hand, I wasn't expecting anything special at that point.

Simple Club
Single-handed weapon
Damage: 6-10
Damage type: bludgeoning
Durability: 80/80

The dwarf then grandly announced, "And now that you hold in your hands your very first weapon in the Fayroll world, remember this moment and never forget it!" That served only to confirm my suspicion that if any of us ever became a serious player in the game, sooner or later he'd come knocking like the ghost of Christmas past.

Auntie Doris lived in an adorable little house seven or so minutes' walk from a beautiful lake. Frori thumped on the carved walnut door and, as we entered, whispered a quick command in our direction, "Wipe your feet. If you track dirt into the house, we'll never see the quest. She's a huge clean freak."

Inside, the house wasn't just clean; it was as sterile as an operating room. Auntie Doris herself turned out to be a little old lady with gray curls, a clean apron, and a white bonnet. She looked exhausted.

"How are things?" asked Frori. "How are you feeling, Auntie Doris?"

"Ah, what a polite dwarf! Not great," replied Auntie Doris sadly. "I can barely sleep with all the noise and uproar every night."

Frori jabbed me in the side and hissed, "Ask why. I already did this quest, so they won't give it to me."

Of course, you did. I imagine this isn't your first time here either...

"Where's the noise coming from, ma'am?" I joined the conversation. "Who won't let you sleep?"

"It's those lake goblins," the old lady threw her hands in the air. "Who knows where those cursed beasts came from, but now they live in my little lake. Every night, they're off rabble-rousing so loudly that I can't go to sleep. They tap on the windows, they make faces, one even climbed up onto the roof recently and ran around up there until the rest joined him. And then they dragged some old trough up and slid down it screaming, 'It's a bobsled, baby, yeah!' What's a bobsled? Probably some kind of goblin curse. It's awful. I barely have any shingles left on the roof!"

The old lady began to weep silently, wiping away her tears with a snow-white handkerchief she pulled out of her sleeve.

"Okay, Auntie Doris, what if we go scare those goblin monsters so badly they never again come anywhere near your house?" I suggested.

"Oh, you dears, please do help," the sweet old lady looked at me hopefully. "I don't know how I could thank you, though. I don't have anything to give!"

"Don't worry about it," I smiled. "We're pioneers out to help people, so we don't ask for anything in return."

You have a new quest offer: Rein in some Hooligans.

Task: Kill 10 lake goblins, so the rest leave the lake near Auntie Doris' house.

Reward:

200 experience

3 pieces of cheesecake from Auntie Doris

3 apples from Auntie Doris' orchard

Accept?

Once everyone had gotten the quest, we once again assured the old lady that the goblins were about to meet their maker and left.

"There are other quests here, but they suck," observed Frori. "Go here, go there. Deliver a letter, fill a barrel of water, make a spit handle. Nothing you need a club for, and certainly nothing that will get a good shot of adrenaline running through your veins. Beating up goblins, though—much better. Experience and some fun at the same time!"

"And the loot isn't bad," I said, taking his thought to its logical conclusion.

By the time we finished chatting, we had gotten to the edge of the lake infested with antsy goblins. A few other players scurried around the shore waving weapons.

"Listen up!" Frori waved his stubby shovel of a hand. "This is the lake with the goblins. We'll lure them over here one by one and take them down together."

"Why one by one?" asked Oygolinn. "Why don't we just get a group up here and be done with it?"

"That won't work," Frori disagreed. "They only come up out of the lake one at a time, first of all, and once they do, they're a lot for you to handle. You're still just Level 1, and they're Level 3. We have to gang up on them, so we'll need a kill queue."

"Well, isn't that a nice way of putting it," I said to myself. "A kill queue. That would be a great title for a detective story."

"Hey, guys!" yelled Frori to the other players who, like us, were anxious to kill some of the watery interlopers. "Who's last in line for the goblins?"

"I am," answered an elf with the proud and hard-to-pronounce name of Euardenalil. "Wait, the five of you are all going to kill just one of them?"

"Yup," answered Frori. "Though not just one. There are five of us, and we want to take out five of the goblins one by one. Fair's fair. Then we'll get back in line to complete the rest of the challenge."

"Ha! Fair!" a dwarf named Forin was outraged. He had arrived after us looking for goblin blood. "And how long do the rest of us have to wait while you five have your fun?"

"No longer than it will take you to kill one of them," Frori said. "We're sitting here yammering on and on, and that moron over there still isn't done."

The whole time we'd been talking, a human named Zubiloff had been trying unsuccessfully to finish off one of Auntie Doris' whiskered and toothy antagonists. Zubiloff wielded a knotty stick that he used to occasionally run up to the goblin and take off some of his hit points. The goblin, in turn, spun like a whirligig, grimaced, and tried to sink his needle-sharp teeth into Zubiloff. A couple times, he landed a bite.

"Anyone want to bet on the winner?" grunted Oygolinn.

Frori looked at him thoughtfully, coins glinting in his eyes. Our enterprising dwarf seemed to have taken what I thought was Oygolinn's joke seriously. Oygolinn was equally thoughtful as he watched the ongoing battle, explaining that there were three types of goblins: lake, forest, and mountain.

Lake goblins posed the least danger to players. They were the least aggressive, so they'd stick to harmless tricks like throwing dirt at you and spitting on your back as long as you left them alone. They ate leaves, snails, and anything else found in a lake, and they only lived in settled bodies of water. Shiny things were irresistible to them, and that's exactly how we planned to lure them over to where we were.

Forest goblins were different. They were much more dangerous and evil, especially in groups, and they were even insatiable cannibals. Humans and dwarves taste equally good to them. Some people said they'd eat anything they could get their hands on—even rocks. They lived in the woods, and you could find them everywhere in Fayroll.

Mountain goblins were the rarest and smartest of all. They preferred to stay away from humans, though they loved sending avalanches of rocks or snow down on anyone they saw walking anywhere near a slope.

"How do you know so much?" I asked Oygolinn with respect in my voice.

"I read through a lot of forums before I joined the game," was his dignified reply. "You need to understand the game if you want to get anywhere."

Just then, Zubiloff made one last valiant lunge, hacked at the goblin, and landed a fatal blow. The goblin squealed, twitched a few times, and gave up the ghost. His body splayed over the grass.

"Let's go, ear boy, cast away." Frori pointed Euardenalil toward a fishing pole lying on the shore. A large coin was tied to it. "Come on, you're holding up the line."

"And next it's your turn," said Frori, glancing at us. "Remember that we're not using the last strike rule, so experience is distributed evenly between us no matter who gets the kill. I'll rile up the goblins, so they only attack me. I have a higher level and more combat experience, so the rest of you need to wait for me and then jump in with everything you've got. With five clubs, we'll crack them like nuts. And remember, I get the loot we collect from them."

A message popped up:

The group leader set a new loot distribution rule: Only the group leader.

Five minutes later, it was our turn to dirty the lake with goblin blood. Frori picked up the fishing pole and cast the lure. At first, nothing more than a few bubbles came to the surface, though they were soon followed by a small whirlpool. A slimy goblin head surfaced, half ears and all wrinkles. His eyes roamed the shore looking for the coin he'd spotted underwater.

Frori grabbed the coin and waved it around to attract the goblin's attention.

"Give it here! Mine!" squawked the goblin, leaping in the direction of the dwarf.

Our leader nodded his head and, once the goblin was close enough, landed a blow with his club.

"Ooph!" the goblin howled, trying to sink his teeth into the dwarf's shoulder.

Four more clubs rained down on him from all sides. The goblin's health bar quickly turned red, and a few seconds later, he whined his life away.

"One down," noted Frori. "Back to work, gentlemen."

The coin flashed off and sank beneath the water.

And so we took a few turns, waiting in line each time. But the third was almost immediately followed by an announcement:

You unlocked Level 2!
Points ready to be distributed: 5

Judging by the satisfied faces of my compatriots, they had also leveled-up. Frori took one look at our faces and shouted, "We're not done yet! There's a goblin coming out of the water!" So we fought on.

About three hours later, we'd leveled-up one more time, at which point Frori announced, "All right, let's be done. They don't give us too much experience, and you're already a few levels in. We could stay here forever, but let's go finish the quest, and we'll do some moose hunting."

We headed for the house, where Auntie Doris stood on the porch. She looked at us with her hand on her head.

"Well, Auntie," Frori happily proclaimed, "those goblins won't bother you anymore. We took care of them."

"Oh, you're wonderful!" The old lady looked like she was about to break into a happy dance. "And I made you something delicious!"

You finished a quest: Rein in the Hooligans.
Reward:
200 experience
3 pieces of cheesecake from Auntie Doris
3 apples from Auntie Doris' orchard

We thanked the kind woman and crunched away at our apples as we walked away from her home toward the town center.

"Okay, sit here for a minute and distribute your points." Frori brought us to the nameless town's central square before heading over to the store, presumably to sell the goodies we got him.

Okay, so what do we have? Ten points. Here goes:

Basic attributes:
Strength: 6
Intellect: 1
Agility: 2
Stamina: 5
Wisdom: 1

I decided not to worry too much about it and invested most of my points in strength and stamina, seeing as how those are most important for swordsmen. One point for agility and that was it. I'll make it somehow without a brain. Brawn—check... Well, future check... Presumably.

The only difference between the moose hunt and the goblin battle, to be honest, was that the moose were much better looking than the slimy goblins with all their teeth and ears. I almost felt bad killing them. Oh, and we had to run after them sometimes, though we could avoid that by strategically assigning positions to everyone in the group. Also, there was no quest. But it was fun hearing everyone yelling and screaming:

"He's running, grab him!"
"By the legs! Grab his legs!"

"Don't let the moose go!!!"

"Yea-a-a-ah!"

The day drew to a close, and it was almost dark when the four of us nearly simultaneously unlocked Level 4. With that, Frori said, "Well, that's that, my children. You're Level 4 now. You got what you wanted, and I did what I said I'd do. It's time you headed over to the big world, so I'll show you the road. I wish I could go with you, but I have some things to do here first. As soon as I finish with them, I'll come find you."

We walked through the trees as nightfall set in, finally reaching a yellow brick road.

"There it is—the road to the city," said Frori. "Just go straight, and you can't miss it. Good luck!" The dwarf melted off into the gathering darkness.

"It's been fun, guys," I said to my soon-to-be former group and left it. "Aegan sounds great, but I think I'll wait until tomorrow. Time to call it a day." I glanced at my groupmates as they walked away to try to get to Aegan the same day. Then I hid behind a tree not far from the road, added three strength points and two stamina points, and clicked the exit button.

Chapter Three
In the Big World

Everything looks better in the morning. You know how it goes: a problem comes up during the day, and by the time you go to sleep, your brain turns to mush trying to figure it out. Thoughts start popping up in your head that no sane person would deem healthy, "Why me?" or "What did I ever do to deserve this?" Then you decide to screw it all and head to bed—tomorrow is another day. Out of the whole cluster of smart, acceptable, and just plain crazy options, one or two start to crystalize into something you can act on. At least, that's how it goes with me.

And on this day, the situation was even simpler. With no problems whatsoever to deal with, I woke up and thought back on my first day in the game. *All things considered...not bad!* Though I still wasn't sure why the Fayroll world was so popular. It may have been great for kids and handicapped people. The former could blow off all the angst puberty threw at them—excessive ego and a frustrated sex drive. The latter enjoyed what they couldn't in this life—people without limbs experienced life with them, mute people talked, and, really, they just got the chance to be treated as equals. Nobody looked at them sideways, and they didn't have to deal with fake attention being lavished on them. They were just a few more players on par with everyone else. I had to give Raidion some props for that.

All that made sense, but what about everyone else? What about all the fully functional and often well-off adults? Sure, the game looked great. It was realistic. The atmosphere was interesting. But games like that were a dime a dozen. Why was Fayroll the one everyone stuck with? That was something I needed to figure out.

I grabbed some food and climbed into the capsule. *Time to throw off the shackles of noobhood and take my first steps in the big world.*

I found myself sitting under the same tree I had exited by the day before. The only difference was the daylight I was bathed in. *Good morning!* Not far away, the same forest crawled with wildlife, and a bit farther away, a pair of elves happily shot their bows and arrows at a beaver that, for some reason, had left its dam and trundled toward me. The elves seemed not to care how wildly they were missing.

"Hey! I thought elves were all about protecting nature? What are you doing to that poor animal?" I yelled.

"Oh, stop it!" yelled back one of the elves. "Who do you think we are, Greenpeace?"

"We're dark elves, so we're allowed to," his friend added more politely.

"You're monsters," I answered. "Torturing animals like that... Just put him out of his misery!"

The poor beaver by this time was stuck full of arrows, though the fact that none of them had landed a critical hit meant that he couldn't give up his digital ghost. There was no blood, of course—humanism in action. The little guy kept trundling along without any dying groans for the same reason.

"Oh, screw you!" the less polite elf announced. "He isn't hurting, and we're getting experience."

I realized there was no changing their minds, gave up, and started off along the yellow brick road to adventure.

I should note that the Fayroll world was seamless, so you never had to wait for new levels to load. Noobland, that safe cradle where players were never bothered and almost never threatened, was, therefore, indistinguishable from the big world. The border between the two worlds, as far as I could tell, was where the forest opened onto a field from which the walls of Aegan were visible.

The walk along the road was anything but boring; there was too much going on. First, a sobbing girl, about six or seven years old and wearing a pink dress, stopped me and plaintively cried, "Sir, would you help me?"

"What happened, sweetie?" I assumed the pose of the Brave and Valiant Protector of Little Girls.

"My name is Mary, and my little lamb is lo-o-o-ost! We're always together, and now I can't fi-i-ind him!" Tears poured from her eyes.

"No worries, let's go see what we can do!" I responded.

You have a new quest offer: Find Mary's Little Lamb.

Task: Find and save Sean, Mary Sue's lamb.

Reward:

300 experience

Accept?

That word "save" had me a bit worried, but I didn't have much choice. The hopeful look Mary gave me saw to that...

The snow-white lamb wasn't far away. Far from it. It was in the next field over—though it wasn't alone. The lamb was there with five or so rabbits, if you could even call those creatures rabbits. They had red eyes, long ears, and nasty, whiskered faces, and they were Level 7. They kicked the lamb from one to the other.

I watched the spectacle and wondered what the developers must have been smoking to come up with that kind of surrealism.

"Sir, please help Sean!" The little girl pulled on my sleeve.

"Right," I responded. "And if I go help him, who will help me? Your little friend's a goner, and we'd better get out of here before they see us."

Mary burst into tears, which attracted the attention of the rabbits. They stared over at us, obviously deciding if they should give us the same treatment as the lamb. Without waiting to see what they concluded, I grabbed Mary and took off in a headlong dash for the road. There, I quickly declined the quest, handed the sobbing girl an apple, and walked away without a backward glance. I felt a little bad, but those rabbits looked nasty. *Level 7—are you kidding me?* Good thing they didn't try to hunt me down.

Suddenly, I heard branches snap to the left of the road. My club in hand, I quickly jumped off to the side. Out of the bushes, leaped five players who then crossed the road and dove into the underbrush on the other side. Behind them, ran a gray-haired old man in the strangest boots I'd ever seen. His enormous beard fluttered in the wind, and he brandished a club in his hands. He, too, crossed the road and followed the sound of branches breaking into the forest.

"Well, hello..." I shook my head and continued on.

Three minutes later, the entire scene played out once more, this time, with everyone dashing from right to left.

Here I am just walking along, and they have someone chasing them up one side and down the other. There's an interesting life for you, I thought wistfully to myself and kept walking.

When the group dashed by for the third time, I grabbed one of them by the sleeve.

"Hey, man," I said. "Where are you running? Is it a quest? Can I come with you?"

"Seriously, you idiot?" I found myself stared at incredulously by a fidgety player named Mastik. "That guy with the beard is trying to get us. We went into the forest to cut some clubs, and he came out of nowhere. 'What are you ruffians doing here?' And bam—he started hitting us with his stick. 'You little good-for-nothings! Coming around here ruining the forest. Get out before I kill every last one of you!' A-a-a-ah!" Mastik caught a glimpse of his pursuer bursting out of the forest and dashed off.

The old man stopped when he got to me and looked suspiciously at my weapon.

"Factory-made," I quickly assured him. "I love the forest. When I was little, all I cared about was protecting wildlife."

"Better be." The old man, who was labeled "Forester," looked at me darkly and melted into the woods.

"Crazy," was all I could say.

Soon, I got to the edge of the forest, the point that marked the end of the starting location. A dwarf had been planted there to make sure everything was clear, and he had a lazy warning for me, "Friend, this road will take you to Aegan, after which who knows where you'll follow it? But you won't be able to come back. If there's anything you still have left to do here, do it before you leave."

"I don't have anything here. I already did it all."

"If you say so," said the indifferent dwarf. "Good luck in Aegan."

The city had me speechless from the moment I entered. In fact, I stood stock-still after my first steps through the gate. I've already mentioned the backwater town in Noobland and how quiet and quaint it was—old people going about their business, children playing pranks on the cats...or beavers, I guess. Hushed tones, soft colors...

But Aegan was a big city that never sleeps—noise, hubbub, everyone running, everyone in a hurry.

Welcome to Aegan!
It is a city shrouded in centuries of legend, renowned for the power of its mighty kings, made famous by its great craftsmen, and built on the bravery of its warriors. The name "Aegan" reaches far back into the oldest annals of the Seven Kingdoms...

I was only too happy to read more about the city's fascinating history. It was built somewhere way back in the forgotten reaches of time, after which it became a fortress city. Later, it was a stronghold of the monarchy, and it was now a hero city.

"They have some good writers," I noted to myself. "A well-written text, easy to read, good presentation."

"Don't just stand there!" A voice behind me boomed, and I was shoved to the side. The voice happened to belong to a hefty dwarf by the name of Gnorin, and he had a following of six other dwarves behind him.

"Hurrying to find Snow White?" I asked in a needling tone.

"What, you need some teeth loosened?" Gnorin responded in the same bass voice.

"No, I'm good," I responded honestly. "I need them all."

"Then don't be a douchebag. Sorry if I shoved you too hard—I'm a dwarf, after all."

"I see that," I noted. "I'm not blind."

"Is there a tavern around here? Or a pub? Really, anywhere they sell beer," asked Gnorin. "Do you know of any?"

"How should I know? I just got here."

"All right, we'll follow our noses. Cheers."

And with that, the gang of dwarves headed down the central avenue leading away from the gate, one after another. Never fear, off to find beer.

"What's with everyone here?" I wondered. "Sadistic elves, alcoholic dwarves... It's like a bad fantasy novel."

I started down the same street, looking around me as I went. The city, of course, was beautifully drawn. The buildings, trees, monuments, inhabitants...everything looked real. If I hadn't known it was a bunch of code, I would have thought I was in some European city from the Middle Ages. And it was obviously huge. I came across empty corners, found alleys packed with players, saw a few squares littered with tents of some kind, noticed some temples, and even walked by a theater—or maybe a courthouse.

And so my wandering and wondering led me finally to a place whose name I could have guessed even without the marker: Market Square. It was pretty simple, really. What else could you call a place packed to the gills with everything you could think to buy? People milled around, noise filled the air, and I was jostled from side to side. Somebody was selling something, somebody was buying something, and everyone was talking, screaming, and bustling around all at once.

"I need a bow, Level 35 to 37! Rare or epic! I can pay!"

"I'm selling elixirs—health and mana! Concentration potions! Poisons discounted when you buy in bulk! Manufacturer warranty!"

"I cook with your ingredients! For free! Pay for me to eat the food with you!"

"Buy a sword, get a sheath free!"

"An eastern dagger, from Sind, sharp as a razor and as long as...your life, eh!"

"Spider eyes, fresh and gray! For crafting!"

"Fish! Fresh, still alive! Dead and dried as well! Fish!"

And stands, stands, and more stands all around, with flags, signs, and even banners. In short, it was a nice place, even a great place, though there was one problem—I had no money. And, judging by the cries I heard from the crowd packing the square, I wasn't the only one.

Just then, as if on cue, a little halfling scooted up to me, "Hey, man, give me 10 gold; I need them for a jacket," he gushed at me in one breath. "Everyone knows me; I'm good for it—I swear. I'll buy the jacket, go farm some loot, and give it back to you…with five extra!"

With that out of the way, he stood gazing at me and even urgently tugged on my hand.

I'll admit, it isn't easy to surprise me. I'm a journalist, and I even served in the army, so anyone or thing that can actually surprise me is worth at least my respect. "Ha!" I coughed. "Well, look at you. You're way too amateurish about this. Use your brain! Write a sign, 'Help needed for mental development, give money for logic tests.' There aren't any around here, so you can cut to the chase."

"Are you going to give me the money?" he asked impatiently, apparently without hearing a word I said.

"No," I answered simply, and he was off like the wind.

"Wow," was all I had to say.

I started to feel left out, as it was very clear I had no business in a place like that with empty pockets. And that meant I had to get out into the world and somehow make some money. I just had clothes—sort of—and a club, so I had nothing to lose and nothing to keep me there. I pulled up the map, found the city exit, and set off in that direction.

A forest began directly outside the city gates. Well, not so much a forest; more a grove of trees. *Huh,* I thought as I walked into the shadows. *I wonder if cities in the Middle Ages had woods right outside them, too. From the movies and TV shows I've seen, they definitely didn't. When invaders (or liberators, depending on the plot) laid siege, they ran screaming across an open plain before the camera swept to their hordes scrambling up the walls and putting the city to fire and the sword. Well, or to free it from the clutches of a tyrant. I wouldn't think they made all that up just for the movies. They probably had some kind of villages right outside the walls and needed grazing land for all their cattle and horses. I guess nothing needs to graze in the game, and there's no point in making players walk forever, so they put the woods right next to the walls.*

The forest was beautiful, both reminiscent of a real forest and, at the same time, different. It was similar in how picturesque it was, with all the grass and clean air. A great spot, and completely unrealistic. In a real forest, you trip over dead wood, mosquitos eat you alive, and there's litter everywhere. I found myself liking the virtual forest better—it was clean, neat, and cozy. And it was full of things I could use to get experience and money. A rabbit ran by with all its experience, fur, and meat. A hardworking badger rustled away while a wiggly snake slunk off. Well, fauna, meet Man, your destroyer. I felt bad for them, but I felt worse for myself. All I had was ragged pants, and I needed to level-up. *Well, if Man is the king of nature, it is time for nature to pay its dues...or tribute, or whatever it is...*

I valiantly ravaged the animal world for four hours or so, twice leveling-up. My bag was packed with all my dead trophies, though by the end, I was pickier about what I kept. At first, I harvested everything I could from my unlucky victims. During the last hour, I only kept the skin, which I knew I could sell. Badger meat wasn't exactly in high demand.

Once I leveled-up the second time, I decided to stop and spend the points.

Basic attributes:
Strength: 10
Intellect: 1
Agility: 2
Stamina: 7
Wisdom: 1
Available points: 10

I decided to go with the obvious. As long as I was going for a tank, I'd go for a *tank*. Six points for strength, three for stamina, and one for agility.

"Well, that was a nice little break. Time to get back to work," I said, pulling out my club and dashing off after a rabbit that ran by me. Having expected more from life than what I gave him, he moaned almost sadly and died.

I bent down to skin him and heard a villainous voice behind me, "That happened to be my pet rabbit. I remember when he was just a bunny—he even ate grass right out of my hands. And now you killed him. What to do, what to do…"

Not only was the voice villainous, but it also had a mocking undertone. I slowly straightened up and turned around. A few steps away stood three goblins. Not just your ordinary ruffians; these were honest-to-goodness goblins, although, judging by their demeanor, they were ruffians, too. They were nasty-looking, with ugly green faces and teeth that stuck out at odd angles.

Wait a second, maybe they were actually orcs? I wasn't really sure what the whole difference was, but that didn't matter. The first thing I noticed was their strange names ("Euiikh"...excuse me?) that glowed red above them. I had the unbelievable luck to meet people who killed other players, most often for fun and loot. That fact and their level (25-27) made it clear to me that there was no way I was getting out of the situation with what I had in my bag. And so it turned out that all I would get for the whole four hours I spent hunting was a little experience. How frustrating.

"Would you look at this, boys? He doesn't even care. But I think he should pay for killing my little fluffykins," the one with the green mug spat mockingly. "My little bunny."

"M-m-m...bestiality. Aren't you the little creeps?" I understood that my imminent death might be fairly unpleasant, as the orcs/goblins appeared to be looking for some fun. At least, I wouldn't feel pain in the game, and I wouldn't get any fountains of blood. Still, it wouldn't be an enjoyable experience. I needed to rile them up and get everything over with, so I could respawn and start over. Although as I thought about it, I had no idea where I'd respawn.

"I heard your kind..." I said with a contemptuous grin. "Wait, who are you? Orcs? Goblins? Either way, I heard all of you and your ugly green mugs are into that animal-loving. The good stuff. Although, wait a second, are you using the animals or are they using you? I guess it makes more sense if they're using you, just judging by your bulging eyes and the way your teeth stick out like that. Yeah, I can see how that could happen after some bison took a good run at you..."

I got them, for sure. Their leader's face turned ash gray, and his eyes narrowed. Honestly, I might have overdone it a bit, though that was when a short (by their standards) orc screamed, "You little fart!"

34

He swung the morning star he held in his stubby hand. My world shattered into something like a photo album. I saw stars...the angry, frustrated face of their leader...a spinning sky. A familiar haze settled in, and I found myself standing in an area near the city wall. No pants, no club—just in my underwear (Apparently, the game's developers didn't want to traumatize the young generation by making them look at naked bodies.) They sent freshly killed players to the nearest respawn point or to the last place they saved, and all cities and villages had respawn points. So the good news was that death wasn't the end. On the other hand, I was resurrected without any of my belongings, which go to whoever killed you. They left me in my underwear, but other than that, nothing. At least until Level 10, you didn't lose any experience, although, after that, you were screwed. If you croaked, you lost everything you had, as well as the experience you were working on.

Just then, I heard my inbox ping. I looked around to see a mailbox that, thank God, wasn't far away from where I respawned and went over. To my surprise, I saw that Euiikh, the green-faced leader, had written me.

> *"You displeased me, my little white-faced friend. You killed my rabbit, said some unpleasant things, and died too easily. That last thing I find especially frustrating. And so, I just want you to know that this was only the first of many meetings, all of which will end in your death. However, you will not die so quickly in the future. See you soon."*

Like a villain pulled straight from some opera, if the email had had audio to go with it, the last words would have been followed by an evil, booming "Wa-ha-ha-ha!" Although I had the urge to respond and suggest that he find a nice little donkey to make love to instead of his rabbit, I decided it wasn't worth it. Those idiots would be trolling me as it was, and a reply like that would start World War III. Much better to keep building my character and get even with them later. I could find a big old mace and wreak havoc on them, though I needed to remember their names—at least in the blacklist. It was like in the old joke: I don't remember evil, so I have to write it down. At least the game had a feature that let me know when they were nearby. I figured that would give me enough time to get away while my level was still low and I hadn't found a super-mega-giga mace.

"This sucks," I complained as I sat down on a bench next to the respawn point. "I don't have anything, no clothes, no weapons, no money. All I have now is a bunch of enemies and my underwear, and that won't get me any further than a virtual church to beg for some change." At one point, I even thought, "Maybe I can just forget the game? I've already seen enough to write an article, and players themselves won't read it. They don't subscribe to our newspaper, and nobody else really cares whether the article is written well from the perspective of the players or not. I can just add some filler, throw in a plug for Raidion, and call it a day."

On the other hand, what was I going to do for a whole month? There wasn't any leaving the city since Mammoth could check to see if I ran off somewhere. And really, was I going to get chased off by a few ugly orc assholes? That wouldn't do. But ramming their heads up where the sun doesn't shine—that would make for a great story.

And, it's not bad here. Before everything happened, the game had been like a free and easy excursion. You know, it's like winning a tour of somewhere in Rostov—it's a nice city, and it's free, so why not go? Although it's not like you'd spend money on it. The city isn't bad, it's just that it doesn't really matter to you. But if it's free, why not? It was the same thing for me; I played because it was free, sort of my job, and not too stressful. But now, everything was different…and I still needed material for my series.

But if the game was going from "Why not?" to "Let's see who gets the last laugh," I needed a plan. Right away, I needed two things: clothes and a weapon. Oh, and I desperately needed someone who knew the game inside and out to teach me the ropes.

That was when I remembered Fat Willie.

Fat Willie was a classmate of mine who cut a rather remarkable figure. Willie was short for William, and I have no idea why his parents gave him a name like that. Maybe they adored Shakespeare, or maybe they enjoyed Tokarev's work and extravagance. Or maybe they'd had one too many drinks after he was born and before they took him to the passport office (that last one seemed most believable to me). Whatever the case, that was his name, and until he was about

12, everyone called him Wilka. It was around that time that he started to put on weight, and by the time he was 14, he weighed around 80 kilograms. That September 1, when we all got to school for the first day of ninth grade, Pashka Kapitanov, one of our class leaders, saw him and said, "Forget Wilka. You're Willie now."

"He's 'Fat,' not 'Willie,'" contradicted Pashka Velikanov, another of our authorities.

The two Pashkas sniffed and looked each other over (the two had vied for the role of top dog ever since first grade).

"Come on, guys, lay off it. You're fine," I intruded, knowing they would soon mix it up if no one stepped in. "We'll just call him Fat Willie."

And so it was decided.

The only one who couldn't care less about the whole situation was Fat Willie himself. The guy never let anything ruffle his feathers. He was as phlegmatic as it gets.

But what he loved more than anything was computer games. When the conversation turned to them, he'd come alive and could chatter on for five or even ten minutes straight. He also had a kind of strange sense of humor. To be honest, I wasn't always sure when exactly he was joking.

So if there was anyone who could get me started, it was him—and I couldn't imagine him missing out on a game like Fayroll. I left my alter ego sitting on the bench and exited the game.

Chapter Four
Fat Willie and His Joke

For whatever reason, my life up to that point had taught me to follow through immediately on the decisions I made. That had something to do with KVN, then the army, and certainly my experience in journalism. After all, putting something off meant giving yourself the opportunity to change your mind, let laziness creep in, or have someone else beat you to the punch. *That's how we humans are: put something off once, and we'll think of a thousand reasons why we shouldn't do it at all.*

And so I immediately decided to get started on both of my ideas. I put some hot dogs on to boil and headed to the attic to look for the box I kept all my old papers, phone numbers, notebooks, and diaries in.

"Where did it go?" I asked myself as I looked for Fat Willie's phone number. "I know I wrote it down in a notebook. Nadya Mamedova was there, we were drinking, and she laughed so hard at me for using a notebook when we have phones, tablets, and virtual diaries. I remember telling her, 'If the electricity ever goes out, and you lose all your gadgets, I'll still have Fat Willie's phone number.' She said, 'Why would you need his number when there isn't any electricity?' And I answered, 'I'll use the paper to light a fire.' Then, while we were chattering at each other, Willie up and walked out without saying a word. He couldn't care less, and I was drunk off my rocker. Ah-ha!"

I found Willie's number and prayed that:

1. Willie hadn't changed his number
2. Willie hadn't gotten rid of his phone altogether
3. Willie was in the real world
4. Willie hadn't found his way (we hadn't seen each other for two years…maybe three) into the loony bin (for excessive gaming) or an obesity clinic (fast food is fast food, after all)
5. Willie was still in the land of the living

So imagine how happy I was when his phone rang three times and was picked up. That same old voice drawled into the line, "Hello?"

"Willie!" I happily shouted into the phone. "You're in the real world! What happened?"

"Oh, Nikifor," Willie responded in his usual hum-drum voice. (At school and even afterward, people called me Nikifor or just Kif.) "I'm at work, who's going to let me play here?"

"You got a job? But you're a nonconformist, fight the system, all of that. Passive, sure. But what happened? Did you switch sides?"

"I still fight the system, and it still fights me. I fight it online; it fights me in real life. I use programming, and it keeps me hungry, cold, and without tobacco. If you're hungry, you'd better go find a job. And hey, go easy on the 'passive' thing. It's a good word, but 'passive warrior'...sounds kind of insulting. Anyway, what's up? You must need something, it's been three years since we last saw each other."

"Have you played Fayroll?" I cut to the chase.

"I play now. I mean, not right now, of course, but every night." He didn't say anything for ten seconds or so, then continued. "Why do you ask?"

"I'm writing an article about it, so I'm in your gamer universe now, too. I played for a day or so, got to Level 5, and someone killed me. Willie, I don't think there's anyone in the world that could show me the ropes better than you can."

It might have just been me, but I thought I heard Willie exhale in relief.

"Sure thing. Where are you now? I mean, in the game."

"In Aegan. At the respawn point."

"Okay, so by the western gate. Go into the city, and you'll see a tavern called the Lonely Troll about three hundred meters on your left. It's cheap, not a bad place. And they have rooms you can go into to chat quietly. Let's meet at 7 tonight, Moscow time—I'll come home from work, grab some food, and head there."

I agreed immediately.

"How many times have you respawned?" Willie asked.

"Once."

"That's it? Phew boy! In the beginning, I practically never left—I must have respawned a hundred times. Okay, see you tonight!"

Fat Willie hung up the phone. I did the same and jumped over to the cooktop, where my hot dogs were past ready. The game's the game, but I was hungry.

Sure, it's humiliating, I thought to myself, *though half the people out there are running around in their underwear. Plus, at least it isn't the real world.* I tried to make myself walk to the Lonely Troll. After all, it was just three hundred meters. But it wasn't just any old city where you might have twenty players milling around. This was Aegan, the capital, and each meter there is like three in most of the places in Fayroll. And then I had to deal with the tavern, where I was sure to be the butt of any number of jokes.

Still, I managed to walk through the gate to the city. Though when I did, the reaction I got was anything but the one I expected.

"Hey bro, they got you, too?" asked a bearded archer walking by.

"I'd give you some pants, but I don't wear any," a mage standing by a bookshelf remarked sympathetically.

"Those damn idiots," muttered a gloomy dwarf. "Open your exchange window."

I opened it and received 10 gold.

"Buy some pants. And a shirt. Can't be looking like that," said the dwarf, who hopped away quickly on his short legs without even waiting to hear me thank him.

"Wow," I said with surprise. "It looks like most people are sympathetic around here."

I had almost gotten to the pub when I heard a laugh that was barely human.

"Get your naked butt over here," yelled a hefty barbarian dressed in iron with an enormous battle hammer strapped to his back. "I'll sing you a lullaby!"

I mentioned that Fat Willie had a very odd sense of humor. Well, there it was.

"You got bigger," I told him when I got closer. "I imagine you have to be careful where you sit down."

"You have to be realistic," roared Willie. "It would be weird if my 140 kilograms decided to play some skinny elf, no? Open your exchange window."

He sent me five pairs of pants, the same number of shirts and coats, a sword, a club, a mace, and a shield. All very cheap, without any upgrades.

"Here's a little handout for you. You'll be killed again, and this way you'll at least have something to wear when you respawn. Put one set on now, and leave the rest in a room."

"Where?" I asked.

"Did you even read the manual?" Willie blinked in puzzlement.

"Well, I read the guides about leveling-up and the history of the world."

"Wasn't that clever of you?" My friend even let out a slow whistle. "Okay, look. You can go into any hotel, and they'll give you a room. Not for free, of course, but you won't go broke. That's your personal space, so the only people who can go in are the ones you invite—and only when you're there, too. The things you leave there never go missing, and you're the only one who can go get them. Leave everything important and valuable there that you don't need to keep on you."

"Live and learn," I said in an ingratiating tone.

With pants and everything else on, I felt much surer of myself.

"Willie, can I ask you some more questions?"

"Let's go find a room, and we'll get you your answers. Or not, depending on the questions."

We walked into one of the separate rooms in the pub.

"So what's your question?" Willie started off, at the same time ordering from a pretty waitress. "Meat and beer. A lot of meat, and five times more beer than meat."

"Not 'question,' questions. The first is what I need to do to get those PKers off my back."

"Level past them, get some serious equipment and a weapon," Willie answered amiably.

"That'll take forever."

"Then buy a character that's already there."

"You can do that?"

"You can do anything you want in Fayroll." There Willie stopped, quickly glancing at me. "A lot of people level-up characters to sell. It isn't exactly legal, but the admins generally look the other away. Still, they're not big fans of it."

"Do they really go after you for buying players?"

"No, they can't prove it, so they don't do anything. Well, as long as you don't make the sale in the game itself. I haven't heard of anyone being dumb enough to do that, though."

"How much does a character like that cost?" I was really intrigued to hear how much you could make providing that kind of service.

"It depends," Willie laughed. "Let's say you decide to sell yours—you wouldn't get a single kopeck. Who needs it? But if I decided to sell mine and threw in all the armor and everything in my room, I could buy an apartment. Maybe not in the center, maybe a one-room apartment on the first floor somewhere in Degunino,[5] but still—an apartment. And if one of the top players decided to sell their character…"

"An apartment for a chunk of code?" My surprise was genuine.

"What did you think?" Willie grinned ironically. "It's a business. A big one. The money pouring through here…damn. I mean, that's true for all the top games. In Korea, some guy sold an account for a game that's been around for a while. Sure, it was an ace account with all the sets collected, all the dungeons beaten, a personal dragon, all the quests, and everything, but still—walked away with 10 million."

"Dollars?"

"I don't remember what they have in Korea, but in dollars, it was 10 million." It was obvious that Willie envied the Korean.

"So what did he do?"

"You're asking me? Maybe he opened a car dealership. Maybe he makes coffee machines or paid off his debts. Maybe he hacks away at a mannequin with a wooden sword day and night. How should I know?"

"You're kidding me," I scratched my head. "I can't believe it. Here I thought it was just a game…"

"Ha!" Willie's considerable girth jiggled with laughter. "People live in the game, and the people on top, live pretty well. Don't forget that you can exchange gold for real money—so there's an underground market and an aboveground market. Okay, tell me this, why do you think people kill other players? I mean, sure, there are some crazies running around, and plenty of assholes. But a lot of people PK to make money. You take out a player, and you get his clothes and everything else. Sure, there isn't much there, but hey, it's like Raskolnikov: 'Ten old ladies make a ruble.' You can sell it all for gold, and then exchange the gold for real money."

"So how many players do you have to kill?"

"PKers aren't really in any hurry. They get something from you, something from the next guy. And they hunt in groups of two or three, and, say, a group of three at Level 23-25 with normal gear can easily take out a Level 40 tank. And it isn't just the money; they get stuff they can auction off, too. So yeah, but that isn't all. You have no idea how much money changes hands in the clans…damn. And the better the clan, the more money there is going around, and the more you get from the clan, obviously."

"What do you get?"

"That you'll have to figure out on your own, my friend. Some things I won't even talk about with old schoolmates, not to mention in the game. Politics, you know? Drink your beer."

While we were talking, the NPC waitress brought over our beer and meat. Willie began pounding the bitter-smelling liquid by the liter, though I just sipped mine.

"Really, if you don't want to keep respawning, you'll need to join a clan," Willie continued through a full mouth. "Just make sure it's a good, strong clan. That way, PKers will know that killing you will bring the wrath of God down on them. The whole clan will blacklist them and hunt them across the entire continent. The only problem is that you can't get into a clan like that."

"Why not?"

"Why the heck would they need you? A Level 6 tank. You're a dime a dozen in Fayroll. Only a noob clan would take you."

"A noob clan?"

"Yeah. Losers nobody needs make their own clan and stick around the starting locations or the Noobland exit to farm and attract more players. They say they're going to take the game by storm, everything's going to be great, they have a solid reputation and steel balls... Though really, they're just stroking their ego. 'Look at me, I'm a clan leader.' There's this one guy, Amendak, who runs a clan called the Great Fayroll Army. He's a clown. Gets a group together to build some kind of army. People last a day or two until they start wondering why they're paying to spend time with him, and then he goes back to Noobland to start over. Clown..."

"Can I join your clan? What's it called, by the way?"

"Messengers of the Wind, but you can't join. I'm getting up there in the clan, but we only take Level 45s and higher. Sometimes, we make exceptions, but only after a group vote or if the clan leader okays it personally. Oh, and only if you have something we need. That's even easy-going, though—the Gray Witch in Hounds of Death, for example, only accepts Level 60 and higher, and even then they're picky about who they let in. Drink!"

I downed a glass and saw the world around me grow a little fuzzier at the edges.

"So what should I do?"

"Keep leveling-up. Work on your abilities. Then, see what you can do. Oh, by the way, I have an offer for you. You're writing an article, right?"

"Yep."

"Mention my clan, say something about how friendly we are, how great it is."

"Why do you care?"

"First of all, a little PR never hurt anyone. Second, I'll give you 100 gold for your trouble. And third, once you get to Level 45, you'll have an ace up your sleeve that we won't forget. So what do you say?"

"Sounds good. And I have a request for you, too."

"Go for it."

"Don't tell anyone that I'm a journalist." I'm not sure why I asked that. Some kind of instinct deep inside me, and I trust my gut.

"Nobody here knows you anyway, but sure."

Fat Willie sent me 100 gold and raised his glass, "Let's drink to working together, and I'll teach you one last lesson!"

I drained my glass in one gulp and realized that I'd lost control of myself. I was a wooden doll, limited to the shortest of thoughts and seeing out of button eyes.

"And there's your last lesson," said Willie as he stepped toward my carcass on the floor. "Stay in control of yourself no matter what. This isn't the real world, where you can just go throw up and feel better. Now you won't be able to move for half an hour."

As if in confirmation of his words, a message appeared:

You're drunk as a sailor. Movement and articulate speech are limited for 10 to 30 minutes.

He rolled me up in a rug lying on the floor and stuck me under a bench near the window.

"Ah," he smiled cheerily as he walked out. "A fine joke! If you need anything, send me a message."

Hilarious, I thought, wrapped up and left in the corner. *He was trying to get me drunk the whole time. I guess he's spent time boosting his alcohol tolerance!*

As I mentioned, Fat Willie's jokes were always unpredictable. I remembered how, one time at school, a classmate of ours tattled on him to our teacher. Willie managed to slip both a laxative and an emetic into the snitch's coffee, after which he stood in the bathroom and watched the poor guy try to figure out which end he should point at the toilet. An unusual sense of humor, to say the least. Still, I was happy with our meeting. I'd gotten some clothes, some information, and 100 gold…better than nothing. Life was looking up! Sure, I ended up on the ground wrapped in a rug, but that I could live with.

Just then, the door creaked and, judging by the sound of their feet, three people walked in.

"Who was that big guy?" asked a female voice.

"Wild Willie from the Messengers," a deep and heavy male voice answered. "Forget about him. Gerv, what do you think?"

"I'm not really thrilled about what you did, Elina, but what's done is done. The decision is made, and the Hounds of Death have our assurance," said the third voice. It was also masculine, though, in contrast to his friend's, it was quieter and ingratiating.

I had no idea what was going on, but the message I got from my intuition was clear, "You're screwed now…"

Chapter Five
Clan Volunteer

"Hey, why are we talking here instead of in the fortress?" the woman asked with some nervousness in her voice.

"They have great beer here," the bass answered. "Maybe the best in Fayroll. Also, it's cheaper—those portal scrolls cost money."

"Penny wise and dollar foolish."

"Oh, sure, look at everyone spying on us. Hey, miss, bring us some beer," he barked.

"Why do you have to be so rude, Gorotul?" The question came from the one they called Gerv.

"It's just who I am. Get used to it!"

"That's a shame," the woman sadly added. "Definitely not good."

"And what you did is good?" Gorotul suddenly asked her. "You betrayed our partners, and that's putting it nicely."

"Betrayal at the right time isn't betrayal. It's foresight," noted Gerv.

"Come on. Maybe we shouldn't talk about this here. Let's go to the fortress. People will find out sooner or later, but I'd rather it be later," the woman said cautiously.

"Oh, stop it," Gorotul brush her off carelessly. "Why worry so much? Ah, our beer!"

I heard some gurgling as the owner of the bass slurped his beer into what sounded like a large stomach.

"Okay," said the woman. "What do we have right now?"

"That's a rhetorical question," Gerv answered positively. "We don't have anything right now, though if things play out right, that might change."

"Exactly," noted the woman. "If we don't support the Plains Eagles and the clans they're allied with, or even if we just announce our loyalty to the Hounds of Death, our reputations will take a beating…"

"Basically, they'll call us traitors and rats," clarified the bass, taking a deep breath after downing his beer.

"It's a risk for our reputations," the woman pushed on, "but that's all since they won't go as far as to openly fight us. And really, sticks and stones... On the other hand, however, we earn the friendship of the Hounds of Death, and maybe even a partnership with them."

"And what do we get from that?" the bass chimed in again.

"Oh, come on, Gorotul... Gerv, I can't do this anymore, explain it to him." Light, feminine steps came toward me, and the bench I was laying under creaked.

"Look, my dear barbarian," came the soft voice of the one she called Gerv. "The Hounds of Death are a powerful clan. An influential clan. A clan with a long memory. And they always remember who their friends and their enemies are. We can't do anything to hurt them since they could crush us without breaking a sweat. But we could help them... Leaving would significantly weaken the clan alliance the Hounds are focusing on more and more. It would be a moral and literal blow to the alliance, and things like that aren't easily forgotten."

"Well, okay. And just like that, we'd look like rats—and we wouldn't even get anything out of it."

"We'd get something out of it," Gerv quietly chuckled. "Our reputation would suffer, but our horizons would brighten. Sure, we would violate our agreement. Yes, we would pull a bit of a dirty trick. Okay, so we would have to grovel a bit... What's that face for?"

"Grovel? Why?!" roared Gorotul.

"Do you want to get to Rivenholm? New lands, new quests, get the clans over there to bend over for us?" the woman chimed in.

"Of course," answered Gorotul. "Why even ask? Everyone does."

"How many ships does our clan have?"

"Two. And we're building two more."

"Is that enough for a full convoy? Enough to get there, considering the competition will be trying to sink us every step of the way? Kraken and his tentacles? Jolly pirates flying the no less Jolly Roger trying to run a jihad on us landlubbers? Whatever else might happen?"

"Of course not," admitted Gorotul. "Although nobody's ever gotten there, as far as I know."

"Exactly. So what's wrong with asking the Gray Witch to let us join their flotilla? As attendants. If we help them and show that we're loyal, she probably won't mind. And if we can prove ourselves to be a reliable, friendly, and useful clan for the Hounds of Death once we're in the flotilla, they'll help us when we get to Rivenholm. And you can't put a price on that. So, my dear, we will do all the groveling it takes. Happily. And it wouldn't hurt to do something else for them, something unusual..."

The woman started rocking back and forth on the bench, which made me rock in my rug. The beer inside me began complaining about the treatment it was getting.

"I heard," Gerv continued insinuatingly, "that the Gray Witch was interested in someone..."

"Yes? What kind of interest?" Gorotul laughed at his double entendre.

"Not what you're thinking," Gerv answered coldly. "Not personal."

"How do you know?" the woman asked with interest and stopped rocking, which made me feel better.

"I just do," Gerv answered evasively. "How... Well, what does it matter to you, Elina?" It's secret information that isn't meant to leave the clan. They call him Wanderer, and he hasn't reached the last level yet. The Witch is trying to find out everything she can about him, and especially wants to know where he's located in the game."

"Unbelievable!" shouted Gorotul. "You have ears in the Hounds?"

"Dear God!" the other two exclaimed at once, obviously shocked at their companion's stupidity.

"Do you know why she's so interested in Wanderer?" the woman asked.

"All I have are rumors," Gerv answered. "They say Wanderer got the Great Dragon quest."

"Oh, come on, that's nothing," announced the bass. "Just one more of who knows how many who have the Great Dragon quest."

"Sure," agreed Gerv. "But why would the Gray Witch be so interested in him? Just for the hell of it? That I doubt."

Okay, Gerv," the woman clapped. "Let's check with our contacts and see what we can find about Wanderer. Maybe someone knows something. That could be a nice bonus for us—we'll just have to do it quietly."

"Well, obviously," Gerv huffed. "If anyone learns that we found out, they'll make life miserable for us—if they don't just destroy us outright. It's no joke sticking your nose in the Gray Witch's business."

"You're telling me," said the woman. "Phew, what a day…"

She stood up quickly, the bench rocked back, and that knocked the rug with me rolled up in it out from under the bench.

What happened next could have been pulled directly from some old comedy. The rug unraveled, leaving me to thud out onto the floor, and I looked up to see the group of three staring down at me in mute surprise. There was a hefty half-orc in armor and wielding an enormous battle axe. At least, I imagined that's how half-orcs look—light-green skin, big teeth that don't stick out of their mouth like my friend Euiikh's, with a well-built, powerful body knotted up and down with muscles. Next to him was Gerv, a small human with a forgettable face dressed in unassuming clothes with a set of metal knives and a small sword strapped to his back. I guessed he was a scout. I wasn't exactly sure what a scout was. Though, judging by what he was saying, it was apparently something like an intelligence agent…or spy. Finally, there was a tall, staggeringly beautiful elf woman. She had almond-shaped blue eyes, textbook-sharp ears, golden hair, and white clothes—probably a mage. Also, she was probably more a girl than a woman.

She crouched down next to my carcass and, in her melodious voice, asked me with some bewilderment "Who are you?"

I don't know what got into me. The time may have expired for my intoxication, or maybe it was the elf's beauty. It could have been the thought that I was royally screwed, or that real life doesn't happen like in books or movies. Whatever the reason, the gift of speech returned.

"Hagen," I answered.

"Well, that's very informative," the elf observed. "How did you get here, Hagen?"

"I came here with Fat Willie for some beer. He got me drunk, rolled me up in the carpet, and stuck me under the bench," I answered truthfully.

"That's probably Wild Willie," the half-orc said, "the one who left when we got here. It's Wild Willie, though, not Fat Willie."

"Who cares which Willie he is?" the elf sadly exclaimed. "What are we going to do with this one now? He heard everything! You heard everything, right?" She turned to me.

"I heard everything." There was no point in denying the obvious. "Though I didn't understand it all."

"Well, at least he isn't lying," said Gerv. "Still, this is a problem."

"Seriously, Gorotul," the elf turned to him and said, "We have a clan fortress with spell protection, comfortable rooms, and everything else you could want. But no, you had to drag us to this squalid pub. I told you! 'The beer is good.' You're kidding me!"

She crossed her arms over her chest and nervously paced the room.

"But it is!" answered the half-orc. "And we shouldn't use the scrolls so often. We need to save money!"

"Yeah, save money. Look at what we saved," the elf responded and squatted down in front of me. "Do you understand how much you've screwed everything up by being here and hearing all of that?"

"Of course. I could tell right away." I wasn't about to argue.

"What's the point of going over everything with him?" roared Gorotul. "We'll add him to the clan's blacklist and smash him if we ever see him again. He won't even leave the city."

"Gorotul, do you even know why you're still in the clan council?" the elf turned on him.

"Because I'm cool!" The half-orc proudly stuck out his chest.

"Because you're one of the founders. And that's the only reason."

"What did I say this time?"

"Gerv?" The elf looked at the scout.

51

"Look, Gorotul," the scout started just as gently as before. "If a serious clan gets all up in arms about a Level 6 noob, everyone will notice. Their analysts will all wonder what we're doing, and soon enough, they'll guess that the noob knows or saw something he shouldn't. And they'll be right. Then, whoever figures that out first will promise to protect him, help him develop, and give him things (which is both easy and cheap), and the noob will tell them everything—and willingly. We're screwed, and someone else has hit it big. That will get the Hounds of Death breathing down our necks if they don't just kill us outright. And to top it all off, once the information gets to our old friends, they'll make life interesting for us as well."

"But aren't they going to anyway?"

"Of course not. If our plan works, we'll have the Hounds of Death behind us," the elf explained to her dim-witted friend.

"So what are we going to do with you?" She looked at me thoughtfully.

"Stalemate," I muttered.

"What?" asked Gorotul.

"Stalemate. You can't do anything much with me holding you back, but you could ruin everything for yourselves. I can't stand up to you, though I'm going to be a threat to your clan for the foreseeable future. Stalemate."

"Good job. You're smart," the elf announced.

"What's wrong with you?" Gorotul snarled. "A threat! I'll eat you right now! A threat…"

"Shh!" The elf suddenly hushed him. "I made up my mind."

"Are you thinking what I'm thinking?" Gerv looked at her sideways.

"It's the best option," she nodded.

Elina the Wise, leader of the Thunderbirds, invited you to join her clan.

If you accept, you will become a member and receive the following bonuses:

+5% experience received

-7% damage done by opponents

+4% ability to see objects' hidden attributes
+4% damage done by all weapon types
+5% protection from cold
+5% protection from fire
+15% healing received (25% when healed by another clan member)
+3% chance of receiving rare and hidden quests

You can fix two items each day using money taken from the clan account.

20% cheaper prices for vehicle rentals in areas that respect your clan

Additional bonus: Because you are joining the clan at the invitation of its leader, you get +10% items in dungeons (when playing with a group made up of clan members).

Your bonuses can be modified or increased by fostering respect within the clan.

I shook my head and said, "Wow!"

"Does shaking your head mean no?" Elina was surprised once again.

"No. I mean, it doesn't mean that. It just means I'm taken off guard. It wouldn't have surprised me if you decided to cut me up and scatter my pieces around Aegan. This is much more surprising."

"If that were possible, we'd have cut you up five minutes ago," said Gerv. "But you'd just respawn."

"So are you going to accept the invitation?" asked Elina, who was starting to get nervous.

"Hey, hey, hey," I cautioned. "Like Spartacus said, let's figure things out before we get into the arena."

"Who said what?" asked Gorotul.

"He was a famous tank," summarized Gerv, giving an answer obviously informed by bitter experience talking with the half-orc.

"Why 'was'?" continued Gorotul.

"They weren't able to buff him fast enough before he got into a fight, and he was killed. They even got his account!"

"Oh, come on, that doesn't happen." Gorotul pressed on, "What server did he play on?"

I couldn't help myself. "I heard of him, too. He played on the Italian server. The Roman server, to be exact."

"See who we have to work with?" Elina said sadly and gloomily.

"It's okay." I tried not to smile as I looked at a perplexed Gorotul. "But back to the matter at hand. I'd like to know what you expect from me and what I get out of it. Who will I owe what?"

Gorotul shook his head in annoyance at the sting of a Level 6 noob rolling out with a bunch of questions. Still, he stayed quiet.

"What do we want? We want you to keep your mouth shut about everything you heard here. Really, that's in your interests too. If that information gets out, we'll be well within our rights to do what Gorotul suggested. We'll name you a Clan Enemy, and you'll die wherever you are in Fayroll—even in the Gray Lands. If nothing leaves this room, you'll have the support and protection of the clan. You can level-up in the areas we control, and you can get clothes and weapons from the clan storehouse. Not epic, of course, but better than the crap you have. Basically, your standard agreement."

"But what if the information gets out, and I have nothing to do with it?"

"There's a spell called True Word. Ridiculously rare and expensive. But if we have a leak and you say it isn't you, I'll shell out for it to make sure."

"There's also Truth Powder, and it's cheaper," noted Gerv.

"Sure, it's cheaper, though it has a 10% margin of error," Elina nodded. "That's fine for little stuff, but not something as important as this."

"Got it," agreed Gerv.

"Well, you obviously wouldn't be buying it for my sake. You'd want to find the rat," I noted reasonably.

"Of course." Elina wasn't going to argue. "I won't spend a copper coin on you. No offense."

"And one more condition," the scout butted in. "You can only leave the clan in two cases. Either you have Elina's permission (and only hers), or you're our sworn enemy. If you leave the clan on your own, we'll hunt you down wherever you are."

"Do I have to sign something? And will I have any responsibilities? As a member of the clan?"

"You don't have to sign anything," confirmed Elina.

"The fortress sergeant will explain your rights and responsibilities to you," Gerv said with a wink that spoke volumes.

"And if anything happens, you'll have me to answer to!" Gorotul was roaring again.

I looked at them thoughtfully, remembering how Willie said that clans are good, and strong clans especially good, and asked my last question, "And what if there are three orcs promising to put me on a conveyor belt to the respawn point?"

"Don't worry about it, warrior," said Gorotul. "We'll make mincemeat of them. PKers don't get a long leash with us. Touch our noobs, and we'll hunt you down. It's a good deed, and we have some fun while we're doing it. We're the only ones who can smack our noobs around." And with that, he guffawed loudly.

"Then I'm in!" I said and tapped the button to accept.

Congratulations! You joined the Thunderbirds.
You are currently a volunteer in the clan.

"Will I be a volunteer for long?" I asked Gerv.

"You start as a volunteer; that's how our clan works. Then, a month or two later (or earlier if you prove yourself), you become a kinsman. That's when you're a full clan member."

"What then?"

"What then? When you get to Level 120, you earn respect in the clan and, if the clan council deems it necessary and possible, you can become an officer. Then, you can invite new members, you get new bonuses, and you get a nice badge next to your name. After that, it's deputy leader and, well…"

"I'm not going anywhere yet," announced Elina. "Though we could skip the volunteer stage. Maybe we should make him a kinsman?"

"Why skip it?" Gerv asked. "First, that's giving him too much. Second, we can't put the spotlight on him like that. People will start asking why he gets special treatment, and we can't have that. Let him run around with everyone else."

"Agreed," Elina nodded her head. "Okay, get over to the fortress."

"Me?" I sheepishly asked.

"Who else?" the elf sarcastically responded.

"How? I have no idea where it is!" I was taken aback.

"As if I didn't know that." I was starting to think the young lady wasn't quite the pleasant person I thought. I was going to have an interesting time of it.

"Gerv, take him there."

Gerv took me by the hand and read from some kind of scroll. The last thing I heard in the room was Elina, "Well, how much money did we save?"

Another blue rainbow spun out in front of me, and I found myself standing on a cobblestone square.

When I imagined their "clan fortress," I thought of something from my distant childhood: Walter Scott, Dumas, or, especially, something from Ivanhoe—some kind of forbidding castle built out of enormous blocks, a drawbridge, turrets, dungeons, and a courtyard in the middle.

There was a courtyard, but that was it. I mean, yes, it was all there, but not how I imagined. It was more like an overgrown country house belonging to some oilman or mid-level delegate somewhere in Nikolina Gora[6].

"Not impressed?" Gerv asked ironically.

"Nope," I honestly replied.

"Well, good."

"Why?" I didn't understand at first, though the truth began to dawn on me. "Ah-ha! I get it! The more unassuming it looks from the outside, the fewer people you'll have trying to figure out what's inside?"

"Exactly. Well done!" Gerv nodded.

"But other people could figure that out, too."

"Not everyone. Gorotul still has no idea why we like to keep things on the down-low."

"Draw it for him," I suggested. "Maybe he understands pictures better than he understands words."

"You're just a volunteer, and don't forget that," the scout turned serious. "We're talking about a deputy clan leader here. Oh, and the clan master for combat. He's no genius, but there's no one better when it comes to planning raids. If he ever invites you to go with him into a dungeon or on a raid, you'll see for yourself. Anyway, let's go find Sergeant. I'll turn you over to him for training, and then I have some things I need to do. Quite a few, in fact…"

As I had imagined, the fortress was much bigger on the inside than it looked from the outside. Either the Thunderbirds were well acquainted with the fifth dimension, or there was an extra paid option I didn't know about when you buy a clan fortress. (I was much more inclined to believe the latter option.) One way or another, there were rooms, twists, passages, and balustrades everywhere.

Gerv quickly ran through the whole maze, from time to time, pointing things out. "That's the training hall," "That's the small clan storehouse. You aren't allowed in there yet," "And that's the big clan storehouse. You'll never be allowed in there," "That's the main hall." After seven minutes or so of that, he stopped at the entrance to a small room.

"We're here. What's with the long face?"

"I'm trying to figure out how I'll find my way out of here. You're about to take off, and I have no idea where the exit is. I'll wander around until I die of starvation."

"Don't worry, someone will show you where to go. Sergeant, are you here?"

"Come in," rang out a deep bass voice. The echo boomed around and across the room.

Once we walked in, I saw that the owner of the voice was a bearded (as if there's any other kind) dwarf with powerfully built arms and a potato of a nose. From the label above his head, I saw that his name was, in fact, Sergeant.

"Huh, so Sergeant is your name," I said, voicing my surprise. "I thought that was just your rank."

"It's both, and it's a way of life," bellowed Sergeant. "Gerv, you've got to be kidding me. What, are we going to be like that Armedakil and start recruiting right in front of Noobland? Why not? We have plenty of leaders, we have so much money to spend on training that we don't know what to do with it, and we have good players coming out our ears…"

"Okay, okay, I hear you," the scout responded, waving his arms in a conciliatory gesture. "This is a one-time thing. Don't worry about the details, but it's true. Elina invited him herself, actually."

"And what now?" the dwarf muttered. "Level 6! We only take Level 25 and higher. We decided that at the council, and Elina agreed. And now you bring me this Level 6 loser."

"How am I a loser?" I was rightly outraged. "Yes, I'm a noob. Yes, I'm dressed like an idiot. But how the hell am I a loser?"

"Volunteer! Nobody said you could talk!" The dwarf turned on me. "Your job is to stand there and shut up!"

"Oh, screw you!" I quickly responded. "What is this, the army? And who are you to tell me to shut up? My parent? My boss? You think I signed a contract to come here so I could have a bunch of beards start telling me off?"

"Wha-a-a-at?" The gnome's hand started toward his belt, obviously going for his battle axe.

"Ye-e-e-es?" I mocked him. "You can't kill clanmates, that's one of the main rules of the game. And if you do, you'll be kicked out of the clan in disgrace."

"He's right," interrupted Gerv, who obviously watched the conflict with interest. "You can't kill him. I mean, you can, but then…"

"I won't train him," the dwarf said in a completely calm voice. "I won't, and that's final."

"It's your job," Gerv replied very quietly and, I thought, with a hint of a threat. "You've been stepping out of line quite a bit recently. Not happy with this, frustrated with that. And twice this month, you disobeyed direct orders from the council. Maybe you're starting to think a bit much of yourself?"

"If you think I'm out of line, why don't I just leave the clan?" The dwarf was getting himself worked up again. "You can train these puppies yourself."

"You think we couldn't find another trainer? Of course, we could. But do you think you'll find another clan that's been as loyal to you as we've been? I'm not so sure. Really, we need to have a serious conversation, and Elina shares that sentiment. We'll revisit this topic when she gets to the fortress. In the meantime, put this volunteer through basic training, so he isn't just standing there doing nothing."

"Though let's stay away from all that military nonsense. I had just about enough of that in the army. Did you serve, by the way?" I asked the dwarf.

"No," he answered shortly.

"I thought so. Paid your way out of it, and now you go around throwing commands at everyone else."

"Nope, didn't pay a thing. I just wasn't right for it, and that's all you need to know. Have a seat."

I sat down in a chair in front of the table while he settled into the one behind it. Gerv looked at us.

"Well, it doesn't look like anyone's killing anybody today, so I'm going to head off."

He pulled out a scroll, I heard a "psh-sh-sh" sound, and he disappeared in a small puff of smoke.

"All right, so the basics," the dwarf began in a slow droning voice.

Covering those basics ended up taking two hours. I heard what I was allowed to do, what I wasn't allowed to do, what I was required to do, and what I had the right to do. To be fair, what I was required to do turned out to be a bit longer list than what I had the right to do. The dwarf went through his spiel confidently, as this obviously wasn't his first rodeo, but without feeling or interest—and obviously thinking about something else.

Honestly, I didn't accept Elina's proposal just because I didn't have a choice. You always have a choice in life. For example, I could have hit the log-out button. Thank God, that was still an option. It's just that I always thought life in a clan was easier, and

Fat Willie confirmed that. But life as a Thunderbird was ridiculously complex. Things were simpler back when I played games; a bunch of people got together to make it easier to get through raids or dungeons. Having proven players that you could trust with your back was way better than just going with whoever and whatever you came across. That also gave you resources you could check with when you were in the middle of a quest, saving you the time it takes to get out of the game and crawl through forums. In some situations, you could even borrow in-game money. And, again, clans gave you pretty good attribute bonuses in a bunch of games.

This was much stricter. I mean, sure, all of that was still true, but at the same time, everyone now had their job to do. Every member, for example, gave the clan 5 percent of the money they earned. Once a week, all members Level 180 and above had to take the clan's newest members through some dungeon or cave, help them beat it, and protect them throughout the process. And there was a strict rule about spending time online—anyone who didn't log into the game for two weeks in a row without letting the game masters know ahead of time was summarily kicked out with no chance of appeal. Everything that happened in the clan had to stay in the clan. The punishment for leaking any secret information was also getting kicked out, and the leak could be named an enemy of the clan if that information was used against it. The reverse was also true: all members were required to report any interesting or useful information they came across.

Then there was information about quests, since all MMORPGs on some level, are based on fighting, beating quests, and how the world is designed. PKs, social life, crafting, and roleplaying all come out of those three pillars, and without them, you simply can't have an MMORPG. If the world isn't well-designed or is imbalanced, the players can't buy into it and go find something else. If the quests are all easy and uniform, players get bored. Sure, you can do a quest like "Kill ten foxes," or "Collect five hip joints from jumping skeletons," or "Take the letter to the old goblin" once, twice, even five times. But who needs a game where that's all you do? And MMORPGs are about everyone fighting everyone else, but nobody would want to play anything that amounted to some kind of meat grinder. You need simple quests to help you level-up and have fun along the way, but the heart of the game has to be storyline quests traced across the canvas of the game. And the Fayroll world had superquests—both epic and hidden. Epic quests let you go through tough, multilevel tasks and get commensurate rewards: the respect and friendship of non-player factions and epic and rare items that were hard or even impossible to get during normal gameplay. Hidden quests were strings of tasks you performed to get something incredibly valuable: the support (including military support) of a whole group of NPCs, items from sets, or unique abilities. They were very hard to find, and players generally came across them randomly by doing something completely unrelated or because someone from the game admin told them about them, which happened very rarely and was frowned on by that same admin. And there weren't any quest guides for hidden quests, which made them unique. Lone players who found hidden quests preferred to keep quiet about them and clans who learned about them immediately classified that information. That last part made sense, seeing as how every clan had its analysts and spies trying to dig up any scrap of information they could find, and they were willing to pay good money to get it—even real-life money. Keeping information about epic and hidden quests from your clan was high treason.

Some things were straight-up forbidden. Clan members couldn't (or, at least, that's what I guessed) kill each other. You could kill other players, but only in self-defense, and each instance was looked at on an individual basis by the clan council. The clan policy toward PKers was simple: they were not tolerated. You couldn't disobey decisions handed down by the clan council, something I imagined was based on imperial policy. Obviously, you couldn't steal from clanmates or the clan storehouse. Giving clan information to anyone on the outside was strictly forbidden. You couldn't ignore a clanmate who needed help if you happened to be walking by (although that went without saying, as that's presumably how any normal person would react).

So, life in the clan wasn't a walk in the park, to say the least, as they had everything pretty locked down. On the other hand, there were quite a few advantages. The clan offered full and complete protection from everyone and everything, unless, of course, it was your own fault you were in trouble. As we had discussed in the pub, any PKers that tried to pick off a member of the clan were as good as dead. They were hunted down by many clan veterans who were only too happy to get in on the chase. They didn't have anything better to do, after all (or at least that's what they said), since they'd already beaten all the quests and explored all the locations, so it was a fun diversion. Actually, there weren't many of those veterans, and that story wasn't exactly true. The Fayroll world was so big—even limitless, I think—that getting around to all the locations and going through all the quests was impossible, not to mention the regular updates... Still, most important was that PKers knew not to touch anyone from the clan if they didn't want problems. And that wasn't just a Thunderbird policy; it was true of all the responsible, respected clans. Although you could still find people out there itching for a suicide who didn't listen to the voice of reason.

The clan had information, weapons, clothes, components, everything one could need to craft things...within reason, of course. Anyone who wanted to learn how to do that could study with the clan master. The clan also had its own hunting lands or a few areas with different levels that newer players could use to level-up, safe from PKers. I would head to one of them the next day with the latest batch of volunteers.

And that was basically it for the rights and responsibilities.

"Got it?" Sergeant looked at me.

"Yup," I nodded.

"Then be on the square in front of the fortress at 9 a.m. Moscow time tomorrow. We'll head to Gringvort to beat up some skeletons and zombies. That's it for now—get out of here."

"Um...Master Sergeant, I can't."

"What? You know, you're really starting to get to me! Stop with your jokes! Why can't you?" The dwarf sprouted red spots, and even his beard turned pinkish.

"I don't know the way out of the fortress..."

I knew better than to hope that a dwarf who was about to crush my skull would walk me to the exit. Still, he had some brain cells left, as he called to a Level 114 mage walking by, "Eilinn, are you on your way out?"

"Yeah, why?"

"Gerv threw this volunteer at me, and he has no idea how to leave. I don't have time, you know how it is—ambushes to plan, betrayals to hunt down."

"Got it. Sure, I'll show him," the mage replied amiably. He seemed nice, with a frank face, middling height, and intriguing staff: four clawed paws holding a crown with broken-off tines.

"Unusual, isn't it?" Eilinn smiled when he saw what I was looking at.

"Yes," I answered. "Epic?"

"Epic. Let me introduce myself, and we'll get going. Sergeant always has a ton to do, and as far as I know, he's leading an excursion to Gringvort tomorrow. It isn't an easy location, takes a lot of prep work. Anyway, my name is Master Eilinn. And yours, my young padawan?"

"Hagen."

"How did you know about our outing?" Sergeant jumped back into the conversation.

"No need to ask, since it isn't polite to interrupt," the mage said to the dwarf reproachfully. The latter was quiet, which I found very surprising. "But I wouldn't expect anything different from you. I'll be coming with you tomorrow to cover the volunteers."

"Oh, you'll be there tomorrow." Sergeant lightened up. "That's great. Who else is coming?"

"Rango, Reineke Lis, and Krolina."

"Wow. It's been a while since we had such a veteran group. What's the occasion?"

"It just worked out that way," laughed Eilinn. "Hagen, follow me. See you tomorrow, Sergeant."

"See you tomorrow," I said to my first boss in parting.

The stubborn dwarf ignored us and walked back into his room, pulling so hard on his beard that it almost grazed the lintel.

"What's wrong with him?" I asked Eilinn immediately.

"Well, two things. First, I've never seen a dwarf who wasn't in a bad mood. Not even once. They're all incredibly feisty and standoffish. And, to be honest, they're all just plain greedy."

"Well, not all of them," I said, remembering the dwarf who gave me 10 gold when I was running around Aegan in my underwear.

"If you saw any other kind of dwarf, you're lucky. All the ones I know are stingy bastards. Anyway, second, Sergeant does have it tough. He can't walk."

"What do you mean he can't walk?"

"He just can't. When he was 16, he got into a car accident. The car rolled, he was sitting in the back, and when it landed, something bent too far and snapped his spine. That's why he started playing Fayroll. He's almost always here, in fact."

I felt terrible. Of course, he'd never served in the army. On the other hand, I couldn't have known. Still, I started to get that gnawing feeling…

"Obviously, it hasn't made him all that humble or pleasant to be around. But believe me, he's a good person. And a true friend. Just believe me. You'll see for yourself at some point."

"What about everyone else who's going with us?"

"You're lucky. You got all three of the clan's best players. Good fighters. Rango and Krolina have been in the clan from the beginning, and Lis joined a bit later. Rango and Krolina are hunters, Lis is a swordsman. So tomorrow, you can just relax and focus on leveling-up.

"Is there something to worry about?"

"Well, put it this way… The location is tricky, and it's designed for Levels 29-32. You would never make it there on your own. The other volunteers are generally between Level 26 and Level 29, so they'll get a good chunk of experience, too, especially at the beginning. That's why they're sending you there. You should get a bunch of goodies tomorrow, so your hamster will be happy. I imagine you'll get some good achievements and 10 or 12 levels. As far as what makes it tricky, well, there are sometimes a few bosses among the skeletons and zombies. There's a Level 46 lich and a Level 48 zombie king. They're tough since they're strong and they cast all kinds of crap. Theoretically, you could take them out, but you'd still die a bunch of times in the process. And you'd lose all the experience you got, so what's the point? Anyway, if they show their heads, we'll take them out."

"That sounds interesting. Oh, and what did you say about a hamster?"

Eilinn smiled, "All gamers have a hamster sitting inside of them. When they get something free, it's happy and sings. When they have to give something up, it whines and complains. Yours is definitely going to come out to play tomorrow. Just don't be late; we'll be porting at 9:05. And we won't wait around for anyone."

We'd gotten to the exit by the time we finished talking.

"It was nice meeting you," said Eilinn. "I have to run, but I'll see you tomorrow."

"Me, too," I responded with complete sincerity. "See you then."

I watched Eilinn walk away and clicked the button to log out.

Chapter Six
Gringvort

A quick glance at the clock when I climbed out of the capsule shocked me; I'd been playing for quite a while.

That Mammoth is a sneaky son of a gun. I was on the job the whole day and even a bit more, I thought. But that idea was quickly interrupted by two more base instincts. I was hungry and...well, I needed to do something else. And that second one needed to happen soon.

Having eaten and cleaned myself up a little, I sat down at my computer. It was about time to get started on my article. The clock was ticking, after all. I looked at the open text editor in front of me. And looked, and looked.

"I need more material first. Then I'll have this thing whipped out in no time... Later..."

I was about to turn off my computer when I remembered lying wrapped up in the blanket and hearing Elina and Gerv talking about the Great Dragon quest and getting to Rivenholm in ships. Nothing Gorotul said could be described as anything but a stream of consciousness. I had made a mental note to look up both of those—really, to figure out what Rivenholm even was. Also, I needed to see if I could dig up anything about that Wanderer. Maybe there was something online? Probably not.

I logged onto a forum and started with a search for the Great Dragon. As it turned out, I shouldn't have skipped reading all the Fayroll lore when I started playing. The history was far-reaching, fascinating, bloody, and varied. It was especially rich in wars. There were the two Skeleton Wars, the three Wars of Loathing, and another dozen that went nameless. However, the most brutal and violent was the War of the Dragon. Some thousand years ago, long before there were ever any players, all the intelligent races in Fayroll clashed. On one side were the undead and unhumans under the command of the Great Dragon—a real one, fire-breathing with wings, the last of the hymenopterans in Fayroll. His ranks included skeletons and liches, specters with their dogs of death, trolls, zombies, and orcs. On the other side, were the light and intelligent races: people, elves, and dwarves...well, and halflings and everyone else who more or less fell into those categories. The fighting started off small, and, naturally, the undead and unhuman started to lose. However, things escalated into genocide as whole dark races were wiped out in their native lands. That was when their leader, the Great Dragon, uttered a pronouncement, "If fate has not deemed us worthy of victory, our time has not yet come."

He disbanded his forces, conceded victory to the light races, and petitioned for an end to the pointless killing. However, in exchange for his forces laying down their arms, he demanded that they be exempt from prosecution aimed at destroying them or extracting reparations in civil courts. The war was over, and they needed to get back to living.

The light powers acquiesced, pointing to both their own war weariness and, they said, their innate goodness. But they didn't keep their word. It wasn't deliberate, and it wasn't all of them, but the damage was done. A few dwarf squadrons either didn't know about the armistice or were goaded on by their eternal stubbornness to keep fighting, and annihilated a large tribe of orcs—green, toothy, and unarmed—after they got into a fight with some dark dwarves. In short, it was a mess.

The Great Dragon learned what had happened and, enraged, pronounced a curse on the light races. But he designed that curse as a quest. A super-mega-extra-rare quest. In fact, it was so rare that not a single player in the history of the game had found it. What it included was a mystery, though its reward was not—the ability to call forth all the dark armies and in essence become the Dark Lord. The rumor went that the ability was somehow limited, but nobody knew what that limitation was. Enormous amounts of time were spent by all the clans trying to find it, though how to get it, who gives it, and what you have to do were all unknown.

A few players had gone on about how they'd found the hallowed quest, though they all later turned out to be False Dmitriys[7] looking for a free ride.

After creating the curse, the Great Dragon went missing, and there were no more mentions of him in the lore. Maybe he died, or maybe he went into hiding. But most likely, the developers pulled him out of the game and saved him on a backup copy somewhere on a backup hard drive.

So if Wanderer actually did get the quest, it wasn't surprising that he'd try to get as far away from everyone as he could. If I were him, I'd have gone off into some desert or cave for a hundred years or so. And if that were true, it wouldn't have been surprising that the Gray Witch was gunning for him either—but how did he get it in the first place?

And then I read some about her, as well. The Hounds of Death were a great, exacting, and merciless clan that came about when two earlier clans joined forces: the Gray Kittens and the Jets. The Gray Witch was the leader of the Gray Kittens and took over the newly formed clan. She was clever, vindictive, unscrupulous, and vengeful, though she was also rational and calculating. She never allowed emotion to get the better of her, and she could ferret out benefits for herself and her clan even when they were hidden behind seven brick walls. She personally compromised the leader of the Jets, who also wanted to be the leader of the new clan, with a detailed and brutally devious plan. It ended in him being denounced as a rat and, based on the clan charter, getting kicked out by a council resolution. Whenever anyone (generally from the old Jets clan) objected, she loftily asked, "And who said you have the right to go against the clan and demand anything contrary to the decisions of the council?"

Still, under her leadership, the clan became the game's best by a number of metrics.

Anyway, judging by all of that, it was logical to assume that Wanderer had uncovered something there. Otherwise, the Gray Witch wouldn't have deigned to go after him personally with an offer. There wasn't anything in the forums about Wanderer, on the other hand, or at least I couldn't find anything.

What I found about Rivenholm was much simpler. When the game began, there was just one continent—Rattermark, the one I was currently on. A year and a half before I joined, however, a global update was released that included an entirely new one called Rivenholm. There were two ways to get there: either you could list it as your starting location (apparently I missed that option when I registered) or you could sail across the ocean, which was much tougher. The problem wasn't even that ships were expensive. It was that getting there was hard and dangerous—so much so that a small convoy didn't stand a chance.

Convoys faced harpies, garudas, and stymphalides from the air, while a Kraken of immense size and monstrous strength ravaged them from below. Anyone left swimming in the water after their ships were destroyed were eaten by sharks. After all, it was an ocean. But the highlight of the trip were the pirates lurking in the waters surrounding the extensive Tigali Archipelago, smack dab in the middle between Rattermark and Rivenholm. They did what pirates always do—steal and kill, eat and drink, and make everyone they took captive walk the plank. Interestingly, they were all NPCs, as there wasn't a "pirate" class, players could choose to be. So, they were our Pirates of the Caribbean. *Jack Sparrow. Sorry.* **Captain Jack Sparrow.**

Incidentally, if you were killed while at sea, you were sent to the nearest respawn point. By default, that was in Rattermark, as there aren't any respawn points at sea, and players respawned there without their ships. A dozen clans had lost their fleets that way.

So, just see if you can get there. And it was so tempting; there was almost nobody there since new players much preferred the settled continent. It had strong clans, guides, and a settled way of life. Sure, there were pioneers and enthusiasts who wanted to try new dungeons, new spells, and new quests... Clans also started sending scouts there, but while those scouts did have some time to level-up and explore...they still wouldn't stand much chance against a landing of high-level players. So all the top clans started readying fleets. The rest simply didn't have the resources. The Hounds of Death had theirs ready, and it was no surprise that Elina wanted to join them.

"Cool," I said, having digested everything I read. "Tolkien doesn't have anything on this..."

And after setting the alarm in my music center for 8 a.m. I went to sleep. I slept like a baby, calmly and free of nightmares. It was just before I woke in the morning that, for some reason, I dreamed about Spartacus, who sat at a monitor and said, "If I'd only known I could get better armor at the auction... I'd have bought some..."

That was when my alarm went off, thank God. *Sometimes fun little twists in life can come back to haunt you—after all, we'd just been talking about Spartacus. But whatever, it was time for battle.* I had a cup of tea and got ready to crush some skeleton ribs under the watchful eye of our elder clanmates.

I got to the square about twenty minutes early, and the first person I saw there was an old Noobland friend: Oygolinn. He'd found a way to get all the way up to Level 27 and pick up some nice equipment. His bow certainly represented an upgrade over my simple club.

"It's an elf up in here!" I waved to him. "Well, look at you. Have you even eaten or slept? We started at the same time!"

"Hey!" Oygolinn greeted me. "Well, not everyone is as lazy as you are. Looks like you couldn't jump more than two levels. How are you here, actually? Don't you have to be Level 25?"

"I can't tell you. It's a big secret. But seriously, how did you level-up so fast?"

"Not that fast," the elf said with a wave of his arms. "Since we were together, I only left the game when my brain started to shut down. Slept four hours and jumped back in. City, location; city, location."

"Why go to the city?"

"I sold everything I got to traders and left the gold in my room. PKers are brutal. It seems like there are a lot of them lately. They got me at least 20 times. The last time they killed me, I decided to hell with it, logged onto a forum, looked through the list of clans, and picked the Thunderbirds. Their terms and conditions aren't too bad, and they're strong on protection: PKers aren't tolerated in the least. So how did you get stuck on Level 6?"

"You know, somehow it just happened...I'm not sure. First one thing, then another... Today, I'll do some leveling-up."

People had been trickling in while we were talking. Honestly, I'd thought there would only be five or six of us, but there were already nine people there... Well, not exactly people. There were four humans: two tanks, an archer, and a mage. Then there were two elves, a lone dwarf, and a halfling named Liutix. I had never seen a halfling before then, and they were definitely unusual. I almost asked Liutix to take off his boots so I could see how hairy his feet were. *I was intrigued!* But just then, my new acquaintance Eilinn walked out of the fortress, counted heads, and said, "All right, we're missing one. Sergeant, who isn't here?"

Sergeant walked out from behind him just as sullen as he'd been the day before (or maybe that's just how he always was) dressed in chainmail. He had a battle axe in his belt, and on his head was a helmet that looked like a teapot with a second spout and lid soldered onto it. After a quick recount, he answered, "We're missing an elf. Gless. Level 26 hunter."

But as soon as the word "hunter" had left his lips, Gless appeared in front of Sergeant in all his elfish glory. Sergeant jumped back.

"You elves," he said angrily, "only care about your entrances!"

"Sorry," stammered Gless, looking sideways at him and sidling off toward the main group.

"Wow," I said. "Sergeant, you're a magician. So, if you say 'cask of beer,' does a cask of beer appear?"

"I'll tell you this much, if I say 'big bruise on your head' and wave my magic wand," he said while tenderly caressing the battle axe at his side, "you'll get your fairytale! And it won't have a happy ending!"

"Okay, quiet," said Eilinn. "Everyone's here, no one's late, and that's a good thing. Okay, listen up. We'll start by going over some information and then port out. We're going to Gringvort, where the monsters average out to around Levels 29 to 34. It's populated by skeletons and zombies mostly, though you'll also come across death dogs and specters. The average respawn is four minutes. Sometimes, there'll be bosses, but you don't have to worry about them; that's what these fine folks are here for." He waved his hand toward the fortress, in front of which stood three high-level warriors (you could tell just by looking at their equipment and weapons). There were two archers—a man and a girl—and a swordsman.

"That's Rango." The male archer waved.

"That's Krolina or just Kro." The girl curtsied.

"And finally, Reineke Lis, or Lis." The swordsman pressed a fist to his chest and did a half bow.

"Lisikins," laughed Krolina.

"They have a ton of experience, and they're guild veterans. So, they'll make sure you don't have to deal with any bosses or unexpected bot respawns. Those don't happen often, though they do happen. We also sometimes get PKers wandering around over there, if very rarely. Generally speaking, they're either really low-level and have no idea what they're doing, or they're part of very experienced gangs. The noobs you can deal with yourselves, seeing has there are ten of you, though you won't be able to handle any veteran PKers. Just don't expect us to take care of bots for you. None of those three will join your group, and none of them will help you in battles you should be able to handle yourself."

"All right, kiddies," clapped Sergeant. "Form up!"

"Who's the leader?" asked a burly barbarian named Ronin.

"How should we know?" Eilinn answered with a question of his own. "It's your group, so you decide."

"But we don't even know each other!" an elf girl said with some surprise.

"So what?" Sergeant asked. "There are lots of ways to choose a leader quickly, even if you don't know anyone."

Just then, I received a group invitation sent by Oygolinn. Of course, I accepted. I couldn't care less about being the leader, so if someone else out there wanted to do the honors—more power to them.

"Why does it have to be you?" Ronin responded sharply, obviously having just received the invitation. "Maybe I want to be leader?"

"Then you should have sent your invitation first," Eilinn agreeably observed.

"The early bird gets the worm," noted Reineke Lis as he walked over.

"Oh, you're kidding me!" Ronin was beside himself, and barely containing his anger.

Everyone else had no problem accepting their invitations to the group, and soon it was official.

"What trophy distribution did you set?" Sergeant asked Oygolinn.

"Who Needs What," the latter answered.

Trophies were a big deal. When you played in a group, there were four ways to distribute loot: to the group leader, to whoever got the last strike in, democratically (get what you can), and who needs what (the best option). While in the first three modes, loot always went to a specific person, in the last mode, players received a message asking them if they needed each item. If they didn't, they selected "no" and didn't participate in the lottery. If they selected "yes," a virtual die was rolled for each person, and the one with the highest number got the item or resource. It was fair and worked well. *Nice job, Oygolinn.* Additionally, the money you got for killing enemies was distributed between everyone in the group equally and automatically.

"Why?" asked a frustrated Ronin. "Let's go with Last Strike. If we do it your way, I might do all the killing and be left with nothing!"

"No problem," said Oygolinn. "Let's vote. Who's for Last Strike?"

Only one person beside Ronin raised their hand, an archer named Kerv.

"Who wants Who Needs What?" Everyone else raised their hand.

"Done. And just so you know, that was the last bit of democracy we'll have in the group. I'm the leader, and I make decisions. If I need your opinion, I'll ask for it. If you don't listen, I'll kick you out of the group."

I happened to see Eilinn glance quickly at Sergeant. Interesting.

"Don't kick anyone out," said Eilinn. "This trip is organized by the Thunderbirds, and you're all volunteers. You don't get to kick people out of the group, though you are responsible for commanding it. You can also demand that they listen to your instructions in battle, and you decide how to distribute loot."

"Exactly!" Ronin was at it again.

"Is everything clear?" asked Sergeant. "Eilinn, open the portal."

"Eilinn barked out some kind of spell, waved his staff, and a portal opened. It looked exactly as I expected it to—a big blue circle with shimmering edges, rolling around and all of that…

"What are we waiting for?" Sergeant yelled. "Get in there! It'll collapse soon, and you'll miss your chance!"

We didn't need a second invitation, as everyone crowded in its direction.

Gringvort

A place where warriors from the great but long-forgotten kingdom of Ringholl gathered for hunts and buhurts. After the second Skeleton War, it fell under a curse laid on it by a powerful necromancer.

The undead now populate it and…

I skipped the rest of the interesting, if very long and untimely story, about Fayroll's attractions. If I'd been alone, I would have read it. In my case, however, I doubted the Sergeant would let me, and I didn't want to miss anything important.

We were standing on a small hill. In front of us, was a modest plain littered with picturesque ruins that looked as if they once could have been small outposts built for something big—to protect the remnants of Darkness, for example, as they slunk away from the west or the machinations of the enemy. A little forest began about a kilometer and a half away from us. In short, it was an idyllic spot.

"Well, there's your field of battle. As soon as you walk down to the bottom of the hill, skeletons will start coming up out of the ground. The zombies start a bit later, closer to the forest. The bosses almost always come alone. One of them, the lich, comes out of those wrecks." Eilinn's finger pointed toward a group of ruins to the left of the hill. "And the zombie king usually comes out of the woods. We'll keep an eye out, so just focus on fighting. Any questions?"

"Yes, I have one." I raised my hand. "What happens if we die? I mean, who knows what will happen. Everything here is pretty strong, and if they catch me once, that'll be it. Where's the respawn point?"

"Good question," Eilinn said, looking at me. "The respawn is here, right behind us."

He waved a finger behind him at (How did I miss it?) a stone covered in runes that had a slight glow.

"You should all link to it. Otherwise, you'll respawn back at the fortress if you die. And no one's going back for you!" Sergeant shouted in his normal tone of voice.

"Just remember to relink when we get back to the fortress," said Krolina, "or you'll find yourself back here, and it's a long way to the fortress or Aegan."

I opened the map and checked to see where we were. Aegan was a ways away. Probably fifteen days away, and the path was full of tough (for me, of course) locations.

Locations in Fayroll were relative, seeing as how it was a world—like all the other latest generation games—that was complete and seamless. The only differences were the levels of enemies you faced and the place names. There wasn't any loading, no "wait a second." When there weren't any more skeletons, werewolves would start coming, and I'd probably be at the next location. Although, sure, they might both be happy living together at the same spot. Leaving Gringvort would put me in the Deisnell Plain so everything around me would change, though there could be who knows how many types of enemies in the plain. In contrast to a lowland area like Gringvort, the plains could be absolutely enormous—hundreds of villages, dozens of cities, a nomad camp…the variety was impressive. And no matter where you went you'd find friends, enemies, quests, skill masters, and traders—whatever you wanted.

Finally, we started down the hill. We were linked to the respawn point, our weapons were drawn, and it was time for battle.

"All right, comrades." Oygolinn stopped us when we were almost to the foot of the hill. "Tactics. Everyone just do your thing for the first five skeletons so I can get a look at what you can do."

At the same time, our commanders came down the hill. Sergeant and Eilinn listened to our conversation with interest, though they made no attempt to come any closer or participate. The veterans laid out on the grass, and Reineke even pulled out a pipe and filled it with tobacco (in contrast to many other games, Fayroll was fine with all legal types of smoking during the game; it just served to get them more players).

"Your poor little eyes will be okay with that?!" Ronin sharply responded. "What, you think we're some kind of experiment? And what can you do?"

"He jumped 23 levels in a couple days," I answered. "You took what, three weeks to go that far?"

"Shut your mouth," Ronin snarled at me. "I still haven't figured out how a Level 6 wimp like you got in with the volunteers."

"Excuse me, but that has nothing to do with us," Eilinn's voice chimed in. "I'd also like to mention that the group has five hours for the raid. The more time you waste now, the less experience you'll get later."

"Everyone be quiet!" barked Oygolinn. "I'm the group leader, and I'll make the decisions. Right now, we're going to kill five skeletons, after which, I'll split everyone up into squads of three... And you'll tag along with one of them as a fourth." He cast a quick glance in my direction.

"Here's the formation," ordered Oygolinn. "I'm in front with Ronin and Fladr." The dwarf nodded, the barbarian grimaced. "We'll get the skeletons to attack us while the hunters shoot them down. Besides me, we have three hunters." Two elves and a human also nodded.

"Flosi and you, Liutix, guard the hunters in case someone goes after them. Make sure they target you."

"But I'm a thief!" Liutix said indignantly while the big paladin quietly received his orders.

"So? I'm an archer, but I'll be on the front lines, too," Oygolinn said. "If it gets to be too much, we'll rotate until the hunters finish them off. Just don't go too far, or you'll attract new ones."

"And who," the leader looked at the mage, "can heal?"

The mage, whose name was Rodriquez (a real-looking one, with a beard and staff, though the staff was obviously much simpler than Eilinn's), gravely nodded.

"Stay close to me, and I'll tell you who to heal if it comes to that. Well, and keep an eye out yourself. Can anyone do any buffing?"

"I can do protection against the elements," Rodriguez's deep voice boomed.

"Can't hurt—go for it."

The mage twirled his staff, shouting something in a language I didn't know, and I saw that we now had a five percent protection against air, fire, and water damage.

"And you," Oygolinn looked at me and exhaled, "stay in the back."

Well, obviously. Where was I going to go with my attributes? One blow from a Level 20 skeleton, and I'd be a memory up there next to the stone on the hill...in my underwear.

"We'll kill five skeletons and fall back to the hill," our leader said before we set off. At the front of the procession, our two swordsmen flanked our commander; several steps behind them were the three hunters with arrows strung and ready; behind them, were Liutix with his dagger at the ready and the paladin, then me; and bringing up the rear was our gray-bearded mage.

About fifteen steps in front of the trio, the ground started expanding almost immediately, with one spot even closer. It grew and grew until skeletons started to climb out. They were straight out of a fantasy novel, waving and shaking rusty swords and shields, rattling bones, clinking chainmail. In the deep eye sockets set in their yellow skulls, burned small red fires. One after another, the bubbles of earth popped, with each...I don't know, pop or explosion...yielding three skeletons. Our plan to take out five targets was discarded before it ever began, and the skeletons hopped toward us out of their craters. The whole scene was especially eerie given the dead (what else?) silence surrounding it all. We were all quiet, watching events unfold. It isn't every day that you have skeletons running at you. As far as I know, not even 10 percent of the people in Fayroll had come across the undead. The veterans, on the other hand, were quiet because it was something they'd seen many times. The skeletons were quiet, of course, because they didn't have anything to speak with.

Oygolinn reacted first, sinking an arrow into a skeleton running at him—and it was a good hit, immediately taking out half the skeleton's health (not his life—what kind of life can a dead skeleton have?). The skeleton then took a slash from Fladr's sword and a cut from Ronin's steel, at which point I received a message:

77

> You unlocked Strength of the Strong, Level 1.
>
> To get it, destroy nine more enemies that are 10 levels or more above you.
>
> Reward:
>
> Daredevil, a passive ability, Level 1: +0.3% to the damage you do with all weapon types
>
> Title: Fearless Strongman
>
> To see similar messages, go to the Action section of the attribute window.

Before I had time to say "wow," I got another one:

> You unlocked Death of Bones, Level 1.
>
> To get it, destroy another 49 warrior skeletons.
>
> Reward:
>
> Mental Fortitude, a passive attribute, Level 1: +0.7% to your mental strength against grave horrors
>
> 0.2% defense against poisons
>
> To see similar messages, go to the Action section of the attribute window.

Everyone else got the message about all the bones and stuff as well, and that tripped up the group. The skeletons used that against us, and our front line began taking hits. The first two skeletons started smacking them in the head, but that was only part of the problem. Right behind those two, were six more.

"Hunters, fire!" Oygolinn's cry rang out. "Rodriguez, heal us! Flosi, get over here! Hagen, Liutix—to the left and right flanks. If you're attacked, get them to target someone else and run for the hill, so you don't trigger more of them!"

I dashed to my left as the archers fired and scanned the area to make sure we wouldn't be outflanked. Meanwhile, things were hopping at the front of our group. Oygolinn's command couldn't have come at a better time, as it shook the archers out of their stupor. They quickly took out two of the first three skeletons and heavily damaged the second trio, making them easy pickings for the three swords of our tanks. When the first fell, I leveled-up.

"Archers, switch to the next three!" shouted Oygolinn as he himself fired at the far group. As he continued loosing arrows, he stepped back, covered by our swordsmen. "Rodriguez, heal the tanks!"

The three hunters also turned their fire on the far targets. The strategy was a good one: only two got to the swordsmen, and they didn't last five seconds against their three swords.

"Fall back," commanded the leader once all the skeletons were piles of bones on the ground."

"What about stripping them?" asked the archer named Kerv, who until then had been quiet.

"Flosi," said Oygolinn, nodding to the piles of bones.

Collecting trophies didn't turn out to be that hard. You just reached your hand out to your opponent's remains and everything he had turned up in your backpack.

In our case, sure, every time, the question popped up, "Do you need this item?" And you took a second to think before replying.

This time, none of the nine skeletons yielded anything interesting—just bones, shards of rusted swords, and a few grave centipedes. A bunch of crap... Although somebody decided they needed it. Who could possibly have taken it all?

"All right, we need a new strategy. We won't split into groups of three," announced Oygolinn. "They'll overpower us since they're in trios, too. Swordsmen, you'll be in the front taking the skeletons on in the center. I'll be right behind you, also working in the center, with the three other hunters working the left and right flanks. You two," he said to Liutix and me, "watch the flanks. If the hunters are threatened, you know what to do. Rodriguez, focus on healing the tanks. Move out!"

And that's how it went. The next nine skeletons were a piece of cake. The archers spread out to the point that only every third skeleton made it to the swordsmen at all, and even their health was in the red. You could almost hear them creaking out something like "Ah, you got me, you living scum," as they crumbled into heaps of tiny bones before Flosi's sword could cleave into them.

I was quite happy with how things were going, as I leveled-up three more times and got another message:

You unlocked Strength of the Strong, Level 2.

To get it, destroy 19 more enemies that are 10 levels or more above you.

Reward:

Daredevil, a passive ability, Level 2: +0.6% to the damage you do with all weapon types

Worthy Reward, a passive ability: +2% chance of finding rare items on defeated enemies

To see similar messages, go to the Action section of the attribute window.

I was especially happy about Worthy Reward since I was sure I'd get the ability. I had just gotten to Level 10, and the skeletons were all Levels 28-30, so I had another ten levels to go. That would be enough time to take out 19 skeletons, right?

"Liutix, Hagen, make sure you watch our back. They respawn every four minutes, so we need to make sure they don't come at us from back there. And keep checking the flanks." Our commander was comfortable in his role, and there was a new steel to his voice.

His instructions were well-timed. I looked over my shoulder, then glanced to my left...and my eyes opened wide. Forty strides away, an enormous skeleton came out of the picturesque ruins. He wore a helmet and had fireballs for eyes.

"Hey, commander, look!" I shouted with all of my strength.

"Form up, face left!" Oygolinn barked as soon as he turned his head.

"Oh no, it's the lich!" the halfling said softly and shakily.

"Stay out of this, let us handle him!" we heard from Reineke Lis.

Without even taking the pipe from his mouth, he covered the ground in three large leaps—the same ground it took us fifteen minutes to cross—and, pulling out his sword as he went, moved toward the lich. The latter didn't react to him in the least, which wasn't a surprise given the difference in their levels. Bot enemies consider you a target until you get 15 levels ahead of them. Then they ignore you. And, really, you ignore them, too, since you don't get experience for killing them. So why kill them in the first place?

I didn't even notice the exact moment the lich died. Two flashes in front of the sun and his helmet and skull were rolling around on the stones and the grass sticking up between them.

"That didn't take long," grunted Kerv from behind me. "Must be nice to be that advanced."

"What are you looking at?" barked Oygolinn. "Form up! Le-e-et's go!"

And off w-e-e-e went. Over the next three hours, I leveled-up nine times, got to Level 3 Strength of the Strong, and finally received another message:

You unlocked Death of Bones, Level 2.
To get it, destroy another 99 warrior skeletons.
Reward:
Mental Fortitude, a passive attribute, Level 2: +1.5% to your mental strength against grave horrors
0.5% defense against poisons
To see similar messages, go to the Action section of the attribute window.

Our friendly team scattered the field with skeleton bones, and in a few places, you could see the ragged remnants of zombies. They were slower than the skeletons, though they could take more punishment. True, they didn't give me an action for some reason. We also took care of a ghost that looked like an overgrown Casper and howled savagely. The howls were probably there to scare us, but I had the distinct impression that it was howling because it was scared of us. Still:

You unlocked Light Drives Out Darkness, Level 1.
To get it, destroy another 49 specters.
Reward:

See the Invisible, a passive attribute, Level 1: 0.5% to your ability to see the invisible—secret doors and crypts

0.5% defense against cold

To see similar messages, go to the Action section of the attribute window.

Sometimes we found more than just bones in the piles our dead friends left behind. There wasn't anything at my level, of course—just usual blue items for levels 27-30. And nothing rare or elite, of course. But that made sense; this was just a normal location with normal bots.

There were five types of items in the Fayroll world:

Usual items were blue, had one or two attributes, and were for any class.

Rare items were purple, had three or four attributes, and were for any class.

Elite items were yellow, had three to five attributes and a class-specific ability, and were for specific classes.

Legendary items were orange, boasted up to six attributes, usually belonged at one point to an ancient hero, and let you learn a new ability or skill. You couldn't find them doing normal quests, though rare ones gave you a chance. On the other hand, you had to kill especially evil and unusual monsters to get them.

And finally, there were set items. They were gold, and they had incredible capabilities. Complete sets could have from 2 to 15 items, and each of those items was incredibly hard to find. Each consecutive item you found gave you huge bonuses. However, they were almost impossible to find out in nature, so getting them meant killing serious raid bosses—one every raid, and not every time. You could also get them from quests, though only from epic and hidden quests. If you had a full set with at least five items, you were closing in on the Gaming Legend title. Though you couldn't get set items in normal combat. I mean, you could, but your chances weren't just close to zero; they were more like one in a billion.

On the other hand, you could get rare and even elite items in normal battles, if very infrequently. We weren't lucky, and I was especially unlucky; there were a few items for my class, though I didn't win any of them. Just not my day.

"Let's get back to the hill," ordered Oygolinn. "We'll rest for a bit and distribute points."

Our formation turned and moved for the hill. There, we lay down on the grass and listened to Eilinn.

"You can rest as long as you want. We have an hour and 45 minutes left. Oygolinn, could I speak with you for a second?"

Our commander headed over, and for a second, I wondered what they could be talking about. I had other things to worry about, however, so I ignored them and set to distributing my points. In total, I'd leveled-up 13 times, earning 80 skill points.

I still wanted to go with a soldier—a simple class that doesn't do much thinking, is strong, and has lots of health. With that in mind, I added 40 points to my strength and 30 to my stamina. After some thinking, I finished up with six agility points and two each for wisdom and intellect. Why not? I ended up with:

Basic attributes:
Strength: 56
Intellect: 3
Agility: 9
Stamina: 41
Wisdom: 3

Yeah, not very balanced. Still, strong and healthy. And now, it would take more than one blow for the skeletons to kill me! Finally, I could go get a class-specific quest and earn some combat abilities.

Nothing really interesting happened during the rest of the hunt. We kept fighting the skeletons for another hour and a half, but still... Everyone else had leveled-up quite a bit as well, if not as many times as I did, and the skeleton trios that just about had us at the beginning of the raid were barely a challenge by the end. Our hunters took them out as soon as they got close enough to shoot at.

As things wound down, we were all relieved to hear Sergeant yell at us from the hill, "Fa-a-all back!"

After we went through the portal and found ourselves on the cobblestones outside the fortress, we were all set to thank Eilinn, Sergeant, and the other veterans and head offline. We were all pretty tired from the stress. However, before we could do so Eilinn said, "Not so fast; line up."

We followed his order, sensing that something was up.

"I'm happy to announce, Thunderbird volunteers, that most of you passed the challenge with flying colors. What we did today was less about leveling you up and more about seeing how you behave in extreme and social situations."

"Did everyone pass?" asked Oygolinn.

"Of course not," Eilinn answered easily. "That never happens. Though you did well—seven out of ten."

"Who didn't pass?" Again Oygolinn.

"Ronin, Kerv, and Aerinn."

"What?!!" bellowed the barbarian. "I was out there killing skeletons right and left!"

"Yes, you were," said Sergeant. "But your ability to wave a sword around isn't the only thing we look at."

"Exactly," confirmed Eilinn. "For starters, you constantly and pointlessly fought Oygolinn's leadership, which everyone else accepted. And then, you were insubordinate. We don't tolerate that in our clan."

"But why us?" asked Kerv, and the elf girl nodded in agreement.

"What items did you take during the game?"

"I got shoulder guards with +3 strength and greaves with +3 stamina and +2 strength," said Kerv.

"I have a mantle with +2 wisdom and +2 stamina and a wristlet with +3 agility," answered the elf.

"And why would archers need any of that? Well, except for the wristlet. It's all for warriors and mages. You knew that, and you knew you had both of those classes in the group, but you took the items anyway. That isn't a huge deal, but it does show that you aren't yet ready to work as part of a team. And that isn't a good thing or a bad thing; it's just that you aren't right for our clan right now. Come back in a month and apply again if you want—except for you, Ronin. Don't bother, because we won't consider it."

The clan badge above the heads of three of our recent comrades blinked and disappeared.

That's why he asked to talk with Oygolinn when we were on the hill, I thought.

"Oh, I won't. Who needs you?"

The barbarian dramatically spat on the cobblestones and turned for the door.

"Listen, elf scum." Ronin turned at the gate and looked at Oygolinn. "We'll be seeing each other. Oh, and I'll have my eye out for you, too, little one." He jabbed a finger in my direction and left.

"Hey, life's more interesting when you have enemies," laughed Krolina. "That way you always have a goal."

"You can also go," Eilinn said, looking at Kerv and Aerinn. "I think the experience you got today will compensate you in full for the time you spent with us."

"Have a good one," said Kerv, and the girl just nodded. It looked to me like she was doing her best to keep from crying. I think she was just embarrassed.

"I think we'll meet again," Eilinn said gently.

"Well," he said when the other two were outside the gate. "And now the rewards for everyone who passed the test. Right this way."

And we followed him into the fortress.

Chapter Seven
Into the Village, Into the Wilderness

"Rewards sound good," muttered Liutix, walking next to me. "But is anyone really going to give us anything good just like that? They'll probably just hand us each a life potion and a mana potion and call it a day."

We got to the small clan storehouse, the one I wasn't "allowed in yet." It was locked, but next to Sergeant stood a halfling with a set of enormous keys hanging on his belt.

"This," Eilinn pointed at him, "is Marcho Bigl, the keeper of the large and small clan storages and the keeper of the clan keys…"

"…for all the doors and locks." I couldn't help myself.

"Very funny. Ha, ha, ha," the keeper of the large and small storehouses, the seven seas, and all the homes of men said emotionlessly, with a quick glance at me. "Somehow, I get the feeling that you'll be last in line to the storehouse."

"That's not good," I said.

"Not good at all," agreed Marcho. "And I think we can say you'll always be last."

"But what if I come alone? And nobody else is there?"

"I'll think of something," said the storekeeper with a smile that spoke volumes. "I've got time, plus a rich imagination…"

"Okay, okay," Eilinn said in a conciliatory tone. "He already knows he made a mistake, and he'll fix it. He's still new. What can you do?"

"New is right," Sergeant butted in grumpily. "Marcho, you should have heard him talking to me yesterday!" Tattletale.

"I'll bet!" Marcho nodded his head in sympathy. "Kids these days."

"Your highnesses," said Eilinn, "we're all aware of how the grass was greener, the sky was bluer, and your socks never had holes when you were new. Maybe we can get on with this?"

Marcho, with a sniff and a groan, pushed open the massive oaken door with gorgeous inlays, and our whole friendly group tramped into the small clan storehouse.

86

My first impression was one of bewilderment. The clan storehouse was drawn like...oh, I don't know... Well, have you seen Warehouse 13? It looked something like that. Racks held all kinds of gadgets and different kinds of armor, and there were weapons and mummified heads of epic beasts hanging on the walls. The heads each sported a plaque that read something like:

Three-legged gorgol, poison-spitter, regenerating. Epic monster, boss. Killed by Harvey Ragnarrson during a clan raid in Khittsbro Cave near Aina.

Well, it wasn't your standard storehouse—more like a locker room. Or our unit's store room. Our storeroom keeper, a hardened warrior had a vivid imagination, and he set it up to make sure nobody would be walking around or stealing anything. You walked in, took three steps, and found yourself at the delivery window.

Marcho stepped behind the window and said, "I'm ready. First!"

"Just one second." Eilinn clapped his hands like some elementary school teacher or tour guide. "After today's test, you are now much closer to full membership in the clan. You showed us—both me and a few of the clan elite—what you can do in combat as well as in personal situations. The fact that you are here means that everything went well. And in recognition of the fact that the clan likes what it sees in you, we would like to give you a small advance in the hopes that you will like what you see in us. To be precise, we will give you equipment and weapons that match your level."

"Step up to Marcho," jumped in Sergeant." Say your name, level, and class. Take what you're given and step away."

"What if I don't like what you give me?" asked Flosi.

"Are you kidding me?" Sergeant choked. "Don't bite the hand that feeds you."

"He wasn't being clear," Oygolinn said quickly. "What he meant was, do we have to wear what we're given? I mean, if we get something better during a raid?"

"Whether you wear it or not is completely up to you," answered Eilinn. "If you don't need it anymore, you're welcome to return it to the storehouse."

Yeah, right, I thought. *Once I get something, I'm not giving it up. And anyway, I can always just sell it.*

The group lined up, and I found myself third.

"Hey, funny guy," said Marcho when he saw me. "Get to the back of the line."

I saw at once that there was no point in arguing with him, so I went and found Oygolinn standing at the back of the line.

"Why are you last?" I asked him.

"I was in charge, so I should be last," he answered calmly.

"You're that proper about it?"

"No, that's just the way it's done. At least, it was in another game I used to play. Whoever was in charge of the group or raid got their handout last."

"Did they hand things out a lot?"

"Yep."

The line moved quickly, as Marcho seemed to be born for his job. Everyone stepping away from the counter looked over their new acquisitions with satisfied faces.

When it was finally my turn, I rapped out, "Hagen, Level 19, warrior."

"A warrior, you say?" I couldn't tell what Marcho was saying by looking at his face, but I had the feeling he had something unpleasant up his sleeve.

"Oh, stop scaring the kid," giggled Krolina, as the veterans had gone into the storehouse with us. She wagged her finger at the storekeeper before jabbing me in the side with it. "And you, don't let him get to you."

"Our hairy little miser here likes to have fun. But he gives you good stuff, and he's honest, so don't worry about it. By the way, King Leer, did you not know that Elina herself invited him to the clan?" Reineke Lis continued.

"Really?" Marcho answered in surprise. "For something he did?"

"Who knows?" Lis responded. "But maybe you'll find out if you give him something nice."

Marcho turned and headed deep into the room, made some noise, rustled around, and shouted back, "What do you fight with?!"

"A mace!" I shouted back.

We heard more noise from his direction before he finally returned holding an enormous shield loaded with different items.

"Here, take this. And remember what old Marcho did for you. When you level-up and decide to get new stuff, stop by and return this—maybe someone else will find a use for it."

"Thanks, Marcho," I said sincerely. "I'll try my hardest."

"Don't try your hardest." The halfling was completely serious. "Just do it."

I only stopped to looked at what he'd given me after I left the storehouse, which was where I found everyone else busy doing the same. The ones who'd gotten their handouts first were already wearing them.

The things I got were pretty good. Maybe not extraordinary, but they would have cost me a pretty penny at an auction. Although, maybe not; I wasn't sure what the prices were yet. The equipment I got included a breastplate, greaves, shoulder guards, a helmet, gloves, and boots—all with two attributes that added strength and stamina. Oh, and Marcho had splurged on the mace. It was rare, it was violet, and it had four attributes.

North Wind Mace
Damage: 25-45
+5 to strength
+7 to stamina
+5% to critical strike chance
+14% fire damage
Durability: 80/80
Minimum level to use: 15

Quite the snazzy little guy, and much more than I expected. The shield was also pretty good, if blue and usual.

Warrior Shield
Protection: 220
+6 to strength

+23% chance of reflecting blows
Durability: 180/180
Minimum level for use: 15

"Well, everyone happy?" asked Eilinn with a smile.

"Yes, thanks, this is great!" we answered without any unison whatsoever.

"Then before you leave, let me say this—remember that the clan has your back. I hope you remember your rights and responsibilities. However, with that said, we have one main responsibility and one main right. Your biggest responsibility is to avoid discrediting the clan in any way, either in word or deed. And for your most important right, remember that you are now part of the clan and can ask for help whenever you need it. I'm sorry if that sounds too dramatic…"

"Everything clear?" Sergeant's voice rang out. "Don't make mistakes, and don't be afraid. That's pretty much it."

Eilinn sighed in frustration and turned to head toward the fortress.

"Regarding transportation," Sergeant bellowed. "Lis will take anyone who wants to go to Aegan with him. The rest of you can leave the fortress, as you'll be fine in this area at your level so long as you don't do anything stupid. The bots around here are Level 33-35."

"You should go to Aegan," Reineke Lis said, walking up to me. "You haven't been to the class instructor yet, right?"

"Right," I responded.

"Then come on, I'll show you where he lives in Aegan."

And we walked through the portal.

Aegan was as loud, colorful, and picturesque as ever. Players and NPCs darted around like pizza delivery boys, arguing as they went.

"Thanks, everyone," said Oygolinn. The portal rolled up, and we were left standing on the street.

"That was great," said Fladr suddenly, and I realized that I hadn't heard a dozen words out of him the whole day. He turned to Oygolinn. "You're a fantastic leader. If you decide to get a group together, let me know."

"Me, too," said Flosi.

Flosi wants to add you as a friend. Accept?

Fladr wants to add you as a friend. Accept?

I accepted all their requests—Flosi's, Fladr's, and everyone else's. Then I sent one of my own to Oygolinn. He glanced at me and nodded his head slightly.
"Well, are we all friends now?" asked Krolina jovially.
I grunted and sent friend requests to her and Reineke.
"That was fast," nodded Lis.
"As lightning," said Krolina with a laugh. "Bottled…"

Reineke Lis accepted your friend request. Added to friends.

Krolina accepted your friend request. Added to friends.

"All right, I'm out," said Oygolinn, slinging his bow over his back and heading toward the market.
A second later, everyone else had scattered as well.
"That guy's a born leader," Lis said quietly to Krolina.
"You think Eilinn didn't notice?"
"What are you still here for?" Lis turned to me.
"You wanted to take me to the instructor," I reminded him.
"Oh, right. Kro, are you coming with?"
"No, I'm going offline. See you, boys!" Krolina stuck her tongue out at us, turned on her heel, and disappeared into a shadow that meant she'd logged out of the game.
"Let's go," said Reineke, and we started off down the street.
"Have you known each other long?" I asked Lis.
"Kro and I? Yeah, it's been a while. We've been through the ringer together. A while ago, we were together in a different clan, then we jumped over to the Thunderbirds. She did a little before me. Doesn't matter. Turn left here."

As we chatted away, we came to a small alley with six or seven buildings lined up side by side. The entrance to each had a carved plywood sign above it: a shield and sword, a staff, a bow, and so on.

"This is the instructor street," said Reineke, and pointed toward the building with the shield and sword. "That's where you're going. Stay here and wait for me when you're done."

I walked in. Fayroll does nothing if not break down stereotypes. I expected some gray-bearded and gray-haired old warrior covered in iron, maybe even missing a limb, who would greet me with a thundering voice of steel, "Hello, hero! Have you come for your lessons?"

Well, something like that.

Ha! The interior of the building looked something like an old wooden hut, just without the fire pit. And inside it, sat a gray old man carving something out of wood. He looked at me and asked, "What can I do for you, sonny?"

"I need skills…I guess. Maybe I'm not in the right place?"

He's probably playing a joke on me. I thought about Lis. *This must be where they teach crafters! What a little joker!*

"Are you a warrior, by any chance?" the old man asked me.

"Yes, a warrior."

"And what level are you?"

"19."

"Then you're in the right place." He smiled again. "Who would you like to be?"

"What do you mean?"

"Well," the old man began, spinning his short knife in the air, "there are all different kinds of warriors. Some attack, others defend, and all of them have their own kind of weapon. Some prefer swords, others go with maces or balls and chains. So who are you? Or who do you want to be?"

"Phew, gramps, I'm not sure. Well, I don't want to protect. I have a shield, so I guess I don't want to go with dual swords. And really, I'd rather do without swords altogether for now. I do have this pretty nice mace, though."

"Well, there you go. So, you're an attacking warrior whose main weapons are the shield and mace, at least for now. Right?" The talkative simpleton suddenly turned serious and got down to business.

"Yeah, pretty much."

"Great. Then I'll make you a warrior. Just bring me ten enemy swords, clubs, or just any melee weapons, but make sure you get them in battle. Then I'll make you a warrior. Okay, that's all for now, off you go. I have to finish this whistle for my granddaughter."

You have a new quest offer: In Search of Steel.
Task: get 10 weapons from defeated enemies.
Reward:
400 experience
Opportunity to get your first class skills
Accept?

I was mad as a hornet when I left the old man. All I needed was a quest back in the lowlands; those swords were everywhere.

"What, the old man got you all confused?" Reineke walked up to me.

"No, not that. Where am I supposed to get ten swords? There are only animals around the city, so I'll have to go a ways to find them."

"I'm starting to feel like the Wizard of Oz!" laughed Reineke. "Calm down, my good man, I'll help you in your hour of need. I'm about to port to a little village where the bots are all around Level 20 and mostly goblins. Well, there are animals, undead, and unhuman, too, of course, but mostly it's just humanoids. You can get everything you need from them, and you'll even do some leveling-up. What do you think, want to come with me?"

"Well, of course!" I nearly jumped for joy. "I'd love to!"

"Oh, and here." Reineke pulled an amulet on a chain out of his pocket. "This is for you."

"For what?"

"Just a gift," Lis smiled. "I carried it around for a while when I was at your level. Someone gave it to me, as well, and I left it in my room after I leveled-up and found something better. Honestly, I almost never sell my old weapons and armor. I feel like I'd miss them. Anyway, you don't need armor, since they gave you a good set, but you could use this amulet. Take it."

I opened my exchange window, received the amulet, and checked it out.

Temple of Strength Amulet

+9 to strength

+13 to stamina

+7 to agility

+14% to critical strike chance.

When combined with the Blow from Below ability, 50% to your ability to instantly repeat it.

Class limitation: only warriors

Minimum level for use: 15

Elite! He gave me an elite amulet. I was in shock, to say the least.

"Cat got your tongue?" Lis asked amiably.

"Like you don't know. You don't mind giving me something elite?"

"My dad once told me to pay it forward," he said. "Let's head to the village."

"The scroll isn't too expensive?"

"Well, I need to go there regardless. By the way, have you forgotten anything?"

"To say thank you?"

"What do I need your thanks for? If the goblins kill you right when we get there, where will you respawn?"

"Oh, da-a-amn!" I even felt a little embarrassed. "Where's the northern gate? I had my respawn point there."

"Whatever, let's go. You can relink in the village. You'll probably die at some point anyway…"

"How will I get back from the village?"

"Well…by walking. You don't have the money or abilities for a horse yet. But it's okay, the locations between there and Aegan aren't too bad. Although there are PKers… And it's far. Or you can go to a different city—Khitskern and Fladridge are nearby.

94

"But I have to get back to the old man to finish my quest."

"You can finish it with someone else. They'll ask you if you've already been to another instructor, and you'll say you have. Then you just tell them what you got, and you'll finish the quest. They all have the same abilities."

After I linked to the respawn point and confirmed it by seeing the stone blink, Reineke pulled out a scroll and used it. We stepped into the portal that opened.

It left us in the middle of a village square. I could tell that it was the square thanks to an obviously communal well, a few stands, and some tongue-waggers sitting around discussing everything under the sun. Well, the respawn stone also helped. I didn't get a message with a story like, "…this village was founded by two brother hunters after a long trek through forests, mountains, and dales…" It turned out that not all settlements and sites deserved their own backstory. Or the developers were just too lazy to think one up for all the different places in the game.

The little village, from what I could tell, was small, with maybe a bit less than 40 homes. It was surrounded by a palisade wall, behind which, judging by the treetops peeking above it, was a forest. My map, which I opened as soon as we left the portal, helpfully told me that the village was called Tocbridge.

"Reineke, where are those two cities?" I asked Lis, correctly assuming that he was pressed for time.

"One is here, the other is here." He pulled his map out of his bag and pointed to them.

"Oh, wow, you have a map, too. Not just the built-in one."

"Yep. You can get one in a quest after Level 40. Or you can buy one, though they're really expensive."

"Does it show everything? The whole continent?"

"Not everything for the quests, no. You reveal it as you go along, and it shows where you've already been. The one you can buy shows everything, though, except dungeons and secret areas. But it's seriously expensive."

If someone at his level thought it was really expensive, then for me it was unthinkable. But who really cares? I had the built-in map, after all. The cities were very close. While it was a five-day walk to

Aegan, the other two were just a day and a half or two days away. One was to the north; one was to the east.

"Okay, I'll see you. Send me a message if you need anything."

Reineke shook my hand and headed for the village gate. When he got there, he turned and called back, "Don't forget to do some quests!"

"I won't," I said to his retreating figure. "Tomorrow."

Afraid to trust my memory, I immediately linked to the local headstone, which is what I had decided to call the respawn points. I sat down near the well and hit the log out button. I pulled myself out of the capsule with a groan and massaged my low back.

"I'm spending too much time lying down. That's not good, I need to move around more," I said to myself. "Maybe I should call up Elvira? Maybe I should eat first. Or I could combine the two: she can come, cook, and then we could get to work. First one, then the other."

My pleasant thoughts were interrupted by my phone ringing. I stepped over to the table and checked the screen—Mammoth was calling.

"Hi, Semyon Ilyich," I answered.

"He-e-ey, Nikiforov! You deigned to pick up your phone! I guess you're just drinking your life away." The boss's roars echoed across the phone line.

"Yeah, right. I'm doing what you told me to do—spending every day sitting in the game...well, laying."

"You aren't doing crap! Where's my article? Where's my article, you twerp?"

"What am I, a meteor?" My confusion was completely sincere. I'd only spent three days in there...or had it been four?

"You have a month to write a nine-part article series. Every three days, get out and write something!"

"What do you mean, nine-part series? Okay, so it may have grown a little, but not by that much. Six-part! We talked about six articles."

"Okay, fine. Six. But the first one needs to be in my inbox tomorrow morning. No matter what!"

"No matter what?"

"No matter what. Make it happen!"

"I'll figure something out," I said dejectedly and hung up the phone. I looked to see who else had called and saw that that was Mammoth's sixth call that day.

Looks like some clients of his are turning up the heat, I thought. *They paid money, now they want to see some results. They should have just paid me. I'd have written the whole thing for them without ever even trying the game. This way...*

But what frustrated me most was that my plans for Elvira were off. Girls and writing serious material generally go together as well as "evil" and "genius."

After scarfing down some pelmeni, I sat down at my computer and confidently typed in my title: "A New World for Millions."

I hammered away until 2 a.m. The article didn't turn out too badly, and Mammoth would be happy, at least, with the gold-star treatment I gave Raidion. I brushed my hair back and said, "Nice work, nice work. Genius! A star in the modern literary firmament."

And with my debt paid, I went to bed with battle waiting in the morning...again...

***

It was morning in the village. Roosters crowed in the yards, some bird squawked away annoyingly from behind the palisade wall, the villagers walking up to the communal well added to the hubbub, and an elder or just some old guy bellowed along. I went over to see if he needed anything, though the noise he made could have just been his normal manner of speaking.

"Can I help you?" I asked him for the third time.

"Definitely," he nodded his head. "E-e-eah, for sure—good timing!"

That "e-e-eah" was starting to get to me.

"E-e-eah what?"

"E-e-eah, I need help!"

"Help with what?"

"Exactly!"

"What, your ear?"

"No, no, no, my ears are fine. My eyes, too! And my teeth…the few I have left. Don't worry about them. I need help!"

"What kind of help do you need, you simpleton?"

"Definite help!"

"O-o-okay… Oh, by the way, how much will you pay?"

"Ah-ha, down to business!" The old man's face instantly went from moronic to focused, and his manner altered markedly. Apparently, he took me for someone in charge, or maybe just some rascal. "We'll write a receipt for 300 gold, and you'll get 230 if you do the job. What do you say?"

"270."

"240."

"285."

"250."

"Got it!"

"What?"

"It's a deal. What do you need me to do?"

"Kill a monster!"

"What kind and where?"

"What kind…what kind…a monstrous one! You leave the village, stay left, and go two miles. Its den is by the swamp."

"And why can't you and the other men here take care of him?"

"They're afraid. They think they'll fail and even be cursed. There's an old graveyard there and a ruined castle nearby. Nasty place. Even a cursed wood!"

"Maybe it's the other way around? A castle with a graveyard nearby?"

"No, my dear sir. The graveyard has always been there—our great-grandfathers are buried there. But the castle's only been there for four hundred years. Although, sure they built it on an older foundation."

"Who destroyed this castle?"

"We fought the skeletons two hundred or so years ago, and they laid siege to our old landlord in there. But the undead came at the castle—experienced warriors who knew the place. Skeletons and their masters, all skeletons, too. With crowns, and glowing candles for eyes. And enormous swords."

"Liches?"

"How should I know? Probably. But the warriors were good, even if they didn't have any meat on them—all bones. They took the castle. The landlord didn't want to become a zombie, so he used some kind of magic and—poof, he, his family, and his warriors were in the afterlife, the skeletons were piles of bones, and the castle was in ruins. And the village didn't have a landlord anymore. It was odd at first—my grandfather told me, and his grandfather told him. But they liked it! Later on, of course, some cousin of the landlord came and told everyone he was taking charge. But then one night he went for a walk in the marsh for some reason..."

"And?"

"And anyone who goes for a walk in the marsh at night is completely taken over by the power of evil... Probably drowned... Or somebody ate him. My grandfather told me something was howling that night fit to burst... Maybe 240?"

"250. And some food."

"Fine. As soon as you bring us that thing's head, I'll write the receipt, and you'll get your money. Okay?"

> **You have a new quest offer: Kill the Swamp Beast.**
> **Task: Kill the monster near the swamp and bring its head to the old man.**
> **Reward:**
> **250 gold**
> **1000 experience**
> **Accept?**

Needless to say, I accepted.

"Okay. What's the receipt for?"

"Once a month, someone comes from the city, from Fladridge, to collect taxes, so he needs a report—who paid who what, if they needed to pay for something."

"Taxes?"

"In life, you always have to pay someone something. We're no different. We pay Fladridge, but if we have a problem, they help us. For example, two years ago, there was a bad harvest after some witches wove a herb wolf into the field and the wheat rotted. They sent us that, um...human-kind aid. Food, sugar, salt."

"Humanitarian."

"What?"

"It's humanitarian aid. It means they sent it out of the goodness of their hearts."

"Oh, right, right," the old man nodded. "That's what I'm saying; they're good people. And we pay them taxes like we're supposed to. They left us money so we could hire one of you passers-by in case we have a problem. But we have to have a receipt: so-and-so gave so much, so-and-so got so much. So, we'll write the receipt as soon as you kill the beast."

"Sounds good! Hey, maybe someone else needs help around here?"

"Of course!" And the old man told me about all the settlement's problems.

Soon, I had a quest from the blacksmith to collect 20 goblin arrowheads, while a heavy-set woman from the local tavern needed me to bring her five boar legs—five left forelegs, to be exact. She must have told me five times, "Left fore, my dear. Don't forget! I'll be sure to have something to thank you with!" She winked coquettishly after that last part.

Given the fact that she weighed more than I did, my capsule, and Mammoth breathing down my neck put together, I had to wonder if going through with that was worth it. She'd crush me... She wasn't a tank, so you couldn't just heave a grenade under there—tanks weren't as dangerous. But my fears were unfounded. It turned out the NPC woman wanted to give me experience, money, and three days' worth of dry rations in exchange for those left forelegs. The old man sent me some food, too, so I was set.

A local shepherd also needed me to find a lost cow and let him know where the poor guy was. Happily, that was it; I didn't need to bring it back myself.

That was all the people I could find in the village with problems, so I set off quickly for the gates. I figured, as any normal person would, that the faster I got started, the faster I'd finish.

Just like in Aegan, the Tocbridge forest began right outside the gate. The only difference was that roads led away from Aegan, while all Tocbridge had were some narrow paths. When I was about a hundred strides from the village, I opened my map and checked the status of my quests. The Fayroll developers had made things easy for players. Zones with quest monsters or items blinked red on the map. Their exact location, of course, wasn't shown, but the blinking zone wasn't that big—five hundred meters or so in diameter. It was much better than in other games, where you were supposed to get a horn from some hairy, seven-legged creature, but they didn't tell you where the thing was or show it on the map. So, you were left wandering around the whole game hoping you'd come across it. Here they gave you a marker.

The closest blinking area was very close, just a few steps away. And, by all appearances, it was the goblin arrowheads. Probably with goblins to go with them. I left the path and moved stealthily (I thought) between the birches and pines.

"Human!" a squeaky voice rang out. "Goblins see human! Goblins love to eat human! Human is delicious! Goblins love to crunch human!"

Suddenly, I took 20 damage, so that must have come from somewhere... About five meters away, stood a short, green, round-eyed thing, and he was again pulling back his bow.

"Goblins will eat human. Human and frog eggs—together more fun and tastier!"

I leaped toward him, leaning away from the arrow he loosed at me from almost point-blank range, and laid into him with my mace. The goblin apparently wasn't that strong, as his health turned immediately red. My next blow drew a long wail and finished him off!

He yielded a few copper coins, a piece of dirty cloth, and three arrowheads.

You have 17 more arrowheads left to collect before you can complete the quest.

"That was Khryk yelling. He said there's good food around, but it's still kicking." I heard a voice say, and a group of five goblins jumped at me from the surrounding trees.

"Yeah, good food!" they gibbered as they rushed me. "Juicy, tasty food! Khryk not lie!"

"It kill Khryk!"

"Okay, then we eat it longer than with Khryk! And then we eat Khryk! Kill him!"

Three of them ran at me waving axes. Two began quickly unslinging bows.

"Phew, boy! They're easy to kill, but there are five of them. Better hurry!"

I met the first goblin with a blow from my mace that took off half his health. Dodging his rusty sword, my next strike found the second goblin for a similar result. The no less rusted saber of the third clanged off my breastplate, and my return swing took his health into the critical zone. Apparently, my item bonuses kicked in.

The first arrows smacked into me, but I wasn't worried anymore. It looked like I wouldn't have a problem finishing off the five goblins. A few more blows took care of the first three gluttons, freeing me to charge the archers.

"Not bad. Not terribly strong, and not terribly smart," I mused as I stripped the dead goblins. My collection of arrowheads (12 of 20) and swords (three of 10) was growing.

"Hey, goblins!" I thundered. "Good food here! Come on!"

Somewhere, in the bushes, I heard a rustling. "Food-food-food." The goblins were hurrying to feed.

The next half hour was spent polishing off one short bugger after another. They ran up in groups of three to five, saying, "M-m-m! Juicy food! Goblins love swallow human!" Their headlong charge was broken only by my friendly smile and welcoming mace.

In the space of that 30 minutes, I finished the blacksmith's quest as well as my class ability quest, watched my pile of copper coins grow, collected an enormous amount of goblin trash (rags, buttons, buckles, half a window shutter...), and even got some things for archery. I would have stopped killing goblins there, but I was close to the next level. A bit longer and there it was.

As soon as I leveled-up, I jumped behind a tree and headed for the path to the village.

The goblins were eternally hungry, but they had no desire to stray very far, so none of them ran after me. I heard them poking around the area, "Khrym not alive! Gryk, too! Where food that kill them?"

I quietly walked out into the clearing and headed for the forest to finish the blacksmith's quest. No point in waiting. After that, I would go see what I should do about that monster. Oh, and I wanted to check out the graveyard and the castle. I was curious, and maybe I'd find something interesting

Chapter Eight
In and Out of the Forest

The blacksmith was surprised. "That was fast! You're obviously quite the warrior. And the arrowheads are perfect! Here's your reward."

> **You completed a quest: Disarm the Goblins.**
> **Reward:**
> **800 experience**
> **35 silver coins**
> **20% discount on smithy services in Tocbridge**
> **+8% friendship shown toward you by the residents of Tocbridge**

"Wow!" I was excited. "So much right away."

"Just like we agreed," the blacksmith reasonably observed.

"By the way," I addressed him once more as he looked over the arrowheads I'd brought, "who can I sell things to around here? I have some stuff I got from the goblins, and I don't feel like carrying it around."

"Talk to Shindlik Torgash," he responded quickly. "He's a complete goon, and he'll squeeze you for every copper coin he can, but he pays in real coin, and he pays right away. His stand is right behind that house over there. If you have anything metal, like swords or armor, I might be willing to take it off your hands."

I unloaded everything I had onto the counter.

"Pick what you want, well, if there even is anything you want, obviously."

The blacksmith quickly dug through the pile of goblin junk, picking out a few items and placing them on the side.

"I'll take all of this," he said five minutes later. His finger jabbed toward a small pile of sword fragments, buttons, and some other metal goods. "I'll give you 40 silver coins."

"You'd only give me 40 coins for this pile of art-house treasure and vintage finery?" My grandmother's voice rang in my head, "You have to haggle. Always haggle. Otherwise, they won't respect you."

"For this assembly of rare goblin goods—only 40 silver coins? No-o-o-o, my friend. I'm better off hanging onto it if—"

"I hope you get cholera," the blacksmith interrupted. "Fifty, and that's it. And no more haggling."

"Fifty it is then," I agreed, sweeping the rest of the pile back into my bag. I pocketed my 50 silver coins and went off to find Shindlik—to haggle some more.

My purse was in pretty decent shape. On the one hand, having more than 100 gold wasn't bad for someone who'd been playing the game for less than a week. On the other, that still wasn't enough to buy anything nice. It was enough for some potions, food, or maybe the plainest equipment out there, though I'd have to find a vendor; I still didn't have enough to go shopping at the auction. Then again, I wasn't too concerned about money. I could always spend real cash at the auction if I had to (though I couldn't think of what could possibly prompt me to do that).

Oh, and the monetary system in Fayroll was as simple as it gets:

One gold was worth 100 silver coins.

One silver coin was worth 100 copper coins.

One copper coin, well, was one copper coin. They didn't have any half-coins or anything like that. And money was converted automatically, so the pile of copper I collected from the ravenous goblins turned into a pair of good-looking silver coins.

And the line between real and virtual money was fine, if clearly felt. Each player could support himself using real money, though there was a limit—$5000 for each account—or the local equivalent, of course. You could invest that amount in your player at once, later, or gradually. You could buy armor, weapons, scrolls. But as soon as you hit that amount, you couldn't add any more. All further extravagance had to be financed by in-game money—the kind you earned in the game. And if you deleted your character and started a new one, the only money you could spend on it was what you had left under the cap. The only thing you could do if you didn't want to put in the work was open a new account. Lots of people, incidentally, did just that.

The only exception was spending money on decorations. For example, you could pay to make your sword look like Conan the Barbarian's. It would look impressive and imposing, but the attributes wouldn't change in the least. Or, alternatively, you could decorate the hell out of your hotel room, hanging works of art all over the walls. That didn't get you anything, but it looked nice. The company made that compromise to please their more aesthetically minded gamers, though there were special conditions, and you had to sign an additional agreement.

Sure, there were attempts to scam people on the black market or poke holes in the code, but none of them ended well for the people involved. The developers turned a blind eye to people selling in-game items for real money and transferring that money to outside accounts, as they might have even had a hand in that pot as well. But attempts to bring unauthorized money into the game were too much for them given the serious problems they could face under money laundering laws. And that could have implications for their gaming license. So anyone operating in the shadows knew Fayroll was a one-way street.

Really, I was surprised by how counter-intuitive the whole thing was. Usually, everything was the other way around—game developers wanted you to pour money into their games. It would have been interesting to sit down with the Fayroll developers and ask them what their reasoning was.

Shindlik turned out to be an unusually stingy and shrewd little halfling who bargained for every copper coin he could get. And when, on the verge of righteous wrath, he pulled a healthy chunk of hair out of his scalp and accused me of wanting to see his family starve, it became crystal clear that he wasn't going to give in. I gave him the rest of my junk, pocketed his 25 silver coins, and headed for the village gate. I still had a cow to find and a graveyard to visit. Oh, and the woods... What was it? Right, there was a monster by the swamp that I needed to kill.

The map showed me that the cow just happened to be moving toward the very same swamp. The blinking quest area on the map was moving quickly toward the east in its direction.

"I'd better hurry," I decided. "That monster can't eat the cow, or the quest would be over. I assume."

After sprinting down the path for a few kilometers, I pulled out my map again and realized I needed to cut into the forest; the swamp was perpendicular to my location. A hundred meters in, I decided to make sure there weren't any goblins around.

"Hey, tasty food is here!" I shouted loudly. "Juicy, crunchy food here!"

Nothing. I couldn't hear anyone crashing through the bushes, drooling as they ran.

"Good thing," I said, and kept going without worrying too much about stealth.

A kilometer and a half or so later, I noticed the landscape changing. Tall pines were replaced by birches and firs. The grass under my feet was thicker—the swamp was obviously nearby.

"Good job by the designers!" I was impressed. "Just like in real life."

I opened my map again to see that the cow was nearby. And so was the monster.

"He's going to eat it!" I quickened my pace.

A couple minutes later, I heard a scared moo, or at least a moo that was as scared as moos can be, and some cracking. Someone was breaking through the birches. Of course, it was the cow, and we broke into a small clearing at the same time from opposite sides. It jumped toward me once I caught its eye, amusingly flaunting its hooves.

"Mo-o-o," it said again. But in that "mo-o-o," I thought I heard something like "mo-o-onsters everywhere, almost ate me!"

And there was a reason for that. Just behind the cow, the monster itself rushed into the clearing. It was a disgusting beast, and the programmers were obviously suffering from a hangover or were just in a bad mood when they thought it up.

It was Level 20, and it had six legs, a scorpion tail, a chitin body, two pincers, compound eyes, and mandibles to round out the picture. Some mix of a fly, a crayfish, a spider, and a scorpion. Above its head were blue letters:

"Burrig—quest monster"

Ooh, a beast from the quest. With its own name! The monsters in Fayroll were both diverse and straightforward. Bots were divided into:

Usual—your different types of goblins, harpies, wolves, specters, robbers, and other types of evil spirits, undead, and even humanoid races. They made up 95 percent of the bot enemies players dealt with.

Quest—opponents created especially for quests. There were both named and unnamed quest monsters, though the named ones gave you a much better chance of finding a good item than their unnamed friends. On the other hand, they were also much more dangerous.

Leaders—a rare type of named monster endowed with remarkable physical or even magical power. They always gave you good things, though killing them was a nightmare. And you couldn't just go looking for them since they only appeared randomly at locations with the right level.

Dungeon masters—formidable foes. Generally speaking, they were the last monsters you dealt with in dungeons, and they were the fastest, most devious, and most dangerous ones in there. The players called them bosses.

Epic—the strongest enemies the game had to offer. Clans sent raids after them, and figuring out who exactly killed who was always tricky. Nobody had been able to kill the Kraken yet. On the plus side, the reward you got for killing them was substantial, on par with the difficulty.

Well, the most dangerous enemy in Fayroll, just like in real life, was Man. Don't forget about PKers. They were hard to kill, and the reward varied…

The cow ran past me mooing, and a message popped up:

You finished a quest: Find the Cow.
To get your reward, tell the shepherd where the cow is.

How simple. Yeah, I can just turn around and march straight over there.

Burrig saw me, hissed, and waved its spiked tail around menacingly.

"Man, I should have been an archer," I hissed back as I circled to my left around Burrig. It bulged out its eyes and circled with me, amiably clacking its pincers all the while.

We had almost done a complete circle around each other when Burrig was the first to crack. It lunged. I instinctively ducked, and its pincers clacked shut above my head. In front of me, I saw my opponent's right chitin side was open. Covering the left part of my torso with my shield, I swung upward to land my first blow, after which I jumped to my right and smacked it again near its tail.

I was lucky again, as one of the two hits was critical. Burrig's health meter went from green to yellow, meaning that I'd taken out 30-40 percent of its health.

Burrig roared, turned toward me, and tried to sting me with its tail. Either I was just faster, or I'd damaged something. One way or another, the strike missed its target. Its tail buried itself in the ground, and Burrig was left posed awkwardly. I took the chance to jump in and slam my mace against its head. Green slime flew, and a nasty sound told me I'd taken out its eye.

I should have jumped back, but for some reason, I hesitated. Burrig shook its head, spraying slime from its eye everywhere, and clamped its left mandible down on my arm.

You were poisoned!
The poison will sap 0.7 health per second for five minutes!

Oh, come on! I had to hurry—I had a lot of health, I wasn't that weak, to begin with, and I'd spent a lot of points on stamina, but poison wasn't something to be taken lightly.

I moved to Burrig's left. Its eye was gone, so I was in its blind spot, and it was weakening; its health was already in the red section.

"Let's do this!" I jumped forward and landed what I thought was a heavy blow to its back leg. It gave way, and Burrig crumpled onto its left side. I landed another strike to its head. The monster's legs flailed upward, and it died.

> **You unlocked Bestiary, Level 1.**
> **To get it, destroy ten more named monsters.**
> **Reward:**
> **Fearless, a passive attribute, Level 1: +1% resistance to mental effects**
> **+1 to stamina**
> **+1 to agility**
> **To see similar messages, go to the Action section of the attribute window.**

> **You unlocked Level 21!**
> **Points ready to be distributed: 5**

Oh, nice. I leveled-up too!

> **You completed a quest: Kill the Swamp Beast.**
> **To get your reward, go show Burrig's head to the old man.**

Oh, right, I needed the head. I leaned over my fallen foe and found that not much was left of it, just the head and a pincer—the left one, for some reason.

> **Burrig's pincer. Can be used by a craftsman to create an item or in other ways.**

That's it. And here I thought I'd get something rare—nope, just the pincer. *Oh, but wait! It had a lair.*

I hurried to the edge of the swamp. It was visible through the birches, especially where there were gaps made first by the cow and then by the monster. On the way, I had an apple—the poison was still active, and it was still damaging me, if slowly. And who knew? Maybe the beast could respawn.

The lair was easy to see. It really was on the very edge of the swamp, and it looked like a deep, although narrow, hole in the earth.

I quickly jumped in and found myself in a small cave littered with rotten leaves. I poked around in the leaves with my mace and found something that first caught on my weapon and then glistened in the semi-darkness.

You unlocked Sharp Eye, Level 1.

To get it, find 49 more tombs, treasure troves, hiding places, and stashes around Fayroll.

Reward:

Riches, a passive attribute, Level 1: +3% to the coins you get from beaten enemies

+1 to stamina

+1 to agility

To see similar messages, go to the Action section of the attribute window.

Well, this has been a productive five minutes. But what was hiding from me?

You found Burrig's lair and discovered:

67 gold

Rough Work Shoulder Guard

Talisman

Okay, so the gold is good, but what's that about a shoulder guard?

Rough Work Shoulder Guard

Protection: 60

+3 to strength

+7% to protection from cold

Durability: 110/120

Minimum level to use: 20

"I'll sell that," I decided. "Mine is much better. But what about the talisman?"

That's when it hit me that I was doing all that in a small lair belonging to what was a pretty tough beast that could respawn at any moment. With that in mind, I quickly crawled out and put half a kilometer between it and me. I looked around and, just to make sure, called out, "Food here, good food!" There was no reaction, so I pulled out the talisman. It was round, with a hole in the center. In the middle of the hole, was something that looked like a tear.

Tearful Goddess Knight Talisman
This talisman belonged to Olaf von Dal, a Knight of the Tearful Goddess Order. Produce it in any of the order's missions (found in all Fayroll cities) and confirm that he was killed to get a reward.

You have a new quest offer: Remembering the Fallen.
Task: Let the brothers in the knight's order know that he is dead.
Reward:
100 gold
500 experience
+5 friendship with the Tearful Goddess Order
Accept?

Well, that works. Easy money, easy experience. Especially since I was planning to head to Fladridge after the village anyway, and the order has missions in every city. Lucky. But I wondered—who was the Tearful Goddess? I thought things were much simpler with the pantheon of gods in Fayroll—there wasn't one. I'd have to check that out on the forums.

Oh, and I needed to distribute my attribute points after leveling-up twice. After adding everything to strength and stamina (in for a penny, in for a pound), with the exception of one point each for agility and intellect, I looked to see what I had.

Basic attributes:
Strength: 91 (60+31)

Intellect: 4
Agility: 17 (10+7)
Stamina: 75 (45+30)
Wisdom: 3

After all that, I took stock of the situation: the cow was found, the monster was dead. All I had left to do was find the boar legs, though I also wanted to stop by the graveyard. I opened my map and saw that the graveyard was nearby, while the boars looked to be about three kilometers away.

"I'll go check out the graves," I decided. "And there was a grove of trees, too. On the way back, I'll take care of the boars."

The graveyard was exactly what you might expect. There wasn't anything pulled from a Romero film—a haze over the graves, crows landing on the gravestones, arms reaching out of piles of earth. Everything was serene and noble; birds were singing, ivy spread between the graves, and gravestones sank into the ground. The whole thing was fairly small, and behind it, through a hole in the wall, the picturesque ruins of the castle could be seen.

Before I walked out into the graveyard, I made sure my health was at the maximum level, and the poison had worn off. I then pulled out my mace and stealthily crept around. Nothing happened. No skeletons came crawling out of the ground, no thunder rolled through the sky, and no demonic laughter rang out. The sun kept shining, the birds kept singing. I spent half an hour exploring, only to find, to my disappointment, that I had wasted my time.

Well, maybe there's something over in the ruins? I thought, climbing through the hole in the wall and wandering between the enormous boulders embedded in the long grass. Before the explosion, the area must have been the castle wall.

I cursed the old man after yet another half hour. "Unclean places, undead...miracles, the devil walking around. Nothing but some stones and grass!"

With that, I left the ruins through what looked to be the old entrance to the castle's inner courtyard. Beyond them stretched a plain, and on the horizon was a small wood—probably the one the old man mentioned.

"It's weird that they built castles here. And where's the moat? Where's the drawbridge?" I noted with surprise. "No wonder the siege was so short."

But what about the woods? I couldn't decide if I wanted to go check them out or not...

I was leaning toward giving up on the whole thing, seeing as how I didn't have a quest in the woods and no longer believed anything the old man said. Not only were there no skeletons, but there weren't even any bones. Although maybe the skeletons came out at night? Maybe that was when they caught passers-by and tore them to pieces. *Whatever.*

I had almost made up my mind. "Yea-a-ah, screw it. I'll go get the boars, finish my quests, and head for Fladridge."

But just then, something glinting in the left-hand side of the arc caught my eye. I brushed aside the grass with my foot and bent over.

You found a hiding place and discovered:
144 gold
Lucky Earring
Deadly Archer Bracelet

Well, hello there! The day is saved! The items turned out to be pretty good, and both violet. I didn't need the archer bracelet in the least, though I was very excited about the earring:

Lucky Earring
+6 to stamina
+5 to intellect
+5% to critical strike chance
+7% to your chances of getting items from dead enemies
+5% gold looted from dead enemies
Durability: 160/160
Minimum level for use: 25

I didn't even care that I couldn't wear it yet—I was a patient person, and I could wait. However, I really needed to get to the city.

If I died, there was no way I would find another earring like that one. It was time to follow Willie's advice and rent a room since I hadn't had time to do so earlier. First, I was rolled up in the carpet, then I was fighting skeletons, then something else... And there wasn't a hotel in the village.

I was about to head back into the forest when a small little something sitting inside me—something we all have—started needling away, "Maybe it's worth checking it out? There were some great items here, so maybe you'll find even better ones there? Or something else valuable?"

I responded to my inner voice reasonably, "But why? There used to be a castle here, but what was ever there? People lived here and would have needed to hide things, but who lived there?"

"You'll regret it if you don't go. It's right there... You'll be back before nightfall!"

"Right, and then I'll have to hunt boar in the dark!"

"Oh, come on. What do you have to lose?"

I realized that arguing with myself was pointless and started toward the wood.

Chapter Nine
Good Intentions

The plain wasn't exactly lifeless. As I went, I occasionally did my part to check any potential overpopulation in the local fauna, bashing gophers and snakes over the head with my mace. I even finished off an emaciated goblin who had somehow found his way there. That proved a handy distraction, as the distance between the castle and the woods turned out to be much farther than I thought at first. It actually took me about two hours to cover it. A bit of an optical illusion there.

The sun had already crested its peak, and on I walked. Though, to be honest, I was enjoying myself and looking forward to dipping my feet in the cool stream that I was sure would be there. A digital pleasure, of course, but one that certainly seemed real enough.

I entered the wood and strained my ears to listen for the sound of running water. However, instead, I heard a woman's cry coming from the bushes a couple meters away from me, "Hey, stop it! Please, don't!"

I pulled out my mace and ran toward the sound. While I may not be the most virtuous guy out there, and I don't recommend trying to play on any kind of civil responsibility I might feel, I can't stand it when people insult or hit women or children. And it sounded like that was exactly what was happening.

Two leaps later, I was into the bushes and saw a rather unpleasant picture lay out before me—a Level 23 player named Gvegory was using his curved saber to chop up some kind of ghastly creature, obviously female. It scrunched up its monkey-like face, burst into tears, and screamed, "Please don't! I'm begging you!"

Gvegory was unmoved and in the process of raising his saber, obviously intending to chop off the poor creature's arm.

"Hey, what are you, some kind of monster?" I asked him.

He wheeled his whole body around wolfishly and brandished his saber. "Who are you? What do you care?" he yelled.

"Doesn't matter," I answered. "Why are you bothering her? She isn't aggressive, she didn't attack you. You'll cut off her arm, and she still won't do anything to you. Look at her; she didn't exactly win the lottery as it is. Look at the poor thing cowering there, and you're going all maniac on her."

"What do you care? I'll cut what I want to cut."

"It doesn't matter to me, it's just crazy…"

"It's crazy? She's just code! Only code!" Gvegory was nearly howling.

"So, she's just code," I answered as evenly as I could. "She still cries. She's hurting. You aren't some kind of wild animal, so just let her go."

"And if I don't?"

"Come on, we're talking like a couple fifth-graders. Let's just go. You can head over to that forest, and you'll find everything you need there. Boars, goblins, even some kind of monster with its own name. And then at night, the skeletons come out! You can grind them into little pieces all you want."

"Listen, you and your human rights," snarled Gvegory. "I'll decide who I kill when. You don't stick your nose in how I play the game. And if you do, I'll report you to the admin."

"Help me! I don't want to die again," the creature whispered to me, seeing Gvegory's narrowed eyes and raised saber.

I really didn't want to be a PKer, since that came with penalties, besides, well… But I also didn't want to leave even that miserable little piece of code with that psychopath. It was time for some mind games…

"Did you cut her, too?" I asked in a lofty voice.

"Cut who?" Gvegory more choked out the words than said them.

"The one who wouldn't put out. I guess you were the only one she turned down, right?"

"Shut up, you bitch!" He turned, his eyes rolled back, and a string of drool leaked from his mouth.

Oh, wow, he's really crazy. This guy needs some big medics to take him to a hospital in a straightjacket. Straight to Dr. Kaschenko. Well, I was right.

"I'll cut all of you!!" screamed Gvegory. "All of you! You, and this piece of trash, and that piece of trash!"

And with that, he thrust his saber at me. We were still standing pretty far apart, so he missed by a wide margin, but the game counted his attempt as a player-on-player attack. I could kill him with a clear conscience.

Gvegory squealed, closed the distance, and tried to land a downward blow. But I was no helpless creature, so I dodged and buried my mace in his right side. His next cut was blocked by my shield and swiped away the arm holding the saber to open his chest—an opportunity I took full advantage of by smashing it with all my strength. The power of the strike sent him tumbling backward, and I quickly jumped in and landed another blow, this time to the head. That was enough to finish him off.

You unlocked Killer Punisher, Level 1.

To get it, punish 29 more players who have killed other players.

Reward:

+1 to strength

+0.1% damage done by all weapon types

To see similar messages, go to the Action section of the attribute window.

Gvegory turned into a shadow that then completely disappeared. That was the first time I saw what happened to players when they died.

"Wow, seriously a psychopath," I muttered. "He's a danger to society, and now he's going to go slit someone's throat in the real world."

I was stunned. I'd been told that many people who weren't right in the head played video games to act out their desires rather than inflict them on the actual public. But to meet someone like that myself...

I found the "Contact Administrator" button in the panel, copied the conversation I had with the mutant to the message, added some comments of my own, as well as a request to pass it and Gvegory's personal information on to law enforcement, and clicked "Send." Obviously, I didn't expect them to do anything—they had a hands-off policy, and they were big into protecting personal information... Still, if he'd been able to, he would have killed me, and he wouldn't have cared if it were the real world or the virtual one.

I didn't help things by provoking him. If he decided to log out of the game then, he'd go pick up an axe and head for the street, or, God forbid, some kind of firearm. I was getting frantic.

> **Thank you for your message. Your information was reviewed under article 14.6 of the Agreement Between the Player and the Company and sent to law enforcement officials along with the place of residence listed by the player at registration.**

Well, now I just had to hope that the psychopath had listed his actual city. But good job by Raidion. It was smart of them to put a clause like that in the agreement. I wondered what else was in it, seeing as how I didn't read it before agreeing to the whole thing—like 99.9 percent of the other players in the game. I would have to go back and read it.

A sob from my left reminded me of the miserable creature over there. She was still sitting on the ground where I first saw her. Her wounds, however, were beginning to close—she was an NPC, after all—that and the fact that the game had a humane policy against causing psychological trauma.

"Here," I said, tossing her an apple from my bag. "Eat it, you'll feel better."

She caught the rosy piece of fruit and gazed at me with enormous green eyes that looked out of place in her wrinkled, ape-like face.

At the same time, I went over to the remains of Gvegory. I couldn't decide if I should collect his things or leave them lying there. "Whatever, all's fair in love and war," I said, adding my voice to marauders of all times and peoples, and reached out my hand.

He didn't really have much. The saber was just average, and everything else was blue or even colorless. In a word, nothing.

A ding told me that I had a new message. *What a surprise!*

"I'm going to find you. I'll find you here in the game, and I'll find you in real life. And you'll die a slow death! I hate you!"

I was really starting to get a following. That was already the third person to promise me a fun rest of my life—in just a couple days. Sticking around for a couple more weeks would accumulate enough for a whole new clan created just to hate me.

Gvegory's letter didn't bother me in the least. It made me feel better, in fact. First, it meant that he hadn't logged out, grabbed a knife, and started slashing everyone he could find with it. Second, let him hate me. What did it matter? If he found me, we'd see who was better. So far, I was up 1-0. And after the army, nothing in real life scared me. Except a shovel. And churches still put the fear of God into me...

"Why?" the creature's voice rang out quietly, if distinctly. "Why did you stand up for me?"

I turned toward her. She was still sitting there clutching the apple, which she hadn't taken a single bite of.

"Well, how do I say this, my green friend," I began with some puzzlement. I hadn't expected her to wonder why I behaved the way I did. I thought she'd just thank me and crawl up into a tree to lick her wounds or gallop off somewhere. I didn't have a quest to protect or kill her, after all. "Well, we don't like it when people kill women. At least, as long as the woman didn't attack you first."

"But you two are the same. Why did he torture me and you didn't?"

"He's a psychopath," I explained amiably. "He's crazy."

The creature scrunched up her face, apparently not understanding.

"You've seen how plants get sick, right?" I asked, and she nodded in response.

"He's sick, too. In the head. But hey, don't worry about it too much or you'll get sick, too."

"I'd like to reward you for your kindness and for saving me," she said quietly but firmly, her eyes flashing.

I perked up—some kind of freebie. I hoped it would be something I could use. But still, I wondered who she even was.

"Ah, don't worry about it, I was just helping," I said modestly. She was still an NPC so her code wouldn't let her change her mind. "But hey, who are you?"

"I'm a dryad. Keeper of the Western Ranges," she responded with a proud tilt of her head.

"Are there other keepers?"

The dryad looked closely at me and said, "You should know the history of the world you're living in. Anyway, nobody remembers us anymore, just the Ancients. You may not have heard of us. There are four keepers, each responsible for their own lands. Though we don't have much power remaining…"

"Yeah, I see that. That guy just about killed you. And you're the keeper…"

"Yes, that's how it is now," the dryad answered sadly.

I hadn't come across mentions of dryads anywhere, and there was another thing—she didn't have a name, a level, a class, or a race above her. I only then noticed that…

"Ah, don't get so gloomy," I said cheerfully. "Don't worry. So, what did you want to give me? And what's your name?"

"I'll tell you about my name later," the creature said busily. "I'd like to give you a friend who will be your devoted and helpful companion. And a strong one, too. Which would you like, a wolf or a bear?"

"Oh, wow, you want to give me an animal to defend me?" I asked.

"Yes. Warriors value them highly!"

"Yes, but," I hemmed and hawed, "they're such a hassle—feeding, watering, cleaning. No, thanks, I don't want to deal with all of that!"

"So you're refusing?" The dryad was amazed.

"Well, yes!"

"You don't like animals?" She frowned.

"I like them," I said to cover my bases, making sure I didn't get her angry unnecessarily. "I just don't have time for them. I forget to eat sometimes as it is, and you can't forget to feed them. And they need walks I can't spend time on. I mean, we're responsible for the animals we have in our care, and I'm not even that responsible when it comes to myself..."

"That makes sense," the dryad said. "Spoken like a responsible man! And well said! Then I'll give you a different gift."

She stood, waved her arms, and three flames appeared in her palm. "These are the seeds of the great tree Tserlusii. Its wood is rare and unusually strong. And valuable, too—it costs three times its weight in gold. Nourish it, and you will find yourself with untold wealth."

Well now, that was something new...

"Thanks, miss. But you have to plant them, water them, take care of them... And more. I'm a warrior, and I don't have time for that. I don't know how to, either, and I don't really want to in the first place."

"You're saying no again?" The dryad's eyes were as big as saucers.

The whole thing reminded me of an old story. A guy found a ruble, ran over it with an iron, and was surprised to find it turn into three rubles. He ironed them again and found himself looking at five. Then ten. Sadly, it didn't end that well. He ironed them once more and was left with just that first ruble. Maybe, I could avoid repeating his mistake.

"Then I'll offer you one more reward: I'll teach you the Forest Paths ability, so you never again get lost anywhere in a forest..."

I stopped to think. On one hand, that wasn't a bad ability. On the other, getting lost in local forests wasn't a big deal, and, after all, I had the built-in map... I decided to see what I could get for dessert—the third offer couldn't have been the last.

"No?" the dryad asked again.

"No, my dear. I told you: I didn't save you to get a reward," I answered, but I felt my soul dying a little.

As soon as I said that, trumpets blared, the dryad was enveloped in a golden radiance, and above her golden cocoon appeared a name: Eiliana the West. I sat down on the grass in stunned surprise. Five seconds later the cocoon exploded in a cloud of gold sparks, and in front of me was a stunningly beautiful girl with green hair. She looked nothing like the miserable beast I had been talking to, with the exception of her eyes.

"The prophecy was fulfilled that was spoken by our protectress, Her Highness the Goddess Mesmerta. Before the Exodus, she said that my three sisters and I would be given our freedom by a warrior who would protect one of us out of the goodness of his heart, and would not accept a reward. There were warriors who protected me, but none of them declined my rewards. You were the first to stand up to the temptations of power, gold, and magic.

"That's all great," I said, a bit dumbfounded, "but what does it mean?"

"It means you have the power to fulfill the divine prophesy and free us!"

> **You unlocked History of Eiliana the West, a hidden quest.**
> **This quest is the key to a series of hidden quests.**
> **Task: Hear the dryad's story and agree to her request.**
> **Reward:**
> **5000 experience**
> **Hrólf the Walker's Sword**
> **Children of the Goddess (series of hidden quests) unlocked**
> **If you do not agree to her request**
> **Reward:**
> **2000 experience**
> **Forest Power Ring**
> **Accept?**

Fantastic! I didn't end up with one ruble! Of course, I accepted.

"Many chasms in time ago, the gods were forced to leave Fayroll. With them, left the goddess Mesmerta, who had created my three sisters and me to protect her ranges and had served as our patron. We wanted to reunite and leave with her, but she said, 'I created you in and for this world. You cannot leave with me, as that would contradict the testaments of the demiurges who created it. But I can give you a chance to follow me, yourselves. The path is long and difficult, full of weakness and pain. You will lose everything—your power, your dignity, yourselves. You will die a million deaths before the day of salvation comes. Only after suffering can you call to me and hear my voice.' The goddess explained that only the pain of her children—she created us, and we were her children—could grant her the opportunity to rejoin us here in this world. But we had to freely agree to that suffering of our own accord, and here you are. So, I ask you: will you help us?"

"Help you how?" I asked.

I wasn't about to just agree right off the bat. Maybe the final quest was to slit open your own veins or eat a rotten tree stump. Or a boiled snake. They were dryads, after all—children of nature.

"You freed me, and now you have to free my three sisters. Only then will you find your way, as the last of us will tell you what to do."

A pig in a poke, I thought. Although...

"Is there a time limit? It's just that I have other things to do too..."

"My heart wishes for you to hurry," said Eiliana, "but I understand..."

Well, if I could take as long as I wanted, and there weren't any penalties, then why not? If worse came to worst, I could just forget about it.

"Okay," I said with a wave of my hand. "Why not? I'm in!"

As soon as I said those words, I heard a distinct boom, after which the golden smoke erupted again and the dryad twisted into the air with a cry:

"May the prophecy be fulfilled!"

> **You finished a quest: History of Eiliana the West.**
> **Reward:**
> **5000 experience**
> **Hrólf the Walker's Sword**
> **Set of hidden quests unlocked: Children of the Goddess**

> You unlocked a set of hidden quests: Children of the Goddess.
> Reward for completing the entire set:
> Experience: variable
> Items: variable
> Skills: variable
> Opportunity to receive epic quests: variable
> Once accepted, you cannot decline the quest.
> Accept?

And immediately afterward:

> You unlocked Heroes of the Gray Days... Level 1.
> To get it, receive 9 more items belonging to heroes of days gone by.
> Reward:
> Lucky, a passive ability, Level 1: +0.6% chance of receiving elite or legendary items
> +1% chance of getting hidden or epic quests
> Title: Scholar of Legends
> To see similar messages, go to the Action section of the attribute window.

Well, that was interesting. The action was definitely nice. But that quest... What was that about? And why all the variables? Everything was "variable." Although, I was sure I would get more than just some trash, and a choice between good and good is always good.

I clicked Accept.

I expected another boom or whoosh, but I was mistaken. The dryad nodded her head, returned to earth, and sat down next to me.

"Look, hero." There wasn't a smidgeon of irony or sarcasm in her voice. Apparently, that's just who I was to her. For the first time in my life, at least for someone... "The first thing you have to do is find my sister, Ogina the East. She'll give you your next instructions."

> **You unlocked Find Ogina the East.**
> **This is the first in the Children of the Goddess series of hidden quests.**
> **Task: Find and save the Keeper of the Eastern Ranges.**
> **Reward:**
> **7500 experience**
> **Piece of dryad armor: variable**
> **Wolf Soul ability**
> **Accept?**

I agreed and immediately asked, "But how do I find her?"

"I marked the spot on your map. Look for her. And hurry—the goddess is waiting for us."

And with that, the dryad evaporated. Naturally. One second she was there, and the next there was just a light haze and a "psh-sh-sh" sound.

"Well," I said to myself, "that wasn't too bad. All right, let's see what we have here before we go looking for dryad number two."

I opened my inventory to check out the sword and was struck dumb, first from elation and then from anger.

> **Hrólf the Walker's Sword**
> **Belonged to a great warrior known for his strength and valor.**
> **Legendary item**
> **Damage: 320-360**
> **+38 to strength**
> **+32 to stamina**
> **+18% to critical strike chance**
> **+15% gold looted from dead enemies**
> **+56% damage done by the Triple Blade ability**

+24% of damage done is added to the health of the sword's owner
Durability: 760/760
Minimum level to use: 110
For class: warrior
The sword becomes a personal belonging as soon as it is received.
It cannot be stolen, lost, broken, sold, or given to anyone else.
It is not lost when the owner dies.
It is destroyed when removed from the owner's inventory or personal room.

What, you don't get it? I had a super-sword, but I couldn't use it or cash in on it. I imagine that I would have been able to get good money for it at the auction—it had great attributes, and would have gone quickly and for a high price. But it was only mine! And I doubted I'd play long enough to reach Level 100. I was almost positive.

Nice job, developers. Well played...

I sat there for a few minutes watching the darkening sky, then headed back across the plain. I'd done everything I could do in the forest, though I wished I hadn't gone in at all...

I'd gone a good distance when, for some reason, I turned and saw a figure running toward the forest in his underwear—probably Gvegory trying to find me.

"Go ahead, go ahead, you're a dead man. Good luck! I doubt the dryad will let you chop her up anymore this time," I chuckled.

And sure enough, a minute after the figure ran into the forest, I saw a burst of flame.

"Well, there's some justice in the world, at least," I said. I spat and turned back toward the ruins.

Chapter Ten
An Earring for Every Sister

It was already dark by the time I got to the castle ruins. Enormous stars littered the sky, and the moon was as large and flat as a pancake. Cicadas chattered away in the grass—or whatever it is that chatters away in the grass at night—beauty and splendor, in a word.

But I couldn't care less. I was dog tired. It had been fifteen years since the last time I'd walked so much. But even there, we didn't walk that much. Back then, my friends and I went on hikes. We just trekked along until we found a spot we liked, pulled out our fishing rods and vodka, and plopped down. That was it.

I walked through the archway, exhaled, and said, "Finally! I'll sit here for 10 minutes and then head for the trees. I can sleep there."

Rattling bones and chattering teeth I remembered so well from our trip to Grinvort told me someone was happy to see me. And, yep, there it was. From a pile of boulders that probably once made up the entrance to the castle, came a Level 22 skeleton, its bony knees happily banging together and its rusty sword waving in the air. In its eye sockets, cheerful, inviting green lights shined.

"One-way ticket coming right up," I said, pulling out my mace in a smooth, already practiced gesture that covered my right side at forearm level. "I jinxed it. Figured they'd come out at night, the restless buggers. I just hope a lich doesn't come check to see who's visiting."

The skeleton got to me and swung its sword with all its might. I reacted automatically, catching the blow with my shield, and smashed my mace first into its ribs from left to right. In the same motion, I swung upwards, catching its wobbling jaw. The double strike took off about 60 percent of its health and knocked it backward. From there, however, it quickly jumped back to attack me again, this time, taking a wild swing at my head. I ducked, the sword whistled overhead, and I buried my mace in its hip. The skeleton crunched and collapsed.

"I'm getting better—that just took me three hits!" I grinned happily and looked around. "Anyone else?"

There were no takers, and the quiet night above the ruins remained undisturbed.

I was just bending over to see what I could scavenge from the last watcher in the proud and daring (if dead) landlord's castle when the silence was interrupted.

From behind the wall dividing the castle from the graveyard, cries rang out, "I'll attract them!"

"Cast, cast!"

"Vitya, you idiot, what are you waiting for?"

"What are you running all around the graves for? You woke them all!"

"Be afraid! Be very afraid!"

A minute later, I saw what there was to be afraid of. The reflections told me that the voices had cast a fireball—and a big one, by the looks of it. It had exploded, apparently, somewhere in the middle of the graveyard. The sky exploded into all the colors of the rainbow.

"It's like Victory Day," I said, grabbing what the skeleton had without even looking at it and running for the breach in the wall.

I looked through it to see exactly what I expected—a group of players had come to put the restless to rest. Three tanks, a hunter, a mage, and a cleric standing off by himself, the latter of which was apparently healing the rest. The group seemed to be playing the Evil Dead, with the only difference being that they were the ones scaring the dead.

"Three to the left! One lich!"

"Tanks!"

"One down!"

"Two down!"

"Heal the tanks!" the mage yelled to the cleric. The mage was apparently in charge of the group. "Take out the lich!"

A bonfire, the remains of the fireball, blazed in the center of the graveyard. There were quite a few skeletons writhing in its flames—at least a dozen. It looked like they'd done a great job awakening the local undead.

On the other side, farther away from my wall, the tanks were finishing off the lich, the last of the three skeletons. It didn't appear to be putting up much of a fight, just grinding its teeth and rolling its burning red eyes as if to complain about its difficult bony life and say, "There was no life in life, and there will be no life after life!"

"Hey, guys!" I yelled, remembering that the local undead fauna would respawn in five or seven minutes and figuring that I should use that time to get out of the graveyard. "Don't shoot—friendly!"

I moved along the wall with my hands in the air.

"Who are you?" the mage asked in surprise. His name, or so said the label above his head, was Grigor.

"I'm the golden fish, and I'm here to give you three wishes!" I couldn't resist. "A player, who else? I was walking along the plain and got held up. My plan was to sneak through here quietly, but then you came along and started throwing fireballs at everything."

"You wouldn't have snuck through," the archer jumped in. "They'd have shredded you. You didn't know this was a cursed graveyard? As soon as night falls, the dead lords come out of their graves and wander around under the moon. They even say that one day, the graveyard will be visited by the Master of the Dead, himself, and that he'll start building his empire from this spot."

There was backstory everywhere you turned. And it would have been interesting to clap eyes on the Master of the Dead—probably an interesting guy to look at.

"Well, I was going to go around the edge," I said with a wave of my hand.

"They still would've eaten you alive," the mage answered.

"So can I go?"

"Of course. What, you think we're going to stop you?" the mage asked in surprise. "We're fair players, not PKers. And what would we even get from you? What could you have collected on the plain? The Sword of a Thousand Truths?"

The group laughed heartily.

"Obviously. Well, yeah…gopher skins…that's about it. Little by little," I confirmed.

"Okay, you'd better get out of here. The respawn is five minutes, so they'll be crawling back out soon," the mage added with some seriousness. "All right, men, let's form a triangle—they'll be coming from the center, I swear."

I quickly ran to the other side of the graveyard and got to the exit. The group had already forgotten about me. The tanks had made a triangle in the center, the hunter was moving along the right flank, and the mage patrolled the left. Only the cleric stood off where I first saw him, and I ended up right next to him. They got to work.

"Hey, be careful. There's a named monster around here," the cleric quickly said without taking his eyes off the center of the graveyard.

"Yeah, I already got him," I responded. "But still, thanks for the warning."

"No worries. Here we go!"

I looked back toward the graveyard to see that the ground around the central graves had opened up, and skeletons were crawling out.

It's all the same, I thought. *First in the lowlands, now here...all the same.*

"Watch the edge!" the mage barked.

I didn't care to watch anymore and started walking home through the dark and already not so scary forest. While I was exhausted, I didn't really care if the local goblin horde heard me.

My map showed that the road I had already traipsed along several times that day was about a kilometer and a half straight ahead. So, I plowed ahead without bothering to look where I was going; I just pulled out my map every few minutes. I had almost reached the road and could just about see it when:

"M-m-m, food coming! Hey, goblins, dinner come! Many food!"

At that moment, I understood how Gandalf the Gray felt when he saw the balrog and said, "There it is. And I'm so tired!"

I took 20 damage. And 20 more. Branches crashed. This time it sounded like there were about twenty of the goblins rather than the five I dealt with during the day.

There's probably some unwritten rule that says I should have turned to fight them. You can't let some hungry little goblins get the better of you. But I didn't care about unwritten rules. It's all well and good to be proud and brave, but it's better to live and fight another day. I sprinted, first to the road and then along it. The goblins ran after me for a few minutes, shooting arrows and screaming at me all the way, "Food run away! Stop food! We eat meat, bury bones! Hard year, dig up, chew bones!"

But then they stopped pursuing me. Maybe they couldn't keep up the pace with their short, bowed legs, or maybe they weren't allowed to go outside their location. Who knows?

To be honest, I was running on fumes. And it was only when I had completely run out of breath and felt like a horse run ragged that, thank God, I saw the familiar palisade wall. I dug deep to cover the remaining ground, tumbled into Tocbridge, sat down by the fence, and logged out of the game.

You know, I've reported on Sensation, I've judged a dozen wet t-shirt contests, and I've participated in Beaujolais Day (and that last one is crazy!), but I have never—I repeat, never—been so physically and emotionally exhausted.

I felt scraped and dried three times over. And I was incredibly hungry… Only I had no desire to cook.

I crawled out of the capsule, laid down on the couch, and said, "I'll relax for a few minutes, then grab something to eat and start writing my article." I mentally patted myself on the head for my gung-ho attitude and perseverance. And with that thought in my head, I fell sound asleep.

My phone woke me up. *Mammoth,* I thought with a sinking feeling in my stomach and looked at my phone. It wasn't him. Instead, it was Elvira, my latest flame, who I was supposed to take to some event that day or the day before—I couldn't remember. Maybe an exhibit, or maybe the theater—I couldn't remember that either. Judging by the fact that it was dark outside, and she was calling, probably the day before. I looked at the time on the display, which told me it was 4 a.m. and tapped the button to answer the call.

"You bastard! You scum! You animal!" She got right into it without so much as a "Hello" or "How are you?"

"Um," I grunted sleepily into the phone.

"You jerk. Look at that; he's sleeping! And here I am waiting. Nervous, trying to call everyone!" I wondered who she might have been calling since we didn't have any mutual friends. "Nobody knows what's going on, and he won't pick up the phone. Because he's sleeping!"

"Yes," I agreed.

"I hate you! I...hate...you!" She added some kind of Tatar curse and hung up.

"Okay," I said. "Time to think about some breakfast."

I turned off my cellphone and landline before going back to sleep, as I still had another two hours. The doorbell rang, interrupted only by the kicks slamming against the door. Elvira wasn't mincing words.

"And here comes breakfast," I said, this time completely awake. I wrapped a blanket around myself and went to open the door. It flew open, and I ducked immediately, which was the only reason I didn't get a purse to the face. I'd seen that trick from her before.

"You animal!" my morning guest hissed, stretching out her fingers in what looked like an attempt to decorate them with my eyeballs.

"An animal," I nodded.

"I hate you!"

"You're repeating yourself."

"How could you do this to me?"

"Not on purpose!"

"What wasn't on purpose?"

"Nothing was. I'm sorry!" There was one thing I did know. Arguing with a woman was like going to the dentist; it's either painful or expensive.

Elvira spluttered and popped like an egg in a skillet for another ten minutes until she mistook my haggard expression for pangs of conscience. Somewhere in the middle, I'd mentioned that I hadn't eaten in a day, and her feminine instinct—feed first, yell later—kicked in. She cooked something for me, we had a romp in the sack (and on a full stomach...phew boy), and finally ended up kissing tenderly. I agreed to do the same for her that night, and she left for work.

"Quite the morning," I observed while smoking on the balcony and watching my little Genghis Khan drive off in her Matiz[8]. "It's enough to kill someone."

Dryads, goddesses, skeletons, Elvira... Too much. Soon, I was going to get a twitchy eye like that one saber-toothed cat. Or an aneurysm. Petrova from the office was lucky; her column had her used to constant craziness, what with her being a cowgirl one day and a nun the next. I, on the other hand, had suffered through nothing more than the cigars, mojitos, various pop stars, starlets, mutant artists, and unrecognized geniuses of the quiet, restrained, and predictable public. And here I was breathing in the heady air of a week's worth of excitement.

I finished my cigarette, and with it, my self-pitying musings before heading online to gather more information. About gods and heroes.

The sun was high in the village, the roosters were long done crowing, and the village people had already drawn their water. Children's voices laughed in the square, while in the background, the blacksmith's hammer clanged away. And I was sitting up against the palisade wall right where I had collapsed the day before. In front of me, were two old ladies, and it appeared that I was the topic of their conversation, "They all come through here drinking just like our old fools!" one said.

"That's what I'm saying. He's sitting there with his eyes all bugged out like that, and he couldn't care less," agreed the second.

I stood up, prompting the old ladies to scurry off to the side in consternation.

"Watch it!" said one cautiously. "I'll tell my son, and he'll show you!" She waved a wrinkled fist in the air.

"Yes, I know, ma'am. He'll show me, and we're all alcoholics, and it's our fault the Soviet Union collapsed—damn democrats."

The women couldn't quite believe their ears—they understood the first part of what I said, but the second... I needed to strike while the iron was hot.

"How about telling me if the shepherd is in the village. Or did he take the cattle out to pasture?"

"The shepherd? Willie? I think he's at the smithy. Trying to get an apprenticeship there." She waved in that direction.

"What do you care?" the second asked, her inner interrogator kicking in.

"I'm looking for a squire," I said. "Off I go. See you later, my dears!"

Naturally, the shepherd was at the smithy, so I told him where the cow was and received in return some experience, a little gold, and a big thank you. But what I appreciated most was that I leveled-up. The blacksmith was surprised and complimented me by fixing my equipment for free. I thanked the good fellow and set off to find the old man, turning over in my head what I'd read online.

There wasn't much to find about the gods. In the official version that came with the Fayroll theology, I read something about how there were entities called demiurges who created the world. They created it, and that was it. They created a planet with seas, continents, forests, and valleys. Oh, and its population: dwarves, elves, humans, goblins, and all the rest. But after they created it, they left—no governing, no interfering. But then later, the demiurges added some additional material. They apparently decided that someone needed to be in charge since without a guiding hand, the whole thing would be a mess of thieves stealing from or killing each other. So they created a handful of gods. But then things went downhill. The gods they made were foul, and, instead of creating a worldwide peace that led to a new golden age, most of them began to divvy up spheres of influence, call themselves Fathers of the People, and turn on each other. That went from bad to worse, until finally, world war broke out that made killing the order of the day…

Demiurges put up with that for a time before getting fed up and telling the gods to go get lost in a parallel universe.

The latter put up a fight, but didn't have the stomach for it, were soundly routed by the demiurges, nearly lost their divine power, and hid in the sunset. They left behind a few confessions, some stray priests, a knightly order, a number of items, and, as it turned out, hidden quests. There might have been something else, but the general public was not aware of it.

But about the quest the dryad gave me, I couldn't find anything anywhere. It looked like no one had yet come across it in the entire history of the game, though there were some people claiming the developers told them about quests having to do with the gods who had left. They said whoever got them would earn mountains of gold or become an enormous force in the game. One of the quests was said to give players the magic power lost by the gods. The rest, of course, were nothing to sneeze at. Although some people said there were quests that led to upheaval, disaster, and genocide.

I was certainly aware of what they could get you, seeing as how the very first, paltry little quest got me a fantastic sword. I may not have been able to use it thanks to the level requirement, but I could imagine what lay ahead. Still, I needed to think hard about whether to keep going. Especially, since I had no idea what lay ahead.

On that note, I checked my map and noticed that there weren't any quest markers. I zoomed out. Still nothing. I zoomed out still further, and there it was.

Dryad Number 2 lived 150,000 miles away from where I was, somewhere in the east. And I had no idea what level the locations there were, seeing as how I'd never been there. The map only showed their names. In short, my dryad was off stuck somewhere in her tall tower...

That was a quest I'd have to come back to. And, incidentally, I had a sneaky little idea.

On a separate note, I decided I wasn't going to say anything to my clan. There was more than just the game at stake; I had my articles to write. And if I were to tell them, they'd go plowing through the rest of the dryads while keeping me locked up in between. Screw them...

And I needed to get that head to the old man. Long story short, he saw me, beamed, and said, "What do you know! The old beast didn't kill you after all. You're lucky!"

"Lucky, shmucky. Here's the head!"

"There it is," he said, happily looking it over. "The very one!"

You finished a quest: Kill the Swamp Beast.
Reward:

250 gold
1000 experience

"Oh, and let's do the paperwork to make sure everything's on the up-and-up," he went on. "Write here that you received 300 gold."

"Here you go. Tricky old guy!"

"Just making ends meet…"

I walked away, checked in again with the halfling trader, lazily haggled a little, and sent him all the junk I'd accumulated the day before. All I kept was Burrig's mandibles; they were unusual, and who knew when they'd come in handy?

That was about everything I needed to do there. Sure, I still had the left foreleg quest, but I really couldn't care less. I pulled it up, found the "Cancel" button, and clicked it. Maybe that was cutting corners, but it was boring, and I was tired of life in the countryside. The city was calling my name. Civilization, a knightly order, and the class ability instructor. I opened my map, got my bearings, and started walking toward Fladridge.

Chapter Eleven
Between *Before* and After

I'm not a big walker. I mean, come on, why couldn't they make it like the good, old games I played when I was young and happy? Everything was so simple and easy. No matter where you were, there was always some griffon-rider or slovenly groom watching over a herd of horses you could borrow. Sometimes, there was just a bearded mage leaning on his staff next to a stationary portal that he kept open for you. You just jumped in and whizzed your way to wherever you wanted to go, for a reasonable fee, of course. Simple, fast, easy.

Not here. There was a downside to the whole immersion experience. Sure, later on, you could find ways to shorten distances by, for instance, buying a horse. But that meant slogging all the way to Level 70, paying a postilion good money to train you, and finally shelling out for a horse that cost something like a Daewoo Matiz.

Somewhere way down the line, you could even buy your own personal mountain eagle. They cost as much as a plane, but as a status symbol alone, they were worth it. I'm not sure if anyone ever bought one, as I never came across any eagles, though the possibility was still there.

Aerial mages had it the best since they could learn the Portal spell at Level 80. That made them the only class in the game that could teleport on their own. Even they had their limitations, however. They could only move around areas they'd already explored in the game, the spell itself cost a mountain of mana, and it took days to recharge.

A more widely available way to move around were the single-use portal scrolls. At first glance, their 1,500-gold price tag didn't seem unreasonable; you read them, picked a destination, and found yourself there. The problem for beginning players was that 1,500 gold was an unheard-of sum. You could find a group going in the same direction and have everyone chip in, but that was much easier said than done. Plus, portal scrolls only took you places you'd already been.

So, there I was three hours into my walk down the yellow brick road. Happily, the developers did their best to throw in quests here and there that broke up the monotony.

My first encounter came about 7 kilometers from the village with an obviously insane girl in a red beret. She was waving her arms and wailing. "Walk me home, brave warrior. I'm afraid of the dark forest!"

Just to be polite, I asked where her home was. As it turned out, she lived with her mom in a hut somewhere in the Very Dark Forest, which was about an hour's walk from where we were standing. Not exactly on the way. One hour there, another back, and besides, I'd heard of girls in red hats. You're taking them home, a wolf shows up, and you have to kill it. Then a couple hunters take its place, and you have to deal with them, too. Oh, and who knew what her mom was like? She could come thundering out of the house with a cleaver in each hand, and you'd have to finish her off just like the rest. All of that, and I'd get maybe 300-500 experience and fifty gold. Screw that. I'd just saved a little green monster, and I was still trying to dig my way through all that got me.

So I sent the girl on her way, though she kept up her wailing for another half a kilometer.

"What do you mean? You're a warrior of the Light! You're supposed to fight the creatures of the darkness who attack innocent people!"

Where did she get that from? Happily, she left me alone, though a kilometer later, an old lady came up to me. She was hauling a bushel of firewood that must have weighed ten kilograms.

"Help an old woman? I think my arms are about to fall off!" She jumped straight in without so much as a "How do you do."

"I'm sorry," I said. "I'm in a hurry. Things to do!"

"Some valiant knight you are, leaving a poor woman alone and helpless!"

"I'm not a knight at all," I said. "I'm just wandering along. How far do you have to go?"

"Only seven miles or so."

"Why didn't you find branches closer to where you live?"

"I was visiting my sister, and I've been collecting this bundle along the way. Here a branch, there a branch. Take it!" The old crone suddenly thrust the whole mess at me.

You have a new quest offer: Volunteer Assistant.
Task: Carry Gerda's firewood to the old sorceress's hut.
Reward:
300 experience
Any one of Gerda's potions.
Accept?

"Ha! Right," I said, even a bit rudely. "I'm not taking it. Seven miles there, seven miles back. Carry it yourself! And why do you even need it? It's summer, it's hot outside."

"Oh, my dear, you'll regret that." The old woman grinned menacingly at me, and I saw teeth that were young and sharp as needles.

I'd have gotten to her hut all right, but that would probably have been the end of the road, I thought.

"Go ahead, old lady, speak your mind," I said, casually placing my hand on my mace. "I have ways of settling disagreements, too."

The grin on her face was replaced by a glower she aimed at me before laughing and lightly flipped the brushwood up over her shoulder. I got one last threatening look.

"No worries, sonny boy. We'll see each other again. You can be sure of that!"

She melted into the bushes on the side of the road with a speed and sprightliness that surprised me.

"Wow. That's one way to spice things up!" I said and kept walking.

My trip would have continued as smoothly and, if not pleasantly, at least as harmlessly as before, except that an alert suddenly popped up.

Attention. Euiikh, a player you blacklisted, is nearby.

Oh boy, an old friend! Not the best time for him, though.

I sprang from the road into the bushes and was about to sprint into the forest when I heard voices. "He's here; find him! Probably in the forest somewhere."

Running would have made too much noise, so I lay still in the bushes.

"Come out, come out wherever you are!" My toothy friend called me. "There are three of us, and we won't stop looking until we find you. You didn't have time to get away, so that means you're still here. Come out and die like a man! I can't promise you it'll be quick, but at least we'll make it simple. If you make us find you, it'll be long and humiliating. And painful."

I weighed my chances and concluded that I was up a creek without a paddle. They'd find me, of that I was sure. And if I ran, a-hundred-to-one they'd find me—orcs can run for days. On the other hand, I was now in a clan, though the orcs didn't know that. Everyone said that PKers, and especially lower-level ones, stay away from clan members. Maybe these guys wouldn't be anxious to risk the reaction they'd get? If they were willing to risk it, well, there wasn't much I could do. It was just a shame I'd lose my gold and silver—and Reineke's gift. He'd given it to me from the heart. Happily, I wouldn't lose the sword or the dead knight's amulet. And if I died, Reineke would be the first person I'd tell. I didn't think he'd take kindly to some ugly green mugs making off with his gift.

I crawled out of the bushes and stood up. The orcs looked at me with tender, anticipatory grins, the way cats look at birds with clipped wings.

"Hello there, gentlemen," I said, smiling back at them. "It's like we never even left each other!"

"You've been leveling-up." Euiikh approvingly nodded his head. "Nice work! Oh, and you even joined a clan! Look at you."

"Yes, and I should warn you that I'm under my clan's protection!"

"Sure, though that won't help you much way out here." Euiikh's voice was quiet. "Go join whatever clan you want, the best and strongest out there. We'll still squash you like a bug."

"What did I ever do to you?"

"You were rude. I don't like rude people. You went too far, and you made us mad."

"What, and you aren't rude?" I already knew I was a dead man walking. I knew my gold and equipment were gone. And I knew I'd spent the whole day walking for nothing. Just then, however, a daring idea popped into my head, and I decided to do what I could to make their lives just as interesting as they were going to make mine. Without further ado, I put thought into action. "Take what you said just now, for instance..."

I quickly turned on my online camera and set it to record.

"What do you mean?" Euiikh asked with a snarl.

"All that you were saying about the clans, what if you said that to someone from—oh, I don't know—the Hounds of Death?"

"Screw all the clans!" His voice rose. "You're going to die regardless, and no one's going to stop us. The Hounds of Death...ha! You seriously think I'm afraid of them? Forget their clan. Screw them! All three of us hate them, and we despise that pig the Gray Witch."

I had apparently struck a nerve. His whole rant had been recorded, so I knew I would at least be avenged.

"And I've had your Thunderbirds roasting on a spit! Oh, and-"

"Who did you have roasting on a what?" A voice boomed out from the bushes on the right side of the road, and two dwarves crashed out of the bushes in our direction. From the badges above their heads, I could tell that their names were Rone and Dorn, they were Level 40 and 42, respectively, and...

I could have jumped for joy when I saw that they were Thunderbirds, too.

"Hey, you green idiot, let me ask you again. Who did you have roasting? Our clan?" Dorn looked less than thrilled.

"Don't worry, volunteer, we'll do this the right way." Rone came over and clapped me on the shoulder. "How did you get them so riled up?"

"The last time they killed me, I might have suggested that they prefer big cow horns to the opposite gender—or even little cow horns." I looked at my feet as I said it.

The dwarves laughed uproariously.

"Yep, that's orcs all right. These guys sound like fun. Hey, stand right there!" Dorn barked at one of the PKers, who edged toward the side of the road, obviously getting ready to make a break for it. "I said we'll do this the right way. I'll take the left one, Rone will take the one on the right. You, little one, will fight their leader, it looks like. That way it's fair. He's a few levels higher than you, but that doesn't mean anything, believe me. You have good armor, and you're angry, so I'm sure you can take him. Whoever wins, walks away with their opponent's loot."

"Ha, right. I'll kill this rat, and then the two of you will jump me." The orc was having none of it.

"Don't pretend that dwarves have the same code of honor you orcs have," said Rone in an even voice. "If we say you'll walk away, then that's what will happen."

"And you don't have much of a choice," Dorn added. "You'll die later for what you said about our clan, and probably more than once. Yeah, don't think I won't tell them. But for now, you have the chance to get away from this alive, providing you can kill one of us. But if that doesn't work for you, my friend and I would be happy to just deal with the three of you ourselves."

"Walk away from you..." An orc with the appropriate name of Grim hissed his dissatisfaction. "Level 50, and covered in iron."

"What, you thought this was going to be easy?" Dorn chuckled, and Rone nodded his head in agreement. "Enough. It's time to answer for your crimes!" The dwarves smoothly and in tandem pulled out the battle axes they had strapped to their backs.

I whipped out my mace as well, before bracing my shield and staring down Euiikh. Now at least, it wouldn't be so frustrating to die. Although, it wouldn't have been that frustrating if the plan I'd cooked up had worked either.

"I'm going to tear you limb from limb," the orc said. He licked his lips.

Oh great, this one's crazy, too, I thought. *With a penchant for cannibalism. How do they always find me? On the other hand, maybe I can use that.*

"Why are you looking at me like that? I don't swing that way," I said. "Besides, I thought you were into animals?"

My crude trick worked. Euiikh howled like a wild animal from deep in the forest, threw his shield aside, and leaped at me. His scimitar, which he held with two hands in an apparent attempt to land a stronger blow, flashed through the air.

He leaped without any attempt to disguise it, so I simply ducked to the left, and a second later buried my mace in his back. Euiikh spun around, and for a second, I caught his eye. The guy was out of his mind. He aimed his next blow at my side, and I caught it with my shield, but before I could deflect it away, I felt him throw his whole weight behind his blade. He was a good bit taller than me, and the six-level difference between us was significant.

I could tell it was a matter of time before he broke through my defense.

"Get down!" I heard Dorn's voice chime in.

Quickly grasping what the experienced dwarf wanted me to do, I rolled to my right, jumped up, and assumed my ready stance. The orc held his scimitar in both hands and swayed a bit. Either he was crazed, or he was trying to hypnotize me.

"They really did a number on you," I said. "Eh, don't worry about it. If you kill me, you can use my money to buy a whole herd of cows. That way you can have fun with them at night and eat them for breakfast in the morning."

"A-a-ah!" The enraged orc again tried to charge me, but he no longer had any sense of where he was going and earned himself a hefty blow to the stomach. He awkwardly turned to find my mace in his breastplate, and I expected his health to turn red at any second. We gradually worked our way to the edge of the road, where Rone had just finished off one of Euiikh's compatriots. Rone had taken his time playing with him, as the difference between their classes and levels was too great to fight on equal footing. I noticed Rone standing there and went around him, but my crazed opponent tripped and fell headlong. I'm not the most honorable person you'll find. Well, let's be honest, I'm not honorable in the least. So, when I saw him lying there, I jumped in and smashed my mace right into his head twice. There was no need for a third time, as Euiikh was dead.

"Whoa!" Dorn said. "You don't go after someone when they're down—"

"Though that was a PKer," Rone interrupted. "PKers get what's coming to them. So, are we going to put them through the ringer again? Think they'll come back here?"

"I doubt it." Dorn shook his head. "Why? They know we'll take everything. No way they come back."

My inbox dinged. Yet another message from my green-skinned fan.

"I swear I'm going to find you in real life. The game doesn't even matter; your life here is going to be a living hell. But I'm going to find you in real life, and I swear you're going to die like…"

I didn't bother reading the rest. He was obviously just a hothead who couldn't string two thoughts together. He was probably really young—they're all like that. There was nothing for me to worry about. He'd be off yelling and screaming for an hour as he bashed in a few walls and thought up a hundred ways to cut me into little pieces. Then he'd convince himself that it would happen just like he thought and go to bed. In the morning, he'd think he'd already found and dealt with me. Just a lot of noise with nothing to back it up.

In the meantime, the dwarves had picked through their victims to see what they'd earned, fair and square. I headed over to Euiikh's body to see what he had. The scimitar was pretty nice, and it was poisoned, too, while his armor was nothing special. Four hundred and sixty gold and some other little things rounded out the picture. *Oh, hold on…*

Sprinter's Ring
+4 to stamina
+5 to agility
+0.5% health regeneration speed
+7% to movement speed
Durability: 96/110
Minimum level for use: 21

Happy birthday to me!

"What did you get?" asked Dorn. "You lit up like a Christmas tree."

I proudly showed him the ring. In fact, I must have looked something like Frodo, which Rone noted with a chuckle. "You have a long way ahead of you, my young hobbit!"

"Yeah, not bad." Dorn pronounced his opinion with the air of an expert. "For your level, at least. Anything else?"

"Not really. Some gold, a scimitar, all poor to middling. Bunch of trash."

They keep everything in their rooms." Rone spat. "The bastards know everyone picks dead PKers to the bone, all the way to their watches and gold fillings. So, they don't carry anything around with them. But what's the point? You kill people, and then you don't even get to use what you took. Idiots..."

"I think they're sick," I said. "Inadequacy complexes. Take Euiikh, did you see him at the end? He wasn't a person, just a charging mule. Hooves kicking and foam flying from his mouth..."

"Who knows if he's crazy or just some mutant," said Dorn. "But we need to let the clan know. They'll take care of him."

I almost wanted to tell them about my idea but decided against it. What was the point? Much better to keep it to myself.

"Thanks, guys." My appreciation was sincere. "If it weren't for you, I'd be leaving Tocbridge in my underwear annoyed and humiliated right now."

"Oh, come on, you could have just let the clan know, and we'd have sent you some money," said Dorn.

I hadn't even thought of that. Complaining to them had crossed my mind, but not getting some financial support.

"We make sure we always help new members. Within reason, of course," said Rone.

"Where were you going, by the way?" asked Dorn.

"To Fladridge." Honesty is the best policy.

"Oh, wow, you have a ways to go. Listen, we just finished an ability quest, and we were going to see the instructor in Khitskern for our reward, but it doesn't matter which city we go to. We have a portal scroll that costs 1,500 gold. If you want, you can give us 500 gold, and we'll all go to Fladridge. We're always up for helping volunteers, but I'm sure you understand that scrolls cost money. No offense?" Dorn looked at me quizzically.

"Sounds great!" I agreed immediately. "I can give you more..."

"No need. Five hundred gold a piece is fair. Plus, we got some stuff from those guys, too, thanks to you. If you're good, we can go now."

Dorn pulled a scroll out of a pouch on his belt and used it.

Fladridge turned out to be a pleasant little city pulled straight from Medieval Europe: tile roofs, neat little houses, ladies in bonnets, and men in frock coats. All it needed was a church steeple peeking above the buildings. But where would they find a steeple, and especially a church to attach it to, in Fayroll? They were pagans, after all. *Although, wait a second—I guess they were atheists.* There were some gods of a sort, but they drove them out. All that were left were legends and four dryads. Even atheists change their minds sometimes, though.

Rone, Dorn, and I split up in the city's central square, as the dwarves were on their way to get some sort of ability. I made them promise to let me buy a round of beer when next we saw each other and sent them friend requests. They laughed and looked at each other, but they accepted. Before they left, I asked if they knew where the class instructors were.

"Kids these days are all so lazy." Rone looked at me disapprovingly. "No running around looking for them. No. Point them in the right direction, so they don't have to bother to even turn their heads."

"Rone, let's adopt him!" said Dorn. "It'll be so much cheaper, and in the last half hour, we've basically become his fathers. There, son, over in that alley between the buildings."

The dwarf pointed in the direction of a small street.

"All right, see you later." Rone thumped me on the shoulder. "Send us a message if you need anything."

"And send us the money when you have it." Dorn clapped me on the other shoulder.

Off they went.

It was time for my revenge. I'm not that mean of a person, but I had to do something. There wouldn't be dwarves in the bushes coming to save my skin every time. It was as clear as day, however, that the orc wasn't about to let me off, and so I had to neutralize him. That or make it so that he would be too busy to worry about me. The good news was that I had an excellent plan.

I looked around and noticed something at the southern end of the square that I needed for my Very Sneaky Plan: a mailbox.

Mailboxes were everywhere in Fayroll, from villages to cities to nomad camps in the Plains to the wildest outposts. You may not find a trader, but you could always find a mailbox. Not only that, but they were always designed to match their environment.

Players could all use the game messaging system, but there were a few occasions when you needed a mailbox. For example, if you wanted to challenge someone to a duel. Clans declared war on each other by mail if they absolutely hated each other. Of course, they just sent couriers to each other with a memorandum of hostilities when they disliked but still respected each other. Mailboxes were also important when you wanted to borrow something, as they were considered strong proof by the developers in their role as arbiters.

All that aside, I walked over and activated the mailbox in the square.

Would you like to send a letter?

No, of course not. Why else would I be here? I entered my name in the sender window, and where it asked for the recipient, I entered "Gray Witch." Then I attached the part of my conversation with Euiikh where he announced what he'd like to do to the Hounds of Death and the Gray Witch in particular. Everything else, and especially the mention of the Thunderbirds and appearance of Rone and Dorn, I initially wanted to take out. Why did the Hounds need to know any of that? After giving that a bit more thought, however, I settled on a better course of action.

Dear Gray Witch,

Today I witnessed an unseemly scene in which a player, in full realization of the consequences of his actions, insulted one of Fayroll's most powerful and worthy clans: the Hounds of Death. Needless to say, simply being a member is a dream shared by the rest of the players in the game, which makes his insult to you, its leader, all the more regrettable. Certainly, the offender was immediately destroyed by myself and my friends from the Thunderbirds clan, as we could not leave such a gesture unpunished given the friendly relationship our clans have. We cannot, however, be sure that he will not continue to profane the name of your clan, one of the strongest and most respected in Fayroll. As proof, I am attaching a video I recorded.

With sincere respect and deference,
Hagen, warrior, Thunderbird volunteer

Something like that. Sure, I may have gone a bit overboard by at least partly acting on behalf of the clan. On the other hand, it only benefited. If all else failed, I would just say I was in shock after the day's events.

I sent the letter and looked up at the sky to see that the day was long past half gone. If was time to head back to the real world. Elvira wanted to take me somewhere that night, and I needed to get some food and work on an idea that had fully formed in my mind. Also, I needed to write up a story. Mammoth wasn't the patient type.

Chapter Twelve
Between Before and *After*

I mulled over everything while I ate, trying to figure out if I should go ahead with my plan. It could very well rile up quite a few players, but it would give me a chance to see how the gaming world would react to a strong irritant. On the one hand, it was all a bit frightening. The other players wouldn't be able to find me, though the developers could. Although to be fair, I wasn't impeding game progress for anyone. On the other, morbid fascination, provocations, and hullabaloos in the information sphere were my bread and butter. Without all that, I'd be stuck running around waving weapons just like everyone else in the game. Either that or, God help me, I'd have to go running off to who knows where in the east looking for material.

"Oh, whatever." I shrugged my shoulders. "What are they going to do, kill me? It's just a bunch of bearded programmers—not quite special forces."

I sat down and, before I did anything else, plugged my USB modem into my computer and unhooked the internet cable. Then I launched a program I had to generate a dynamic IP address.

"You can't be too careful" was my motto when it came to making up stories online. I doubted anyone would try to hack me, but still. God helps those who help themselves…and orcs kill those who don't.

I logged onto the game site, registered as Buzdigan, headed over to the forum, clicked on the "quests" section, and then went to the "Epic and hidden quests" subsection. A second later, I had created a new topic entitled "Bringing back the gods: nonsense or a real quest?"

"I haven't been playing long, but I'm making some progress—Level 23 already. The game's cool, everything looks great, you fight but have to use your brain, too, and the quests are fun. The PKers are a pain, but that's always true. I have a question about quests, though. I read on the forums that there are hidden and epic quests and that they give you the best stuff. It's hard to get them, though. Anyway, I was chatting with some guy recently. A few friends from college and I were at a bar after class on Friday, and he came with one of them. He just started playing Fayroll, too, his level's about the same as mine, but he said that he just got a hidden quest. It was a complete accident that happened while he was saving or killing something for some other quest. Long story short, he's supposed to help some NPCs and might get something in return from the gods that left.

"So my question: Is that real? Does that happen? If it is real, can you do the quest in a group? What do you get for it? Someone has to have come across it at some point, so speak up!"

I reread what I thought was a great example of charming, not-exactly-articulate writing that could plausibly be written by your average Joe—a mix of truth and lies. There was no point in thinking up some fake quest when I knew about a real one, after all. Still, it wasn't worth unveiling the whole truth. I wondered what kind of reaction it would get and clicked the send button.

Then I called Elvira and found out that we were scheduled to go to some exhibit for new artists that had supposedly discovered a new style of art. Basically, a bunch of long-haired women standing around in scarves smoking their slender little cigarettes. Who knows what they actually drew? Maybe an eye, maybe somebody's ass, but it was art. *New age! Gag.* Still, I had to go, since Elvira liked all that crap. I'd sit through it, she'd make me some food later, and at least that way, I wouldn't be stuck eating pelmeni yet again.

The next two hours were spent hard at work on my article, and I was nearly done when I had to start getting ready. I headed over to the wardrobe and thought for a while about what to wear. The previous occasion had been a failure. Elvira had dragged me to yet another exhibit, and I figured it would just be a bunch of half-crazed avant-garde men in their eyeliner standing around with flat-chested, pimply-faced dames squawking on about how, "It's genius! Genius, I tell you!"

So I dressed accordingly: jeans and a t-shirt featuring the likeness of a popular TV show doctor wagging his finger above a caption that read, "In this hospital, I'm king and god!" It was a cool shirt the girls from advertising gave me for my birthday. As it so happens, they were the only decent people in our snake pit.

How was I supposed to know that it wasn't a modern art exhibit? Or that it was actually a showing of pieces from the collections of different oligarchs? The "Little Dutchmen," Polenov, Aivazovsky, Serov... There was even some guy there from the Ministry of Culture, judging by the dejected way he was taking the whole picture in. It was much more impressive than what they have at The Tretyakov Gallery... Although to be fair, he may have just been shocked by the fact that what he was seeing was hanging there rather than in The Tretyakov Gallery.

The people in attendance were dressed accordingly—ladies in their pearls and furs hanging on the arms of their walking wallets, B-list sluts with expensive phones in one hand and tiny terriers in the other, equally B-list non-traditional pairs (at least I got something right), celebrities, a fellow journalist flagging down waiters with canape?, politicians, and all dressed to the nines. Dinner jackets, Burberry Prorsum and Frankie Morello suits, evening gowns... Elvira was in something decked out in crystals, too, and next to her was me with the doctor on my t-shirt. We had people staring at us all night—at me and the doctor with surprise, at Elvira with sympathy. I couldn't care less, but she was of a somewhat different opinion.

She looked like she wanted to cut me when we got home. I stayed awake all night I was so worried she might try to smother me in my sleep. Don't think I'm joking—she's Tatar, and they're crazy.

Eventually, I decided to make sure my bases were covered and went with a linen suit that was as comfortable as it was universal. All set, I left for Krymsky Val[9], where the event was being held.

The exhibit wasn't worth describing except to say that I could have done better. Just give me a canvas and a few tubes of paint, as apparently squeezing the paint out of them is now an actual skill. Still, quite a few obviously well-off men and women came to see the artwork and even buy some for themselves. I walked behind Elvira for a bit as she darted around the gallery before I decided to sit down on a bench in a corner behind a palm tree. It was a nice little spot that was quiet and peaceful. I even began to doze off as I listened to the music softly wafting down from the ceiling. However, just as I started to drift away, a couple of men stopped on the other side of the palm. I couldn't help but overhear their conversation.

"...called in all the veterans."

"Because of one thread? Some kid obviously wrote it, or maybe it's just there to throw people off the track."

"But why? What track would they be trying to throw people off of? Information wars always have a goal, whether they're trying to attract people or weaken the opposition. But if you don't stand to gain anything, there's no reason whatsoever to do it! This isn't your first time around the block. You should know this doesn't sound like your usual provocation."

"I don't know...maybe just an attention grab...laying out a position..."

"For a Level 23 player? Besides, it's obviously someone still in school, and the only way they try to grab attention is by screwing the players around them. We both have to deal with that constantly. No, this looks real. Some dumb kid found an equally dumb source that stumbled over something he didn't understand. And now, they're walking around the game with an incredibly rare quest. Let's just hope they don't get tired of it and give up."

"I leaned on my people to try to get them to give me the thread author's IP address, but you know how Raidion is with confidentiality. It's no State Duma[10] in there—they're serious."

"If all else fails, we can find some hackers to break into the server."

"That's daring, but it's stupid, too. They'll find your hackers; you know that as well as I do. Then we'll have to send you-know-who money, and he'll..."

The pair walked away from my palm and left me wide awake.

Four-to-one they were talking about me, I thought. *That's crazy—a couple of important guys like that playing games.*

I broke cover from behind the palm to see that they had stepped away toward a corner and were talking on their phones. They weren't the only ones, as a lot of the men in the room appeared to be getting ready to leave despite the frustration written on their dates' faces.

No, I thought, *that has to be a coincidence. There can't be so many people playing the game, and especially old rich guys.*

Elvira walked over.

"There you are! I was about to call missing persons. Let's go, everyone's about to leave."

"Why?" I asked.

"I'm not sure." She shrugged her dark, bare shoulders, her heavy chest swinging under the thin fabric of her dress. "A lot of people are talking about some kind of quest, something unique or whatever. Sounds like an adventure game or flash mob of some sort."

"Yeah, probably." I may have miscalculated somehow, but something somewhere told me that things were definitely about to get interesting.

The first thing I did when we got to my apartment was turn on my computer. I logged into my Buzdigan account and found exactly what I'd suspected. I'd gotten much more than I dreamed possible. I had hoped to generate a little buzz, maybe get people talking a bit, and see how the community reacted to something out of the ordinary. Maybe I'd even participate.

I participated all right. In the four and a half hours that had elapsed since I started the thread, it had grown to eighty pages. It wasn't even a thread anymore; it was now a new section entitled "Legacy of the Departed Gods." There were seven threads in it, and the comments covered the gamut. Some were happy to hear the news, others thought it was a fake, and still others asked me to get in touch with them. Nobody seemed to remember that I wasn't the one with the quest.

My forum inbox was also packed with more than fifty messages. Reading the first few subjects didn't make me feel any better: "I'll buy your information. Good money." "You'll tell me what's going on if you know what's good for you." "Welcome to the Great Fayroll Army!"

I let out a stunned sigh—I may have been in over my head. To be more specific, it appeared I'd underestimated how interested the gaming community would be in what the gods left behind.

The screen refreshed, and a new message appeared: "The Thunderbirds invite you to join their ranks." My clan was behind the curve. Here they were taking their good old time, and the Great Fayroll Army was trying to poach me.

"Hey, Nikiforov." Elvira's voice rang out from behind me as annoyed as ever. "You care more about that computer than you do me?"

"You know, El, you're great, but sometimes you say the most ridiculous things."

"Then turn off your idiot box and let's go eat. We can have a little to drink, too—it's been a long day."

Well, I thought, *I'll tackle this tomorrow with a hangover.*

Elvira's "a little" was less than convincing.

The next morning was dreary with a gray sky. I had the hangover I'd anticipated, as well—"a little" turned into "a little more," which gave way to "one more drink." The whole thing was complicated by listening to her nag as she looked for one of her stockings. "You animal, you hid it somewhere! Another one of your fetishes." Then it was her phone: "You were reading my texts? How dare you!" That reminded me. I needed to change the password on my phone. God help me if she were to find it. She'd kill Lena from advertising, and me, too. Lena would die quickly, but she'd probably keep me around for a while. She's refined that way. Then she was looking for her keys…which were found where? Obviously, in her purse ("Whatever, you mixed everything up again like you always do.") Finally, we finished with a goodbye kiss and, "I'll call you. Don't you dare not pick up the phone."

I didn't have the least desire to smoke, but I went out onto the balcony and lit up anyway. She was leaving, and I needed to be sure that happened. I only breathed a sigh of relief when her Matiz pulled into traffic and disappeared around the corner. Women are great—they're fun, pleasant, and appetizing. But they're exhausting…

I turned on my computer, made sure my USB modem was plugged in, and logged into my Buzdigan account. My eyes widened in shock. The number of threads had tripled, and the debate about whether the whole thing was true or not dominated the forum. True, I didn't have that many new messages—just about a hundred, though there were more threats than I'd seen the day before. "If you're lying, I'm coming for you." "We'll find you and squeeze you until you give up the information." "We have your IP address. Tell us what's going on, or we're stopping by for a visit." The kids were having their fun. Why weren't they in school, though? What does the Ministry of Education even do? Or are they all on holiday?

There were offers, too, and other clans had invited me to join them. All in all, a success. Anyway, what was done was done, and it was time to head to Fayroll. I just hoped the sun was shining there. Without further ado, I switched the computer over to my regular connection and lay down in the capsule.

Fayroll greeted me with a gorgeous, sunny morning. That was probably true of most locations, with rain, fog, and everything else that is delightful about the weather probably saved for areas where they fit the script or were part of a quest. I'd have to see that at some point.

The square was crowded and noisy. The last couple days had made me forget how many players there really were in the game, and so it took me a few seconds to reacclimate myself to the running, trading, and cursing going on all around me.

Two symbols grabbed my attention from the lower left corner of the gaming interface. They were both envelopes, meaning that I had mail waiting for me both in my personal inbox and in the game's postal system. I'd have to go find a mailbox. The fact that I had something in the postal system didn't surprise me—it was probably the Hounds of Death replying to my message. But who would have sent me a personal message? Maybe Euiikh was at it again.

I checked to see who wrote me and whistled. The message was from Gerv. I wondered what he, the clan's gray cardinal, would want from me, a random volunteer.

"Come find me as soon as you log into the game. Gerv"

Short and sweet. I was about to respond when...*Ah, no need.* "Gerv. Ge-e-erv!" I bellowed across the square and waved my hand. He was there fifteen steps away from me getting food from an NPC, and, when he heard me, he turned, nodded, and waved his hand as if to tell me to wait where I was. Well, if the boss tells you to wait, that's what you do.

Three minutes later, Gerv came over and jumped right into what he had to say.

"Do you even get what you did?"

I was taken aback, not exactly sure what he was talking about. My letter to the Hounds or my escapade with the quest? I immediately ruled out the possibility that he'd sniffed out something about the quest, seeing as how I was the only one who could possibly know about that. There were no witnesses.

"I was just trying to do something good." I decide to play it safe and be vague.

"If you wanted to do something bad, I'd say you were insane. Are you aware that there's an official protocol in place for interclan communication? You did write an official letter from the clan, after all. Let's just imagine that Merkel got a letter from…oh, I don't know, Vasya Pupkin, a locksmith from Building Maintenance 18. 'Some guy at the pub told me that the Germans are about to go to war with us again, but don't worry, I gave him a jab to the nose. You aren't idiots, and you don't need us in Berlin for the third time. Russia and Germany are friends and all. Oh, and do you have skirts in your closet, too, or just pants?' That's basically what you wrote. Sure, maybe the context is a little different, but the idea is the same."

"But everything's okay?" I breathed a sigh of relief when I realized he was talking about my letter to the Gray Witch.

"Yes, of course. More than okay. Our two clans are going to sign a cooperation and mutual assistance agreement. The Witch was apparently so touched by how our clan feels about hers that she contacted Elina herself to offer us their friendship. Elina was shocked, obviously, because she had no idea that was coming. But she quickly let the Witch know that anyone who insults the Hounds of Death is insulting the Thunderbirds. The document will be ready to sign tomorrow. As soon as we figured things out with the Gray Witch, we all left to find you, and you were logged out. So we tried to find anyone who'd talked to you recently, and the acrobat brothers, Rone and Dorn, got in touch. They figured you'd done something wrong, so they immediately started telling us how you were a good guy and couldn't have meant any harm." Gerv's imitation of Dorn's booming voice was dead on. "'He did everything by the book, they were the ones who started it.'"

"Ha! And they went on and on about how helpless I am." I was moved.

"That sounds like them." Gerv nodded his head and continued. "When we figured out what was going on, Elina started yelling about how you didn't let us know first. Then she quieted down, thought for a bit, and gave a speech about how it was fate that led us to you in the pub. We let you into the clan, and you helped us meet a goal you heard about. Then she said how we need to reward you, seeing as how you acted in the interests of the clan."

"Of course I did!" I puffed out my chest.

"I don't exactly agree with her." Gerv looked past my gesture and stared closely at me. "I think you couldn't care less about the Hounds, and I don't think you really care about what we need. You handed that orc over to the Hounds, just handed him over so you wouldn't have to deal with him. You only wrote about the clan to make yourself sound more impressive—I don't think it had anything to do with our interests. Maybe that crossed your mind later, but I doubt it."

Damn, he's smart, I thought. *I need to keep an eye on him. That wasn't a terribly difficult deduction to make, but still.*

"But I still helped you!" I began my defense.

"Yes, you did. Elina wanted to formally present you with something in the clan fortress, but then this whole firestorm broke out, and now we don't have time."

"What firestorm?" I blinked for effect.

"Do you even read the forum? Do you care about what's going on in the game?" Gerv was suddenly angry. "You can't be that oblivious! Apparently, someone got a quest from the Departed."

"The Departed?"

"The Departed Gods."

"Is that good?" I kept up my façade.

"It's impossible. The clans are all on edge now, and even lone players are trying to find out what they can. Although they're all on the outside. What chance do they have?"

"What do you mean?"

"The chances of finding the player with the quest are almost zero. Miniscule—it would be pure randomness."

"Wow! So what's the quest?" I was enjoying myself thoroughly.

"Nobody knows."

"Then how did everyone find out about it?"

"That's what I'm saying; read the forums. Yesterday, some Level 23 player wrote that he was chatting with someone else at the same level who told him about a quest they got from the Departed Gods. Now, the clans are all looking for him so they can find out about that second player." Gerv shook his head. "You know, you read it all on the forum, and it's all fine and good, but it sounds crazy when you explain it like that."

"Seriously. Maybe that first player was just playing a joke? Or someone's trying to trick everyone?"

"Maybe, but that doesn't make sense. You'd need a reason to run a ruse like that, and there isn't one here." Gerv could have quoted the two businessmen from the gallery verbatim. "Either that or it's just absolute nonsense."

"Maybe he just wanted a laugh!"

"There's nobody like that here." Gerv was confident in his reply. "Plus, the message isn't written like that. And even if that were true, believe me, the clans have gone all out to check out worse stories. So, everyone's been on edge since last night. The high-level players are all scouring Level 18-30 locations, talking with NPCs and players to see who saw what. The NPCs answer, the players don't."

"Why not?"

"There are tons of clans. Just imagine having someone ask you for the hundredth time if you've seen anything. What would your response be?"

"I'd tell you to screw off. Not everyone, of course. You could get something from some people."

"That's exactly what everyone's saying. Nobody likes it."

"Are there really that many clans?"

"Just look around you!"

I looked around. There were plenty of players running around, but not that many.

"Look more carefully."

I did what he asked and realized what he was talking about. Everyone running around was Level 100 or higher, and clearly in leadership roles.

"The guilds all sent their best people out to question witnesses, but they're going at it so hard, there's nobody left to question. Everyone has a different method—some are more pleasant about it; others try to scare you into talking. Everyone's angry."

"Pay them 3 gold, and they'll tell you everything." I had a piece of advice for him. "Pay them 10, and they'll even make things up to tell you."

"Good idea." Gerv fell silent and clapped me on the shoulder. "Well done, I should have thought of that myself. You haven't seen anything, have you?"

"Nope, I'd have told you right away. By the way, what's the reward you were talking about for me?"

"Oh, right, sorry."

Gerv waved his hand.

Your status in the clan was changed to kinsman. You are now a full-fledged member.

You have the right to access the small clan storehouse.

Your clan bonuses now include:

+7% protection from mental effects

+4% protection from poison

+5% to movement speed

Your bonuses can be modified or increased by fostering respect within the clan.

"There you go. We wanted to do it up in the clan hall, but sorry, no time."

"This works for me. Do you have any clues about the guy everyone's looking for?"

"Not really. The thread was started by someone named Buzdigan, and he was at Level 23 as of yesterday. All anyone can find about him is that there was a player with that name in the game, though the last time he logged in was two years ago. The Buzdigan, who wrote the message, probably registered on the forum using a different name from the one he plays with. Everybody does that. So who knows what his name in the game is. Some people talked about rounding up all the Level 23 players they could find, though there are just too many of them—and not all of them play regularly. Plus, they're always jumping between locations. He could be up to Level 24 or 25 now, too. There hasn't been a response from him on the forum either, so I guess he realized that he got everyone too riled up. Maybe he's scared and waiting until it all blows over."

"What about the second player?"

"The one with the quest? Nothing. We know he exists, but we don't know who he is, what class he is, what his name is, absolutely nothing. Just his level, and even that isn't a sure thing. So, everyone's looking for this Buzdigan, both in the game and in real life."

"Wow, that's serious."

"Well, of course. It's a hidden quest from the Departed Gods. Okay, anyway, I have to go. So much to do, it's crazy. Oh, Elina may ask you to stop by for a private conversation. And wipe that smile off your face—we're talking about our clan leader. If anyone from the Hounds of Death asks you to come talk with them, who are you going to tell first?"

"Elina?"

"Sounds good. And second?"

"Gerv!"

"Good job. Have a good one!"

"Gerv, wait a second. Where's the Tearful Goddess Order mission?"

"Oh, interesting. Why do you need it?" Gerv perked up.

"Look." I pulled the unlucky knight's medallion out of my inventory. "I found it in some loot I got, and it came with a quest."

"Oh, deliver the medallion." The scout's interest waned immediately. "Well, yeah. They'll give you something decent, no worse than rare. I've heard of people even getting epic things from them, though that was just rumor. They did give MaryAnn from our clan something legendary, though. Anyway, the mission is over there, to the right of the well. Is that all?"

"Yup. Thanks, Gerv."

"See you."

He went off to talk to the next NPC on his list.

For my part, I decided to act on what he told me later, and instead headed off toward the mailbox.

"Halt!" A forceful, Level 100 elf with a clan badge reading Unbroken by Evil stopped me. "A couple questions."

"Twenty gold."

"For what?" The elf was taken aback.

"For my answers."

"A little expensive, don't you think? And maybe a bit brash?"

"You don't have to pay if you don't want to."

"Fifteen."

"Done."

The money found its way to my pocket, and I graciously invited him to continue.

"Ask away!"

"Do you know a player by the name of Buzdigan?"

"No."

"Have you heard anything about a quest that brings back the Departed Gods?"

"No."

The elf waved his left hand and enveloped me in a cloud of something like a glistening powder. I sneezed.

"What the heck?"

"It's just truth powder. If you were lying, it would have turned black. Simple and effective."

"You're kidding me. What about warning me? It's magic!" I was indignant.

"I'm paying you." The elf coldly rebuffed me. "I have the right to check your answers. Okay, see you."

How lucky am I? I thought. *Good thing he phrased that second question awkwardly. I could have talked my way out of knowing about Buzdigan, seeing as how everyone's heard of him now. But if he'd asked me if I know who got the hidden quest about the departed gods, I'd have been screwed five ways to Friday. Serves him right.*

I told the next high-level player who ran up to me that I didn't know anything right off the bat. All I wanted to do was get my mail.

There was a message in my inbox. It was from the Hounds of Death, just as I suspected. On the other hand, I never would have guessed that it would be from their leader—the Gray Witch.

Dear Hagen,

It sure is good to hear that there's still some decency in the world. Why else would someone from another clan, one that isn't even allied with the Hounds of Death, stand up for the honor and dignity of that same non-allied clan's leader? And that's exactly what you and your friends did. Lots of people say I'm a strict and ruthless leader, almost a tyrant. And, you know, I'd have to agree with them. But I always add that I respond in equal measure to both the good and bad things done to me and my clan, no matter if they were done by friends or enemies. You reap what you sow.

You've shown yourself to be a true and devoted friend to me and my clan, and so I would like to extend to you the friendship of the Hounds of Death. If you ever decide to leave the Thunderbirds, you can rest safe in the knowledge that you have a place waiting for you here.

I'd also like to sign a friendship agreement with the Thunderbirds. Judging by Elina's response, it sounds like you haven't yet told her about what you did or your letter. What you wrote confirmed my good opinion of you, though, obviously, clan leaders need to know about letters like that.

But moving on to more material matters, please accept the ring attached to this message as a token of my gratitude. We have decent jewelers, and I had it made especially for you. I hope you like it.

That's all for now.

Your friend, more than you can imagine,
Gray Witch

P.S. I don't think that orc Euiikh is looking at a very easy future. Well, really, I don't think he has a future at all. G.W.

P.P.S. I sent your friends Rone and Dorn small gifts as well. Hopefully, they like them. G.W.

Huh. Things were looking up.

The Hounds of Death offered you their friendship.
The benefits you will get if you accept are:
Title: Friend of the Hounds of Death
10% cheaper prices for transport rentals in areas that respect the Hounds of Death
8% cheaper prices offered by NPCs for goods sold in areas that respect the Hounds of Death
6% cheaper repair prices in areas that respect the Hounds of Death

That decision couldn't have been any easier. Of course, I accepted. Oh, and there was the ring attached to the message.

Hounds of Death Friendship Ring
An object handmade by Flader
+17 to strength
+15 to stamina
+5% defense against all weapon types
+50% chance that 25% of the damage inflicted by enemies will be reflected back on them
+25% defense against the Sepulchral Chill spell
Durability: 260/260
Minimum level for use: 25
For use by Hagen
Cannot be stolen, lost, or given to anyone else.
If the owner dies, does not remain at the location of their death.

"We have decent jewelers." That was quite the understatement—their jewelers were incredible if they were capable of something like that. I could only imagine what materials they used to make it and how much they cost. One thing was for sure: she had an awfully nice and respectful "thank you" coming her way.

Esteemed Gray Witch,

I deeply appreciate the honor of being named friend of another clan, both as a member of the Thunderbirds and as a simple player named Hagen. You can count on my assistance whenever it is needed, so long as it does not harm my clan or my honor.

Thank you for the ring. I couldn't imagine anything better. Your jewelers are fantastic. My best regards to them.

With respect and deference,
Hagen, Thunderbird kinsman

Once I was done writing the letter, I sat down to mentally go through my list of things to do in the city. There didn't turn out to be too many of them:
Visit the Tearful Goddess Order mission.
Visit the instructor and finally give him the ten goblin swords.
I decided to start with the instructor. Remembering where Dorn pointed, I was able to find the little alley fairly quickly and noted that the buildings there were identical to the ones in Aegan. I picked the one with the shield and sword hanging outside and went in.
As you may recall, the first old man was carving a whistle. This one was making a kite—your everyday, diamond-shaped kite. When I walked in, he was attaching the string to the tail.
"What material did you use? There isn't any good paper around here, is there?" I was so surprised I forgot to say hello.
"Parchment. They make great parchment in the eastern lands." He answered without a hint of a boast. "It's thin, it rings—it's perfect for flyers."
"We call them kites." I jabbed my finger at the old man's creation.
"No, my friend. Kites are a kind of bird. They fly in the air, too, but they're different from flyers."
He put his work to the side and looked at me.

"And who might you be? I don't think we've met."

"We haven't. I'm a warrior, still new, I want to get some abilities."

"Sounds good to me. Have you been to any other instructors?"

"Of course!" I wasn't about to hide that. "I went to see the instructor in Aegan. He told me to collect some enemy weapons—swords or clubs."

"And did you?" His eyes narrowed.

"Yes, though it's a ways to Aegan. I decided to just come here."

"That's for sure. It's especially far if you don't have skills or abilities... All right, let's see what you have for me."

I dropped ten rusty swords onto the table in front of him.

The instructor looked the pile of unsightly metal, counted it, even sniffed it.

"Goblins?"

"Yep."

"Little buggers. Okay, what's your level?"

"Twenty-two." *In those brief moments, the game mechanics peeked through and ruined the atmosphere,* I thought.

"Okay." The old man scratched the back of his head. "Here's what we'll do. I'll give you some options, and you can decide which one works best for you."

"Really?" I was surprised.

"Really. I can teach you two active abilities and two passive abilities, though they'll be very average for attack and defense. I can also teach you two active abilities and one passive ability—they'll be decent, but that's all. Finally, I can teach you one active ability and two passive abilities that are the best for your level. It's up to you."

"How much do they cost?"

"The price? It's the same for all of them: 200 gold up front."

I stood there thinking. Sure, the last option sounded the best, and the abilities were obviously really good, but something held me back.

A few seconds later, I realized what that something was. First, a strong, active skill would probably take a lot of mana, and I didn't have much of that. It might very well take a while to recharge, too. Second, the abilities would be best for my current level. In another ten levels, everything would change, and I'd be left with something ordinary and not terribly useful. And that was all I'd get if I picked the third option. With the second I'd get two active abilities—not as good, but at least solid.

"I'll take option number two. Here's the money."

You unlocked Good Choice, Level 1.

To get it, make 14 more good (as judged by the game masters) decisions in game situations.

Reward:

+2 to wisdom

Logician, a passive ability, Level 1: +1 to intellect

To see similar messages, go to the Action section of the attribute window.

You learned a new active ability: Sword of Retribution, Level 1

Boosts the strength of your blows by 75% and increases your chances of landing a critical hit by 50%

Activation cost: 30 mana

Recharge time: 45 seconds

You learned a new active ability: Bloodletting, Level 1

Gives you a 50% chance of causing bleeding

Bleeding damage done: 7 health per second for 50 seconds

Activation cost: 35 mana

Recharge time: 1 minute

You learned a new passive ability: Strong Shoulders, Level 1

Lets you wear light armor and chainmail

"Happy?" The old man watched my face closely.

"Certainly!" There was no sense in hiding it. They were good abilities, they didn't take much mana, and they did decent damage. Plus, I could wear light armor. "Can I ask you a few questions?"

"Go ahead."

"How do I use abilities in battle?" It sounded funny to ask, but I hadn't looked that up on the forums yet. I guess I hadn't thought that far ahead.

He patted the bench next to him in an invitation to sit down. "Look, when you're in battle, and you want to use one, just say it—either out loud or to yourself. That's it. Just remember that you can't have more than five active abilities. If you want to learn a sixth, you'll have to pick one of your existing five to forget."

"How many passive abilities can I have?"

"As many as you want."

"And the second question, these are all Level 1. What happens later? Do they level-up?"

"Good question. The more you use them, the better your chances are of having one of them level-up. They each have their tipping point, but I couldn't tell you exactly when that is. Fight a lot, use them a lot, do a lot of damage, and you'll be fine."

"How many levels do abilities have?" I figured I'd asked the old man everything I could think of seeing as how I had him right there.

"Three. Only three."

"When can I learn new ones?"

"When you get to Level 25. And then Level 30."

"Got it. Levels divisible by five."

"What?"

"Thank you, I said. Time for me to go."

"Hang on a second. I see your path lies to the east." The old man threw me a look that spoke volumes.

"What? Why do you say that?" I was surprised, as I hadn't even thought about where I'd go next. I had too much to do right where I was.

"I don't know, I just had a feeling. Anyway, if you're in the east, get me some parchment for my flyers, okay? My granddaughter loves flying them, but if she breaks this one, I don't have enough parchment to make a replacement."

168

You have a new quest offer: Acquire Parchment.

Task: Get some parchment from the eastern end of the continent and bring it to instructor Serhio in Fladridge.

Reward:
1000 experience
Your choice of active ability.
Accept?

Yes, of course. Though I wasn't planning on heading east—yet, at least.

"All right, I'll see you." I gave the old man a deep and grateful bow.

"Good luck, sonny!" He waved and got back to work on the kite's tail.

I left the instructor, whose name, to my shame, I only found out thanks to the quest description, and smiled. Life had new meaning and looked to be much more fun thanks to my new abilities. All I had left to do was visit the knight's mission, give them Olaf's amulet, and get my reward.

Chapter Thirteen
A Knight and a Mayor

The mission turned out to be a little building marked by a sign identical to the amulet—a circle with a tear in the middle. I pushed the door open and walked in to find myself in a small room centered around a desk. Behind it, sat an old man who could not have looked less like a knight. He was wearing a robe and writing something. *This was the representative of a powerful order of knights? Where was his chainmail, sword, mustache?* He looked up from the parchment in front of him.

"How can I help you?"

"Is this the Tearful Goddess Order?" I thought I might have been mistaken. Maybe the building belonged to...oh, I don't know...Who could it have belonged to?

"Yes, the Tearful Goddess Order." He immediately dispelled my doubts, cutting short my attempt to think of what else might be going on. "What do you need?"

"I have an amulet for you." I pulled it out and showed it to him. "Here, I think it belongs to one of you."

"Wait a second." He jumped up from the stool he sat on and ran into the next room. He returned almost immediately, throwing open the door and announcing grandly, "Master of the Tearful Goddess Order, keeper of the lost temple secret, member of the Council of Involved, Majordomo Hugo von Shlippenshtain awaits you!"

That was impressive. Involved in what? And what was that about a secret?

I walked through the open door with as dignified and measured a gait as I could muster.

The inside of the room looked much more fitting for a knightly order. The room was spacious, weapons hung on the walls, an enormous bearskin sprawled over the floor, and a fire crackled in the fireplace. I found myself looking at a tall and sinewy older knight. He had a drooping Polish-style mustache and could have been pulled straight from Dragonlance or the movie *Crusader*. Shlippenshtain

170

seemed like a strange name for him, as I would have expected something like Pan Tadeusz or Sir Ogloblya.

"Welcome, warrior." The knight nodded his head slightly in greeting. "I am Master of the Tearful Goddess Order Sir Hugo von Shlippenshtain. You can call me Master Hugo. And what is your name?"

"Hagen," I answered. "Hagen from the Thunderbirds clan. I don't have quite as many titles, as I haven't had time to acquire them yet. So you can just call me Hagen."

"Well, if you have bravery in your heart, strength in your arms, and a brain in your head, titles and glory will come. You just need to understand if you really need glory." Master Hugo was being very diplomatic. "Brother Tsimiskhy said you brought an amulet belonging to one of our brothers. Could you give it to me?"

"Of course. That's why I'm here." I offered it to him.

"Olaf von Dal." The knight looked at the amulet sadly. "He was a fun, carefree boy, and all he wanted was to write the chronicles of our order. You know, Hagen, he even bought a thick book that was orange for some reason. We joked that it turned blue for fear of what he would write in it, but he said that sooner or later his stories about our order would be called the Orange Chronicles. How did he die?"

"I don't know, Master Hugo. I found his amulet in a den belonging to a creature I killed named Burrig. I imagine it was responsible. He was probably just unlucky since he must have been a strong knight and the creature wasn't that dangerous. Maybe he twisted his ankle or was already wounded... Who knows?"

"It's not important anymore." The master nodded his head in agreement. "You say you killed the beast?"

"Well, yes."

"Can you prove that?"

"Yes, as a matter of fact." I pulled out Burrig's claw, which I had been carrying around the whole time.

"Will you give it to me? I'll keep it with Olaf's amulet to show that his death did not go unpunished."

"Of course." I gave Hugo the claw.

You completed a quest: Remembering the Fallen.

You let the brothers in the knight's order know that he is dead.

Reward:

100 gold

500 experience

+5 friendliness from the Tearful Goddess Order

You also completed an additional action and may receive a variable reward.

"Thank you." The knight clasped his fist to his heart. "I think it would be fair to give you something more than the standard reward offered for returning the amulet belonging to our fallen brother."

Ah-ha! That's what Gerv was talking about! I thought.

I had been trying to figure out what weapon he was talking about, seeing as how there wasn't a mention of one in the quest description.

"The Tearful Goddess Order is very old," continued Shlippenshtain. "Our storehouses have accumulated many things needed by people in search of fame and great exploits. We also have much gold, which people treasure so highly. Finally, the order has knowledge we can share."

Choose one of the additional rewards available for completing the Remember the Fallen quest:

3000 gold

An item from the order's storehouse matching your class

An ability matching your class

"Choose carefully, Hagen. Pick what you need most."

"What would you pick?" I asked.

"Me?" The knight smiled. "I have not been asked to make that choice, as I am usually the one giving it. I can only say that there are three things the order values above all else: personal honor, a purposeful philosophy, and soldierly abilities. Those are our founding principles."

I found myself looking at what was obviously a trick question for the second time in the space of ten minutes. Just as with the instructor, I was sure there was more behind it than just gold, some item, or an ability.

"I choose the ability."

"And why?" Hugo was intrigued.

"Gold is just metal, and I can get it whenever I want. Items I can purchase with the gold I get. But abilities... You can't mine them, and you can't simply buy them. Plus, they're combat abilities so they could save my life."

"Bravo!" Hugo was effusive with his praise. "I was right about you!"

> **You learned a new active ability: Strength of Fire, Level 1**
>
> **Inflicts fire damage on your opponents: 5 health per second for 30 seconds**
>
> **Activation cost: 55 mana**
>
> **Recharge time: 30 seconds**
>
> **The Tearful Goddess Order offered you their friendship:**
>
> **The benefits you will get if you accept are:**
>
> **Title: Friend of the Tearful Goddess Order**
>
> **You can always count on the physical, magical, or financial assistance of the order, whose missions are in all the cities in Fayroll, if you need it to defend your honor, protect the defenseless, or destroy evil.**
>
> **All knights of the order, when they see that you are in need of assistance, will consider it their duty to help you.**
>
> **If you commit a dishonorable deed and the order learns of it, you will be stripped of their friendship and declared their enemy.**
>
> **Accept?**

That made things interesting. On the one hand, it was help from lots of NPCs and a wallet I could dip into if needed. On the other, if you happen to just kill someone, and an NPC sees it, you're toast—the enemy. I didn't need any help figuring out what knights do with their enemies. It would be straight to the respawn point for me.

Still, I leaned toward accepting their friendship and ended up clicking "Yes."

You unlocked Friends by the Bushel, Level 1.

To get it, become the friend of nine more orders, factions, or societies founded by NPCs.

Reward:

Charmer, a passive attribute, Level 1: 5% discount for all traders and all products in Rattermark

Title: Everyone's Favorite

To see similar messages, go to the Action section of the attribute window.

"I'm very happy our order has a new friend. In days gone by, many of your kind were our friends, though these days, they prefer to get what we have rather than enjoy a relationship with us." Hugo seemed entirely sincere in his regret.

"Things aren't the way they used to be." I sighed. "No romance in the world anymore…"

"These are bad days. Everyone's chasing gold, and meanwhile evil is awakening."

"It's awful. You can't even walk down the roads." I thought back to the unpleasant woman with the bushel of sticks.

"There's actually a reason I'm still here." Master Hugo leaned in and confided in me. "There's a very powerful witcher in our city, or maybe somewhere in the outskirts. Be careful out there, Hagen, and especially at night."

"Can I help?"

You have a new quest offer: Witcher in the Shadows.

Task: Find out something about the witcher living in Fladridge or its outskirts and get the information to Hugo von Shlippenshtain.

Reward:

1200 experience

Other rewards: variable

Important note: If you do not get the information you learn to Hugo von Shlippenshtain, and instead use it to find and kill the witcher, you will fail the quest.

Accept?

"I'd be happy to help the order."

I left the mission very satisfied with the ability, experience, gold, action, and quest I'd gotten. Not bad!

Ten steps later, I found myself staring at a sign: "Hotel."

"What an idiot!" I smacked my forehead. "I almost forgot. I'd have been stuck lugging everything around yet again."

The hotel was small and cozy. The bell hanging on the entrance rang softly, and the face of the cute blonde girl behind the counter lit up with a smile.

"Welcome to the Starling and Lira! I hope your stay will be pleasant."

"I'm sure it will be. Could I have a room?"

"Of course." She smiled again. "Room 15, second floor, up the stairs and to the right. Five silver coins a day. You pay when you return your key and leave the hotel."

She handed me a key.

You're now renting a hotel room. It is your personal space, meaning that you always have a place to leave your things no matter which city in Rattermark you're in. You are the only one who can enter unless you bring someone with you, and they are only allowed in when you are there. Don't forget to pay on time. If you do not, you will not be allowed into your room. Don't worry, however, your possessions will remain there waiting for you.

"Got it!" I looked at the girl again, and she smiled one more time. "What's your name, cutie?"

"Lubelia." She blushed.

"Beautiful. Lubelia, here's 30 gold. That's enough to cover rent for... Well, for a long time. And here's one gold for you. Buy yourself some candy or something—something as gorgeous as you are!"

"Thank you, sir." Lubelia blushed again and looked at me coquettishly. "Maybe I can come by this evening to fluff your pillow?"

"No, no, no," I said. "I won't be there tonight, I have things to do. But thanks."

I walked upstairs thinking about what I'd turned down. She was great, and I enjoy sex as much as the next guy, but sex with a piece of code seemed a bit much. Some perverts somewhere probably can't get enough of it, though...

The room was simple: a table, a bed, chairs, a window, and a large chest. The latter was all I cared about. I unloaded all but 30 gold, taking the time to pat myself on the back for what was a decent haul for Level 22. Although, it really wasn't that hard—a thousand here, five hundred there. I also decided to leave the lucky earring there until I got to Level 25, and the sword followed it. Sure, I couldn't lose it, but what was the point of carrying it around? I did keep the ring the Gray Witch gave me, remembering that I couldn't lose it either.

Once I had everything in the chest, I stepped back and looked at my collection proudly. Then, having slammed it shut, I left the room.

"You're leaving already, sir?" Lubelia scrunched up her nose adorably. "That quickly?"

"You bet, babe." I handed her the key. "Exploits await! You don't happen to know where I could find some villains to protect the city from, do you?"

"Of course I do." She sighed. "We can't even go into the forest anymore. There's a witch living there, and the magistrate even put a price on her head. Go talk to the mayor, he'll tell you everything. Will you be coming back here?"

"Well, certainly. I'll be back!" I said in my best Austrian accent.

"What?"

"Ah, forget it, it's from a movie."

The magistrate building was the tallest in Fladridge, and it had the most NPCs and players running around it. I was already sick and tired of the inquisitive high-level players running around asking questions, and I almost got into a fight with one of them after he grabbed me and tried to shake some information out of me. Obviously, he outweighed me by a large margin, so I had to think of something quickly.

"A-a-ah! Game admins! He's stopping my game progress! Help me!"

"Are you crazy?" Volosat from the Children of Sin clan dropped me. "What are you talking about? If you don't know anything, just say it!"

"I did!" I looked at him in annoyance. "You came here to kill me! Kille-e-er!"

"Who needs you, you squirt?" He wheeled and walked off.

"Why did I have to start all this?" I berated myself as I clambered up the steps of the magistrate building. The mayor's office was on the third floor, and nobody had bothered to invent the elevator yet. "I saw what I wanted to see, but this is getting out of hand."

The mayor looked, well...like a mayor. Remember Evgeni Leonov from An Ordinary Miracle? One and the same, although this one was in a black frock coat. He had an enormous nose, red cheeks, and crafty little eyes—the kind of person who never gives and always takes.

"What do you need, sir?" he asked.

"Someone told me you have a witch problem. I can help take care of it."

"Yes, exactly. She's awful, sneaking all over the place!" The mayor smiled as he realized why I was there.

"Witches are all the same."

"It's true." The mayor cocked his head and looked at me. "If it weren't for knights like you, altruistically helping us simple people..."

"Altruistically?" I was indignant. "Evil always has its price!"

"What's that?" The mayor cupped his hand around his ear.

"Its price, its cost. I was in Tocbridge and dealt with a monster there..."

"Oh, that was you! By the way, how much did the old man pay you?"

I thought back to him and realized he wasn't such a bad guy. There was no sense blowing his little game.

"Three hundred. Why?"

"Oh, nothing, we've just suspected that he's been skimming off the top for a while now. Okay, let's see, how much should we pay you for the witch? I think 300 gold is fair, the same as for that monster."

"Well, one is a brainless swamp animal, and the other is a devious, magic forest witch out for blood." I reproachfully shook my head and looked into the mayor's disgustingly honest eyes. "They're completely different!"

"Completely what?"

"The witch costs more, I'm saying!"

"Yes, I get that. How much more?"

"About 500 more."

"No, not that much more. If we say, for example, something like 200..."

"You don't know anything about evil creatures, my good man." I put on a mysterious face. "The horrible ragged skirt. The terrifying crooked nose. The awful broomstick and boiling pot of nastiness. Add 400 gold to the standard 300, and you have yourself a deal."

"We have an upstanding city and upstanding witches." The mayor looked hurt. "Crooked nose and boiling pot—please! This is an upstanding evil creature and look at you going on and on. Five hundred even, and that's it. Go kill it already. They're still feeding cows hay, and it's summer out! The whole city is in a panic... I'm sorry, I got carried away. Anyway, the herder's afraid to take the cattle outside the city. But what kind of witch would go after a grimy wretch like him? So what do you say to 550?"

"Okay, Mr. Mayor." I was about ready to give in. "Six hundred and we'll start the hunt."

"Deal. But bring me her book of magic to prove you killed her." His tone made me realize that there was no bargaining on that point.

> **You have a new quest offer: Kill the Forest Witch.**
> **Task: Kill the witch living in the forest near Fladridge.**
> **Reward:**
> **600 gold**
> **1500 experience**
> **10% to your reputation in Fladridge**
> **Additional condition: Bring the witch's book of magic to the city mayor as confirmation that you killed her.**
> **Accept?**

"Done! Just give me some gold to buy food with."

"After the quest." The mayor stopped me with a gesture.

"An old man in a tiny little village gave me an advance so I could grab a bite to eat before my daring feat of heroic valor. But the mayor of an enormous city can't match him. Well, whatever you say... Just don't expect the minstrels to sing your praises in my ballads!"

"Fine, fine." The mayor amiably buckled under my reproaches. "I don't care about ballads, but the city's reputation... Talk to the storekeeper on the first floor. Tell him I sent you."

"No, no thank you. I know those storekeepers. 'We'll write up a certificate. Give the bearer food. Sign here. Stamp here.'"

"Are you sure you're a hero in search of adventure?"

"Yes, I am, don't worry."

I left the magistrate building pleased with myself. Pausing to look around the square, I remarked to myself how great the developers were. It was a good world they'd thought up. Very diverse.

So where was the local headstone? I had a witch to kill.

Chapter Fourteen
The Hunter and the Hunters (Part One)

Having visited the headstone that, per the usual, was close to the city gate, I stood by it for a second mulling over my options. Was it worth going back to wander around the streets and find some side quests? In the end, I decided it wasn't worth the extra hassle—after all, the most fun I'd had in the game was when I explored areas off the beaten track. Plus, I wasn't terribly interested in anything like "bring me ten wolf fangs" or "collect ten medicinal field dandelions." Quests like that were too straightforward and boring. Don't get me wrong, I have nothing against the people who try to beat every quest in a particular game, and I don't call them nerds. That's just the kind of people they are—nothing wrong with that.

I smacked my forehead in disgust at my forgetfulness once more, headed over to the nearest vendor, and unloaded everything I'd accumulated in my bag: some pelts, the scimitar belonging to my now-defeated friend Euiikh, and the rest of the trash. The total came to six gold. Sure, my mom and grandmother told me to always bargain, but I was too lazy that time.

At the Fladridge gate, I expected to see the usual yellow brick road, but I was mistaken. It turned out to be paved with planks, giving way to a normal dirt road after about a kilometer. Maybe the developers were having a little fun, or maybe the mayor was just too stingy to fork out the money. Either way, the pattern was broken.

There was a ways to go: five miles by road, I estimated, and then a trek through the forest. *Covering distances like that every day,* I thought, *would get me used to it in a hurry, and in the end, I might even start to enjoy it. Especially since I had something to think about.*

My thoughts covered the social experiment that had yielded such unusual and fascinating results, and my third article, which I had already written in my head and just needed to get down on paper. I even started organizing my thoughts for the fourth article. I thought back to how I'd promised Elvira a trip to Spain that we never took. And, you know, I was having such a good time that I was thoroughly disappointed to see three figures straddling the road and a message pop up.

Attention. Euiikh, a player you blacklisted, is nearby.

"You didn't think you were going to get away that easily, did you?" The voice belonged to my already good friend Euiikh.

"Wait, are you following me?" I asked. "Don't you have a life? You killed me once, I killed you once, and so we're even. Call it a day and move on."

"Where's my scimitar? You probably sold it, you dog."

"You won't believe it, but I just did half an hour ago." My answer was completely honest. "In Fladridge. If you hurry, you might be in time to buy it. Look for the vendor closest to the gate. Off you go!"

"First, I'll kill you, then I'll go get it." Euiikh licked his lips, obviously anticipating the unpleasantries he had planned.

Yes, go get it, I thought. *They'll catch you there—I saw at least two Hounds. They'll give you a scimitar you won't soon forget, and they'll give you a lot more, too.* Although, it was weird that he wasn't afraid to go to the city. Maybe he didn't know he was being hunted?

Incidentally, my opponents were dressed much worse than when we'd last met, and it struck me how shabby they looked. They'd apparently grabbed whatever they had in their rooms and didn't take the time to visit the auction.

"You aren't looking your best, boys. No money?" My question was equal parts gloating and sympathy.

"We were in a hurry," answered Euiikh. "We didn't want to miss you."

"What made you think you'd find me here?"

"There's only one road. You were obviously on your way to the city, and this is the only road going in that direction. As soon as we died, we picked up some things from our rooms and used our last scroll to get to Fladridge. Then, we set up this little ambush, figuring you might decide to go back to Tocbridge. We've been here for days, haven't touched anyone, just taking turns logging out to catch some sleep. And here you are."

There was some logic to their plan, I had to give them that. Also, that was why nobody from the Hounds had gotten to them—they'd been hiding here the whole time. It was true: they had no idea they were being hunted.

I was completely satisfied in the knowledge that my death would almost immediately be avenged and that I wouldn't lose much. After all, my most valuable possessions were now in the hotel, along with my money, and I could just replace my current equipment and weapon at the auction. Maybe even splurge on an upgrade. But thinking about the surprise awaiting my sworn enemies set my mind completely at ease.

I started the battle coolly and calmly. "Let's go, you animals! Thieves, onward!" I assumed my stance.

The orcs appeared shocked by my composure and impudence. At least, the two moving to surround me on either side did so cautiously and even uneasily, apparently not sure what to make of a Level 22 warrior ready to take on three higher-level opponents.

I calmly watched their pincers close in on me. Euiikh himself clearly wanted the kill to sate his complex. The other two were there to back him up and, if worse came to worst, kill me before I could hurt their leader. There appeared to be no thoughts of drawing out my pain and suffering. That might have been because Euiikh had come to respect me, or it might have been because he was afraid of someone popping out of the bushes again. That latter option was more plausible, and the thought put a smile on my face.

"Go ahead; smile," the orc said. "You won't be for long!"

"No, no, no," I answered. "You have no idea how to do this bad guy thing. You're supposed to say something like 'My steel's about to wipe that smile off your face!' Or 'That smile will still be on your face when I separate your head from your shoulders.'"

"Hey, boss, someone on a horse is coming!" The warning came from one of the other two, whose name was Gryk. We could hear hooves clopping along not far off. Somebody was riding up, though they didn't sound like they were in a hurry.

"It's an NPC. They stay out of this stuff," Euiikh answered. "Players don't ride that slowly, and why would anyone around here have a horse? The people here don't have money or the abilities to get a horse. And high-level players just use portals."

"Yeah, right!" I jumped in. "That's the cavalry coming to save me. Seriously! They're about to tear you a new one."

"Oh, who needs you?" Doubt had already crept into Euiikh's voice. "You got lucky once, so now you think it'll happen every time?"

"Lucky once, lucky twice."

Euiikh responded with a downward cut of his saber that I caught with my shield. I deflected it to the right and jabbed my mace into his stomach in an attempt to at least knock him backward if I couldn't do any damage.

"Hang on, friend! I'm coming!" I heard a voice coming from somewhere above me accompanied by the clatter of hooves.

"What the—" Gryk was interrupted by a long lance held by a rider astride a prancing horse.

"You're kidding me! Who are you?!" Euiikh turned his full fury on the rider. "You're an NPC! Why?"

"That's why!" I buried my mace in the side of his head, muttering to myself: "Sword of Retribution."

Why pass up the chance to try something new? I'm all for self-education. The blow was intensified by the ability and, apparently, was critical, as the orc's health quickly turned red.

"A-a-ah!" He screamed and tried to catch me with an upward slice of his saber.

I jumped to the side and swung my mace, landing another shot to the head that ended my third meeting with Euiikh. The count was two to one in my favor. At the same time, the NPC I still didn't know hurriedly pulled out a long sword, and with the deftest of strokes, dispatched Euiikh's other companion, an orc named Mruk.

"Is that all? Are there any other enemies, sir?" The knight took off his helmet and addressed me.

"It doesn't look like it." I looked for his name.

"Allow me to introduce myself. Gunther von Richter, Knight of the Tearful Goddess Order."

Gunther von Richter was a very young knight with a frank face, unruly red hair, and a shining white smile. He was also the owner of a long sword, broad shoulders, and a warhorse to which I owed my life.

"Well, look at that," I said aloud. "Though I'm still trying to figure out why you helped me."

"The holy duty of all knights of the Tearful Goddess Order is to help everyone in need, especially if they are a friend of the order." It was less than original, but he said it with complete sincerity.

"That's not a bad responsibility to have." I was a fan. "Do good on earth!"

"Where? What does the earth have to do with it? I'm no plowman!" The knight looked at me perplexed.

"Forget it. Thank you, Gunther von Richter. They would have killed me if it weren't for you. I wasn't scared, but it would certainly have been unpleasant."

"Death is never pleasant and always scary. Still, there are different ways to die." Richter was on his soapbox. "But, knights are always prepared to die. It comes with the job."

"Of course. Samurais have to always bear in mind that they could die at any moment and that when the time comes, they must die with honor. That's their biggest concern."

"Well said. But what's a samurai?"

"They're way off in the east." The knight listened with interest. "All in white pants, white jackets, and with a sword. Tough warriors. They invented the 'warrior code,' or Bushido in their language. Later, one of the main ones, a guy by the name of Daidōji Yūzan, wrote it all down."

"I'd like to read that." The knight appeared to be inquisitive as well as noble. "We have a code as well, though it's small and not so well written. Where are you going, by the way? If you're on your way to Fladridge, we can go together. I enjoy chatting with you, and my father always said that trips with a good companion go by twice as fast."

"Sorry, my friend, but I actually just left Fladridge. There's a witch bothering the locals, so I was contracted to go deal with her."

"A witch?" The knight perked up like a terrier catching the scent of a fox.

"Yep. She lives somewhere around here."

"Would you mind if I joined you? I took a vow to destroy all witches wherever and whenever I see them."

"Would I mind?" I even clapped my hands. "Are you kidding? It would be my honor and great pleasure to have you along with me."

I was thrilled to get an NPC knight as a companion. He may have been crazy, but at least he had a sword. He could go first and take the first blow.

"Is the wicked creature far from here?" Richter was all business.

"No, not really," I answered. "Three miles or so, though it's through the forest."

"Miles?" The knight's eyebrows shot up.

"Well, just not far." I would have to watch my language, as Gunther appeared to be collecting material for his own encyclopedia. "A fifteen-minute walk."

"Then what are we waiting for?"

The knight hung his lance in a special holder in the horse's harness, unhooked his shield from the saddle, and slung it behind his back.

"What about your horse? It won't be stolen? Or run away?"

"No-o-o." Gunther patted the horse's withers. "He's too smart to be caught, and he definitely won't run away. Ready?"

I heard something rustle behind me.

The sound was unexpected, and I spun around while pulling out my mace. When I saw the person in front of me, my mace dropped, and my mouth opened. It was a lanky man in a black suit, a white shirt, and a black tie. He held a small suitcase.

"I haven't seen Gordon Freeman, and I don't even know what's going on." My response was automatic. *What did you expect me to say after I saw a person like that in a game? A fantasy game, no less.*

"Let me introduce myself." The man in the suit bowed his head slightly. "Game admin Number Nineteen."

"And your name?"

"Number Nineteen. That's my name."

"Sir Hagen, who are you talking to?" Gunther couldn't figure out what was going on.

"NPCs can't hear us," explained Number Nineteen.

"Sure, he can't hear you, but he's worried. You'll say your piece and then leave, and he'll think I'm crazy. I still need him to help me kill a witch."

"If it will make you feel better..." Number Nineteen snapped his fingers, and Gunther froze.

"I am informing you that player Euiikh lodged complaint number 14,347, claiming that a non-player character of the knight class inappropriately interfered with his game progress. He says the interference resulted in his death, that of his companions, and their loss in a battle. Is there anything you wish to communicate to the game administration through me?" Number Nineteen's voice was emotionless.

"Of course," I said. "Quite a bit. First of all, he would definitely have won—it was three against one."

"Irrelevant." The administrator jumped in quickly. "Player-killing is built into the gameplay. Also, the complaint was not lodged against you; it was lodged against an NPC with you as a witness. If there is nothing you wish to attest to, you can decline to discuss the matter further. In that case, the non-player character will be deactivated, and the situation will revert to how it was before his interference. If you can prove that the non-player character was at fault, the same will also be true."

I realized that holding my peace would leave me in the company of three angry orcs thirsting to kill me. Plus, I'd lose a good and very helpful knight. "I would like to give a statement." I decided to have some fun. "And I would like to do so immediately. The non-player character by the name of Gunther von Richter acted reasonably in all respects—both in terms of the gameplay and human decency."

What nonsense—human decency? He was just a program!

"And your proof?"

"I would draw your attention to the fact that the non-player character in question belongs to the Tearful Goddess Order. Further, you will note my personal status as a friend of the aforementioned order and the responsibility that places on the non-player character named Gunther von Richter with respect to me."

Number Nineteen was quiet for a minute, apparently reviewing the information I gave him.

"Complaint number 14,347 has been reviewed. The non-player character was found to be acting within the bounds of his program. Player Euiikh has been denied his request."

"He did that on purpose, the rat!" I tried to get in a complaint of my own. "He tried to confuse the admin. That's the kind of person he is."

Number Nineteen shook his head.

"All players have the right to lodge complaints, and we are required to promptly and impartially review them. Player Hagen, the help you have voluntarily and objectively provided in this matter deserves a reward from the administration. Would you like to receive one?"

I almost let out a sarcastic "of course not," but decided against it. Number Nineteen could have taken that to be my answer.

"Obviously!"

Number Nineteen snapped his fingers.

> **You received a blessing: Left Hand of the Creator**
> **+20% protection from fire**
> **+20% protection from cold**
> **+15% protection from mental effects**
> **+20% vitality**
> **+15% health restoration speed**
> **+15% mana restoration speed**
> **Active for one hour**

"Wow!" I was impressed. "And that's just the left hand! I wonder what the right hand is like."

"If you don't have any pertinent questions, I will leave." Number Nineteen drew the meeting to a close.

"Thanks for the buff." I decided to be polite. "And please unfreeze Gunther. I need his help with that witch."

"He'll wake up as soon as I leave. Have fun playing the game."

And with that, Number Nineteen disappeared—you know, how the image on a TV screen disappears, bam, and it's gone, just darkness and heat.

Gunther started.

"Did I fall asleep?"

"No, you just blinked. For a long time." I reassured the nervous knight. "Ready to go?"

Off we went.

I really liked the local forest. Everything was open, there wasn't any dead wood laying around, the terrain was flat, and we were left alone. We walked to the sound of birds chirping, the grass crunched under our feet, and we enjoyed the pleasant, fresh smell in the air.

"Sir Hagen, what else is in that book they wrote in the east?" I had apparently piqued Gunther's interest.

"Well, there's a lot," I answered.

I needed to be careful. If I quoted it to him, I'd have to explain what a shogun was, what a kakemono was, and why samurais can't lay down with their legs pointing toward their suzerain's residence.

"Tell me a piece of wisdom they have."

"If a samurai loses in battle and is about to die, he has to say his name proudly and die without doing anything that would humiliate him." I had to think for a while, but I came up with something simple.

"Exactly. We've talked about that, too. I think I'll definitely make a pilgrimage to the east. You aren't going that way, are you?"

Again with the east. I had the feeling I was literally being pushed in that direction the whole day. Could it have been more than just a feeling? Maybe it was true.

A small house appeared behind the trees. It was neat and tidy, the roof was red, and it had white walls with green shutters. The clearing was charming. The sun gleamed down on it, and it was covered in flowers.

"Is that the witch's den?" I stared at the house. "It can't be!"

"Witches are tricky." Gunther nodded his head. "Our eyes could be playing tricks on us, so don't believe anything, Sir Hagen."

I glanced at the house again and pulled up my map. We were standing in the very center of the red circle.

"Yes, this is the place," I said to the knight. "Let's go see what we can find."

We walked out into the clearing and were greeted by an adorable old lady with white curls, a ruddy, wrinkled face, and a white apron. She was sitting on a bench knitting something that looked like a large stocking, and the whole picture could have been pulled from a Christmas card. Our footsteps caught her attention, and she looked up at us.

"Hello, noble knights!" Her voice was as pleasant as could be. "What brings you here?"

Chapter Fifteen
The Hunter and the Hunters (Part Two)

"No, I'm not a knight. He is, though," I said, flicking my thumb over my shoulder. "I'm just a warrior."

"Then what brings one knight and one warrior here?" The old lady continued knitting as she asked her question. For a second, I thought the ends of her needles flashed red.

"We're looking for someone." There was little sense hiding the truth. "A scary witch."

"What do you mean, we're *looking* for her?" Gunther cut in, having unslung his shield with his right hand. "She's right in front of us! You can't see her?"

"Of course I see her," I said. "And she knows that we know. This is how the game works, Gunther."

I took a few steps forward until there were no more than ten meters between the witch and me.

"It's true," she said, her needles clicking ever faster. "But you can still leave—no harm, no foul. I'm in a good mood, and my belly's full, so you may be able to make it back to Fladridge in one piece."

"But maybe not?" I asked.

"Maybe not," she said with a shrug. "I'm in a good mood right now, but who knows how I'll feel in another ten minutes? I'm a woman, and our mood is always changing."

"You're no woman!" Gunther's outrage surged. "You aren't even human! I should destroy you on the spot!"

"So we're going to do this the hard way. Don't say I didn't tell you so," she said in an even, controlled tone as she rose from her chair.

Above her head appeared an inscription written in blood-red letters.

Witch Frida
Level 26

She stretched out her hands to either side, each holding a needle, the tips of which glowed bright red.

"Time for your exercises, grandma?" I crouched and prepared for battle. "Let's go—feet shoulder width apart!"

Frida, the witch, grinned ferociously, brought her hands together, and thrust them in Gunther's direction. She shouted a spell in some gibberish language. It could have been Ancient Chaldean, or it could have been Hindi—I was none the wiser. Or maybe it was some kind of local dialect? Who knows?

Gunther may have been young, but he obviously had some experience under his belt; he very nearly ducked out of the way of the fireball hurtling toward him. Very nearly, but not quite. The fireball—a word that perfectly describes what the evil woman conjured up—glanced off his left side, and the shock wave threw him all the way back to the edge of the clearing. He smacked into a birch tree and collapsed, feet twitching. When he made no effort to get up, I realized he had been temporarily knocked out of our little game.

"A-ha!" Frida was apparently satisfied with her handiwork and turned toward me. "Now you and I can have some fun!"

"Aren't you a bit old for that kind of thing, grandma? Besides, I'd prefer someone a bit younger and maybe a little bustier."

"Oh, I won't be enjoying you like that." She nodded toward Gunther, whose head now twitched in time with his feet. "That one's canned like a peach, and it's a pain to claw him out of all that armor. Plus, knights like that are too stringy. But look at you: fresh, soft, juicy. I'll have you for dinner with some roots and cabbage!"

The witch was obviously trying to keep me talking as she crept closer. Still, I maintained some distance between us. At the same time, she kept her needles spinning relentlessly in an effort to distract me.

The needles flashed, one with red lightning and the other white. I kept my attention firmly fixed on them and was ready. My knees were bent, and, realizing that the sizzle coming from them meant something bad was in the offing, I rolled forward. It didn't turn out exactly the way I wanted because my shield caught on my jaw, but I sprang up much closer to Frida and swung my mace at her. She dodged, grazing my arm with one of her needles.

You are taking cold damage.
You will lose 0.8 health per second for three minutes!

This is really bad, I thought. *Another couple of those, and I won't have to worry about the merciless blows of evil—she'll finish me off with her spells, even with my protection buff. If it weren't for Euiikh and his stubborn orcishness, I'd really be in a pickle.*

"Well, my dear not-a-knight, how do you like my needlework?" The old lady's evil smile was playful as she toyed with me.

"You'll knit me a scarf and hat later," I said in the same tone, keeping one eye on her hands.

The old hag obviously knew her way around a fight, and we spent the next minute warily circling each other. It dawned on me that sooner or later, she would outwit me. Plus, eight-tenths of a health point may not seem like much, but I was losing a full 48 health a minute.

I was just about to attack when I heard a rumble and a shout. "In the name of the Tearful Goddess!" From somewhere off to the side, Gunther crashed into the witch, apparently having recovered from his stupor. The collision sent the hag flying sideways. Her needles clattered to the ground and, with a crunch, shattered under the knight's iron-clad feet.

Gunther landed two blows that luckily left the witch stunned. They had some heft behind them, too; her health turned yellow. After a second, she realized something was wrong and quickly figured it out with a screech.

"My needles! You broke them!"

The witch sprang backward, avoiding yet another crushing blow from Gunther, and screeched out what was apparently a powerful spell. Lightning sprang from her hands and pierced the knight.

The witch snarled, lightning pulsed, and Gunther shook as if he were sitting in an electric chair. It struck me how much she looked like Emperor Palpatine—all she needed was a hood.

"My needles!" Frida shrieked crazily. "They've been in my family for centuries, handed down from mother to daughter for generations. My sister is going to kill me!"

Gunther shook with more violence, and his head swung lifelessly from side to side. I felt rage pulse through my veins.

"Kill the Sith!" I roared, throwing my shield to the side and gripping my mace with two hands. I ran at the witch and sank my weapon into her head with every bit of strength I could muster.

She stopped her electrical roasting of the knight and tried to wrap her claws around my throat, spitting out one spell after another.

You are taking cold damage.
You will lose 1.3 health per second for two minutes!

You are taking grave horror damage.
You will lose 0.5 health per second for three minutes!

You are taking fire damage.
You will lose 1 health per second for three minutes!

Ignoring the stream of messages, I evaded her stranglehold and thrashed her with my mace.

"Sword of Retribution! Strength of Fire!"

"A-a-ah!" The witch lit up as my ability kicked in. "Fire!"

My health turned red. I had no idea how much health the witch had left; I was too busy to check. I rained blow after blow down on her, though she answered with fire spouting from her fingertips, searing its way through me.

"That's it, that's i-i-it!" the witch screamed at me from inches away. I looked into her eyes and saw neither pupils nor irises—nothing but liquid fire and hatred, all as real as I'd ever seen in any human. Adrenaline pounded through my body, and my hands found her throat. She mirrored my new tactic, and I felt her fingers squeezing the life out of me.

"Do-o-o-ne!" The word choked out of her and a moment later, she dissolved into a pile of ash. I looked up. A step away stood Gunther von Richter, and in his hand was the sword he'd used to land the killing blow. His armor was dented like an old teakettle; his eyes were black and blue; his helmet was still laying under the birch tree; and he was as pale as a ghost—but he was victorious.

You unlocked level 23!
Points ready to be distributed: 5

Thank God. If it hadn't been for that, I'd have earned an honorable death along with my victory thanks to all the crap the old devil threw at me. But when you level-up, you get your full quotient of health and mana, so…

"Here, eat this." I tossed Gunther a crust of bread and a piece of dried meat.

"How can you eat after a battle like that?" The knight looked at me in bewilderment.

"Just eat it. Forget the battle, eating something will help you regain your strength. And while you're doing that, I'll go see what I can find over here."

I walked over to the pile of ash that was once Frida, —quite the powerful witch, as it turned out. And what did I find?

Witch glasses. Serve as proof that you killed the witch.

That works. In the old days, games would give you the head, but this was the era of tolerance and humanism. So glasses it would be, torn straight from the witch.

And that was it; nothing else. Where was the gold? Where was the book? Also, why didn't the mayor want me to bring him the glasses? It didn't really matter, glasses or a book, as long as I finished the quest.

"I'm going to check out the house," I called over to Gunther. "You look around here."

"I wouldn't go in there." The knight pursed his lips. "You'll trigger some kind of wizardry, and that will be it."

"I have to. There's something I need to find so I can prove that the witch is dead."

"Things aren't how they used to be." The young knight shook his head. "Nobody believes the word of a warrior without material proof anymore."

194

"We'll talk later." He didn't know what a respawn was, but I did. The witch was quest-specific and probably wouldn't respawn, but you never knew. Plus, she mentioned something about a sister; maybe they lived together.

Inside, the house was small, neat, and even rather cozy. There was a good-sized wood stove, and cooking utensils were everywhere. It looked like the old witch had told the truth about her cannibalism.

In the corner, hidden under some kind of cloth, was a chest. I walked over, uncovered it, and lifted the lid.

Frida's Chest

In the chest belonging to the evil witch Frida, you found:

The witch's magic book, which describes spells and voodoo rituals

700 gold

Greaves

Magic ring

8 bundles of Drianod grass

Goblin-shaped chess piece made with extraordinary skill, perhaps from some incredibly rare chess set (Who knows how or why the witch came to have it?)

I emptied the chest into my bag.

You completed a quest: Kill the Forest Witch.

You killed the witch living in the forest near Fladridge.

To get your reward, bring the witch's book of magic to the city mayor as confirmation that you killed her.

I left the house and called out to Gunther, "All right, let's get out of here!"

"Maybe we should burn the house down?"

"What? Are you some kind of pyromaniac? If we burn it down, an hour from now, some forest devil or terrible ghost will crawl out of it. Witch houses are better left well enough alone. Burning them never ends well."

"What could happen?" Gunther was intrigued.

"Anything. And, really, the less you know, the better you sleep."

"I'll sleep fine," he said, laughing loudly. "I always sleep well. It takes me a while to fall asleep, but I'm fine once I do."

We talked as we walked back to the road, where we found the knight's horse grazing as it waited for him.

"Sir Hagen, if you want, you can ride Duke. I'll run alongside." Gunther's offer was kind and gracious.

"Who? His name is Duke?" I looked at the horse.

"Yep." Gunther nodded. "The Duke of Orny gave him to me after I saved his daughter from a lich lurking in their castle dungeons. He marched me right into his stable and let me pick a stallion."

"You saved his daughter, and that's all you got?"

"What are you talking about?" The knight said, incensed. "Everybody knows that the Duchy of Orny has the best horses in all of Rattermark. They're worth their weight in gold. Do you have any idea how much horses weigh?"

Worth their weight in gold? Nice. I'd heard of swords being paid for that way, but not horses...

"So that's why I named him Duke—to show my appreciation. Well, up you go?"

"No, no, no. I don't like horses, and I don't know how to ride them. You go ahead, and I'll just walk."

"Duke isn't a horse; he's a stallion. But if you're going to walk, I will, too. We're brothers in arms, and we should share everything."

"By the way!" I slapped my forehead with my palm. "Thanks for reminding me; we need to split the loot."

"Split what?"

"I found some gold and some other things in the witch's house. Half of it is yours!"

I was well aware that NPCs don't need gold or anything else you could find in the game. But I would have felt like a rat if I hadn't offered my worthy—if digital and naïve—knight his half.

"No, no, Sir Hagen. I don't need any of the witch's belongings." The knight was indignant. "You should probably forget it, too. Nothing worthwhile comes of anything—good or otherwise—that you get from a witch."

"Whatever you say. If you change your mind, your half is waiting for you."

I realized I had forgotten to take a look at the greaves and ring. The greaves turned out to be pretty nice, and the ring as well.

Ivy Greaves
Protection: 340
+9 to agility
+8% to attack precision
+6% additional damage done by Toxic Shock (if it is learned)
Durability: 230/230
Minimum level to use: 27

Now I just needed to find that Toxic Shock ability...

Woven Grass Ring
+4 to wisdom
+3 to stamina
+0.7% mana restoration speed
Durability: 110/110
Class limitation: only mages
Minimum level to use: 26

They were pretty good items, though I didn't need them in the least. It was a shame; I would have been happy to wear the ring. The extra wisdom would have been nice if it weren't for the class limitation. I didn't have any of my own, after all.

The battle with the witch exposed how weak my mana was, as the two abilities I used spent nearly half of it. The ring would have helped.

"Ah well." I sadly sighed and spent all five of the points I had on wisdom. It was a shame, but I had to do it.

That out of the way, I looked the herbs over thoughtfully. They were obviously for a quest I hadn't gotten. I decided to walk around the city the next day and figure out who gave the quest.

As for the chess piece, it was obviously trash, but it sure looked nice. I decided to leave it in my bag for the time being.

By the time I had thought through everything and checked it all out, I realized we were almost to the city. Gunther's mind was also occupied, though he sometimes wriggled a bit in his boots; that birch tree had apparently done a number on him.

We walked into the city and went our separate ways.

"Where are you off to?" I asked Gunther.

"The order mission. I have to inform the master of what happened, give him a full report of the journey. I'll tell him about our battle, too."

"I'm going to stop by tomorrow. I'll tell him what a hero you were and how well you fought."

"You don't have to do that..." Gunther blushed and stuttered. Once again, I was stunned by the good work the developers had done; he could have been a living person. "What did I do—"

"The samurais said something else," I interrupted, and Gunther perked up. He was obviously fascinated by the samurais, and he could barely hide how excited he was to hear what I was about to say. "True bravery is living when it's time to live and dying when it's time to die. You proved your bravery, you live fairly, and you were ready to die for a cause you thought was right. There isn't anything wrong with me telling that to your direct supervisor."

"To who?"

"To the master."

The knight walked off in the direction of the mission, his badly mangled armor clanging with each step, and I set off to talk with the mayor.

"Well?" He waited on pins and needles, and his eyes kept flicking over to my bag. "Did you kill the witch? Did you?"

"Yes, yes, I did. Here." I gave him the glasses and book.

"Oh, you even got her glasses! That's very nice of you. Or do you have to use them to read the book?" The mayor put them in a desk drawer.

You completed a quest: Kill the Forest Witch.

Reward:

600 gold

700 experience

10% to your reputation in Fladridge

There was one more surprise.

You unlocked level 24!
Points ready to be distributed: 5

What a day!
"Well, thank you. The city is in your debt."

The mayor stood up, handed me a purse full of gold, shook my hand vigorously, and started pushing me out the door with his ample midsection.

"Hey, do you really need those glasses?" I had a sneaking suspicion dawning, and I wanted to check it out.

"You want a souvenir?" The mayor playfully jabbed a finger into my chest. "To remind you of your great feat?"

"Something like that. I'll hang it on the refrigerator like a magnet."

"Where?" The mayor's face looked exactly like Gunther's.

"On the door to the icebox," I said.

"Well, aren't you the art lover!" The mayor waved a sausage-like finger.

"Pretty much."

"Eh, here you go. Whatever."

He opened the drawer, pulled the glasses out, and tossed them to me.

"And now you'll have to excuse me. So much to do! The city awaits." The mayor's face turned serious.

"Agreed, lots to do. Send me a letter if anything comes up."

I walked out and thought for a bit.

"You know what? Tomorrow's another day, and I can think over everything then."

I headed over to the mailbox, sent the greaves to Oygolinn, and sent the ring to Rodriguez. Maybe they could use them. I knew I wouldn't get much if I sold them, so I was better off helping out a couple of friends.

Then I walked to the hotel, smiling at Lubelia as I went in.

"See? Never believe a word I say."

"What do you mean?" she asked.

"I promised I wouldn't be coming to spend the night, but here I am. Anyway, make sure no one bothers me before morning."

"No one at all?"

"No one."

I climbed the stairs to my room and tossed the chess piece into the chest. Then, after adding two points to my strength, one to my intellect, and another two to my wisdom, I logged out of the game.

Chapter Sixteen
The Hunter and the Hunters (Part Three)

I pushed my chair back from my desk, stretched happily, laced my fingers behind my head, and surveyed my handiwork. There was a folder open on the screen in front of me, and it held four files where, just four hours before, there had only been two. I had churned out two more articles. Well, I'm not positive "churned" is the right word—they had practically written themselves. One had been bouncing around inside my head since the road from Fladridge, and all I'd had to do was put it down on paper. (Okay, type it up in my word processor.) Its sequel popped out of me like a champagne cork. The first looked at game mechanics: items, quests, magic. The second described the world itself: geography, history, fables, and folk legends. Regardless, the job was 65 percent done, and I was only a bit more than a week in. That gave me pause to think. I had a whole month, and at my current rate, I would be done in another week. What was I supposed to do with the last two weeks? There had to be some way I could turn that to my financial advantage. A thought popped into my head...

Anyway, I sent the files to Mammoth after a quick internal discussion regarding whether I should send them both right away or stagger them a bit. In the end, I decided to make his day, picturing his gray mane quivering in happiness as I did. Maybe he'd even do a little dance.

Now, the articles were making waves; I'd checked the Capital Herald's website, and the forums were abuzz. I was surprised to see that everyone, from kids to retirees, was reading the first two articles, especially the middle generation.

All the older progressives were putting up a united front against me, as the author, and my findings. I'd made my position fairly clear: there was nothing wrong with games themselves, but they shouldn't be used to escape from real-world problems. They're just a quick breath of fresh air.

The older generation and some of the middle generation accused me and the gaming industry as a whole of brainwashing young

201

people, trying to keep them away from civil life, misleading them, and just about everything else under the sun. I think I may have even been blamed for the burning of Rome, not to mention working with Grishka Otrepyev[11], the runaway monk, to seize Moscow and assassinate Archduke Ferdinand. It wasn't anything I hadn't seen before, and I was just happy to see that my work was getting traction.

I was surprised to see that the younger generation read newspapers, to begin with, though one of them may have happened upon an article and shared it on a forum; I'd have to check into that. However, they and the rest of the middle generation were standing up for me and the gaming industry. They couldn't figure out what was wrong with just doing what they wanted to do. The older generation screwed the country up and then turned on them. *Civil life? Give them raids and dungeons!*

That all had to have Mammoth jumping for joy. There was traffic, there was noise, and ratings were climbing. The perfect storm.

I was really excited, too, of course. A quick search showed me that my articles had been shamelessly copied onto twenty or so other sites—needless to say, all with blatant disregard for copyright law. But the popularity was what had me so elated. It was at that moment, however, that my stomach interrupted my reverie.

"I'm hungry!" it told me in no uncertain terms. I stroked it reassuringly.

"Let's get a couple sausages into you. Maybe even three. With some pasta!"

My stomach growled back its satisfied response. A second later, that response turned sour, however, when it discovered that I'd misled it. The refrigerator was a cold wasteland populated by nothing more than a jar of mustard and a shapeless piece of something that looked like it might have been cheese in a past life. A sickly sprig of dill rounded things out.

I looked at the clock to see that it was 9 p.m. Still, there was nothing for it—I had to make a trip to the store. Fayroll had wreaked havoc in my apartment. The refrigerator was empty, there was chaos everywhere, and, I realized, it was getting awfully stuffy.

With the windows open, I put on a coat and headed for the nearest market, putting the next day's problems out of my head for the time being. They weren't helping my digestion.

***

I woke to the sound of my phone ringing. No surprise, it was Mammoth. The fact that it was 6 a.m. didn't surprise me either.

"Nikiforov, what do you think about writing eight articles after all?" He jumped right in without so much as a "good morning" or "I hope I didn't wake you."

"No, Semyon Ilyich, not happening."

"Why not? Everyone loves them—go online and see for yourself. The paper's owners are patting me on the back for a job well done. And really—"

"Really, Semyon Ilyich, the perfect is always the enemy of the good. We don't want to overdo things. Let's just wait six months and come back for another cycle following up on this one."

"You may be right," Mammoth grunted and paused. "Now that I think about it, that's a great idea. It looks like you still have some brain cells left! Oh, and head over to accounting once you're done with this cycle. The owners said to give you a bonus when you're done. Our numbers are up. Not just thanks to you, of course; don't flatter yourself. We're all doing a great job under my excellent leadership. You just happened to be in the right place at the right time."

"Did you see that I sent you two more articles?"

"Yep, one's being published tomorrow, the other two days later. So, in five days, I'll need another one."

"Sounds good."

"See you." Mammoth hung up.

What a guy! He calls, wakes you up, insults you, and gets you all worked up over work. I paused to be happy I had such a great boss and jumped in the shower.

When I logged in two hours later, Fayroll met me as it always did—with great weather and birds singing outside the window.

I walked down the stairs and winked at Lubelia. "Good morning, beautiful!"

"It isn't good at all!" The lovely girl answered me with a haggard and gloomy look on her face. "Someone killed Yanka, our shepherd, during the night. Who would do such a thing? He wouldn't hurt a fly."

"How was he killed? With a knife? Or did they crack his skull open?"

"If only! It's like he was fried. His clothes were all scorched, and he was covered in burns. Harry Budochnik says he saw lightning flashing during the night."

"Well, maybe he was just struck by lightning?"

"What lightning, sir? We haven't had a cloud in the sky for two weeks now. No, there's some kind of black magic afoot. You got rid of one witch, and now there's another one."

"Looks like it." I was thoughtful.

The suspicions I'd had the day before took on new meaning.

I left the hotel and walked quickly in the direction of the Tearful Goddess Order mission.

"I need to speak with Master Hugo immediately!" I stepped through the door and barked at Brother Tsimiskhy, who was sitting behind the same desk drinking what looked like milk or kefir.

Service in paramilitary organizations is enough to change even the most inveterate clerical workers. Brother Tsimiskhy sprang from his stool, reminiscent of Jackie Chan springing to his feet from a prone position. A second later, he was back and had flung the door open wide. "Master Hugo is ready to see you."

"Good day to you, Sir Hagen." The master greeted me from his chair by the fireplace, nodding his head in my direction.

"It's good to see you, master. I suspect I know who the witcher is." I had barely crossed the threshold when I gave him the news of the day.

The master stood up and walked over. "You suspect, or you know?"

"Oh, that's just a phrase from a bad novel. I have a few facts and a few small details that all point to one person. I'll give them to you, and we can decide what we think. Okay?"

"Go ahead." Von Shlippenshtain crossed his arms over his chest.

"Yesterday the local mayor gave me a quest that had me kill a witch in a nearby forest. You know, kidnapping people, dark rituals, all that."

"I'm aware. Gunther von Richter told me about how you killed the creature in a desperate battle."

"Me? No, it was Gunther who killed her. We fought together, but he landed the killing blow. He really did a fantastic job. I doubt I would have been able to do it alone."

"Still, he probably wouldn't have been able to do it alone either. You both did good work. Continue."

"You should give Gunther some kind of appreciation or acknowledgment. He'd like that."

"We will, we will. Please, continue."

"Anyway, the mayor said that I had to bring him the witch's book of magic to prove that I'd killed her. There's nothing out of the ordinary there—you did the killing, now prove it. But here's the thing: all I got from the witch were her glasses. And I think that's what I was supposed to use to prove that she was dead."

"What do you mean?"

Whew boy. How was I supposed to explain to an NPC what was written in the quest?

"There was an engraving. 'Witch Glasses.'"

"Okay, and?"

"There was nothing like that for the book. It looked like it had been in the witch's family for ages, handed down from generation to generation. And that's what the mayor wanted. He didn't care about the glasses, but he'd need them to justify the expenditure to the city council. They'd want proof, too, after all."

"Yes, that is strange. Is there anything else?"

"There is. The book contained all the spells Frida knew. The strongest and most effective was the lightning she cast from her hands. And did you hear that the shepherd was killed last night? Did you hear how he was killed? The mayor even mentioned how much he didn't like the shepherd; I heard him myself. That's all circumstantial, but—"

You completed a quest: Witcher in the Shadows.

Task: Find out something about the witcher living in Fladridge or its outskirts and get the information to Hugo von Shlippenshtain.

Reward:

600 experience

"That is circumstantial, you're right." Hugo walked around the room and rubbed his temples. It struck me that if he didn't have a mustache and you stuck a pipe in his mouth, he'd be the spitting image of Sherlock Holmes. "Still, it paints a picture."

"I don't know if you've noticed," he continued, "but a lot of people in the city have been saying that the mayor has changed over the past six months. He used to spend time chatting with the people in the city, and he took charge of the feasts for all special events and especially weddings. They even used to joke that your marriage was only valid if the mayor was at your wedding. He always made sure the roads were in good repair. But in the last few months he's been unwilling to leave his office, he doesn't go to feasts, and he always says he's too busy for anything. I think it's fair to say he's the witcher."

The master stopped. "We need to hurry."

"Why?" I asked.

"He got what he needed, and he was only living here until he could find that book. Witchers are different from witches. While witches live with the knowledge handed down to them, witchers are always trying to find new spells. He has the book so he could take off at any moment."

Hugo opened the door and shouted into the other room. "Von Richter! Where are you, you lazy, good-for-nothing imbecile?"

Thirty seconds later, a sleepy Gunther tumbled down the stairs leading to the second story. He was still just in his long johns, but his sword was in his hand.

"Well, look at that. And you, Laird Hagen, were telling me this walking mistake we somehow let into the order is a great warrior?" Apparently, I was already a "laird." The old master had promoted me.

"At least he has his sword!"

Gunther stood there, blushed, blinked, and looked like he wanted to sink through the floor.

"Yes, though he won't need it to kill his enemies—they'll die of laughter as soon as they see this sorry excuse for a knight."

"Good morning, Master Hugo. Good morning, Laird Hagen." Gunther managed to choke out some mumbled words.

"A good morning for some, the last morning for others if that's how you're going to be behaving in the future, von Richter. We're going to spend all night training—get dressed, get undressed. I even have my supply of switches." Master Hugo said that last part in what could only be described as a fatherly tone.

Wow. The game may have been virtual, but the army is still the army. I almost mentioned the burning match and my sergeant, but I decided against it. The poor guy was already in an unenviable position.

"You have two minutes to get yourself ready. I'm going to hunt the witcher, and you, of course, are coming with me. Laird Hagen, I have a question for you."

"Yes, Master?"

"Would you give this lout and me the honor of your company? You're a good fighter and an honorable comrade. That creature is bound to be pretty strong, and I don't have much hope for this cephalopod."

You have a new quest offer: Kill the Witcher.

This quest is a variable reward for Witcher in the Shadows, a quest you completed earlier.

Task: Kill the witcher.

Reward:

1500 experience

Other rewards: variable

Important note: You should probably attack the witcher with 2-4 other players. He is a high-level monster that far exceeds most opponents you will find in Fladridge.

Accept?

Wow. Where was I going to find those 2-4 other players? Although, wait a second, I could ask some clanmates, of course.

"Master Hugo, of course, I will come. And I have an offer for you."

"Let's hear it."

"From what I can tell, we're up against a strong opponent, and all we have from your order are you and Gunther."

"And Brother Tsimiskhy."

"Well, yes, though he doesn't look like he'll do that well in battle. At least, that was my first impression."

"That is correct. He's a good writer, but put a sword in his hands..."

"I can talk to some of my friends. I think they'd be happy to help your order."

"Sure, but that will take too long. By the time they all get here, the witcher will be gone. And I'll be back to square one trying to find him."

"My friends are in the same clan as I am. They have some pretty powerful mages who can send them here very quickly. It isn't cheap, but—"

"The order will reimburse them." Von Shlippenshtain broke in. "This is a matter of honor. How fast can your friends get here?"

"Give me five or ten minutes, and I'll tell you."

I pulled up my list of friends. Logged into the game at the moment were Rodriguez, Flosi, Reineke Lis, and Krolina. Perfect. The first two, with my apologies to them, would have been nothing more than cannon fodder. But the last two...

I wrote Reineke: *Hi! Happen to be interested in killing a witcher?*

His answer was instantaneous. *A witcher? I've seen my share of witches, but a witcher... How strong is it?*

Judging by the description, much higher than Level 27-30.

Much higher? Probably 65-75. Piece of cake. Who else is coming?

Me, the master of the Tearful Goddess Order, and one of their knights. They're Level 55 and Level 30 or something like that.

Kro's logged in, invite her, too. She likes this kind of thing.

One more tank wouldn't hurt either.
Oh, come on. There's the two of us as well as you three.
I'm serious. Better safe than sorry.
Fine. Where?
Fladridge, the order's mission. By the way, they're paying for the travel scrolls.
Nice. We'll be there in ten.

I turned back to von Shlippenshtain. "Master, three of my friends will be here in ten minutes."

"Great!" The knight clapped his hands loudly. "I'll go put on my armor. Von Richter!"

"Here I am, Master!" Gunther flew into the room, as he'd apparently been standing behind the door afraid to walk in.

"Help me put my armor on."

The knights left, leaving me to my thoughts. Why had no one killed the witcher yet? The quest obviously wasn't hidden, or it would have said that in the description. A little more thinking brought me to the conclusion that quests were all linked. Players who went directly to the mayor were given a quest that had them bring the witch's glasses back as proof of her death. The book wouldn't have even come up since nobody was looking for the witcher, and the mayor was just the mayor. And nobody would be looking for the witcher since the master only gave the quest to friends of the order. Only players who took the ability were named friends of the order, and it had been forever since someone had preferred the ability to money or items. So the quest had never been activated. It was all a big, complex puzzle.

Three minutes later, the front door banged open, and I heard Krolina's voice.

"Hi, baldy. Where's Hagen?"

"Laird Hagen is in Master Hugo von Shlippenshtain's office. Would you like me to let him know you're here?" Brother Tsimiskhy's voice was obviously annoyed. I could tell why, what with all the people barging in and traipsing around. For all he knew, he might even have to feed them later.

"You sit there, I'll go find him myself."

The door creaked, and in flew Krolina.

"Hey! You're already a laird? Nice!"

She turned back toward the door and shouted through it.

"Hey, baldy, there are two more of us coming, so send them right in when they get here."

"Yes, fair lady." Tsimiskhy's voice grated obediently.

Krolina's shoes tapped their way around the room.

"It's so cool in here. A fireplace! Wow, what an enormous bear. Oh, nice blade!" She pulled the katzbalger[12] off the rack, weighed it in her hands, and tried a couple parries. "This is a fun toy. I want one!"

Master Hugo walked down the stairs, armor clanging. He saw Kro and bowed his head.

"Good day, fair lady. Let me introduce myself, Hugo von Shlippenshtain. Forgive me for not knowing your name, and for being unable to greet you on one knee as I should. It's the armor, as you can see."

Kro curtsied and responded.

"Ah, who cares? I'm Krolina, a friend of this little guy. Nice to meet you! We have another two friends coming. Speaking of which..." Kro raised her index finger.

"Hi, there!" Reineke Lis' voice rang out. "I'm looking for a friend of mine named Hagen."

"Lis, in here!" Kro called to him. "We're all here!"

Reineke walked into the room, and behind him marched another warrior named Romuil.

"Hi, everyone." Reineke nodded to the group. Romuil waved.

"Master." Reineke gave Shlippenshtain a personal bow.

The latter responded in kind.

"So what's going on?" Lis jumped right in.

"There's a witcher who's pretending to be the mayor." I started my report. "We have to kill him. He's quite a bad guy!"

"Are you sure he's a witcher?" asked Romuil. "There'll be hell to pay if we kill an NPC!"

"I have a quest to look for the witcher," I said, "so I'd say there's a 90 percent chance it's him."

"If you have a quest, it's definitely him." Krolina nodded her head grandly.

"By the way, Master Hugo, my friends haven't gotten their quests yet."

"Of course," said the knight. "Ladies and gentlemen, would you help us kill the villain?"

Everyone responded in the affirmative.

"Then let's go kill him." Hugo finished the report.

"Hold on a second," said Lis. "If he's the mayor, he's where? In city hall? There are tons of NPCs there, and we might kill someone by accident. Plus, there's no room to maneuver. No, we need a plan."

"Exactly!" Gunther chimed in from the corner where he was sitting meekly. "People could get hurt!"

He earned himself two simultaneous responses.

"Von Richter, who gave you permission to speak?" That was the master.

"Oh, he's adorable!" That was Krolina, who just then saw the young knight.

"Stop!" And that was Reineke. "Here's what I propose. We all go outside the city walls. By the gate, there's a small field in front of the forest, and we can wait there. Once we're in position, someone, even that doorman, the one sitting at that table writing—"

"Brother Tsimiskhy," said von Shlippenshtain.

"Yes, then Brother Tsimiskhy can go tell the mayor you're leaving the city and ask him to see you off. You're an important guy, so he'll have to say yes. And there—"

"Wait a second," I interrupted. "How are we actually going to attack him? He's still the mayor, after all. He might see us all, realize that we're about to knock him silly, kiss Master Hugo goodbye, wave a handkerchief and scurry back to city hall. Then he can get away once it gets dark."

"That's true." Reineke was taken aback.

"We won't have a problem." The master chimed in. "Our order has a powder prepared by the Old Gods. Just a handful of it is enough to reveal the true identity of evil spirits and the undead."

"Perfect." Reineke perked up. "Then let's make our way to the gate in pairs, and you tell Tsimiskhy to go see the mayor."

Krolina had a question. "Why don't we all just go together? The more, the merrier!"

"That's our strategy, Kro. Pairing off."

Our friendly group found itself outside the Fladridge gate discussing the upcoming battle, though I had the feeling nobody was listening to anyone.

"We'll go straight for him, with Kro doing her thing behind us," said Reineke, and Romuil nodded his head in agreement.

"I'll be doing the fighting!" Von Shlippenshtain was insistent, and he tapped his weapon, an enormous flame-bladed sword, with his finger.

"Is that your horse? Will you take me for a ride?" Kro asked Gunther, who turned crimson from embarrassment. He nodded, dropped his glance, and, I imagine, regretted bringing Duke with him.

I stayed silent and kept my eyes fixed on the gate.

The entire picture was enough to attract a number of people in the vicinity, from beginner players to the high-level players, of whom there were still plenty in Fladridge. It wasn't every day that you saw a group like ours: three serious players, one noob, two NPC knights, and a horse. *Ah, my apologies—a stallion.* And everyone was explaining something to everyone else, with the stallion occasionally snorting in the background.

One dwarf from the Hew Orcs, My Axe clan had an idea. "Looks like a flash mob!"

"In the game?" An elf from the Forest Children clan was less than convinced.

"Maybe the quest is to see who can out-argue everyone else?" A tiny elf girl from the Lake Fairies clan squeaked out her alternative.

More and more people showed up, and everyone had their own idea.

Suddenly I saw the chubby mayor striding through the gate.

"Oh, wow, look how many people are here to see off our hero, valiant knight, and Master of the Tearful Goddess Order Hugo von Shlippenshtain! The entire city is here, and even some of its guests. Well, my friend, have a safe journey."

"Right, that's why we're here." A giggling voice coming from the hushed crowd could be heard.

But then everyone was silent as they realized they'd soon be getting the answers to their questions.

The mayor walked over to Hugo.

"Well, how about a hug goodbye?" He stretched out his arms. Hugo wasted no time and threw a handful of powder into his face. Something hissed, wisps of dirty smoke curled up, and the smell of burnt hair filled the air. The mayor disappeared and was replaced by a tall old man in a dirty robe. His greasy hair framed a bony, unshaven face.

"Ah-h, Mikali powder. You figured it out, you snake!" The witcher gnashed his teeth. It was definitely him.

I looked at his level and staggered backward in horror—107!

Reineke glanced in the same direction and exchanged looks with Kro and Romuil. I was no longer a part of his plans, that much was sure. Honestly, I no longer had any illusions about being part of the fight either.

"Yes, I did." Hugo's answer was even. "You'd probably have jumped me somewhere along the road if I'd really been leaving."

"Of course! I can't tell you how happy I was to hear the news. I'd have waited until dark, caught up to you, and finished you off. What's with your band of rabble?"

"My friends. They're here to make sure everything is fair."

"Fair with a witcher? Don't make me laugh!"

"A-ah, it's a witcher! That's definitely a quest." A voice rang out from the crowd. "I've heard of a rare one here. And yep, the knights from the order are involved."

"A hidden quest?"

"No, damn it. Just a rare one. There are all kinds of conditions apparently, but you get a really good reward. A guy I know got something rare for it."

So my suspicions were on the money.

"You're kidding!"

"Seriously!"

"But check out that witcher—no walk in the park, that's for sure."

"Yeah, Level 107. Probably has some tricks up his sleeve, too."

"The Thunderbirds were ready for him, though—three high levels."

"Twenty-to-one the Thunderbirds win!"

"Oh, aren't you clever! Obviously, they'll be able to take care of him. Three-to-one says the cute one finishes him off!"

"Done. Five-to-one says that one…Reineke does it."

"Agreed."

The crowd began to make some noise as everyone haggled and bet. The witcher and the knight looked at the orgy of gambling with surprise. Kro, meanwhile, wasted no time jumping backward while the two warriors circled around to the flanks. Gunther realized there was no escaping the fight and tied Duke to a low-hanging oak branch.

The witcher finally found his voice. "Where'd you find these jokers?"

Hugo quickly retorted. "They're the people who live here. And our guests. Well, shall we begin?"

The knight grabbed the hilt of his sword with two hands and hoisted it above his head.

"Why not?" The witcher grunted, thrust his hands forward, and shouted a spell.

Frida's lightning was one thing, but this was completely different. Pulses of energy leaped from his palms toward the knight. The latter barely had time to bring his sword in front of him when the pulses shattered it, flinging shard of energy into Hugo's chest and throwing him onto his back.

Everything else happened in quick succession.

"Unbelievable!" The crowd gasped and murmured in response.

"I told you he had some tricks up his sleeve!"

"Damn, just like Saruman!"

"Seriously!"

A gray-haired, long-bearded mage named Peronius was more thoughtful. "I wonder what that spell was?"

"I'm going in, Kro. Hold your fire!" Reineke shouted over his shoulder before rolling toward the witcher, landing a blow, and looping around him.

"Master!" A distraught Gunther jumped over to the fallen Hugo and began unlacing his helmet.

The witcher flung lightning bolts at Reineke, who, incredibly, was able to dodge them all. An arrow thudded into the witcher and was soon followed by another as Kro joined the battle. The witcher jumped back and sprang toward Reineke.

"I got him!" Romuil shouted and slammed his sword into the witcher as he ran by, only to see him turn, catch another arrow, and try to cast another spell. Before he had time, however, he was startled by a blow to the back from Reineke and an arrow to the shoulder.

I let my frustration get the better of me as I watched everything going on without me, and jumped around behind the witcher to smack him in the hip. He dismissed me with a hand to the torso that sent me flying back five meters. My health bar turned red.

Someone from the crowd shouted to me. "You got off easy, my friend!"

That was for sure. Why did I go poking my nose in? I didn't even want to!

Reineke and Romuil continued battering the witcher with their swords, and Kro landed another arrow. It looked like he was about to go down when suddenly he sprang up, barked a spell, threw his arms in the direction of the tanks, and flung them back in opposite directions. Without pausing to survey his handiwork, he immediately extended his right hand with an outstretched index finger pointing toward Kro and released a fireball that left her choking and smoking on the ground.

A warrior from the Rublins clan was jubilant. "He did it!"

"Not so fast." An indefatigable dwarf from the Axes clan disagreed. "He's already in the red, so if they can knock him down, they'll finish him off."

The witcher laughed, threw out his arms, and, I think, was very surprised to see the tip of a sword protruding from his chest.

Gunther von Richter, the only one of our group still on his feet, stood behind the witcher and clung to the hilt of his sword. The witcher stepped forward to dislodge the sword from his back, turned on his heel, and shoved Gunther square in the middle of his torso.

I didn't think the blow had much force behind it, but I wasn't too far away to see how the knight's armor melted where the witcher's hands made contact with it. Gunther staggered and collapsed.

Still, the young knight had done his job. The ten seconds he'd bought let everyone else regroup, and the witcher turned back to the battlefield only to have an arrow bury itself in his head, and two swords slice their way into his ribs. His health was nearly gone. Reineke raised his sword to finish him off.

"Wait!" It was Hugo von Shlippenshtain. "He's mine!"

Reineke lowered his sword.

The master walked over to the dying witcher and picked up Gunther's sword.

"And you said I wouldn't kill you." The old knight gazed at his enemy.

"If you didn't have your pack of dogs, you'd never have killed me. You'd be the one dying instead!"

"It isn't a pack, and they aren't dogs," answered the master. "They're my friends."

And he buried the sword in the witcher's chest.

Chapter Seventeen
By the Fireplace

You unlocked Level 25!
Points ready to be distributed: 5

The game couldn't have picked a worse time.

You unlocked Level 26!
Points ready to be distributed: 5

Oh, come on!

I frantically paged through the level notifications. There were quite a few—six…or even seven. I figured I could come back and read them later.

You completed a quest: Kill the Witcher.

You killed the witcher, so go talk to Hugo von Shlippenshtain to get your reward.

Reward:

1500 experience

Other rewards: variable

That sounded great, but I didn't have time for it either right then.

I tried to get up. The hairy bugger had gotten me good. My legs shook, and I was starting to feel a kind of pleasant pliability deep inside. I tottered over to Gunther, who was lying motionless and lifeless face-down on the ground.

"Hey, buddy, what's going on?" I turned him over. Through the hole in his breastplate, I could see a jagged wound that looked to almost reach his heart. Or maybe his lung? I wasn't a pathologist.

Gunther groaned almost inaudibly and mumbled something.

"What's that?" I leaned directly over him.

"Is he dead?"

"Who? That devil? Yes, of course. Master Hugo carved a big old hole in his sternum."

"That's good. Now, I can die, too. Like a samurai."

"What are you talking about?"

I looked at the crowd standing by the Fladridge gate and listened to the chatter going on.

"That's so cool! There wasn't even anything like that on the Klaternah raid."

"Seriously. Wait, who bet on the guy with the mustache?"

"Not me."

"I bet on the hot one."

"Nobody bets on NPCs!"

"Ruslan from the Collectors actually bet on him. Everyone was picking favorites, and he said the NPC would do it. He was right."

"But what about the loot?"

"The players get it."

"No, that can't be. Nobody bet on the NPC."

"That's crazy—nobody won."

"Ha, sometimes everyone walks away with nothing."

A dwarf, who was obviously in the know, had figured the whole thing out. "We should have bet on how long it would take them to kill that guy."

The elf girl snapped back at him. "Hindsight is 20-20."

"All right, show's over. Let's head back to the city."

The group stirred and started moving toward the gate.

I shouted at their retreating figures. "Hey, hold up! Someone heal Gunther!"

The players stopped and looked at me.

"Are you crazy?" The dwarf stared at me and circled a short, fat finger around his temple. "He's an NPC!"

"He's a good guy, and he saved my life yesterday. Well, and he helped us today, too."

"Really, boys. One of you is probably a healer." Kro piped up in support as she rummaged through the witcher's corpse. "Gunther's cute, and he promised to give me a ride on his horse."

"Oh, come on. He'll die and come right back to life. Maybe not here, of course, but still…" The dwarf stood his ground.

"This one won't. His kind just leaves amulets behind," I answered gloomily. "Fine, if no one wants to heal him out of the goodness of their heart, I'll be happy to pay."

"Relax," the gray-bearded Petronius said calmly. "I'll do it."

He walked over to Gunther, reached out his hand, and whispered a spell.

A blue ray of light flashed into Gunther's chest, and the knight quivered slightly.

"Done. Healthy as an ox," the mage said.

I turned to him happily. "How much do I owe you?"

"Kids these days are all about the money. That isn't all there is, not even in this world." The mage shook his head reproachfully. "Some things don't come with a price tag."

Gunther pulled himself up on his elbows, lowered his head, and studied the gaping hole in his armor.

"I've heard of mages healing wounds so well you can't even see where they were, but I never thought I'd see it happen. And certainly not to me. Thank you!" He hopped up and bowed to Petronius.

"No problem." An obviously touched Petronius smiled. "That's what we mages are here for."

"Can you fix the hole in my breastplate?" the knight asked shyly. "It's just that my dad gave it to me, and if he finds out that I didn't take good care of it…"

"Don't get cocky, knight!" Petronius' tone was sharp, but I could tell from his face that he was enjoying Gunther's naivety.

"I would like to thank you, wise one, on behalf of myself and our order, for saving this blockhead's life." Hugo von Shlippenshtain walked over. "Know that you will always be a welcome guest at the Tearful Goddess Order."

"I'm flattered and grateful." The mage bowed his head. "But with that, I must take my leave."

Petronius nodded to us all, as the rest of our witcher-hunting band had come up to join Hugo, Gunther, and me, and turned toward Fladridge. The rest of the crowd was already moving in that direction, and the dwarf was still going on about how if you heal NPCs, then you'll stop killing goblins, too. Soon we'd all be nothing more than farmers growing turnips and tobacco. Dwarves will be dwarves.

"I'd like to invite you all to the order mission," Master Hugo said. "We'll celebrate our victory and tie up some loose ends."

"One second, let me untie Duke." Gunther ran over to the oak, where his stallion was already tired of waiting.

"Hey! You promised to take me for a ride!" Kro ran after him incensed. "It would have been fine if you died. But you didn't, so a man's got to keep his word! Well, okay, not a man. Yes, I get it, you're not a man; you're a knight."

"This is ridiculous." Reineke shook his head. "Master, do you have any drinks at the mission?"

***

"Tsimiskhy!" Von Shlippenshtain bellowed out to the little brother as soon as he walked through the door. "Bring our best wine to my office for my friends and me."

The scribe, who had apparently observed the entire battle, was somehow sitting at his desk. He stoically sighed, though he went off to get the wine without argument. The wine looked to be somewhere in the basement.

"After you, my friends."

Less than an hour after leaving for the battle, we once again found ourselves in the cozy room. A fire was again crackling in the fireplace. We had chalices of wine in our hands, though it still felt like the battle never actually happened.

Also, Kro and Gunther weren't there. Kro was off riding the horse and driving Gunther crazy with her questions. "Do you have a girlfriend? Have you ever?" She had plenty of stories for him, too. "So he came at me, and I smacked him in the mug with my sword—bam! Oh, sorry, you're blushing. You're so adorable!"

"That was quite the witcher. Level 107 is no joke." Romuil jumped in suddenly. "When he knocked us off to the sides and smacked Kro with a fireball, I thought we were goners. If it hadn't been for your guy…"

"Yes, von Richter performed admirably. In another year or so, I'll recommend him for the order's Chapter. That's why I'm so hard on him—things will be tougher there. The supreme master is a tyrant, and the Secret Keeper is no slouch either. He'll be smashed right up there in the armpit of power. I hope he'll be ready."

"That's for sure." Reineke exhaled. "I'm just afraid even you will be a piece of cake after he finishes dealing with Kro."

"She's a nice girl and a good warrior," the master said. "I saw how she got up after she got hit by that fireball. She was smiling."

"I don't think that was just bravery. She isn't the brightest tool in the box." Reineke chuckled. "Though, to be fair, we all underestimated that guy. Good thing Hagen convinced me to bring another tank, otherwise who knows what would have happened. He'd probably have killed us all and gotten away."

"No, he wouldn't have gotten away," I said. "Everyone there would have jumped in and killed him just to see what would happen."

"Agreed." Reineke nodded. "Players have a policy of their own, regardless of what they write in the papers. It's just that their policy differs from the government's policy. Well, put it this way: it's in a different dimension."

Romuil laughed. "You're high as a kite! I have two questions for you. First, where do you get weed that strong? Second, how do you find the time to smoke it?"

Reineke and I laughed with him. Von Shlippenshtain diplomatically smiled, obviously not understanding the joke.

"Boys, that horsey is incredible!" Kro whirled into the room like a little hurricane. Behind her was Gunther, and I could see that it was all over with him.

Kro turned to Master Hugo. "And your Gunther is a peach! By the way, can he name me the lady of his heart? You know, do feats of valor in my honor, praise me in different countries, tell everyone that I'm the most beautiful in all the land, that type of thing? Like a normal knight?"

"That is not forbidden." Von Shlippenshtain's answer was somewhat evasive. "So long as he himself wants it."

"What say does he have in the matter? Kro got an idea in her head, and she's not going to let it go. Gunther, just be done with it and do what she says," Reineke said.

Gunther, who was less embarrassed than scared of the actually frightening expression on Kro's face, hurriedly addressed the group. "Yes, I am proud to announce that, from this moment on, Lady

Krolina is the lady of my heart. I will cherish her devotion and, if need be, die for her honor and for her smile."

"That's so sweet!" The lady of his heart was touched and clasped her hands to her chest. "Dear von Richter, I give you my kiss and, to remember me by..." Kro dug in her pockets, coming up with a bunch of little knick-knacks: feathers, an earring, part of a chicken bone, a small diamond, and some sticky candies. "To remember me by...Oh! My hairpin!"

She thrust a hand into her long mane and dug out a shiny hairpin bedecked with a jewel.

"Tie it to some string and wear it on your chest. That way you'll remember me when you feel it or see it." Kro let out an emotional sob.

"Of course, fair lady." Richter got down on one knee and accepted the hairpin from her.

When he stood up, Kro kissed him on the cheek and wiped a dutiful tear from her eye—for some reason, from her right one.

"And with that, let's move on to business!" Reineke clapped his hands and pointed toward us. "Krolina, please tell everyone here what you got from the witcher's body. I saw you stripping him!"

"I didn't strip him—I gathered the fruit of my victory." She sniffed with dignity.

Romuil jumped in to correct her. "Our victory."

"Our victory." Kro wasn't about to argue, and instead began counting on her fingers. "Okay, let's see. There was a magic book, 5,000 gold, two rings, and that's it."

Von Shlippenshtain jumped. "Speaking of gold, I just remembered my promise to reimburse your mages for sending you to Fladridge."

"Please, don't mention it," Lis said firmly. "We're now friends in arms, so... Plus, the gold we got from the witcher will more than compensate us, and there'll still be 500 left over. We can't forget to split that, by the way."

"Well, now that the gold's out of the way, let's discuss the book," continued Kro briskly.

"I'd like to ask you to give the book to me. Neither I nor von Richter nor our order asks or will ask for any other part of the loot." Von Shlippenshtain's voice was quiet, if very distinct.

"You need it that much?" Kro looked at him with a seriousness in her eyes that I did not expect.

"It was created by evil, it serves evil, and it was left by evil. And never again can it fall into the hands of evil." The old knight's tone was still just as soft.

Romuil chimed in, though he wasn't looking at or addressing anyone in particular. "A book like that probably has lots of spells from the dark side, with eighty or ninety percent of them for battle."

"Take it." Krolina held a fat tome out to the old knight. "If I have to, I'll answer to the clan council myself."

The book was thick and old, with red leather binding and bronze clasps. Master Hugo weighed it in his hands.

"That's strange," I said. "I thought I gave him a different book yesterday."

"You did give him a different book." Von Shlippenshtain looked at me. "I told you, witchers collect knowledge. They find magic books and other documents with spells, and then they perform a reunification ritual. The knowledge from all the different sources is gathered in their magic books."

"That makes sense." I nodded.

"This," Hugo said as he shook the tome in his hands, "is quintessential evil. There's only one thing to do with it."

He shook it one more time before sending it hurtling into the fireplace. The fire flared, hissed, turned green, and...the book was gone. Von Shlippenshtain thoughtfully looked on and sat down in his chair.

"Screw the book," Reineke, who was also looking at the fireplace, said. "There never was a book in the first place. Right, Romuil?"

"What?" Romuil was staring in the same direction. "What are you talking about, Lis?"

"Nicely done!" Krolina clapped. "All's well that ends well."

"Of course," smiled Reineke. "So what about the rings?"

"Oh, come on!" Kro visibly deflated. "I was hoping you'd forget. They're nice. One's rare, for mages, with four attributes. The other... Lis, please, it's so cool, and it's for archers. Look!"

She pulled it out.

Ring of Wind and Sparks
+15 to agility
+10 to stamina
+11% to accuracy
+13% damage done by the Triple Strike ability
+9% chance of doing critical damage when using the Straight Through ability
Durability: 330/330
For class: archer
Minimum level for use: 65

"You'll turn it in to the clan storehouse," Reineke said sharply.

"But Lissie, please! It's even for the abilities I use. Please, please, please?"

Lis finally had enough. "Oh, stop it! You can keep it, but you're turning in the mage ring."

"Of course. You're the best!" Kro gave Lis a peck on the cheek.

Gunther frowned from the corner where he was sitting.

"Well," said von Shlippenshtain, who got up again from his chair, "now it's my turn to hand out some rewards. The witcher is dead!"

For completing the Kill the Witcher quest you get:
1500 experience
Other rewards: variable

I heard another ding. What a day!

You unlocked Level 31!
Points ready to be distributed: 5

Fantastic. Level 31 was much better than Level 22, where I'd been stuck for so long.

"I would also like to reward each of you individually. Although...there's one more reward I have for you all." Hugo waved his hand. "Forgive my presumption, but I consider friendship with the Tearful Goddess Order a reward as well."

"Of course, master," Reineke said with a nod. "This is an enormous honor for my friends and me."

Master Hugo looked at our whirling dervish, who was, for the moment, quiet. "Lady Krolina, I am pleased to give you a scroll that has been kept here in the Fladridge mission since time immemorial. It contains an ability called Through Walls that you will find useful as an archer."

"Thank you!" She did a small dance. "I've never heard of that!"

"As far as I know, it gives your arrows incredibly destructive power. I would also like to personally give you this katzbalger. I believe you took a liking to it."

"Thank you. Really, thank you!" Kro spun around to face us. "An ability, a gorgeous sword, and my own knight. How lucky am I?"

"An entire order," von Shlippenshtain said with a knowing smile partially concealed by his mustache. "When the young men in our order hear about you, they will certainly wish to take the place of von Richter in your heart. I suspect your smile will be the cause of many a duel."

Gunther frowned deeper in his corner and drifted off into his thoughts.

"And now, you, gentlemen." Hugo looked at Reineke and Romuil. "I give you swords. Both were bound for warriors of our order, and I am sure that in your hands they will serve only the cause of good."

"Wow," whistled Romuil. "Elite!"

"Yeah," Reineke said in confirmation. "Thank you, master. Know that our swords and those of the entire Thunderbirds clan will always be ready to serve the Tearful Goddess Order."

Von Shlippenshtain turned to me. "And for you, my friend, I would like to start by giving you this."

He pulled a shield off the wall and handed it to me.

"It belonged to a great knight, one of the founders of our order. The legends say it was the Goddess herself who gave it to him. She also gave him a sword, but, alas, it was lost. Derek von Lichtenshtain is a legendary figure in our order, as he left the common people, taught himself the ways of a knight, and was knighted by the crown for his deeds of valor and true greatness of spirit. He was a mighty man."

You received an additional reward for completing the Kill the Witcher quest.

Reward:

Shield of Derek von Lichtenshtain

A shield? They're always good.

Shield of Derek von Lichtenshtain

Belonged to one of the founders of the Tearful Goddess Order, and is said to have been given to him by the Goddess.

From the Shield and Sword set

Set includes:

Shield of Derek von Lichtenshtain

Sword of Derek von Lichtenshtain

Protection: 880

+22 to strength

+30 to stamina

+32% to dodge ability

+14% to critical strike chance

+7% gold looted from dead enemies

+24% life energy restoration speed

+18% mana restoration speed

+12% experience received by killing enemies

Durability: 1160/1160

Minimum level for use: 45

For class: warrior

Cannot be stolen, lost, or broken.

The following bonuses are unlocked by using the complete set:

Flash of Light ability

Bloody Mark ability

Life-Giving Tree ability

+15% to your chances of getting items from dead enemies

+17% gold looted from dead enemies

"Oh wow," I said. "Legendary. Cool!"

Hugo raised his eyebrows, not understanding me. A second later, they dropped back down—the wise old man understood and understood correctly.

"Legendary?" Reineke said. "We all got lucky. Seriously. What level is it for?"

"Forty-five. And I'm not turning it in to the clan storehouse!"

"Of course not. Turning a fair reward in to the clan storehouse? Who do you take us for?"

Hugo coughed. We turned back toward him.

"But that's not all. Lord Hagen, I would like to officially invite you to join the Tearful Goddess Order."

You were invited to join the Tearful Goddess Order

If you agree, you will become a member of the order and earn the following bonuses:

+12 to strength

+6 to wisdom

+88 to health

+3% experience earned

+7% damage done by all weapon types

+5% chance of finding rare and hidden quests

Additional:

You will gain access to the order's hidden knowledge, and will most likely unlock chains of rare and hidden quests.

Note:

Only 75 players have ever been invited to join the Tearful Goddess Order. Of them, only one accepted.

Limitations: You will join the order on the side of good. Committing evil deeds will cause your reputation within the order to fall, and you will be expelled from the order and declared its enemy if it falls too far.

Accept?

"That's crazy!" Reineke exchanged glances with his friends. "Join a non-player order? I've never heard of that…"

I stood there, lost in thought.

Chapter Eighteen
Choices

I wondered why everyone else had declined. I mean, I knew why I would turn down von Shlippenshtain's offer, but why did the rest? For the same reasons, I was about to or for different ones? And if they had different reasons, what were they? I was especially intrigued by the one person who had agreed to join. He was probably a veritable fount of information, and he was off walking around somewhere.

"Thank you, Master Hugo, but I have to decline. I have some pretty good reasons, and there are also some promises I have to keep that don't really line up with the order's mission. Two circumstances, in particular, are keeping me from joining your order. For the time being, at least."

The knight's face fell. "I'll be honest, your answer disappoints me. Our order would gain an excellent warrior and a good person if you joined. Let's do this: I'll leave the invitation open. If you decide you can join the order in the future, just come find me and tell me you're ready. Does that work for you?"

"Absolutely," I said. "That would be an honor, but is it a problem that I'm a member of the Thunderbirds?"

"Of course not." Hugo was firm on that point. "Your clan is your clan, and your order is your order. Besides, my order and your clan now enjoy a very friendly relationship, am I right?"

We assured von Shlippenshtain that yes, players and NPCs are friends forever, and we all meant every word.

Then we had another drink to toast our achievement and took our leave to attend to other matters. What point was there in sitting around? The job was done, everyone had their rewards, and it was time to go.

Out on the street, life in Fladridge was as ordinary as ever: children were playing, old ladies were carrying water in buckets, and players were rushing every which way. The only thing that stood out was the angry shouting coming from the pub next door.

"Seriously? Healing NPCs! Let's…let's…let's find some pandas who know Kung fu and let them into the game, too. Why not? We'll give them their own continent! Got to be kidding me…"

"He's still at it." Reineke shook his head.

"Ah, he'll stuff his face and fall asleep," Kro said placidly. "All right, who's going where? I'm on my way to Hostig."

"I'm on my way to Gorrint. Some friends need me," answered Romuil.

"I have to go to the hotel first," Reineke said. "Hagen, want to come with me?"

"Of course," I said. "I'm going there, too."

"And then where?" asked Kro. "Fladridge doesn't really have anything else for you at your level."

"I'm not sure," I answered honestly. "Everyone's pushing me eastward."

"Who is 'everyone'?" asked Reineke.

"Well, all the NPCs." I twisted my hand around in the air as if screwing in an imaginary lightbulb. "The instructor, and Gunther, too—just go east."

"In that case, you need to go east," Reineke said as if pronouncing a verdict.

"Definitely." Romuil seconded his opinion, and Kro nodded her crazy head in agreement.

"See, you always choose your own way and make your own decisions in the game." Reineke smiled humorlessly. "Where you go, how you go there, who you go with, and why. You're the only one who can decide if you want to be a dark elf or a thieving halfling. Just a minute ago, for example, you made a choice. Thousands and thousands of players would never even dream of joining a non-player order—they're way better than any clan. And you turned them down, which is your right. Neither the clan nor I will ever ask you why, though having you join would have been incredibly valuable for us: access to information, access to the order's storehouses, and an army of friendly warriors. But you turned them down, and you are perfectly within your rights to do so. The game is made up of choices like that, both big and small. You decide for yourself and bear the responsibility for your decisions."

'Why, why?' Just because. Of course, it would be great, but not with the limitations I had. Anything I did in the "minus" column would have hurt my reputation. That category includes lies, and I was a constant and willing liar. After all, that was my profession. Executioners cut off heads, beekeepers kept bees, florists grew flowers, and I lied. Okay, fine, not all the time, but I never really told the truth. I was a journalist, and journalists never speak the whole truth. It's always better or worse than it really is because nobody cares about reality. We live there already. And who knows what I'd end up doing in the game? Maybe I'd beat someone up or kill them. My reputation would suffer, seeing as how I wouldn't be evaluated by a person—they might miss things or not take emotion into account. No, it would have been a machine that simply records what happens. Sooner or later, and almost certainly sooner, my rating would drop below the threshold. I'd be kicked out of the order, declared its enemy, and hounded through all of Fayroll. *And they have missions in every city!* Anyway, I didn't need that. The benefits were outweighed by the drawbacks. Besides, I wouldn't be getting most of the benefits; my clan would.

"Still, the game reserves the right to give you friendly advice," Reineke continued. "Once you've done everything you need to do in your current location, it uses NPCs to give you hints and push you in the direction that will be best and most interesting for you...from its point of view."

"But how does it know what's best for me?" I was pretty sure I knew the answer to my question.

"Big brother is always watching!" Kro opened her eyes wide.

"Basically, yes," agreed Lis. "It's true. The game analyzes all of us constantly, checks to see which quests we'd like, looks for adventures we'd find fun—at our level—and then it decides which way is best. But you decide if you want to go that way or not. I'd have to agree that the east is the best place for you right now."

"Why?" I was intrigued.

"Your level, for starters. Most locations there are levels 32 to 45. I mean, sure, they have high-level locations, too, and even a raid boss. But on the way to Selgar—"

"Sel*gar*?" I asked, putting the emphasis on the second syllable.

"No, it's *Sel*gar," said Krolina helpfully. Romuil nodded. "The biggest city on the eastern side of Rattermark. Well, like Aegan here. Lots of traders, an auction, herds of players, a few major clans, tons of quests. You should go there regardless, but besides that, the only people who don't want to visit an entire section of the continent like that are ridiculously noobish or lazy. The question is how to get there."

"Exactly, that's what I'm talking about." Reineke pulled out his map. "Look, there are two ways you can go. The best option is to follow the Crisna River, or, as it's normally called, the Great River. It flows across half the continent, starting in the Sumak Mountains and ending in the Nameless Sea. All you have to do is follow it, and you won't get lost. That way is longer, of course, but you go from town to town doing quests along the way. All in all, you should be in Selgar a month or a month and a half from now. There are lots of towns along the way, and it takes a day or less to go from one to the other. You always have something to do."

"Just make sure you go around Snakeville." Krolina poked her finger at a spot on the map. "Right here."

"Why?"

"It's a bad place," Romuil said. "There used to be a village there called Snakeville. Then, three years ago, two clans went to war. Someone didn't do something—someone's toes got stepped on or whatever... Anyway, they really went at it."

"So what happened?"

"Then," continued Reineke, "one of the clans started losing. Their mage, apparently an incredibly powerful one, cast Universal Flood. It's a spell that starts water pouring out of the sky like, I don't know...like from a bucket. No, more like from a hose—a ton of water for a long time. But he must have missed something because the whole flood swept right through Snakeville."

"And?"

"And washed it into the river. The whole village. With its roofs, well, cows, and NPC villagers. Everyone drowned. All that was left were the chimneys. Well, and picturesque ruins of houses."

Kro jumped in. "The admins were furious. They added a rule saying you can't touch NPCs unless it's part of the script, and also another rule against large-scale combat in cities, villages, and really anywhere people live. And the penalties they added...damn."

"The admins also disbanded those clans, holding them responsible for catastrophic losses and casualties in the game world even though it's all just a bunch of code," Romuil said in closing. "And they left Snakeville as a warning. It's a bad place. They say it's terrible there at night."

"What do you mean?" I still didn't understand what was bad about it.

Reineke rejoined the conversation. "You always know you're playing a game, right? And no matter what you're going through, it's never really all that scary, no?"

"Of course."

"Well, when you're there, you have a hard time distinguishing the game from reality. You think that if you die, it won't just be the game. At least, that's what people who have been there say."

"But they don't tell you what's actually there," confirmed Kro. "All they say is that it's 'terrible.' I wanted to go check it out, but I haven't yet."

"Long story short, just go around," said Reineke to sum up.

"Why are you sending him along the river?" Romuil interrupted and pointed at a different spot on the map Reineke was still holding. "He could go through Foim Plateau."

"Right, the plateau, where the yetis live." Reineke snorted.

"It's twice as fast. And Amadze crossed it alone two years ago, and his level wasn't that high either."

"What is Amadze?"

"A scout."

"Exactly. And Hagen is a warrior. The yetis will be all over him, and they respawn every five minutes. Plus, Gruskat Valley is after the plateau. He'd have to deal with hordes of orcs and wolves."

"It's up to him." Romuil stretched and continued. "Anyway, see you all later. I'm off."

"Hold on, let me give you your gold." Reineke froze for a second.

Once they'd finished, a portal opened, and Romuil stepped into it. I probably could have added him as a friend, but for some reason,

I didn't want to. Maybe that was one of the choices Reineke was talking about.

"He has a dark side. And there's something going on with him and Murat, by the way," Kro said with a glance at Reineke.

"We don't have to have anything to do with him." Lis gestured my way with his eyes, obviously reminding Kro of my presence.

I figured it was best not to inquire.

"Lis, show me the map again. How do I go there, and what's the final destination?"

Lis opened his map, and I estimated the distance, pulled up the game map and tried to compare the two. Then I activated the quest for Ogina the East and checked the red circle. It turned out to be about five days' walk from Selgar, right on the border with the notorious Gruskat Valley, where all the wild orcs were. Hordes of them. Romuil was right: it would be easier for me to cross the Foim Plateau. But the yetis...

"Look, there's a crossroads you have to go to either way." Reineke had obviously realized what I was trying to figure out and pointed to a city on the map. "You need to go here, to Montrig, and that will take two weeks. By then you'll have made a decision."

"Maybe you'll find someone to go with you!" Kro was trying to be encouraging. "Want me to give you my knight?"

"Alas, Lady Krolina," said Gunther as he walked down the steps, "while I would be happy to go with Laird Hagen, I cannot. The master is sending me to the Supreme Chapter at Grondar to tell them about the death of the witcher and other news."

"Grondar. That's somewhere way off in the south." Krolina scowled. "How long will it take you to ride down there?"

"A long time. But I don't have a choice. He gave the order, and that's final."

Krolina looked at the knight compassionately. "Let me take you with me. I'm taking a portal to Hostig, and that will save you 1,500 leagues or so."

"Are you serious, Lady Krolina?"

"No, I'm joking. Come on, get your things together."

"I'll be back in three minutes." Gunther sprinted back up the stairs, his armor clattering as he went.

"That's a shame—he'd make things easier for you." Reineke looked at me. "Good NPCs always come in handy."

"Sometimes, the opposite is true." I smiled. "You're responsible for whoever's in your care. Life's simpler when you're alone."

"Yes, I'm aware. Just don't miss the moment when the game stops being a game. If you don't see it coming, it'll make it harder for you later."

"I'll do my best." I knew what he was talking about. More and more, I was thinking about the NPCs as real people rather than digital creations. It was unusual, but kind of fun. And not that healthy.

"Lady Krolina, I'm ready." Gunther bounced down the stairs and froze in front of Kro. "All I have to do is bring Duke here."

"Don't worry about it," said Kro grandly. "We'll go find your little stallion and port from there. Okay, boys, send me a message if anything fun happens. I'll come save you."

"Goodbye, Sir Reineke. Goodbye, Laird Hagen." Gunther bowed his head in farewell.

It was odd, but in those two days, I'd grown attached to the young knight and his belief in honesty, friendship, and the eventual triumph of good over evil. That was certainly the least of what I believed in when I was younger…

"Goodbye, Sir Gunther von Richter. I think we'll cross paths again," I said.

"Of course," said Gunther with conviction and without a shadow of a doubt. "Did you think we wouldn't? You're on your way to the east, and I'll head that way soon. Just make sure you wait for me there. I'll find you."

"I'll be sure to wait," I promised. "I don't have anywhere to go."

"We're off. Mwah!" Krolina blew us kisses and took the young knight into the stable behind the mission, where a minute later we saw the light of a portal.

"The valiant von Richter dragged off like a lamb to the slaughter," I said matter-of-factly.

Reineke grunted.

"Well, to the hotel?"

"To the hotel."

Lubelia was at the hotel looking as beautiful as ever, and she handed us keys. I noticed she didn't ask who Reineke was, even though she'd never seen him before in her computerized life.

"Don't leave without me," Reineke said. "Let's meet by the entrance in ten minutes."

"Sounds good."

I stretched out on the bed without taking off my boots, something I—dirty swine that I am—had always dreamed of doing, and I finally distributed my points.

There were thirty-five of them. All of five went to wisdom. I added fifteen to strength, another ten to stamina. Intellect got three, agility got two, and I was done.

Next, I set about sorting through everything I'd gotten. Where was that super earring? And what ear were you supposed to put it in? I definitely remembered that fruits wore them in one specific ear—but which? I decided to just go with the left. Later, I'd look it up online.

All that was left was the highlight of the evening: the Hounds of Death Friendship Ring. I could feel myself turning into a killing machine...probably. One thing was for sure: I was becoming a prime target for PKers.

Next, I collected everything I needed to dump in my chest and hoped there'd always be as much. There was extra gold after saving thirty for myself to buy bread and some treats. Then there was the shield. I wasn't sure I'd use it even after I got to Level 45, as it was too valuable an item to have with me regardless of the bonuses that came with it. Plus...there was still a ways to go before Level 45, and I was far from certain that I'd even get that far. And I wasn't bothered in the least that my clan didn't know I had a set item. I certainly wasn't going to turn it in to the clan storehouse. It was my shield, and that was final.

So where was I, having turned yet another page in my online life?

Basic attributes:
Strength: 128 (80+48)
Intellect: 13 (8+5)

Agility: 19 (12+7)
Stamina: 100 (55+45)
Wisdom: 15

Not bad. Sure, I was a little one-sided, but that die was cast. We can't all be mages.

And then it was time to go—Reineke was probably waiting for me already.

He had a question waiting for me as soon as we met on the stoop. "Hey, do you remember when I gave you the amulet? I told you that I don't like selling things I don't use anymore."

"Well, yes." I was a bit surprised—did he want me to give the amulet back?

"I'm selective about what I save, but I never sell the weapons I've used. And I never will. I do like to give them away, though. You're a good guy, even if it's always a bit hard to tell what you're thinking. Anyway, take this."

He held out a blade.

"I ran around with this beauty from Level 30 to Level 41. Before that, I had a morning star until one day a friend told me it was time to switch to a sword. He said that blunt weapons don't work as well as edged ones, and he was right. I didn't really want to use a regular sword, so I got this broadsword instead. Here."

Scorpion Broadsword
Damage: 73-114
+11 to strength
+9 to stamina
+12% chance of doing fire damage
+9% chance of poisoned strike
Durability: 160/180
Minimum level for use: 28

"You're my personal Santa Claus," I told him. "I don't think I'll ever repay you."

"Don't worry about it." He clapped me on the shoulder. "You'll take care of me in the next life. Well, you didn't forget me either. That reminds me—here's your 100 gold from the witcher."

The coins clinked together pleasantly.

"Hey, did you give Kro her gold?" I asked.

"Nope," he answered calmly. "She forgot, and you didn't remind me. I'll mail it to her. Oh, and about Santa Claus, you're a lucky son of a gun. Something came up in Mettan, which is right on the river. If you want, you can come with me."

"Can you show me on the map?"

"Look. Here's Fladridge, and here's Mettan. You'll save at least five days."

It looked like I wasn't going to have to deal with the Very Dark and Very Scary Forest. Instead, I'd jump right into the river I needed to travel along.

"Hey, are there any boats on the river? Do you have to ride, or can you take one of them? Maybe a ferry with the big old wheel, a boatswain, and some gypsy music?"

"Yes, there is, though—no offense—you don't have the money."

"It's that expensive?"

"That depends on who you're talking to. For me, 10,000 gold per day isn't bad. I don't know about you, but I imagine you can't afford it."

"You imagine correctly. Why is it so expensive?"

"They want you to walk. Otherwise, everyone would take the boat."

"So that's the only option?"

"No, there's a quest ferry, too, but it's a really tough quest that doesn't even let you ride for free; you just get a discount. But that's your call. If you want, you can go talk to the pier boss in Mettan. Or just walk around the city—there's a lot that's fun to do."

"What if I just build a raft?"

"Everything in the river will eat you alive. It's teeming with all kinds of things, and they're all carnivorous. You think you're the first one to have that idea? Anyway, are you coming with me?"

"Of course. Just give me ten minutes to take care of a quest."

Reineke nodded, and I hurried off to a stand I'd noticed earlier. The sign above it read "Life-Giving Power of Nature: Herbs, Roots, Ointments." A herbalist named Felga quickly asked me to find eight sheaves of Drianod grass, though she had her doubts that I'd be able to find them.

"They're so hard to find…so hard!"

To her surprise, I simply pulled them out of my bag, receiving in return 150 gold, 400 experience, and a charming smile from the lovely herbalist to boot. She also promised me a 10% discount on all her inventory. I doubted I'd ever need it, but it didn't hurt.

That done, I walked over to Reineke, who was sitting on the step outside the hotel.

"Ready?" he asked.

"Sort of," I said, and rolled my eyes. "I wouldn't mind picking up some abilities. I have at least two waiting for me."

"Oh, you can get them in Mettan. I definitely remember seeing instructors there."

Lis opened a portal, and we stepped inside—Lis to see his friend, and me in search of new adventures. Or maybe just yet another headache.

Chapter Nineteen
The Great River and Other Issues

The smell of river water is unmistakable. It's a bit sweet, with a smack of freshness, different underwater plants, and a touch of sand. That was the smell that met us, making our hearts skip a beat when we exited the portal.

We were standing on a perfectly standard pier. As expected, it was wooden, and it reminded me of Bobili Pier in Krasnoslobodsk, where I'd been sent the year before chasing a story. Mammoth had heard that the city was being called the Rublevka of the Volga, so he decided to cover his bases and collect some material just in case. Petrova was actually supposed to go, but, you know, a young woman alone in a strange city and all. Something might have happened... But what could happen to her that she hadn't already been through? She'd worked as an oligarch's servant, and then she spent time with some Bedouins in Egypt. And both the former as well as the latter liked to have fun, or so she told us once at a corporate party after we'd gotten her thoroughly drunk. I guess it was one thing to chow down caviar in Rublevka and experiment in a tent with some exotic nomads, while wandering off into the depths of Russia and chatting with the people there was something much worse.

Krasnoslobodsk turned out to be a very nice little city, even if it wasn't well taken care of and was stuck in the roaring 90s. Still.

There were three boats at the end of the pier: one big one and two smaller ones. I wasn't expecting a ferry with staterooms, but honestly... The boats were pleasantly reminiscent of ships I'd read about in pseudo-historical and pseudo-Slavic fantasy novels. At least, they looked exactly how the books had described them. And, to be frank, I doubt I'd have ventured out on a river like that one on those boats in real life.

I could see why it was called the Great River. I'd seen the Volga, the Dniester, the Seine, and the Thames. They had nothing on the Crisna. I've also heard that the Amazon is a big river, but I don't know since I haven't seen it. Still, I don't think it would be anything next to what was in front of me.

The Crisna was enormous. The opposite bank was so far away that it disappeared when the water swelled higher. It flowed lazily as if still feeling out its greatness and size. The waves gently washed ashore near the pier.

"Powerful, no?" Reineke was obviously enjoying watching my face. "I couldn't believe it either the first time I saw it. Beautiful and enormous!"

"Seriously," I agreed. "Impressive. What's on the other side?"

"It might as well be the moon for how far away it is for you, my friend. Over there is Mirastia, the dark kingdom of the dead. The raid zone there is for strong, high-level clans, and nobody, no matter their level, ever goes alone. Zombies, skeletons of all shapes and sizes, hell hounds, blood ghosts, wyverns, probably, and lots of all of them. And as if that weren't enough, at the end you have to deal with the Emperor of the Dead, sitting on his throne of bones in Skull Palace. Sitting there with a grin on his face and a sword in his hand. A lot of people said his sword was from a set."

"Was it?"

"Nope, not in the least. Legendary, and really incredible, but not from a set. Clan after clan has died trying to storm Skull Palace… In the entire history of the game, only three clans have ever taken the palace and killed the Emperor: the Vultures, the Wild Hearts, and, if I'm not mistaken, the Forest Beasts."

"And our clan?"

"We're not that strong, or, at least, not yet. We took out some lower-level bosses around the outside a few times, and that was all."

"What about the Hounds of Death?"

"They tried four times, but they weren't able to do it. The last time, the Gray Witch and two of their warriors got all the way to the Emperor. He piled them up one on top of the other in the throne room, though, and the Witch was livid for two weeks. She really wanted that sword, I guess."

"Or she wanted even more prestige for their clan."

"Could be."

"So does the kingdom of the dead cover that entire bank?"

"Oh, please, no. You can see how wide the river is now, but in three weeks, you'll also realize how long it is. Two weeks after that, you'll lose your mind completely. Everything's different on the other side. Farther downstream, which is where you're going, right next to Mirastia, is the Forest of Spiders, and then another forest—apparently without a special name. And after that, there's everything you could think of. The thing is that it's tough to survive alone. You have to go with your whole clan or with a big group, and you need to be at least Level 100. Oh, and you should have a bunch of healers with you since there aren't any respawn points there. If they kill you, you come all the way back here. That's why storming Skull Palace is so hard. If you die and manage to get back over to that side of the river, you still have to wade through a sea of skeletons, and that can take a while."

"But what about the three clans that killed the Emperor? How did they get back? There couldn't have been many of them left."

"One of the bonuses you get for killing the Emperor is a portal that opens. You walk in, say where you want to go, and you're there. Well, within the known regions, of course."

"But why did the developers make it so hard?"

"Well, aren't you inquisitive today? Everyone has their own opinion. Personally, I think they made the locations over there just in case the world gets too crowded. That way they can gradually start to open things up, start cities, populate them, write quests, and add actions, none of which are there now. There isn't anyone living there, so there aren't quests or actions. If there were, people would try to head over. That lets them preserve it for later, so to speak."

"And Rivenholm? If all that is true, why would they need Rivenholm?"

"Why did people imagine El Dorado? It's a pipe dream. You need them, so you have something to work toward, something to discuss, something to think about. It's just that it's far away across the ocean, and that side of the river is right there. Well, it's close compared to Rivenholm, at least. Oh, Ruh, hi!"

A big, high-level warrior barbarian came up to us, and his size immediately reminded me of Fat Willie. For some reason, I'd thought that he was part of our clan, but he turned out to be in the Valley Children clan.

"Hey, Lis. Who's this?" Ruh more boomed than spoke.

"Hagen. He's a good guy from our clan."

"Hi, Hagen! How's life?"

"Getting there, Ruh. Doing my thing, taking my time, killing some monsters."

"Quick on his feet!" Ruh winked approvingly at Reineke. "I like that. Anyway, you ready?"

"More than. Okay, Hagen, see you around. If you need anything, write. Oh, and, again, go around Snakeville. Don't try to get fancy."

"Agreed," Ruh said. "Rotten place. Zoren, a friend of ours, was there, and it changed him. Eventually, he was so gloomy he quit the game. He was even at Level 128 and respected in the clan. So just go find your jollies elsewhere. All right, let's go."

A portal flashed and Reineke dove in behind Ruh.

Once again, I was alone. It struck me how that was the norm for me, save for when I was in a full-on crowd. I didn't seem to have a middle ground.

I had a strong feeling of déjà vu. Something like that had happened just recently, and that time I left the game. There was nothing for it but to stick with tradition, so I clicked the button to log out.

There was one more good tradition starting to take shape: as soon as I exited the game, my phone rang. I climbed out of the capsule, rubbed my stiff low back, and answered.

"Hi, son." It was my dad.

"Hi, pops," I said with some suspicion.

My father was the kind of person who thought kids should learn how to live life on their own. You know, throw them in and watch them sink or swim. And if they sank, well, that was their problem.

"Well, kiddo, what are you up to?" My suspicions grew. He obviously needed something.

"Ah, you know, we're slammed at work..." I decided to get out in front of him.

"Oh, stop it. I called the office first and asked to talk to you. They said you wouldn't be there for another three weeks."

"Whatever, just tell me what you need." There was no avoiding it this time.

"We need to go patch up the roof at the dacha[13]," he said, putting his cards on the table as well.

Oh, no—anything but that!

In addition to the apartment I was living in, my grandfather gave our family twelve acres in Mozhaysky District. The land also had a house that was built during the communist years out of anything they could find or steal back then. Needless to say, the old dinosaur regularly tried to end its miserable existence and collapse in a heap. My father, however, was stubbornly insistent that that would not happen, and he was constantly ready to buy materials and bring it back to life. Year after year, it groaned and creaked in the wind, frustrated that its humans wouldn't let it die. It was apparently time for yet another resurrection.

"Dad, I really can't. I have work."

"Son, it's our family nest." Ha, right—he meant our plywood nest. "It's just something we have to do. Plus, you know I won't let it go, so just give in and come. Your mom will definitely be happy to see you."

I sighed, knowing that he was right.

"When?"

"Tomorrow morning I'll stop by to pick you up, so be at the building entrance by seven. And hey, we'll get some work done, then in the evening we'll roast some meat, have some drinks...it'll be great. No?"

"I guess so. See you tomorrow," I said gloomily as I hung up the phone.

Great, now I had to explain to Elvira that I was off to the dacha and not to see some girls. She wouldn't believe me anyway, though, and she'd just get on my nerves, so I decided to do my due diligence and send her a text. I wasn't about to call her—my mood was already bad enough without dealing with her. And I decided to leave my phone at home.

The dacha adventure took all of three days, and I only got back to Moscow on the fourth. Life in the country wouldn't have been too bad if it weren't for my parents hounding me constantly. My dad kept trying to teach me life lessons, explaining that "they're all thieves. Or homos." I needed some clarification

"Who is 'they'? And who is 'all'?"

"Everyone you see on TV. All of them."

My mom took another tack: she fed me. Constantly. "Come on, eat something. It's good! Why do you think I cooked it?" Three days of that.

No, I mean, I get that parents love their kids, especially when don't see them for a while. But it's hard to get through that much love without a little weed…

The morning I got back, I walked into my apartment and started by turning on my phone to read the texts I'd received. I'd turned it off when I left, knowing full well that I'd have gone crazy if I had to deal with my parents and everyone calling me at the same time.

Elvira, Elvira, Elvira, Elvira. I opened one at random. "Where are you? Missing you." Wait, was that really her? It was, and I got an uneasy feeling. Nothing good could come of that.

Oh, Mammoth. Typical: "Call me when you sleep off the booze. If you don't call before the end of the week, you're fired."

"Hello? Semyon Ilyich, it's Nikiforov."

"Ah, the lost sheep. Where were you?"

"Playing the game, reading the forums. I decided to turn off my phone so I wouldn't be distracted."

"I'm expecting your next article today."

"Why today? It's due tomorrow."

"Deadlines, Harrikins, deadlines. And ratings. Our readers like your work, and we have to give them what they want. Have you even seen our site?"

"Um-m-m…"

"Exactly. 'Um-m-m…'"

"I'm not sure I can have it done in time."

"You will. And in three days, I want the last one."

"Come on! You gave me a month, and now I'm supposed to fit it all into two weeks?"

"You're almost done already. Okay, let's do this: if you can get me your fifth article today and your sixth in three days, I'll owe you one."

"I have a counter offer. If I get everything done, you give me a two-week vacation. The one I was supposed to get back in May."

"He wants a vacation. For two weeks. That's a bit much, don't you think?"

"It's just the time you cut off my deadline. You weren't expecting me back before then anyway."

"Fine. I'll give you a vacation, and for that... Well, we'll talk about what you'll do after your vacation when we get back. Deal."

"Can I stop by around four with my article and fill out the vacation form while I'm there?"

"You're a clever son of a gun, Harrikins. I've never seen this side of you. Fine, stop by. You can get your money while you're here, too, and that way the accountants will get off my back. I don't even get half of what they talk about."

I hung up.

Score! The whole thing ended up being even simpler than I thought it would be. Here I was planning a grand campaign for how I could squeeze those two weeks out of him, as the articles were just about ready. All I had to do was write them down—I'd left my netbook at home when I went to the dacha. Although... I determined that, after chatting with Mammoth and shaking his hand, I would count to make sure I had all my fingers with me. On both hands. I'd check my toes, too, for good measure.

Without going into the details, everything went well. I wrote the article, dropped by the office, filled out the form, and got my money—quite a decent amount, as it turned out. That night, I decided to take care of two things I'd been putting off: calling Elvira and checking out the game forums as well as the paper's site.

I started with my favorite representative of the Golden Horde. To be honest, I really wasn't looking forward to it, given my distaste for scandals and fights. But I have an even stronger distaste for putting off anything unpleasant I have to do. Once upon a time, I was more like everyone else on the planet and did my best to avoid those conversations. You know how it is, there's a tough conversation you need to have, and you start thinking up any excuse you can to kick the can a little further down the road. Unfortunately, that just means you won't get to pick your battlefield and, worse, you'll have wasted a whole day trying to figure out what you want to say. After that, your karma is in the toilet, and you've burned through nerve cells you'll never get back. What good does that do you? People who choose that road remind me of men trying to wade into cold water. They tiptoe in, splashing themselves with water, as if that warms them up, clenching their stomachs, doing girly little squats, and squealing when the water gets to their waist. Isn't it simpler to just jump right in? You get the whole thing over with in one fell swoop.

"Hey, El."

"Where were you?"

"At the dacha helping my parents. You didn't see my text?"

"No. You wrote me?"

"Of course! As soon as I found out I had to go. I called, too, though your phone was unavailable."

"I was worried."

That really got me going. Maybe she was pregnant? I mean, children are great in general, but right then...

"El, do you have a Schengen[14] visa?"

"Sure."

"And your friend works at a travel agency, right?"

"Still does."

"Listen, what do you think about taking a trip in a few days? Just not to Turkey. Maybe to Spain or Greece? Ask her if she has any good deals going on right now."

The phone was silent. Finally, she responded, though her voice was almost inaudible.

"Are you joking?"

"Why would I joke about that?"

"Okay, but if you tell me in a few days that you can't do it after all, I'll kill you for real."

"I won't."

"All right, let me call you back."

That was one more thing done and one more thing that pleasantly surprised me by how well it went. I was still worried by how strangely she was acting, but it takes a woman to understand another woman.

There was nothing unexpected on the paper forums. Battle lines were formed, and everyone for and against video games was going at it from one end to the other. I wouldn't say my handiwork was responsible. It was just a happy coincidence that the articles had been released at the right place and the right time. Still, as I scanned the debates, I felt the same sense of satisfaction a craftsman looking at his work might have.

The gaming forums, on the other hand, had quieted down. Most players had decided that the whole epic quest idea was a myth, and they'd left for greener pastures. On the other hand, I was struck by the fact that most threads on the topic were written fairly professionally. I had the feeling that there was a PR specialist behind the scenes pulling strings to get everyone focused in the right direction. Perhaps, a clan or group of clans decided to smooth things over and get rid of potential competitors while they looked for the quest holder. If that was true, they did a good job. I silently wished them luck in their search, wondered if they'd find him, and went to sleep.

***

I stretched and heard my phone ring.

"Kif, it's me. There's a trip to Costa Daurada, Salou. A resort city in Spain."

"Ah, Catalonia. Sounds great. When's the flight?"

"The 15th, in four days. 4:15 p.m. from Sheremetyevo."

"Perfect. And it isn't a charter, so we won't have to wait at the airport."

"So should I reserve seats?"

"Go for it."

Elvira paused before quietly muttering a goodbye.

"Okay, see you tomorrow."

Catalonia, fruit, sangria, Port Aventura... All I had to do was write one last article and turn it in before I was on my way to a sunny piece of heaven.

I really didn't need to log into the game, since I knew what I would write about. There wasn't anything else to do, however, and, strange as it may sound, I was starting to miss the blue sky of Fayroll.

Once again, I found myself standing on the pier. The early morning sun was playing on the water of the Great River as seagulls flew overhead. A peaceful scene for once. To the left of the pier, some fishermen sat on the bank, occasionally jerking on their rods.

I stood there for another couple minutes, enjoying the picture of universal calm and stability, and then started toward the city. The very first thing I had to do was go talk to the instructor and get my two abilities. Knowing my luck, if I didn't, I'd soon find myself neck-deep in some drama or other and wouldn't have the time.

The town was small. There were about thirty buildings, and I saw the familiar sign for the instructor I needed before also noticing the town's Tearful Goddess Order mission. I also came across the port building, which had just one floor and looked like a barracks, as well as a tavern, a hotel, and a squat little building with a sign that read "town hall."

I paused for a second by the order mission and considered dropping by to tell the local leader hello from Master Hugo, but thought better of the idea. Who knows what kind of witcher I'd have to go catch if I did? Instead, I turned and walked straight toward the sign with the shield and sword.

We'll see what kind of hobby this instructor has, I thought. *The first carved and the second made kites. Maybe this one weaves sandals or plays the balalaika[15]?*

I knocked on the gate.

"Come r-r-right in!" It was a child's voice, and it seemed to get caught on the letter "r."

I walked in to see a girl about five years old sitting on the porch with a straw doll in her arms.

"Hi," I said.

"Gr-r-reetings," she responded.

"Why do you like the letter 'r' so much?"

"I just lear-r-rned how to say it, and I like showing it off!"

"Got it. What's your name?"

"Adele."

"And where's your grandfather, Adele? I came to see him."

"Gr-r-randpa is fishing. As soon as he catches something, he'll r-r-return home and br-r-ring me a lollipop. Do you have a lollipop?"

"Nope, I don't." I held up my hands.

"That's a shame." She sighed.

"It is," I agreed. "Where does your grandfather usually go fishing?"

"By the pier-r-r. R-r-right on the other side. He's the only one there with a bear-r-rd."

"What's his name?"

"Gr-r-randpa!" The little girl looked at me in bewilderment, as if to ask what else she was supposed to call him.

"Of course, but what do the neighbors call him?"

"Dar-r-rn old Gr-r-rod." She lowered her voice and stomped her foot.

"Got it. Well, I'll bring you a lollipop. And your 'r' sounds great!"

"R-r-really? You'll br-r-ring me a lollipop?" She beamed at me.

I nodded. "Of course I will!"

On the way back to the pier, I stopped by the tavern and found only three people there, all of whom were NPCs. The tavern keeper sold me a lollipop, though the surprised look on his face told me that players usually just bought beer. Apparently, I was the first to ask for a lollipop. But what was wrong with buying one for Adele? I'd promised I would, after all, and I could have her grandfather give it to her. Grandparents are always tickled when people like their grandchildren. Of course, I'd give it to him before the conversation turned to my abilities.

After Fladridge, its restless residents, and the crowds of players rushing up and down the streets, Mettan seemed calm and peaceful. I only saw two players on the road, and it looked like they were focused on finishing quests.

I finally arrived at the pier and was happy to find that only one of the people fishing there had a beard.

"Master Grod?"

He turned and motioned for me to be quieter.

"I need to talk with you."

"I'll be fishing for another two hours, so stop by the house later. Do you know where I live?" the stocky old man asked softly.

I nodded.

Grod nodded in reply and waved his hand as if to send me on my way.

Well, there was nothing for it. I had two hours to kill, so I decided I might as well walk around the city and head over to the port to see what the twisted quest was about. The ships were anything but reassuring, but it sailing poorly was still better than walk in comfort.

I stopped at the port building and knocked on the door like any decent person might.

A gruff voice answered from behind it. "Come in, whoever you are! Just wipe your feet."

I made sure my feet were clean and pushed open the door.

Chapter Twenty
On the Shores of the Great River (Part One)

The port master was pleasantly reminiscent of Mammoth. I mean, outside of their height and how hairy they were, they didn't resemble each other much on the surface. One big difference was that this salty, wind-driven sailor was one-eyed, one-legged, and incredibly grizzled. His face was marked by a permanently spiteful grimace, and there was a cigar stub jutting out of the corner of his mouth. Still, there was something about his eyes and the way he carried himself that reminded me of Mammoth. His name was Neils Holgerrson.

"What the hell do you need?" Mr. Holgerrson's greeting was more an interrogation.

Ah-ha, one more thing he and Mammoth had in common. I recognized him by his amiability and cordiality, and my heart warmed.

"I'd like a seat on the boat," I informed the sea dog.

"Oh, is that all? Belay and ballast! Well, if you're a rich little kiddie and your mommy gave you a sack of gold to go along with your Rosa-Mimosa perfume, hand over 10,000 coins a day and the spot is yours! I'll take you straight to the Kraken if you want."

"Where am I supposed to get that much money?"

"Then take a hike. I'd rather drop a hundred thousand squids down my pants than make an exception for you."

I imagined the squid, saw where they'd be going, and shuddered...

"Maybe there's something else we could figure out?" I winked at Holgerrson.

"Get the hell out of here!" The old sailor roared at me like a wounded hippo. "They said you landlubbers are all turning into women, but I didn't believe them. Yeah, right, we'll figure something out! You know what I do to people like you—"

I doubled over with laughter when I realized what the devil thought I meant.

"Oh, calm down," I told him. He had already unstrapped his wooden leg and was whirling it around his head, taking aim at me as he did.

"That's not what I meant!"

"No?" Holgerrson puffed on his cigar butt, which had somehow stayed in his mouth even while he was bellowing at me. "Then what did you mean? I thought you were one of those...rear-wheel drivers... And you're like a girl with that earring..."

That did it. I had to see which ear normal guys pierce. And which one they stay away from.

The sailor snuffled and grunted as he started strapping his leg back on. The cigar didn't move a millimeter.

"I meant that maybe I could help with something. I could help you, and you could give me a good deal on that ticket. Sure, you can't give it to me for free, but you could take fifty or seventy percent off the price."

"Oh, yes? Well, there is this one thing. It's very odd, though."

"What do you mean?"

"The captain of a tub called the Firefly runs between cities here in the lower reaches of the Crisna. That's the one you're trying to get on, but it's gone."

"What do you mean, it's gone?"

"Just that. Two days ago, it left the city with a full crew, and nobody has any idea why, bosons and bluster. Since then we haven't seen hide nor hair of them—gone!"

"How big is the crew?" I pictured a squadron of sailors bedecked in ribbons and vests, their dashing captain in front, marching three by three to the tune of a merry shanty and disappearing into a forest.

"Have you seen their bathtub? Where would they fit a big crew? Three mates and Gul, that's it."

"Oh, so the captain's name is Gul."

"Right. So, want to go looking for them? They were supposed to set sail yesterday, buccaneers and bootleggers. Everyone's worried something will happen to them. What do you say?"

You have a new quest offer: Find the Captain.
Task: Find Captain Gul.

Reward:
700 experience
Significantly discounted passage on the Firefly
Accept?

"Why not? Let's go find us a captain."

"Excellent. As soon as you find the old octopus, send him this way. I'll do my best to get him to knock something off the price, brandy and brigands. Oh, and stop by town hall. That dried squid went there yesterday to ask about something. Maybe Mayor Glopkins knows what's going on, that landlubbing rat."

Their town hall was just a few steps away from the port. I peered cautiously through the doorway to the mayor's office, knowing as I did what those local politicians are capable of. This one, however, did not appear to be anything out of the ordinary. He was long and bony like some kind of dried fish. His long nose was knobby, and his eyes were sad. In short, he looked nothing like a Glopkins. I knocked on the door as I took a step inside.

"Hi, there," I said in greeting.

"Hello!" he answered cordially.

"I have some questions for you. Do you have a minute?"

"Yes, of course." The mayor stretched his face into a smile. "My job is to make sure that everyone visiting or coming through our city has a comfortable stay while they're here."

"Wow!" I said. "I'm not here about that, though. I was just talking with Mr. Holgerrson..."

"Ah, that old drunk. 'Brandy and booze'...straight down the hatch!" The mayor had apparently had his fill of the port master. "And?"

"Well, he hired me to find Captain Gul. He said Gul apparently came to talk to you before he went missing."

"Yes, he was here. He asked me for directions on how to get to Marion the herbalist. His rheumatism was acting up, and you know how hard rheumatism can be on sailors. I told him where he could find her."

"Could you tell me, too? I need to get Captain Gul back here so the ship can set sail."

"That's a good deed you're doing, young man. I'll tell you how to find her and even write her a note. Otherwise, she won't talk to you. She can be petty, that one, though her mother was no better. She was a rat, rest her soul. But both of them—the deceased mother and now Marion—are first-rate herbalists.

"Thank you, Comrade Mayor!"

"What did you call me?"

"Oh, that was just a habit. In my parts, it's what we call respected officials."

"Got it. It's a good word, we'll have to start using it."

The mayor sniffed as he jotted a few lines down on parchment with a red quill pen, sprinkled some sand over his work, shook it, and handed the parchment to me.

"Give this to Marion, and she'll be happy to answer all your questions. Good luck!"

"But where should I go to find her?"

"That's easy. As soon as you leave the city, turn left. You'll walk through a grove of trees, then a clearing, and finally you'll see a field with an enormous elm tree. Her house is right next to it."

"Thanks!"

I turned toward the door.

"Wait a second, young man..."

"Hagen. You can call me Laird Hagen."

"Laird Hagen, I can see you have some experience under your belt." The mayor walked over from behind his desk. His voice also took on a more respectful tone as soon as he heard the word "laird." *So that's how you join the nobility...squatter's rights.*

"Well, a little," I said modestly.

"Come on! Just look at your sword and shield. And your eyes, too...there's war in them. It's hard to tell what you're thinking— maybe you're cracking a joke, or maybe you're about to crack someone's skull. In August, we celebrate Royal Guard Day, and our local veterans have the same look. They pull on their chainmail and helmets, drink too much wine, and go to town. Sometimes, they'll turn over the Sindhi traders' fruit stands, others, they'll chop clay housing tiles in half with their bare hands. Then, when night falls, they jump into the river shouting 'for the Guard!' We're never sure if they're cooling off or going crazy. Oh, and they break empty pitchers over their heads."

"Soldiers are insane... Not all of them, of course, but still..."

"Soldiers, yes. But you're different."

"So what do you need?"

"We have a problem; our water monster is missing. Someone stole it..." The mayor sadly scrunched up his large nose.

"What water monster? An animal?"

"No, it's a statue. Our city was founded by three large and illustrious families: the Diamonds, the Garfunkels, and the Flanders. Once upon a time, they landed here, and the fathers of the three families all remarked on how good a place it was for a settlement. So they started building the first houses."

The mayor sat down again behind his desk and motioned for me to follow suit.

"Anyway, they were sanding logs and building foundations when the Water Monster crawled ashore. It was terrifying, with fins and eyes like two torches, and it glowed! There it was, ready to destroy and eat them all."

"All three families at once?" I was having a hard time believing the story.

"Those water monsters...o-o-oh!" The mayor shook his fist in the air and continued. "Then Josly Flanders grabbed an axe and started hacking away. Everyone else followed his lead and jumped in to help."

"So did they kill it?" I asked without a shadow of a doubt.

"Yes!" the mayor answered proudly.

Bravo! It only took the fathers, sons, uncles, and everyone else in the three families to kill one water monster. And who's to say it wasn't just a local seal coming ashore to get some sun? Or maybe some exercise?

"Their glorious achievement complete, the three families finished building their houses and celebrating the founding of a new settlement. We only later became a city. That was when Martin Flanders, Josly's son, showed everyone a statue of the water monster he'd skillfully carved out of wood. It became the first heirloom in Mettan, and it has been kept and passed down from generation to generation all the way until today. Except now, it's been stolen." The mayor hung his head.

"Who stole it? Do you at least have any clues?"

"Yes. There are two local good-for-nothings named Bill and Ted Thatcher. They're both lazy blockheads. The last time they got into trouble, I promised I'd kick them out of the city if it happened again. They told me they'd get me good for that, and so I suspect this is their handiwork. Maybe you could find them and get the statue back?"

"I can certainly try. But I have two questions," I said uncertainly.

"I don't care if you have ten—we just need to find the statue!"

"First. I can find them, but I'll have to take the statue by force if they don't give it up willingly…"

"Understood. Nobody will have a problem with that." The mayor winked.

"Second. What's in it for me?"

"You're doing a good deed, helping an entire city!" He blinked, obviously perplexed at my poor grasp of the situation.

"Well, of course. But what else?"

"The city's coffers aren't large…"

"What's your relationship with the port master?"

"He answers to me. Not always well, but he's supposed to."

"What about a discount on ship passage?"

"Got it." The mayor realized that he might not have to pay me for my services and was visibly cheered. "I'll make it happen! So do we have a deal?"

> **You have a new quest offer: Symbol of Renown.**
>
> **Task: Find and return the statue to the citizens of Mettan, for whom it represents the glory of their forbearers.**
>
> **Reward:**
>
> **600 experience**
>
> **10% to your reputation in Mettan**
>
> **Additional reward: Discounted passage on the Firefly**
>
> **Accept?**

"Now we're talking business!"

"What did you say?" The mayor's ears perked up again.

"I'm just saying that's a good offer. And you have a great city—clean and beautiful."

"It really is. You should come in September when we have our pumpkin festival. You can see the city all decked out and enjoy some great pumpkin pie!"

"I'll be sure to come. Anyway, I'm off—time is money, after all."

I left the town hall and checked the game time. The old dog would be fishing for another hour and a half. I decided to forget him and his abilities for the time being and headed toward the city gate, reminding myself as I went that I needed to find a headstone to link to.

The forest, in good Fayroll form, began immediately after you left the city limits. I pulled up my map to see where the two thieves were. It turned out, they weren't that far, and they were also somewhat on the way to the herbalist described by the mayor. I turned left after walking out of the gate. Ten minutes later, I reached the grove he'd mentioned, walked through it, and saw the clearing.

I paused to figure out where I should go first—right to visit those two social outcasts or straight to start with the herbalist. Dealing with the ruffians was probably simpler, I reasoned, given the fact that I was sure the herbalist would just send me off somewhere else. The two brothers were the end of the line, and the outcome was straightforward: either I'd end them, or they'd end me. I turned right. From the map, it looked like their forest home was just another ten minutes' walk away.

I was right on the money. Ten minutes later I found them, though, to be fair, I'd started hearing them much sooner. Apparently, they were drunkards in addition to being ruffians and thieves. Their songs rang through the forest.

"*I can tell a goblin by its ga-a-ait!*"

"*He carries, carries arrows to the si-i-ide!*"

"No, no, no, Billy." Another inebriated voice interrupted the vocalist. "This is better."

"*The forest, the woods, the wooded plains,*

Orcs in a line marching off to the wars!"
The two voices then joined in chorus.
"A-a-a-a-ah!"
The Alexandrov Sing and Wail Choir, I thought to myself as I walked into a small clearing that featured...I don't know...I guess you could call it a structure. It was something between a hut and a hovel. Near it, sat two heavily boozed-up and incredibly ragged brothers singing arm in arm. They occasionally passed an enormous bottle filled with an awfully muddy-looking liquid between them.

I called out a greeting. "Hi, there, outcasts!"

"And you be well, too." The one to my left looked at me with bleary eyes that had no idea what was going on.

"I need to talk to you."

"Talk away," said the second burglar.

"Did you steal the water monster statue?" I decided to cut right to the chase.

"And what if we did?"

"Then you need to give it back. People are worried."

"Who cares about people?" The one on the left spat. "Right, Billy?"

"Right, Teddy. Screw them!"

"Guys," I said, trying to get through to their digital brains, "I don't want to hurt you. Just go ahead and give it to me."

Before I could even finish talking, the two blockheads were rolling on the grass laughing.

"Hurt us?" Billy guffawed, holding his stomach with one hand and pointing a dirty finger at me with the other.

"O-o-ooh!" Teddy was still rolling on the ground. "I'm dying!"

"Okay, boys. You have one minute. If you don't give me the statue, I'm going to start knocking you around." I pulled out my broadsword.

The laughter ceased. Both brothers looked at each other before running into the shack behind them. They returned with hefty clubs in their hands.

"Well, my friend, you brought this on yourself," said Teddy.

The two began to circle me from either side.

"So you aren't that drunk after all," I noted, taking three steps backward and holding my shield up to my chest.

"Nope. It's just that we're never sober, so this is how we always are," Billy said, stalking cat-like around the grass to my left.

I'd better attack, I realized. Waiting any longer would leave me caught between them.

I rolled to my right and just had time to see the surprise in Ted's eyes when I half stood and drove my broadsword into his ample midsection. Then I yanked him to the right, shouting the first of my abilities. "Bloodletting!"

I slid my sword out of him, moved to my left, and turned. I crouched behind my shield, just in time. While Teddy looked with wonder at the gaping wound in his stomach and the insides pouring out of it (somehow, while there was no blood, it was okay to show intestines), Billy raised his club, bellowed a war cry, and ran at me.

"A-a-a-ah!"

I took the blow on my shield, realized how strong he was by how my arm went limp from the force, and let his club slide off my shield to the right. I slashed him across the chest, and he staggered backward, giving me an opening to run his stomach through—brothers should share everything equally—using Sword of Retribution. Billy collapsed to his knees, his health bar sliding into the red zone.

I looked back at Teddy, who was unsteadily walking toward me, his club in one hand. The other held the contents of his stomach in place. Before he could get to me, he also fell to his knees with a whisper. "Don't kill us! Don't kill us, okay? We'll give you everything."

"I'll take it myself," I said, and cut through his neck.

"Teddy!" hissed Billy, who looked at me. "Curse you! You killed us."

"No, you killed yourselves," I answered, finishing the job.

Rummaging through the two corpses got me nothing more than a few dozen silver coins. The brothers were anything but wealthy. The statue, however, was nowhere to be found. I realized I'd have to check out their shack, something I did not want to do in the least.

There in the corner, buried in a pile of trash, was the statue of the water monster. Just as I'd suspected, many years ago, three valiant families had vanquished some unfortunate seal.

You completed a quest: Symbol of Renown.
To get your reward, return the status to the mayor of Mettan.
Reward:
600 experience
10% to your reputation in Mettan
Additional reward: Discounted passage on the Firefly

As I dug through the garbage, I found an unsurprisingly filthy scrap of paper with something written on it. There was even some kind of map. I held it up to read the writing.

Teddy, bring the supplies to our new camp. Here's the map.

A "new camp"? Where was the old one? And who was "our"?

You have a new quest offer: Thieves' Map.
Task: Show the map to the port master.
Reward:
200 experience
Additional: You can get an additional quest when you complete this one.
Accept?

Ah-ha—it was a starter quest. That made sense.
I accepted the quest and stopped to think about where I should go next. I looked up at the sky. About an hour and a half had passed since my conversation with the instructor.

I'll head to the city, I decided. *The herbalist isn't going anywhere.*

One clearing and one grove later, I was back in town. I decided to start with the mayor.

He drooped when he saw me. "Couldn't find it?"

I silently placed the statue on the table.

"There it is!" he gasped happily. "Exactly!"

He grabbed it and clasped it to his chest.

You completed a quest: Symbol of Renown.

Reward:

600 experience

10% to your reputation in Mettan

Additional reward: Discounted passage on the Firefly (speak with the port master to get your additional reward).

"Don't forget to go see Holgerrson," I reminded the mayor, "to make sure he gives me that discount."

"Don't worry," he said reassuringly. "You'll get it. Just come talk to me if you need anything, and don't be a stranger!"

"I won't," I said and left to go find the instructor.

***

I pushed open the familiar gate and saw a familiar girl named Adele.

"Hi, again. Has your grandfather come back?"

"You pr-r-romised me a lollipop. R-r-remember?"

"Of course. Here it is." I held out the candy—a rooster on a stick—to the girl.

"Fanks," she said, having already stuffed it into her mouth.

"So where's your grandfather?"

"Gra-a-a-andpa!" Her scream was right next to my ear and so loud that I jumped back automatically. "Ther-r-re's someone her-r-re to see you!"

"Someone who?" The bearded man peeked out of the house. "Oh, it's you," he said, immediately recognizing me. "So what do you need?"

"Abilities," I answered truthfully. "You're the instructor, right?"

"He gave me a lollipop!" Adele announced to her grandfather. "Pear-r-r!"

The instructor's face warmed.

"Well, come on in. I'm certainly not going to teach you out there." He swung the door wide and stepped aside.

"Who else have you talked to?" he asked me.

"The instructor in Aegan and Serhio in Fladridge."

"The old rogue's still alive." The instructor's face creased happily, and I could tell the two were old friends.

"Sure is. Spends his time making kites. Do you know each other?"

"We fought together at Krakatuka...but that's not important. So what would you like?"

"I'd really like some new abilities," I said with some surprise. *What else could he give me?*

"I can tell you're a good kid, so I'll be up front about absolutely everything I can teach you. Then you can decide what you want. Okay?"

"Perfect."

"I have two combat abilities: Wind Power and In Passing. Wind Power is for when you want to knock your opponent back a couple steps and give yourself time to regroup."

"You knock them back with your shield?"

"No, you use your shoulder or your torso. The ability for your shield is different; you do damage in addition to knocking them backward. This one just pushes them back. And now, In Passing. Learning it gives you the chance to do serious damage even if you just barely nick your opponent with your blade."

"A good chance?"

"Well...40 percent or so."

"Okay, so that's two. What other pairs do you have?"

"I also have non-combat abilities. They're very helpful, though. One is passive, meaning it's always there for you and doesn't need to be activated. It's called Last Chance. When you're almost dead, it kicks in by itself to get you back to half health over the course of thirty seconds."

"That sounds great. And the other one?"

"Wake Up. You get 400 health when you use it. What do you want?"

"Can I take a minute to think about it?"

"Yes, of course. We're talking abilities here. You can always find another wife, for example, but you can't just go back and pick a different ability."

I stood there, lost in thought. Last Chance was a must-have, that much was certain. Those thirty seconds would save my life many times over. Plus, it was activated automatically. Like a notification. But the second one...

Wind Power—not bad, not bad. It didn't do any damage, but it gave you time to re-grip your sword and get your shield situated the way it should be. The few seconds would be priceless.

In Passing—a 40 percent chance of doing critical damage... Also intriguing...especially when paired with Bloodletting.

Wake Up—I had 1,700 health at the moment, having started with 150 and gained 50 with each new level. Wake Up's 400 health would be a big boost.

So what do I want?

"Okay, gramps, I'm ready." I turned to the instructor.

"Well? What do you want?" He looked back at me inquisitively.

"Last Chance and In Passing."

"Good choice," he said approvingly. "That'll be 100 gold."

"Oh, wow, you aren't cheap," I said with eyes wide open.

"What did you expect? I'm not just giving you some *thing*; I'm giving you the chance to live longer. Do you have any idea how many times what I'm teaching you will save your life? Me neither. So... I mean, if you don't want the abilities, you don't have to take them."

"Of course, I know all that. I'm not arguing with you."

I gave him the gold I got from Reineke.

You learned a new active ability: In Passing, Level 1

Gives you a 40% chance of doing serious damage to your opponent even with a weak or glancing blow.

Activation cost: 45 mana

Note: Using this ability frequently and effectively can give you a better chance of doing damage.

Recharge time: 50 seconds

And then the next notification popped up.

You learned a new passive ability: Last Chance, Level 1

Activates when you have 5% or less health left and restores 50% of your health over the course of 30 seconds.

Activates automatically.

"Thanks, pops," I said to the instructor.

"No problem. Just remember—don't hurry into battle, but don't ever freeze either. You'll miss your chance if you hurry, and you're dead if you ever stop moving."

"Basically, hurry unhurriedly."

"Exactly." He nodded his head in affirmation. "Okay, see you later then. I'm off to feed my granddaughter dinner."

With that, he respectfully, if insistently, pushed me out the door. *Fayroll hospitality at its finest. He could have fed me dinner, too, or at least have offered...*

I wasn't getting fed, so I headed off to go see the port master. Buckets and brass tacks! Something like that.

There was no sense in knocking. Holgerrson couldn't care less about etiquette and cared even less about me.

"Oh, it's you!" the one-legged seaman bellowed. "What do you need? Did you find Gul? Broadsides and bulkheads!"

"No, not yet. I found something else, though, after I met the Thatchers, brothers from around here."

I handed the sea dog the note and map I found in the dead bandits' den. Holgerrson took it, sniffed, and started to read. It took him more than a minute and a half, which I found fairly odd for a note with less than ten words. He then took even longer to study the map just as thoughtfully. Then he looked at me.

"Quite the interesting little paper you brought me, brandy and bullfrogs."

You completed a quest: Thieves' Map.

Reward:

200 experience

"What's so interesting?" I asked. "It's just a piece of paper, and there's not much to the text."

"No, not much," he answered. "Still, this is quite the little thing. Sit down already—you won't find the truth in your legs."

He motioned at a chair.

"There's no such thing," I said, sitting down. "I've never seen it, at least."

"Doesn't matter." Holgerrson waved his hand. "No sense arguing over the truth. But this note, on the other hand... We've had someone mucking things up on the river the last few months."

"Mucking things up?"

"Someone's out there pirating ships. They attack, send the crew overboard, and take the cargo. Then they bore holes in the ships and send them to the bottom."

"Oh, wow. Some bad guys for sure."

"Yep. But here's what's strange: they only attack ships with small crews and large cargos. And they always know ahead of time. A couple times, we've sent out trap ships loaded with the Royal Guard instead of cargo, and nobody's ever attacked them. That means—"

"You have a rat," I broke in with the tone of an expert. "They're passing information on to the pirates about the ships that are coming and going. And it has to be someone local."

"That's what I'm thinking, too. In fact, I'd say I'm positive. A little while back, I started to suspect those flesh-eating Thatchers. They were always the poorest of the poor, but then suddenly they came into some money."

"Sure sounds suspicious to me."

"Exactly. Okay, bring those little squids over here so we can interrogate them. Where are they now?"

"Um-m, that's going to be a bit difficult. I left them in the clearing."

"What do you mean, difficult? What clearing?"

"Just that. I left them in the forest clearing. Dead. Long story short, I killed them. Completely."

"Whew boy. Not that I care—dogs deserve a dog's death. I'd have killed them myself when we were done. But that way, we'd have been able to find everything out from them. Now, though..."

Holgerrson looked at the map one more time.

"Hey, why don't you head over there? Judging by the map, it isn't far. You can do it—you're smart, and you like taking risks. And I'd give you something nice in return, buccaneers and booty. Over there—I'd give you a cutlass from my collection," he said, pointing to a wall that was covered in different kinds of cutlasses.

You have a new quest offer: Quieter than Grass.

Task: Scout out the pirates' lair and see how many there are.

Reward:

400 experience

Additional reward: A cutlass from Neils Holgerrson's collection.

Accept?

"Done," I said. *And why not? It was a piece of cake, and, even if I couldn't get there by road, it still wasn't that far. Like Mark Twain said, "Hurry to do good deeds, especially when they aren't a threat to your wallet."*

Chapter Twenty-One
On the Shores of the Great River (Part Two)

I left the city gate, confidently headed toward the clearing, having decided to start with a visit to the herbalist. That was my primary quest at the moment, after all. I wasn't sure I'd end up taking a boat down the river, but who knew where the rich tapestry of life would lead? All I could do was work on the quests that cost the least and earned the most. And I was set up to save quite a bit on the river passage. Plodding along from city to city would take forever. Plus, I just wasn't in the mood...

As I walked, I thought back to the old instructor and wondered if I'd picked the right abilities. My conclusion was that I had. Last Chance was a passive ability, meaning that I didn't have to worry about it kicking in when it was most needed. I'd have the opportunity to come back from the dead, so to speak. As far as In Passing was concerned, my logic was simple. Thanks to what I was carrying, the 40 percent chance of landing a critical hit gave me the same chance of getting more health from my opponents, and that was highly valuable.

The other two abilities weren't quite as effective. Wind Power didn't do any damage whatsoever. Wake Up was very tempting for the time being, but it wouldn't amount to much later on. What was 400 health at, for example, Level 60? At that point, I'd have 3000 basic health, not to mention what my inventory would add. I figured I'd made the right decision.

By the time I'd run through all that in my head, I had made it through the grove I'd grown to know so well, crossed the clearing, and walked out onto an enormous field with an enormous tree in it. Under the tree was a neat little house with black smoke wisping out of the chimney.

"Looks like she's brewing a potion," I said aloud as I walked toward the front door.

There wasn't a fence of any kind. Instead, there was a small yard with chickens and ducks running around a cooking stand set on a tripod. I was obviously where I was supposed to be.

I walked up onto a small porch and knocked on the door.

"Who is it?" asked a deep, but lovely voice. Well, perhaps not girlish; maybe even womanly. As we all know, there are two things about women that don't change with time: their voice and their earlobes. Therefore, I had no way of knowing how old the girl or woman behind the door was, though, given her profession and the timbre of her voice, I pictured a tall, slender, red-haired beauty with green eyes. She had pearly teeth and dimpled cheeks, and she was wearing well-fitting clothes that showed off every curve of her body.

"A wanderer," I answered.

"Hold on, I'll be right there." The voice added emotion to become even richer. It appeared travelers were welcomed and respected at this home. The mayor had been awfully critical, but there was nothing wrong with her at all.

The door swung wide with a creak of its hinges. On the threshold, stood a young lady who looked nothing like what I'd imagined. She was a girl, young and tiny, with fairly sharp, even coarse facial features. She was wearing a man's shirt and woven pants, I couldn't tell what color her eyes were, and she had a wet, mousy ponytail tied back with a colored thread.

"You aren't a wanderer," she said somewhat nervously as she looked me in the eye. "I don't know you. Who are you? Where's the wanderer?"

"That's me," I said. "I walk around cities and villages looking for people to help."

The girl smiled. "Got it. And here I was wondering what you meant. What do you need?"

"Nothing much, really. Mayor Glopkins said that you were the last one to see Captain Gul and his sailors. I'm looking for them. So, Marion, is it true that you saw them?"

"You know my name? Have we met before?" The girl looked closely at me.

"No, the mayor told me about you. That's how I know. So, what about the captain?"

"Oh, the fine captain and his people. Yes, they were here." She laughed, and it struck me that there was something off about her laugh.

"Where did they go?"

"Into the forest. And don't look for them—you won't find them."

"What do you mean?" I liked this conversation less and less.

"Rarely do you find the people I send into the forest."

"So why did you send the sea wolves there?"

The girl grinned, baring her small, sharp teeth. "That's just how it happened. Your fine young men somehow concluded that I needed some male companionship and decided to solve my loneliness by all joining me here at once."

"Sure sounds like sailors," I said. "Straight and to the point. Heave ho, and all."

"I don't know what 'heave ho' means, but I'd have been in a pickle if I hadn't thrown some Livitsitis Tsulendarius powder at them." The herbalist's smile was more reminiscent of a snarl.

"What kind of powder?"

"Just a normal magic powder. If you smell it, you think you hear voices calling you."

"Calling you where?"

"Just calling you. 'Come here,' 'Hurry over.' The voice is sensual and usually belongs to the opposite gender."

"Got it. So did they follow it?" The whole situation was starting to go south.

"Of course. What else could they do?"

"All four of them?"

"Certainly, and each in separate directions. The captain, for example, went that way." The little herbalist's finger pointed in the direction of some spruces growing on the edge of the field behind the house.

"Phew boy." I scratched the nape of my neck. "This isn't good."

"Are you going go to find them?" Her eyes met mine.

"There's nothing else for it. I promised the port master." I nodded. "Why? Do you need something?"

"What do you think a herbalist would need?" Marion smiled, this time normally. "You can gather herbs for me. If you do that, I'll tell you where your sailors might be. Well, that is, if they're still alive."

You have a new quest offer: Herbs for Marion.
Task: Collect herbs for Marion.
Royal hawthorn - 5 branches
Montevina celeia - 5 buds
Black crabon - 1 ovary
Reward:
500 experience
Strength potion (variable)
+10% to your reputation with Marion
Accept?

So that reputation bump came with the quest. I'd have never agreed to collect herbs except that I desperately needed that little monster to like me. A better reputation meant a chance at her telling me where the poor sailors were exactly.

"Certainly, I'll go get everything for you," I said.

"Be careful," she said almost amiably. "The celeia and hawthorn are easy to find since they grow pretty much everywhere, but the crabon is a much rarer plant. The undead like hanging around them, too, since they say a crabon ovary once gave life to a lich. Those walkers don't have any brains, though their instincts are much better. They even have some of their memories still. So be careful when you're looking for the crabon. Remember, you can only find it around ruins, and the only ruins in these parts are near the old pond."

"What's by the old pond?" I asked to clarify.

"There used to be a castle there belonging to one of our first landlords, but he was killed, and his castle was torn down. He was tortured for a while before he was killed, and they say he still comes back to his castle, or rather what remains of it, because of that. If he finds anyone there alive, he does what he used to do back when he was the landlord."

"What does he do?" I knew the answer but asked anyway.

"Judge, jury, and executioner," the herbalist answered casually. "All in one."

I pulled up my map. The first two herbs were everywhere. The crabon, on the other hand, was about three leagues away, near a place with the poetic name of Ainville. Happily, it was a stone's throw away from the pirates' lair.

"You're talking about Ainville, right?"

"Yes. Be careful."

"All right, I'm off," I said to the herbalist. "I should be back soon."

"Maybe, maybe not," she answered calmly. "The forest only appears safe; it really isn't. Anyway, give it a try. If you're lucky, we'll see each other again."

I trudged into the spruce grove and started walking in the direction of the old pond.

A couple minutes later, I noticed a bush right ahead of me that shimmered all the different colors of the rainbow. I almost logged out of the game, thinking it was telling me I was tired and couldn't think straight but I realized that the shimmering bushes were the ones I needed to collect.

I walked over to the bush, crouched down next to it, and looked at it closely. One branch was obviously shining brighter than the rest, so I reached out and broke it off.

You found an object for the Herbs for Marion quest.
Royal hawthorn - 1 branch. You need to find 4 more.

Got it. So this is what it's like to care about preserving nature— break off four more branches.

I walked around the forest craning my neck to find more of the colorful glimmers. Ultimately, by the time I got to Ainville, I'd broken off three more branches and found three buds—tough berry bushes that looked like...how can I describe them? Something like chokeberries.

The spruce forest ended, and right beyond it, I saw ruins on the bank of a small pond covered in duckweed and surrounded by bushes. The spot had clearly been a small fortified manor once, though it was now nothing more than a collection of picturesque rubble. One of the boulders somehow stood out from the rest, so I squinted to see it better. Yep. Something shimmered on it. Definitely crabon. I walked out of the forest and toward the ruins.

As I got closer and walked into the small square in the center, I had a chance to look over the rubble once more and realized I'd have to do some climbing. The boulders hadn't looked so big from the forest. Luckily, time and rain had eaten away at them to create footholds I could use to climb.

I spat on my hands and started up the boulder with the crabon. It was enormous, its top something like two or three stories high. At some point, it must have been part of the castle's foundations. Maybe it hadn't been so small after all.

I'm getting too old for this, I thought as I clambered higher up the rough, sun-warmed side of the boulder. There wasn't much to hold onto closer to the top, and I started getting some butterflies in my stomach. There was no one around to collect my bones if I fell.

I finally got to the top and pulled myself up one onto a fairly large, flat area, where I sat down, panting hard.

"This is what mountain-climbers do all day long?" I asked no one in particular.

I looked around and noticed the plant I was there to find. It was a small bush covered in berries and some kind of pods. One of the pods shone brighter than the rest, so I quickly plucked it.

You found an object for the Herbs for Marion quest.

Black crabon - 1 ovary.

Note: This plant is highly magical so your decision to harvest it may have unpredictable consequences.

"Wow, a little scarlet flower right here in my hand. Now some kind of hideous monster is going to crawl out." I chuckled, preparing to climb back down. Before doing so, however, I looked down at the ground, which was pretty far away from where I was, and froze.

The courtyard was surrounded by a circle of boulders and had been empty five minutes before. Now, a hefty skeleton paced around with a sword in one hand and a dagger in the other. In contrast to all of the other skeletons I had seen in the game and their naked bones, this one was dressed. On his head was a crown, on his left leg was a knee pad, and he had a bright blue belt with gold embroidery tied around his waist.

"Where are you off to, looking so fine?" I asked him with surprise. "Going out clubbing?"

That probably wasn't the smartest question to ask, but I really was stunned. *Where could he have come from?* Then things got even curiouser. He stopped, turned his skull in my direction, and looked at me with the dark blue balls of lightning in his eye sockets.

"The flower. You picked my flower," he rasped in a mechanical voice.

"So what?" I responded, picking my own jaw up off the top of the boulder. *What did you expect? Some kind of skeleton came out of nowhere and started talking. How was that possible without a tongue?*

"Give me the flower, climb down here, kneel before me, and prepare to receive your sentence," the resurrected dead man continued.

"But what's the sentence? For example, if I'm supposed to give you my youngest daughter, I'll have to turn you down. I don't have a youngest daughter. I don't have an oldest daughter either. I'm not even married," I told the skeleton.

"Your sentence will be just and swift. I, the lord of these lands, don't have time to give every thief a long trial."

Now, everything made sense. I'd picked the crabon ovary and triggered the quest mechanism. The herbalist had mentioned how the dead like to hang out around the flower, and the fellow in the crown was the dead landlord. As I'd been told, he played judge and executioner for his lawful lands. Wow, for a second, I was actually scared.

"I don't need your daughters. Come here and accept the punishment for stealing in my castle," the landlord continued drolly.

"Why just me? What about the rain that washed away the foundation of your castle, the birds that pooped on it, and the bugs that crawl all over it…"

"Are you coming down or not?" The skeleton's voice betrayed his annoyance.

"No."

"What right do you have not to submit to my will?" He was really getting angry. "I am the lord of these lands, and all living and unliving creatures must bow to me!"

"But not me. I'm a free man, and I don't bow to anyone."

The skeleton ran a lap around the courtyard before again stopping to stare up at me.

"So what's the plan?" I looked at him amiably. "If I'm not coming down to you, why don't you come up to me? It's great up here! The sun, the breeze..."

"Come down on your own," the skeleton hissed, "or else."

"Or else what?"

"Come down!" The skeleton stomped his foot, which made the knee pad slide down to his shin. He pulled it back up like a woman pulling on a stocking, and I broke out laughing.

He kept going, which I found even funnier. "I don't see anything funny!"

I rolled around, holding onto the top of the boulder with two hands to make sure I didn't fall off. The skeleton stared at me, utterly clueless as to why I was laughing at him instead of being afraid. He scratched the back of his vertebrae, which pushed his crown down onto his forehead. That made me laugh even harder, and I started to worry that I might slip into hysterics.

"Stop, please, don't do anything else," I choked out between shrieks of mirth. "I don't want to die of laughter up here!"

"Are you coming down?" the skeleton asked trustingly and hopefully.

"Yes, yes, I'm coming," I answered. "Just stand there quietly for a few minutes without doing anything. I'm begging you. Please!"

"Don't give me orders, commoner!" He shook his head, which sent his crown back down onto his forehead and sent me back into fits of laughter.

"What's with these people?" The skeleton was indignant. "The landlord gives them an order, and they just laugh. You come down here!"

"I'm coming already," I told him, wiping away tears, and started down.

Going down was much easier than coming up, and soon I was on the ground. I shook myself off and looked at the skeleton, who stood ten strides away from me.

"Well, what did you want? Here I am."

"Come closer and get down on your knees," he said grandly, pointing at the ground in front of him with the point of his somewhat rusty sword. That was apparently where I was supposed to kneel and, presumably, lose my head.

"No, thank you." I waved my arms. "I'm too lazy, for starters, and I'll get dirty. I just won't, basically."

The skeleton lowered his arms. "What do you mean, you won't? By what right?"

"No right in particular," I said. "I just don't want to."

The skeleton tramped in place, as the situation was clearly not one his creators had designed him for. I highly doubted that any other players had knelt down as he ordered, but figured that they'd all probably just run at him waving their weapons instead. That's what he was coded to deal with. But conversations were not in his arsenal.

"How are you doing, by the way?" I decided to finish the job. "How are things? Your joints, they don't creak too much? Does the weather bother you?"

The skeleton stopped tramping and looked at me again. "Maybe you can just kneel down?" he said tentatively. "It's the way things are done..."

"What way are you talking about?" I asked. "I'm a citizen of a different country, so I'm not under your jurisdiction. Your complaints are completely unfounded."

"But, did you pick the flower?" the skeleton asked litigiously. "It grows in my lands!"

"Where is that written?"

"It doesn't need to be written anywhere; everyone knows that!" The skeleton threw up his arms.

"Right, so all of Fayroll knows that the sovereign of a pile of stones and one flower is a skeleton."

"Landlord Drauh!" he clarified grumpily.

You unlocked Names of Evil, Level 1.

To get it, convince 9 more representatives of Evil to tell you their names voluntarily.

Reward:

Seeker, a passive ability, Level 1: 0.5% to your chances of unlocking hidden quests by understanding the importance of objects

Title: Unmasker

To see similar messages, go to the Action section of the attribute window.

"Okay then, Landlord Drauh," I said, very pleased with myself. Getting an action out of nowhere was always nice. It was like finding 100 rubles—it isn't much, but for the rest of the day you're in a great mood.

This really is pretty funny, I thought. *A person standing here arguing about something with a skeleton. If I happened across this situation, I'd definitely think about drinking less. Seriously...*

"Fine!" The skeleton assumed a battle stance. "I'll ask you for the last time, will you accept my harsh, if fair, judgment of your own free will?"

"I'd rather not," I said, slinging my shield onto my arm and pulling out my sword. "I question its competence and impartiality. Though, I don't doubt there will be a sentencing."

"Correct." The skeleton ground forward and brought his sword down on me from above. I caught it with my own sword. At the same time, he tried to get under my shield with his dagger but failed there as well.

I knocked his sword away and took a couple steps backward. The dead landlord stuck his sword and dagger out in front of him and inched toward me.

"You, Comrade Landlord, are as petty as you are vindictive," I said, keeping my eye fixed on him.

"Well, I have to keep an eye on you living folk constantly. Turn your back for a second, and you'll tear up anything—flowers, stones—that isn't nailed down."

"Oh, come on. Why do you need all this? You're dead!"

"So? It's still mine. A-a-ah!"

He sprang at me again. This time he wasn't so lucky, as I pricked his right side with the point of my sword after knocking away his blow. Or was it his bone? Anyway, I got his right side, also taking the time to shout "In Passing!" The strike went straight through, though I couldn't tell if the ability added force. One way or another, it didn't look like his health dropped by that much.

We traded a few more blows, though this time, I missed my chance and he grazed me with his dagger. Then, after another series of attacks, I broke through his defense with Bloodletting. I thought that was odd. *What blood did a skeleton have to let?* We kept fighting.

"That's it, mortal, I'm tired of you! It's time for you to die!" He tried once more to break down my defenses with the same move he'd been using. This time, I caught his sword with my sword, as usual, but I brought my shield down on his dagger. My trick was successful, and the dagger clattered out of his hand. I immediately brought my shield back up to crunch against his jaw, landing blow after blow to push him back from where the dagger was laying. The skeleton tried to parry my strikes, but a few still landed. Then I saw my opening.

"Sword of Retribution!" I thrust straight through his ribcage.

The skeleton's health dropped lower than low; I couldn't even see the red. I decided to strike while the iron was hot and raised my sword to finish him off.

"Wait, mortal," the skeleton mumbled. "Maybe we could come to an agreement?"

"About what?"

"Well, I could tell you where I hid my treasure. Or share a secret with you!"

"What secret?" I was intrigued and let me sword drop.

"I didn't become this way on my own. I was made undead by a powerful witch named..."

The skeleton's jaw dropped away from his skull. His bones collapsed in a pile. Damn it. Bloodletting killed him! Apparently, the bony fellow had a quest, and probably a big one. Damn.

I rummaged through the landlord's temporal remains to find a few gold coins, some bones, a rusty sword that wasn't even blue, and... *What is that?"*

Dead Landlord's Crown
Quest item
It cannot be stolen, lost, or broken.
It can be sold or given away.
It is not lost when the owner dies.

Huh. So, the crown has a quest, too. What a doubly interesting undead fellow. It's a shame I didn't get anything good from him. Where's the kneepad? The belt? At least I have the crown—maybe somebody will give me a quest for it, or I'll come across it later.

I pulled up my map and looked to see how far it was to the pirates' lair. It turned out to be less than a ten-minute stroll away by my estimation, so I set off briskly in that direction.

My stride was steady, I wasn't afraid of anything, and I didn't even stop to take more care when I heard voices up ahead. I was king of the world.

"Well, look at this, brothers, who do we have here?" A bearded pirate stepped out from behind some bushes to my right.

"Probably some idiot from the Royal Guard," said a second pirate, this one pushing out of the bushes on my left.

"Oh, stop it, Gromio," said a half-elf with a bow on his shoulder who slid down out of a tree right in front of me. "What Royal Guard? Didn't you hear him traipsing through the forest? How did you miss the crashing and cracking? He's just an idiot in the wrong place at the wrong time. And it'll cost him his life."

That was a lesson for me—no more thinking I was king of the world. I did have one option left, and I hoped it would work.

The pirates with their knives circled me on either side. The half-elf started taking his bow off his shoulder.

"You have thirty seconds at most," I said to myself before turning around and sprinting back in the direction I'd come from. I didn't get very far before the eighth arrow killed me; not more than 500 meters. The half-elf fired quickly and accurately.

The world around me spun in circles, and I found myself back in Mettan—in my underwear. There was some kind of person sitting next to the headstone. He was smoking and apparently contemplating eternity.

"PKers?" he asked me philosophically as he looked me up and down.

"Bots," I answered succinctly.

"It happens." The soulless smoker continued smoking his pipe.

I quickly ran over to the hotel more than in a hurry. The girl behind the counter jumped and stared at me when I dashed in. *What would you have done if someone in their underwear ran in yelling something?*

I barked an order. "Give me the key!"

"Here, room number nine," stammered the brown-haired beauty named…What was it? Jacqueline!

"Thanks!" And off I ran up the stairs.

Once in my room, I grabbed one of the sets of clothing and a mace Fat Willie gave me way back when then sprinted back down the stairs.

"You're leaving already?" The squeak in Jacqueline's voice told me that she was really scared by this time.

"Things to do, my dear!" I yelled back over my shoulder.

I flew out the city gates and dashed along a path I'd come to know so well, just at a speed I was less accustomed to. I ran without caring about the branches lashing my face. Did I have a choice? I had to get there before some adventurer did, or all my beautiful possessions would be crying hot tears of anguish without me. Not all of them, of course, as I still had the ring with me, but everything else…

If I'd tried to run that far in real life, I'd have probably died. In the game, however, I was fine. Not far from my destination, I stopped and crept forward more cautiously. I moved from tree to tree, getting closer to where I figured my things were laying.

When I saw the half-elf just before I died, I realized immediately that I was screwed. If they killed me right there, what I had with me would probably be lost. The NPCs wouldn't take them, but sooner or later some other player would come, kill the trio, and get what I'd left. I decided to run as far as I could, realizing that I'd have a chance to come back when the gang went back to their camp. I didn't get far, but still...

My things were laying on the grass. Oddly enough, that was the first time I'd seen what the remains of a dead player looked like. There was a transparent cocoon with all my possessions inside it like some kind of suitcase. I laid prone on the grass and crawled forward, doing my best to not make a sound and expecting to be hit with an arrow at any second.

When I got to the cocoon, I poked it with my finger and saw my things fall out on the grass—noiselessly, thank God. I quickly and quietly stuffed it all in my sack before crawling back where I came from. Five hundred meters later, I crouched and continued on just as quietly until I got to the ruins at Ainville, where I changed, sat down behind a rock, and thought about what to do next. I certainly didn't want to give up on the quest, since I wouldn't get the cutlass if I did. And, judging by the fact that it was a tough quest, I figured the cutlass would be pretty good or at least unusual. But I also didn't want to just keep dying time after time.

I opened my map, scrolled over to the red area, and took a closer look at it. On one side, I noticed a marsh.

"Oh, that's good," I said aloud. "That's very good. Well, it's wet, dirty, and putrid, but it's also good."

I figured the devious pirates probably set guards on all the roads, but they very well may not have had anyone watching the marsh. Maybe that was the way to go? I certainly didn't want to, but I was beyond that at that point. First, however, I had to finish things up with the herbalist. I checked to see what else I needed to find and set out to look for it.

A half-hour later, I was knocking on Marion's door.

"Oh, wanderer," she said with an odd smile. "Did you find the plants?"

"Sure did," I said. "Here they are."

Surprise flashed across the herbalist's eyes. "And the black crabon?"

"That, too. It wasn't easy, as I came across someone there, but we hammered out our differences, and he gave me the plant."

"You fought the landlord?" Marion asked incredulously. I nodded. "And killed him."

"Wow. Well, give me the herbs." She reached out her hand.

You completed a quest: Herbs for Marion.
Task: Collect herbs for Marion.
Reward:
500 experience
+10% to your reputation with Marion

"That reward is too small for someone who killed the landlord," the herbalist said. "I'd like to give you one of my most powerful potions, though you need to decide which one you want. Let's take a walk around the house."

Yet another choice; I went along behind her to see what she'd offer.

We walked over to a sideboard standing in the corner, and Marion pulled out a sling equipped to hold five beakers already in their holders and a lone flask with a bright scarlet-colored liquid in it.

"See for yourself, warrior. Here," she said, giving the belt a shake, "are five strength potions. They give you another quarter of your normal strength for an hour when you drink them."

"And the sling?" I asked.

Marion nodded and continued, showing me a flask with a blue liquid.

"This is a potion, also for strength, only it gives you a permanent boost. Unfortunately, I don't know how much the boost is. I'm sorry. It could double your strength, or it could barely move the needle. Pick which one you want."

I didn't even need to take time to think.

"The one that's permanent, of course."

Marion raised her eyebrows. "If you don't mind me asking, why is that?"

"It's not a secret. I'll go through five potions quickly, no matter how good they are. This one, however, will stay with me forever.

Even if it gives me just one point, I can keep that point. You have lots of strength over there, but it's borrowed."

"Good choice, warrior. I think you're right. Here."

The herbalist handed me the flask, and I quickly drank it.

You drank Strong as a Bear, a rare potion, and gained 8 strength.

"Well, happy?" Marion smiled at me.

"Thank you," I said with a bow. "That wasn't a potion; it was a dream come true. Oh, don't forget that you promised to tell me about the captain."

"Everyone who wanders off into the forest without their memory sooner or later finds themselves in the marsh with the vilas. Look for your friends there."

"Vilas?"

"The materialized souls of girls unlucky enough to die of true love. They aren't aggressive, but be very careful about making them angry."

"I'm already afraid of them. Are you talking about the marsh over there?" I waved in the direction of the marsh I was headed to next.

Marion nodded her head. "Yes."

"Got it. All right, I'm off. Thank you."

"And thank you, too. Mm…wanderer. Oh, wait!"

I turned. "What?"

"Did you find anything when you killed the landlord? Maybe a symbol of power?" There was a strange ring to her voice.

"His crown. Why?"

"Nothing, don't worry about it. Take care of yourself."

Marion, clearly turning something over in her mind, went back inside and closed the door.

"Interesting…weird." I shook my head, checked the map, and walked off toward the marsh.

Chapter Twenty-Two
Vilas

There wasn't really anything to say about the marsh. A marsh is a marsh. Some kind of annoying insect buzzed around incessantly, gasses bubbled and stank, and snakes occasionally slithered by, drawing lines in the muddy water. A nasty place.

I pulled up my map every minute or two to make sure I didn't miss the place I figured the pirates' camp would be. At the same time, I kept my head on a swivel looking for the vilas whose voluptuousness took out Captain Gul and his sailors. I wondered what they looked like...

A few seconds later, my question was answered. A slender womanly figure with blonde curls, flowing clothes, and wings on her back sprang out from under my feet.

"Whoa!" I lost my footing and fell backward into the water.

Laughter rang out as the flying beauty soared over the top of me. "You're so fu-u-unny!" Her sonorous voice giggled, and her wings flapped, drawing out the sound.

"I'm wet and dirty," I muttered. "And all thanks to you. What did you have to jump up from under me like that for?"

"It's fun!" The hovering girl's nose scrunched up. "Where are you going?"

"I'm looking for some friends of mine," I said. "A brave captain and three sailors. Have you seen them?"

"A captain and three sailors? Well...what if I have?" The adorable girl again scrunched up her nose.

"Would you mind telling me where?" I asked smoothly.

"What's in it for me?"

"What would you like?"

"Oh, I don't know." The vila thoughtfully twirled one of her curls. "Maybe you'll marry me?"

"Doubtful," I said with a cough.

"Why? Am I ugly?" A change came over the vila's eyes. While they were blue, to begin with, crimson flashed across them.

I started before responding with complete sincerity. "No, of course not! You're incredibly beautiful. It's me, not you."

"What's wrong with you?" The crimson faded from her eyes and the happy tone returned to her voice. "Are you sick?"

"Yes," I confirmed hurriedly. "I was cursed. Not completely, but there."

"Where?"

"Well, there." I glanced down with my eyes.

"Completely cursed?" The vila's eyes filled with tears. Her full lips quivered.

Come on, girl, what an idiot you are, I thought. *Just listen to the tale I'm about to spin for you. Get ready for the waterworks.*

"Completely. I once loved a girl, and she loved me, too. But you know how it goes: a powerful wizard took a liking to her. He needed to get rid of me, so he put a curse on me so I wouldn't be able to, you know…" I sadly shook my head as if in disappointment at my poor luck.

"You po-o-or thing." The vila flew down and took me by the hand. "Who would do such a thing…and what about the girl?"

"What about her? She said she didn't need someone 'unproductive' like me."

"Someone what?" The vila obviously didn't know the word.

"Unable to reproduce, put it that way…"

"I understand. What a horrid creature!"

"You don't know the half of it," I said. "And now my only hope is to find Captain Gul."

"Who?"

"Your guest, the sailor. He'll take me to a mage in the big city, and maybe the mage can help me."

"And then you'll go back to that girl?" I thought I detected something not quite right with the vila's question.

I stared at her, doing my best to look puzzled.

"To her? After what she said to me and, more importantly, after I found you? Of course not. You're the only girl for me! By the way, what's your name?"

"Elmilora. But is what you're saying true?" The vila let go of my hand and clasped her own hands to her chest. "Honest?"

"Elmilora. Look me in the eyes. Could they lie to you?" I looked deeply at her.

"Then let's hurry over to the island. I'll ask the Supreme to let your sailors go so you can sail wherever you need."

The vila led from above, and twenty minutes later, we arrived at a fairly large island littered with green trees, each with something like a crown on top of them. The roar of voices swept over the island, as something like twenty of the beauties flew above it chattering away. Not one of them was listening to anyone else, from what I could tell.

"So where's the captain?" I asked Elmilora.

"We have to go see the Supreme first." She was serious for once. "Nothing on this island can happen without her permission. Let's go."

She took me by the hand and led me deep into the island. The forest grew thicker, and the aerial hubbub grew more distant the further we went. Finally, we arrived at a large round field, in the middle of which was a raised area capped with an empty throne.

Elimlora's voice rang out. "I request an immediate audience with the Supreme! By right of the bride!"

The whole thing made me uneasy. *What is the "right of the bride"? Am I being played for a fool?*

My thoughts were interrupted by the flutter of wings. A stunningly beautiful, if no longer young, vila flew down onto the throne. Her wings were larger than those of the others, she was wearing a golden cloak, and there was a thin gold ring around her head.

Elmilora bowed. I thought for a second, decided that my back would be fine if I did the same, and figured I only had one shot at a first impression. That vila could have been smarter than the others, after all.

"Come closer," said a melodious voice.

I straightened up. The supreme vila—it was definitely her—sat on her throne looking at us. Suddenly, two more girls appeared from goodness knows where behind the throne, and they were also different from all the others I'd seen on the island. They had sabers hanging from their belts that were clearly magical—light blue electric sparks flashed up and down their blades.

Elmilora took me by the sleeve and motioned forward with her dimpled chin.

"Right," I said and nodded.

We walked over to the foot of the hill.

"Who are you, traveler? Where are you from, and what are you looking for in my lands?" The Supreme lowered her head slightly as she grilled me.

"I'm Hagen. Hagen from Tronje," I replied courteously.

Where did Tronje come from? I needed to say something, but what subconscious depths was that buried in? Anyway. Tronje it would be. It sounded nice, anyway.

"I'm a warrior and an adventurer."

"I see that. But why does my subject Elmilora call herself your bride? Did you propose to her?" The Supreme let a half-smile flit across her face, though there was ice in her eyes.

Damn doll. She had me between a rock and a hard place. If I said no, Elmilora would probably tear me to pieces. Either that or the Supreme herself or one of the beauties from behind the throne would do the job for her. If I said yes…I had no idea what would happen, though I doubted it was anything good. My heart was in my throat. Marriage, I decided, was the better of two evils, and that way I'd get to see who could out-talk whom—and I was a professional.

"This is the first I'm hearing of Elmilora's plans for our future, though I don't have any problem with them. Unfortunately, I can't get married right now due to extenuating circumstances. I would be happy to do so, however, once I handle my business, though I need your help for that."

"So you are willing to marry Elmilora, a vila?" The Supreme flew toward me.

"Once everything I need to do, my mission, and my problems are taken care of. Certainly."

The Supreme shook her head and smiled again.

"Well, then that settles it. Elmilora, Randiana, get everything ready for the betrothal. In the meantime, Hagen from Tronje and I will discuss the help our people can give him."

My, apparently, bride (*What?*) and one of the guards flew off with a rustling of feathers.

"Simalina," said the Supreme to the second guard. "Tell them to prepare for the great rite."

"Yes, Great Mother." The guard nodded and leaped into the sky.

"Well, Hagen, you're a fool." The Supreme reclined easily on her throne, threw one leg over the other, dangled her shoes from them, and looked at me from under her cloak. "You're an idiot. You obviously don't know that vilas who marry mortals of their own free will become mortal?"

"No," I mumbled.

"That's what I thought. Or that when mortals promise to marry vilas and don't keep their word, they are subject to one of Fayroll's most powerful curses?"

"No." I wasn't enjoying finding out what a blockhead I was. I was enjoying even less the fact that she was telling me that to my face.

"Or that if they keep their word and marry a vila but aren't faithful to her, they get the same curse—you didn't know that either?"

"No."

"Fool." The Supreme was obviously enjoying the situation.

"What do you get out of the marriage?" I was very interested to hear what she would say.

"Nothing at all. I'm just having fun. Also, I'm the ruler, and I take care of my subjects. May they be happy!"

"Got it. So what am I supposed to do now? Get married?"

"Get married."

"But I have things to do!" I replied nervously.

"Nobody's rushing you. Finish them, and then get married. Go through the betrothal rite, and then go do what you need to do. By the way, you obviously played on Elmilora's weakness for masculine fragility. She has a thing for that, though the rest aren't any better. So, what do you really need?"

"Captain Gul and his three sailors." I realized there was no need to try to impress her anymore.

"We have them. They're stubborn, and they don't want to marry anyone. They're smarter than you are, apparently."

"More experienced. But really, what's so bad? Elmilora is beautiful, and she has a great figure. I'll buy her a house and have somewhere to come home to."

"Yes, yes, of course." The Supreme smiled once again, and there was something about it that I didn't like at all.

"So, can you give me the sailors? As a present for our betrothal?" I smiled back at her.

"Maybe." She kept smiling. "Maybe not. But if you do one thing for me…"

Oh, thank God. Finally, a normal give-and-take relationship.

"Tell me, your honor." I prepared to listen.

"It's easy. Or it may not be. Anyway, we have some pirates settled in not far from the marsh. I need you to kill their leader and get something for me: a signet ring he stripped from our seer Horala when he killed her."

Look at that—the stars were aligning. "No problem. I do have some questions, though."

"So will you do it?" The Supreme was obviously capable of taking the bull by the horns.

You have a new quest offer: Horala's Signet Ring.

Task: Kill the pirate leader and get Horala's signet ring from him.

Reward:

900 experience

Captain Gul and his sailors will be released from the vilas' island.

+10% affection for you from the Supreme Vila

Warning.

This quest will be almost impossible to complete on your own. You should probably take 4-5 friends with you.

Accept?

"Sounds good. But on the condition that I get some help from you."

"That depends on what you need. I won't send my girls to fight."

"I'll do the fighting; I'm used to it. But I need to see where their camp is. So I can plan my strategy."

"That's easy," the Supreme said with a wave of her hand. "After your betrothal, Elmilora will take you wherever you want to go and tell you everything you need to know."

"And guards? Do you they have any guards?"

"Oh, please." The Supreme pursed her lips. "Just distract them."

Simalina and Randiana flapped back onto the field. "Supreme, everything is ready for the rite. They're all waiting!"

"Well, Hagen from Tronje, let's go. Your rite is waiting."

There was nothing for it but to do what I had to do. The Supreme got up off her throne, though she walked next to me instead of flying.

"So, what will I have to do?" I asked.

"Nothing much. I'll perform the whole thing, so just do what I tell you to do and answer my questions."

"Whatever you say. I hear and obey."

We made our way through a small copse of trees and walked out onto an equally small open area that appeared to be the very center of the island. It was just starting to get dark and, perhaps just for the romance of it, a bonfire was burning. Around it, stood a hundred or more chattering vilas. A stone column covered in runes was next to the fire.

The Supreme pointed me to a place to the left of the fire. On the other side, I saw Elmilora, who looked very nervous. She waved when she saw me looking at her. I waved back, of course. Obviously, I was a gentleman.

The Supreme flapped her wings to fly up a meter and a half off the ground.

"Sisters, today is a happy day! One of us found herself a man, a destiny, and a chance at a new life. Each of us dreams of getting that chance—our last chance. Elmilora was successful, and I would like to believe that each of you will be, sooner or later, as well. May you each have your chance at happiness and life."

The clearing was completely quiet, which I found surprising and somewhat frightening. A hundred girls, even if they weren't exactly real, not making a sound—that didn't even happen in Goethe's *Faust. Have you ever seen even two quiet for more than a minute? And here there were a hundred of them!*

"Elmilora Krakh Taug, come here and lay your hand on the vila altar given to us forever by the Fair Goddess Mesmerta to hold the warmth of her heart and memory of her blood."

"Elmilora walked over to the column and rested her palm on top of it.

"Hagen of Tronje, do the same."

I walked over and put my hand on the column. It suddenly grew warm, and a ray of light unexpectedly shot up.

The vilas grew nervous and murmured to each other. Elmilora's eyes widened.

"What's wrong?" I asked her. "Is that not supposed to happen?"

"Not like that," she said. "That's never happened!"

I glanced at the Supreme and noticed an entire range of complex emotions chasing each other across her face—confusion, fear, and everything in between. Still, she quickly regained control of herself and addressed the group.

"The Goddess consecrated the union of these two hearts with that sign. The light signifies that their life will be easy and bright!"

The vilas calmed down, with the more delicate ones among them wiping away tears.

"Elmilora Krakh Taug," continued the Supreme, "are you prepared to bind your life to that of this person, to be his true and loving wife?"

"Yes, Supreme," said Elmilora in her lovely voice.

"Laird Hagen of Tronje, are you prepared to bind your life to this vila, to be her respectful and faithful husband?"

"Yes, Supreme, I give you my word, though, of course, I first need to finish a quest I hold dearer than life itself."

I prayed she wouldn't ask me to be specific about which quest I meant. Children of the Goddess guaranteed me eternal bachelorhood, but I didn't want to mention it out loud. Not even to NPCs.

"A man's debt is holy, and his word should be kept," said the Supreme with a nod. "But your union is blessed by the Goddess, and with the power vested in me, I, therefore, call you Betrothed. From this moment onward you are one of a chosen few: the bridegroom of a vila."

You are the bridegroom of a vila.

You get:

Friendship with the vilas throughout Fayroll.

Title: Bridegroom

You can always count on the support of the vilas throughout Fayroll.

All marshes are 50% more passable.

Note: If you do not fulfill the conditions of the betrothal rite, the following will occur:

You will suffer from the Scourge of the Goddess curse.

In addition to the curse, you will also have several penalties:

All marshes will be more difficult to pass through, and you will have a 75% higher chance of dying in them.

You will be 50% less attractive to female NPCs.

Title: Betrayer

Apparently, swamps and marshes were now home sweet home. So what was next?

"I will now announce the conditions of the Betrothal," proclaimed the Supreme. Sparks from the bonfire shot skyward.

"Elmilora Kraukh Taug, you are charged with waiting for your bridegroom, Hagen of Tronje, patiently and honorably. If your behavior is considered to defame you, the Betrothal will be considered annulled. Do you agree?"

"Yes, Supreme!" Elmilora clenched her fists and clasped them against her chest.

"Hagen of Tronje. How much time do you need to fulfill your promise?"

"I'm not sure, Supreme. Maybe six months, maybe a year. It's anyone's guess."

"I rule that in six months, you will return here to continue this conversation. Be very afraid of deceiving us—the holy altar detects all lies, and the vengeance of the vilas will be terrible!"

"I understand, Supreme," I said, somewhat disappointed.

"The rite is complete!" The Supreme threw her hands in the air, and they were accompanied by another shower of sparks.

From the altar, another column of light again shot skyward. Judging by the Supreme's nervous face, it, too, was not what they were used to seeing.

She came down to earth and started speaking in her normal voice.

"Okay, girlies, go have fun. Hagen and I need to talk."

Elmilora's lips started to pout, though her friends grabbed her by the elbows and dragged her over to the fire.

"Let's go, warrior," said the Supreme. "You can tell me what you have going on with Mesmerta."

We walked off to the side, and I asked her a question. "Are you sure you want me to tell you? In much wisdom, there is much grief."

"Your grief isn't my grief." The Supreme looked at me coldly. "These little fools trusted my explanations, accepting them even though the altar had never lit up like that before. But I would like to know about your relationship with Mesmerta, who long ages ago left the created world."

"Well, look," I said, as I thought about how best to tell her. "Not long ago, I helped a funny little green creature, and she asked me to help her sister. They have something to do with your goddess—and that happens to be the small but important thing I have to do, you know?"

"So that's what the changes in the magical fabric of Fayroll have been about," the Supreme said, fixing her enormous green eyes on me. "Apparently you helped one of the Keepers. We're all in for some interesting times if you're successful."

"What will happen?"

"It'll be interesting." The Supreme obviously had no intention of explaining anything to me. "If you live long enough, you'll get to see it. If you live long enough, and if you finish in less than six months, of course, come right back here. Understood?"

She walked off into the darkness. I decided that enough was enough and logged out of the game.

After a visit to the shower and the refrigerator, I called Elvira.

"El, hi!"

"Hey, let me call you back." She hung up.

"Whatever you say, my dear," I said and pressed the button to end the call.

I sat down to write my next article. The text was, as was becoming my custom, already in my head, and I just needed to get it down on paper. That took me two hours, and I had just entered the last period when my phone rang.

"Okay, Kif, listen. We're flying in three days, not two. Well, if we don't count today, then in two."

"So the day after tomorrow?" I said. "You have me all confused. What are we counting?"

"Yes, in the evening, the day after tomorrow. We'll be there for nine days and ten nights. Do you have everything you need?"

"What do you mean, 'everything'? My honor, my conscience, socks, sausages, canned fish, a modem? What's 'everything'?"

"Yes, and socks. A swimsuit, sunscreen, body lotion?"

"El, body what? Relax. I have a swimsuit, sandals, shorts, and my bandana. I'm ready. Oh, I just need to buy a couple packs of cigarettes."

"But I'm not! Tomorrow morning at 10, we're going shopping. I'll be there in a few minutes, so I'll spend the night, and we can leave from your place. Otherwise, it'll never happen—I know you. Okay, that's it, over and out."

Phew boy. In the space of three hours, I'd been snagged by two women. It was becoming a trend...

294

Chapter Twenty-Three
The Calm Before the Storm

Shopping with a woman... It's a trial all mature, traditionally oriented males go through. It starts innocently enough at school and university.

"You girls go buy the food, and we guys will get the alcohol."

Then you start dating and get married, at which point it becomes a merciless battle of wills to see if the woman can wear you down.

"Does this look good on me?"

"You can't even tell that this color doesn't match my eyes!"

"I don't have a purse for these shoes!"

"I can't wear the same thing nine days in a row!"

"Those aren't the right curlers. What are you standing there for? Go look for them!"

"You're looking right at it—it's jojoba! Jo-jo-ba! What don't you understand?"

I didn't understand anything! What's jojoba? The word alone was giving me a headache. I had no idea what curlers were for and why those weren't the right ones. A better option would have been to hand me a pistol—preferably recoilless—and let me blow my brains out.

Why does she need rye bread? Does she think they don't have any in Spain? Oh, not that kind. Come on, you'll be eating desserts by the ton for dinner and cakes for lunch at cafes. No? Right.

Listen, you have two boobs and one ass. Why do you need six bikinis, or whatever those rags—really just piles of string—are called? Why piles of string? Because some strands of spaghetti would do just as good a job! What? They cover all the important bits? My dear, all your important bits will be spilling out all over the place. And for that money, you could get a whole spool of string. Fine, buy whatever you want! Me? I already got everything I need. Two swimsuits, sandals, and a bandana, just like I said. And two cartons of cigarettes. I don't need anything else—I have shorts at home. Yes, I'm an animal.

And that's how the whole day went. Just one long, never-ending marathon. We didn't even stop for lunch since fast food is bad for you—too many carcinogens and additives. Sure, that's true, but it's also true that I have the right to a lunch break. They even get lunch in prison. And dinner. They get pasta...

Finally that night, I dropped Elvira off at her house, telling her that I'd paid off all the tribute we hadn't been giving her people since the last time we were under their yoke. I got my last marching orders in reply.

"The flight is at 11:30 p.m., and we need to be at the airport an hour, no, an hour and a half beforehand, so I'll get to your place at 9:30. I'll call a taxi since you'd either forget or have us riding in some death trap. At 9:30—are you even listening to me? At 9:30 you need to be packed and standing in the hallway with your suitcase. Got it? Nod your head. Now tell me what you heard."

"9:30 at the door with my suitcase. Can I go?"

"Yes."

What if she got me to marry her? I decided I'd be better off with my winged woman. At least she was an idiot...

At home, it took just one gloomy look at the capsule to realize that the last thing I needed was some fighting. I checked my computer, nodded my head in satisfaction that I'd sent Mammoth the article that morning, and went to bed for what I knew could be my last good night's sleep for ten days. Who knew what my favorite little Tartar steppe child would think of in Spain? Going to a nightclub, looking for local street racers, heading up into the Pyrenees to see the sunrise in the mountains and swim in a mountain stream...the possibilities were endless, though I was afraid they didn't include much sleeping. I needed to rest up before we left.

I slept in and might have slept even longer if my stomach hadn't growled to wake me up around 11 a.m. After a big breakfast and a smoke, I sat down to think about what else I had left to do before we flew out. I settled on two important things: call my parents to let them know that I'd be out of the country for ten days and deal with that band of pirates so I could find Horala's signet ring.

I figured the one-legged port master would also give me a quest to take out the pirates—no need to visit a fortune teller for that one. I decided to start with reality and finish with my virtual world, though maybe I wouldn't even get that far. We would see.

My parents were happy I was taking a trip. Rather, they weren't as happy that I was going on a trip as they were that I wasn't going alone. They regularly harped on about grandkids, and this time they were hoping that the rich sea air would have me thinking about making one. Right. I was afraid of Elvira enough as it was—if we had a baby girl together, I was a goner. I shivered.

I was just about to stick my phone in the pocket of my sweatpants when it rang. The screen read "Mammoth."

"Yes, Semyon Ilyich?"

"Nikiforov, I got your article—good work. The whole cycle is good. Everyone's reading them, and the clients are happy."

"Clients?"

"Oh, lay off it—you knew all along. I think they even want to give you some kind of bonus."

"Well, that's good."

"Certainly not bad. So stop in tomorrow—"

"I can't tomorrow."

"Why not?" Mammoth assumed a gentle tone that didn't fool me for a second.

"I'm on vacation. You signed the form yourself."

"I did? I don't remember that."

"Check with HR. Everything's in order, and you can read the form if you want."

"Okay, okay. Just make sure I can call you. There's something really important we're going to need to talk about. For your articles. Got it? I'll be in touch."

I hung up. Not so much as a "hello" or even "goodbye." *Quite the role model, I had to say.*

But thanks for the heads-up, I thought, pulling the sim card out of my phone and dropping it onto a shelf. None of that. I was going completely off-grid. And if Elvira needed me, well, she had a knack for that as it was.

I packed my suitcase, grabbed a bite to eat, and checked the clock. It was 4 p.m., and I was out of things to do. There's nothing worse than sitting and waiting, so I decided to jump into the capsule.

Nothing had changed on the island. Beautiful women flew back and forth under the trees, the sun was shining, and the leaves rustled in the breeze.

"You're here!" Something blonde and blue-eyed swooped down on me. It was, of course, my betrothed, all prettied up in a white robe.

"Of course," I answered soulfully. "How could I live without you? You're my destiny."

Elmilora blinked and appeared to be about ready to cry.

Maybe everything they say about blondes is true? I thought. I don't generally believe in stereotypes, especially since I've seen a thing or two in my day, but that little creature had me rethinking that.

"Listen, sweetie..." I began.

Elmilora thought the better of bursting into tears, wiped her eyes, and came forward, letting me know that she was all ears.

"Your Supreme told me you'd take me to where those scary pirates are. Just without them noticing."

"I'll take you there," the vila said with a willing nod of her head. "It isn't far. They're building a camp in a small valley that's just on the other side of a hill from the marsh. There's no guard on this side since they think the mountain is impassible. But I know about a path that's tiny and deep, but crosses it. Well, it isn't exactly a path. We don't usually go that way since we fly and it isn't good for wings. Aren't my wings pretty?"

From that stream of consciousness, I concluded that, one way or another, I had a shot at our friends' backs. But what should I do with the patrols? It would have been hard enough if they just had soldiers, but there was that nasty half-elf to deal with too...

"Hey, how did they kill your seer? Especially since you can fly?"

Elmilora frowned, and her eyes again filled with tears.

"She went to go talk with them. Just because. We don't do anything bad to anyone else, and nobody does bad things to us. But they killed her. For no good reason."

"Well, don't worry about it; we'll be killing them this time," I said to reassure the girl.

298

"Yes, you'll kill them all! You're the best. And the strongest!"

Elmilora puffed out her cheeks and held a hand out in front of her as if she were holding a sword. If she was doing an imitation of me, I worried that the game was portraying me in a less-than-flattering light.

"Exactly!" I said. "Let's go. Time to show me the mountain and the path."

"Come on," my bride said as she nodded her head and took off.

I don't know if she took me the short way or not, but we were there, almost completely dry, in almost no time. A mountain rose smoothly out of the marsh where the latter ended. It wasn't that tall, but still.

"Where's the path, my dear?"

"There." The vila flew over to a thick bush. I had no idea what it was called in the game, though it reminded me of a lilac bush. *Or is it a lilac tree? Anyway.*

"Crawl deep in there."

I followed her directions and saw a small opening in the mountain. Once I stepped in, I realized that it was more the opening to a small, arched tunnel, at which point I realized what my bride meant by "deep" and why it wasn't easy on her wings. I poked my head out of the tunnel.

"Elmilora, wait for me here. Don't fly over to the other side, okay?"

"Sounds good," she answered. "Whatever you say. Will you be long?"

"No."

"Is it safe?"

"Yep."

"Maybe I should come with you? I'll be so worried!" The vila clasped her hands to her chest and batted her long eyelashes.

"Everything will be fine, just wait here," I said before diving back into the tunnel.

I heard her voice calling after me, "Please be careful!"

She's worried about me, I thought and paused for a second to enjoy the feeling. Then I turned to wonder why it wasn't dark. I was in a tunnel, after all. Instead, there was a good bit of light filtering in.

The answer was simple: it was only about twenty strides from one end to the other, and the light coming in from both ends was enough to keep the whole tunnel fairly well lit.

The tunnel exit on the other side of the cliff—it was definitely more a cliff than a mountain, as my bride had led me to believe—was also masked with shrubbery. I crawled through it, sincerely hoping that I wouldn't find a snake and doing my best to keep the leaves from moving. Suddenly, the view in front of me opened up onto a meadow twenty meters or so below me. I appeared to be on an overhang that jutted out over a deep cave.

How did I know it was a cave? I could clearly hear two voices below me, though I couldn't see their owners. One of them was obviously in charge, and the other was quieter. The band's leaders evidently enjoyed more comfort than the rest of them.

I glanced across the meadow and saw a picture-perfect pirate camp that looked like it could have been pulled straight from an adventure story or movie. About five bandits were lounging on the grass or walking around dressed in exotic clothing. Two more were roasting a boar over a fire; one kept it rotating, while the other jabbed at it with a knife.

You completed a quest: Quieter than Grass.

To get your reward, go see the port master and tell him what you saw.

Reward:

400 experience

Additional reward: A cutlass from Neils Holgerrson's collection.

Plus guards in the woods, I thought to myself. *Seven here, at least three in the woods, and two more in the cave. Not good. There's no way I can take them on myself—and it'll even take a pretty strong group. Okay, I'll head back to Mettan and try to think of something.*

I inched my way back to the tunnel just as stealthily as I'd left it, made my way through the tunnel, and walked out to see Elmilora sitting on a rock with her arms wrapped around her knees.

"Waiting for me?" I smiled at her.

She nodded. "Yup!"

"Okay, show me how to get out of the marsh."

She chattered on about something or other the whole way there. I wasn't particularly listening, as I was busy thinking about what to do next.

I had three options. The first was to forget both quests and keep going to the next town. In that case, I'd only come back once I was capable of taking out the pirate band by myself. The second was to ask my clan for help. The third was to screw it all and give up on the game. After all, there was nothing keeping me playing anymore. None of my choices were optimal, but they did all have their advantages.

I didn't want to forget the quests since they both gave me obvious benefits. Plus, that Supreme was more than your ordinary NPC. She knew quite a bit, and the quest gave me a 10 percent reputation bump with her. Asking my clan for help was the last thing I wanted to do. I'd already dipped into that well, and soon they'd all just laugh at me for being so needy.

But giving up...well, sure, I could. Maybe later. Not yet.

I soon found that we'd made it to the edge of the marsh.

"I'll be waiting for you," said Elmilora. "And missing you."

"Me, too. Don't you worry. I'll be back before you know it. By the way, how can I find you? It's a big marsh, and I don't want to have to comb it looking for you."

"You can use my name?" My bride looked at me in surprise. "Just come to the edge of the marsh and call for me. I'll fly right over."

"Okay," I said. "See you soon."

And off I headed in the direction of the city.

"I'll be waiting for you here!" Elmilora said to my retreating figure.

I wasted no time when I got to Mettan and immediately went to see Holgerrson. On the porch outside the door, I bumped into a broad-shouldered barbarian warrior on his way out.

"Hey, Holgerrson," I said to the old sea dog, "we have to talk."

"There sure are a lot of you today, bilges and brass," he said. "What do you need?"

"The same. I found the pirate camp, and there are more than a few of them."

"Ah-ha, so you found them, too. Well done!"

You completed a quest: Quieter than Grass.

You received a reward:

400 experience

Additional reward: A cutlass from Neils Holgerrson's collection.

"Here you go." Neils hobbled over to the wall and pulled down a cutlass in a black sheath with gold trim. "I promised you, so here you are. A sailor's word is his bond forever. Barnacles and bosons!"

I took the cutlass and looked at it.

Neils Holgerrson's Cutlass

Reputation item

Show this cutlass to the port master of any city on the Crisna to get a discount on river passage.

The amount of the discount depends on your reputation in the cities on the Great River.

It was a good thing I came to see him; the cutlass was handy to have. I wondered if Holgerrson, himself, would give me an additional discount if I showed it to him.

"So, there are a lot of pirates?" The sailor had already gone back to the topic at hand.

"Yes, maybe ten, with a leader." I pursed my lips in annoyance.

"We need to get rid of them, but I don't have anyone I can ask to do it. I'm a leg short, and the mayor's a useless octopus."

"A what?"

"An octopus. Can't tell his head from his…well…behind. And the Royal Guard is off somewhere. What do you say, want to help out the city and port? I'll make it worth your while. You'll have some gold and even something else from me coming your way."

> You have a new quest offer: Get Rid of the Land Pirates.
> Task: Kill the band of pirates robbing traders on the Great River close to Mettan.
> Reward:
> 1100 experience
> 800 gold
> An item from Neils Holgerrson's storehouse.
> +10% to your reputation in Mettan
> Warning
> This quest will be almost impossible to complete on your own. You should probably take 4-5 friends with you.
> Accept?

Did I have a choice? I accepted. One way or another, I had to take out the gang.

"So what will you give me?" I asked, my interest piqued.

"I have all kinds of stuff in my storehouse. Some people lose things, and I get some things left over after those traders are robbed. There's always something there for a warrior."

"That's good. But where can I find someone to go with me?"

"What, you don't have any good friends?"

"Sure, I do, though none of them are around here."

"You know, did you see the warrior who was leaving when you got here?"

"Yes," I said, looking at him carefully.

"I just asked him to do the same thing, and I think he had a group with him."

Actually, yes. I'd noticed a few people hanging around the port building when I got there.

"Thanks, Captain. Let's hope they're still here."

"See you, sonny boy. Hurry up!"

The old sea dog whistled through his nose as he puffed away at his pipe.

I rushed out onto the porch and looked around. The warrior I'd bumped into was standing with his back to me in a group of four other players. They were already close to the city gate and in the middle of discussing something hotly.

"Hey, guys!" I called them as I ran over, worried that they were about to walk out the gates. Who knows how long it would have taken me to find them in the forest...

The warrior turned around. "Are you talking to us?"

His name was Olgerd, and he was a Level 40 swordsman who was obviously in charge of the group.

"Yes. Do you have a quest to kill the pirates in the woods, too?"

"What do you care?" Olgerd asked coldly.

I decided not to be clever. "There are five of you and ten of them, maybe another two, then two more in the cave and who knows how many on patrol. Don't you think that's a lot for you?"

"It'll be tough," said a halfling scout named Bulkins with a sigh.

Besides him and Olgerd, there were also two human warriors in the group and an archer elf named Farainil. I chuckled to myself at the stereotype—if you're an archer, you're going to be an elf. That's just how it was.

"I have that quest, too," I said, cutting to the chase. "I'd be happy to come with you unless you only want clan members. An extra sword certainly wouldn't hurt you, and I wouldn't have to find my own group. You know how tricky that will be around here."

"Why not, Olgerd?" asked a warrior named Reger. "We'll get the same experience, and we can figure things out with the reputation bonus later."

"Agreed," said the second warrior, whose name was Uncle Fedor. "We all just happen to be going that way anyway."

"Then it's a deal," said Olgerd. "But let me just say right off the bat that I'm the leader."

I nodded. "No problem—lead away! Where are you guys thinking of going?"

"Through the forest. Where else?" asked the scout.

"We don't have to. We could go through the marsh," I said quietly.

"How?" Olgerd looked at me suddenly.

"Have you seen the marsh to the north? The far side ends next to a big cliff with a tunnel in it leading right to the meadow."

"Okay," said Uncle Fedor. "That's one option."

The archer was less than convinced. "But how long would we have to slosh around in the marsh?"

"We wouldn't. My bride is there, and she'll show us a shortcut," I said with pride.

"A bride in the bog?" Uncle Fedor looked at me with sympathy. It may have been because I was marrying a marsh spirit, or it may have been because I had some gray matter missing.

"A vila?" Olgerd, who apparently had more experience than the rest of them, grunted.

"Yep."

"What an idiot! Still, that's sure nice for us," said Olgerd happily.

"They have an archer on guard, by the way—a half-elf. And he's good, too," I said.

"Yes, we saw him," said the little scout.

"Okay," Olgerd said, "we'll go through the swamp. There are seven pirates in the meadow: two by the fire and five more walking around. I'll take the first two while you all get the rest focused on you. They're all Level 34, so we should be able to take them. Farainil and Bulkins, you hang back and wait for the patrol."

"What if there's more than one patrol? Maybe there are more?" I asked.

"Why? There's one patrol. Two warriors and an archer," answered Olgerd.

So I just got lucky. If I'd gone just a little left or a little right, I'd have missed them. But no, I had to march my butt right into their sights.

Olgerd continued with his battle plan. "When the patrol gets there, we'll take the warriors."

"What if we still haven't finished with the first group?" asked Reger.

"We'll have two, two and a half minutes, so we should be fine."

"How do you know?" I asked.

"You need to read the guides," he answered pointedly. "Smart people write everything up. Anyway, we should have time. If we don't, you'll get the warriors to attack you." That last part was said with a finger pointed in my direction. "Bulkins!"

"Yes, general?" The scout puffed out his chest.

"You look for the archer and get him to attack you. He'll probably be able to take you out if you aren't quick enough. But by that time Farainil will have a shot at him, and then it's just a matter of hitting him. Far, you'll have about thirty seconds, since I think that's about all Bulkins can give you. He'll refocus his attack after every second arrow, too. Oh, and we need to get a look at their camp."

"No worries there," I said. "The tunnel opens onto the meadow right above the cave where their leader is. It's perfect."

"Definitely. And the distance?"

"About three hundred meters to the forest." I looked at the archer.

He nodded. "No problem, I can do it."

"Won't the leader come out when he hears the noise?" I asked.

"Of course." Olgerd looked at me. "But he won't come out until we're done with the last of his fighters. Then he and his lieutenant will come out. At that point, we'll have to see who's still standing. Farainil, make sure you kill the leader. Questions?"

"How are we distributing trophies?" asked Uncle Fedor.

"By need. Other questions?"

"Respawn?" That was the scout.

"They're part of the quest, so they won't climb back out of hell until we kill their leader. And we'll have another ten minutes after that, too."

"Guys, there's one thing," I said. "I have a quest from the vilas for the leader. I need to get a ring from him."

"Not a problem," said Olgerd. "Nobody else cares about it. Okay, ready? Let's go!"

"Hold on," I said. "Send me the group."

"Oh, right," answered Olgerd. "Good? Roll out."

Chapter Twenty-Four

Press the Button

Elmilora was sitting right where I left her: on the edge of the marsh. She saw me, jumped up happily, and hovered in the air, wings flapping.

"You're back!" She clapped her hands. "I missed you."

"Yep, I'm back," I said, out of breath. We'd been moving fast, and I'd even broken a light sweat. The day was drawing to a close, but the sun was still burning in the sky. "These are my friends."

"Hi! I'm Elmilora, Hagen's bride," she said with a wave.

Part of the group grunted while the other part waved in reply.

"You're kidding," Uncle Fedor said to me.

"Nothing wrong with that," I replied.

"I like her! She's cute," squeaked the scout.

"That's not the half of it," I said. "Dear, we need to get to that mountain again. The guys and I are going to have a talk with the group over there."

"Isn't that dangerous? They're so evil. You know how they killed Horala," Elmilora said with a sob.

"Just look at us," I answered soothingly. "Look how strong we are. What are they going to do to us? Anyway, dear, it's going to get dark soon, so let's go. The marsh at night..."

"Oh, that's no problem. I'd just light some fires," said the vila. "But if you're in a hurry, let's go."

Everyone was giving me a hard time about marrying a vila, but there was certainly an upside. Who knows how long it would have taken us to plod through the marsh on our way to the cliff. We may not have even gotten there. This way it took us all of twenty minutes—and we got there mostly clean and dry.

"Thank you," Olgerd said to the vila with a smile. "And good luck in your marriage."

"Thanks. Haggy, dear, we're going to invite your friends to the wedding, right?" So I was already "Haggy."

"Do we have a choice?" I said. "They'll be there whether we invite them or not."

"True," said Uncle Fedor, laughing. "No getting out of it!"

"Okay, you had your laughs," Olgerd said. "The tunnel is up there?" He pointed at the bush.

"Yes," I answered. "Short and sweet."

"And on the other side?"

"The same thing. There's cover for everyone."

"Then let's go."

Olgerd disappeared into the underbrush, followed by Uncle Fedor and everyone else.

"Fly home, don't wait for me here," I told my vila. "There's going to be a lot of yelling and screaming over there, and you shouldn't have to hear it."

"I'm worried sick about you," said the vila. "I don't think it will be very safe over there."

"But I'm a warrior—danger is my life. And now it's yours," I said to her with a smile.

"You're right. Will you come to the island soon?"

"As soon as I'm finished, I'll come right there. Okay, fly home. Drawing this out won't make it any easier."

I kissed her on the cheek, waved, and crawled into the bushes. Without looking back. Real men don't look back.

The group was situated comfortably on the other side. The elf was looking around, obviously trying to find the best spot to shoot from, while the scout was shuffling his feet and looking around timidly.

"What's wrong?" I asked him.

"There are probably snakes around here," he answered with embarrassment.

"What are you talking about?" I had already forgotten my own recent fears on that account.

"Cobras...or copperheads."

"Shush!" Olgerd, who was surveying our position, abruptly broke in. "Who cares about snakes? If that's all we had to deal with, we'd be home free. Look at all of them down there. On the bright side, they're all in the same place, so we won't have to split up."

I looked to see what he was talking about and noticed that they were indeed all in one spot. They were sitting around the fire eating the boar they had apparently finished roasting. Judging by the pile of bones, their feast had been going on for some time.

"Well, what are we waiting for?" Olgerd pulled his sword out from behind his back.

"Let's do this," agreed Uncle Fedor.

Before we moved out, Olgerd had some last words for Bulkins and Farainil. "Remember, you two, wait for the archer. Don't move a muscle until you see him. If anyone else sees you and comes after you before them, we may not be able to help, and the half-elf will kill us all. If only we had a healer...ah, well. Okay, let's move!"

He leaped down from the cliff, glanced quickly into the cave, and sprinted toward the unsuspecting pirates. The three of us were right behind him.

I checked the cave as well once I jumped down. There was an opening that appeared to lead to the cave where the entire group's leader was holed up.

I hope you're right, Olgerd, about him not coming out until we kill everyone else. If you aren't, we're all goners, I thought as I dashed toward the fire.

Olgerd got there first and brought his sword crashing down on the neck of the pirate closest to him. The pirate's health immediately turned yellow, though the advantage of surprise was over. The group jumped up, cleavers and long knives in their hands. I didn't see a single sword among them.

"Get them," a red-bristled pirate shouted. "Brandishing their swords around here."

He took a swing at Olgerd with his knife. Olgerd ducked gracefully behind the pirate he'd already wounded and landed a powerful blow to his head.

His voice rang out a second later. "One down!"

Two pirates rushed at me at once, and I no longer had time to keep track of everyone else in the group. They grunted in concentration as they slashed away at me with their butcher knives, getting in each other's way as they did.

I was able to catch their knives with my shield, though I couldn't find an opening for a strike of my own. They were both going at me hard, by accident or on purpose, and I knew that taking a swing at one of them would mean taking a hit from the other.

"Two down!" That was Uncle Fedor.

Reger chimed in. "Three down!"

And here I am retreating, I thought. *Nice.* But that's when I caught a lucky break. The pirate on my left stumbled, and, as he tried to regain his balance, I grabbed my chance. A quick slide to my right put me in a position to catch yet another knife slash with my shield before swinging my sword left to right into the second pirate's side and stomach. As I did, I shouted, "Bloodletting!" He staggered back two steps and clutched the gaping wound in his abdomen.

Without losing another second, I jumped back to the first pirate. He had his feet back under him and his knife at the ready, though he was obviously not expecting such a whirlwind attack. I knocked his knife to the side, buried my sword in his chest, and called out another ability.

"Sword of Retribution!"

"Four down!" Olgerd again.

"Hagen, I've got this one," I heard Uncle Fedor shout from behind me. His sword whistled and thudded, followed by another cry: "Five down!"

The pirate in front of me wobbled, my next blow landed true, and I seized the moment to slice downward through his chest. He croaked and collapsed.

"Six down!" It was finally my turn to chime in, and I could feel the adrenaline coursing through my veins.

"Seven down!" Reger and Olgerd shouted together.

"Bunch of children," added Uncle Fedor.

Olgerd quickly took charge. "Watch the forest—two more are on their way. Bulkins, you're up. Find the archer, go, go!"

The little scout jumped down from the cliff and sprinted off into the woods.

We formed up into a semicircle and started scanning the trees for our next wave of opponents.

"They should be here any second," said Olgerd quietly. "It's been more than two and a half minutes."

An arrow whistled through the air and smacked into his shoulder.

"Damn it," bellowed Olgerd. "Find him, Bulkins!"

Two hulking beasts lumbered out of the woods. They had swords in their hands and were wearing leather armor, in contrast to the group we'd just finished off.

Olgerd began barking out orders. "Hagen, come with me to the left; the rest go right." Another arrow hit his shoulder, but he had just started moving, and this one only grazed him.

"There he is!" Bulkins yelled at us as he pointed at a tree. "He's on that branch. Far! Bring him down!"

"Hagen, wake up!" Olgerd shouted at me.

I looked over to one of the two tanks rushing me, sword at the ready. *Every action has an equal and opposite reaction,* I thought and threw myself at his legs. He tripped and fell headlong on the grass. Judging by the prolonged "a-a-ah" that followed, Olgerd had read the situation correctly and plunged his sword into the pirate's back. I jumped up quickly, saw that my opponent was still on the ground, and, without further ado, followed Olgerd's lead. Another few strokes and the poor guy gave up the ghost. His sword clattered to the ground unused.

A branch cracked at the edge of the meadow and Olgerd and I turned to see the half-elf falling from the tree. Two arrows were already sticking out of him—Far was hard at work. He had, however, overestimated his abilities, as several arrows were sticking out of the ground far short of their target. And the two arrows he had landed weren't enough to finish the half-elf, who was firing away at Bulkins. The latter was ducking in and out of shadows, though a few shots found their mark and left his health well into the red.

"Look at him," I said, "picking on the little guy."

I charged the half-elf, brandishing my sword.

"I'll help the others," Olgerd shouted as he ran toward Reger and Uncle Fedor. They were off trying to bring down the second burly pirate.

I was a few steps short of the half-elf when he, marksman that he was, caught Bulkins leaving a shadow with an arrow to the head.

The scout squeaked and melted into the air, leaving behind a transparent cocoon with his belongings.

"We lost one," I shouted back. But an arrow slammed into my chest—the devil shot better than Legolas. My health turned yellow, apparently from a critical hit.

"Oh, you monster!" A voice rang out from somewhere above me. "Stop shooting arrows at my bridegroom! You beast!"

The half-elf looked up to see Elmilora soaring above us. Her fists were at her sides, and her eyebrows were creased with righteous indignation.

"How dare you! Don't you know who I am? I'll let you have it!" She threw her arms forward and cut loose bolts of lightning from her fingertips that crackled into the half-elf's chest. His health turned red. Farainil finished him off with an arrow through the eye. The half-elf dropped where he stood.

"That one was brutal!" Apparently, the rest of the group had taken care of the last pirate.

"Sweetie, are you okay?" My bride fluttered down.

"Yes, I'm fine," I said, out of breath. "Thank you. Although I did tell you not to get involved. What if he'd killed you? What would I have done then?"

"Oh, that's so sweet! You were worried about me?"

"What do you think? Okay, get out of here. Please meet Bulkins at the edge of the marsh—I think he'll probably be coming there."

"The little halfling? Okay." Elmilora took off. "I'll be back soon. You're done here, right?"

"Of course. We killed everyone," I said. "Right, guys?"

The group murmured in agreement. Yep, everyone was dead.

Elmilora blew me a kiss and flew off. We watched her go before turning our gaze on the mouth of the cave. Nobody had come out yet.

"Maybe we have to call him?" said Uncle Fedor uncertainly.

"Yeah, right, in chorus. Like Santa Claus," answered Olgerd. "He'll be out in a second. Where else is he going to go?"

"Uh-oh," we heard from inside the cave. "What's all that noise out there? Who's keeping Silvio from going to sleep?"

A pair of figures walked out of the cave. One was taller and well-muscled, with a handsome face, expensive clothes, and a longsword. The other was short, squat, wild-haired, obviously dressed in whatever he could find, and holding a boarding saber in his hand.

The taller one looked at his companion. "Look, Rufus—these fine folks just cut up our crew. That wasn't nice. What do you think we should do about that?"

"Let's cut their throats, master. What else?" answered the shorter one.

"Agreed." Silvio turned to look at us. "Gentlemen, this was awfully rude of you. You just came crashing through my meadow and killed my people. Quite the outrage, wouldn't you agree?"

"Oh, please," jumped in Olgerd. "You're the one sinking traders, and you think you can talk down to us."

I added my two cents. "Plus, you killed a vila. And they wouldn't harm a fly."

"Yes, that was a shame about the vila. We made a mistake," agreed Silvio. "But, now that we're talking, so you killed these good-for-nothings—forget them. Maybe we can all just walk away right now? An eye for an eye, so to speak?"

"Yeah, right," said Uncle Fedor less than politely. "Walk away after all that?"

"What are we waiting for?" Olgerd took charge. "Hagen, Uncle, you take the hairy one. We'll—"

He didn't have time to finish his order. Silvio took one enormous leap that covered the distance between us and buried his blade in Reger. The strike was a good one, Reger's health turned red, and he collapsed backward under the force of the blow. Silvio tried to follow up with a hit to Olgerd, as he was standing next to Reger, but this time, steel met steel as Olgerd blocked the attack with his sword. Reger, with complete disregard for his remaining health, dauntlessly jumped into the fight and quickly seized his opportunity to land a hefty blow to Silvio's back. The latter obviously was not expecting an attack from that quarter, having thought he'd finished Reger in one go. He turned, broke through Reger's defense with a powerful stroke, and Reger was done. However, Silvio paid dearly for his revenge. He quickly spun back around, but Olgerd was quicker, and his blow took out a good chunk of Silvio's health. That was followed by two arrows from our archer, who, up until that point, had been supporting us with his fire.

Our situation was much better. The little fellow ran at us with a wave of his saber, shouting some words in a language none of us knew. Far buried two arrows in his back before he got anywhere close to us, and, unlike our friends off to the side, we had time to brace ourselves. Two swords met him as soon as he got to us. One—Uncle Fedor's—was blocked, though the second—mine—landed with Bloodletting to boot. Rufus' health started slowly draining. We alternated hits that began wearing him down, and Far kept up his stream of arrows. As a result, by the time Reger died and left Olgerd to handle the pirate leader on his own, we were about done with Rufus and his surprising amount of health. Olgerd called over.

"We lost another one!"

"You finish him off," I told Uncle Fedor. "I'll help Olgerd."

Uncle Fedor nodded and jabbed his sword into Rufus, who was already on his knees and barely putting up any resistance.

I dashed over to the pair still locked in combat and buried my sword in the back of Silvio's legs.

"Sword of Retribution!"

Silvio collapsed to his knees. Another arrow thudded into his chest, while Olgerd cried out and sliced into his neck. I decided to add my contribution and stabbed him with my sword. Judging by the result, mine was the finishing blow.

You completed a quest: Get Rid of the Land Pirates.
To get your reward, talk to Neils Holgerrson.

"Finally," said Uncle Fedor.

"We did it," added Olgerd in relief.

I turned to him. "Boss, go ahead and loot him, then I'll take the ring."

"Sounds good," said Olgerd. "Just so long as he doesn't respawn—I don't want to deal with all that again."

He bent over the dead leader's body.

A message popped up asking me if I wanted to participate in a lottery for warriors' pauldrons. I was about to say yes when Olgerd jumped in. "If nobody minds, I'd like to give them to Reger. He sacrificed himself, after all."

I agreed with his gesture and declined the invitation. Once everything was done, I went over to the body myself.

You completed a quest: Horala's Signet Ring.
To get your reward, go talk to the Supreme Vila.

"Okay, I got it," I said with a sigh of relief.

"Great," answered Olgerd. "Then I'm going to go see what I can find in the cave."

The raid was, in sum, a success. I finished with 270 gold in my pocket, not to mention the quests I'd completed.

"Good work, everyone," said Olgerd. "Let's head for the city before they can respawn. Hagen, are you coming with us?"

A thin voice interrupted us as Bulkins scrambled down the cliff and ran over to his belongings. "Hey, I'm back!"

"There you are," Uncle Fedor said cheerfully. "We're about to head back. I'll send a message, so Reger knows to meet us in the city, and I can grab his things, too."

"Thanks, guys, it was a pleasure doing business with you. I'm headed to the marsh so I can finish my quest for the vilas."

"Tell your bride I said hi," asked Olgerd. "She's a cutie."

"And from me, too," Bulkins said.

"Will do. Nobody minds if I send friend requests, do they?" I asked.

Uncle Fedor answered for everyone. "Go for it."

Elmilora was waiting for me by the tunnel.

"Have you done anything the last two days besides sitting around waiting for me?" I felt bad.

"At least you come back," she responded. "Soon, you're going to sail away, and then I have no idea when I'll see you again."

I tried to cheer her up. "I don't think it will be that long. Anyway, let's go talk to the Supreme."

We soon arrived at the familiar clearing, and I belted out my request. "I'm here to see the Supreme Vila on important and secret business."

With satisfaction, I heard the rustle of wings somewhere above me. It was a sound I'd already grown to appreciate.

"So, you did what I asked you to do? And faster than I expected." Her voice was deep and dripping with sarcasm.

"Anything for a friend," I said impertinently.

"Don't forget who you're talking to," the Supreme replied. I quickly sobered up. "Where's the ring?"

"Here you are, your highness," I said with a bow.

You completed a quest: Horala's Signet Ring.

You killed the pirate leader and got Horala's signet ring from him.

Reward:

900 experience

Captain Gul and his sailors will be released from the vilas' island.

10% affection for you from the Supreme Vila

The Supreme turned and quietly spoke to one of her guards. "Bring the four here, the ones who came a few days ago."

At the same time as she was speaking, I got another, no less heartening notification:

You unlocked Level 32!
Points ready to be distributed: 5

The Supreme looked back at me. "Also, by way of, oh, I don't know, a reward, let me tell you something. Maybe even a piece of advice. Be careful with the dryad quest. I'm not talking about the danger, though it's incredibly dangerous. Just be careful. There might be something going on that has nothing to do with what you were told, and you could end up with something completely different than what you're expecting."

I had no idea what she was talking about, and so I drew the only conclusion I could: that 10% affection bonus had already kicked in.

Four gloomy-looking men in jackets were brought up.

"Captain Gul?" I asked the gloomiest of them.

"The one and only," his deep voice answered.

"Great. Supreme, are they free to leave?"

She nodded. "Just as we agreed."

You completed a quest: Find the Captain.
To get your reward, go talk to Neils Holgerrson.

"Serafina," said the Supreme to one of the guards behind the throne. "Take these fools to Mettan. It's getting dark, so they'd get lost on their own."

"I can take them," I said.

"I don't doubt it. No, you go say goodbye to your bride. And don't forget, you have six months. When that time's up, I expect you back here."

"I'll be here. What choice do I have?"

It took us about twenty minutes to say goodbye. But finally everything had been said, cheeks had been kissed, vows had been reaffirmed, and I was back at the Mettan gate. Once there, I was shocked at how many dwarves were on their way in.

"What's going on?" I asked Bulkins, who I found nearby.

"Their clan is going over to the other side, to Merastia. They want to kill the king and take his sword," he answered as he munched on an apple.

"They have nothing better to do?" I shook my head.

It was true. The dwarves were all from Hew Orcs, My Axe, a clan I'd already come across, and they were dragging wood around, building rafts, launching some kind of ships, and loudly arguing about who would get to the other shore first. Two of them, Artemi and Partavi, were standing by the pier and arguing especially loudly.

"You have no idea how cool I am," shouted Artemi. "Do you know how much money I get? I milked two clans for all they were worth."

"And you're proud of that?" shrieked Partavi. I couldn't tell if it was a he or a she since dwarves all look the same without their beards. "Who cares about money? It's all about being cool!"

"I'm trying to tell you how cool I am! I could take out anyone. You set them up, I'll knock them down."

"Set them up? Knock them down? I have a butt made out of bones!"

It was completely true. He (or she?) had a bone plate attached to the seat of his (or her?) pants in an apparent attempt to ward off more shameful wounds. I imagined it also made sitting in wet or cold areas more comfortable as well.

Unfortunately, as they argued, the first group set off in search of the Skeleton King's sword. It was followed by the second, and then even the third.

I shook my head, looked at the quickly darkening sky, and turned to Bulkins before leaving to see the port master.

"Dwarfs—what can you do?"

Mr. Holgerrson was celebrating the end of the workday by chugging away at some ale.

"A-a-ah, it's you, bowsprit and boatswain. Good work. Old man Gul came by and told me about your adventures.

You completed a quest: Find the Captain.

Reward:

700 experience

Significantly discounted passage on the Firefly

"You kept your word, so I'll keep mine." Niels pounded his glass back onto the table. "Want some ale? It's fantastic, by the Kraken!"

"No, thanks. So what kind of discount do I get on the boat?"

"Seeing as how you found that drunk, oh, and that cuttlefish Glopkins came by—"

"I have the cutlass you gave me, too."

"...plus the cutlass. A day's passage on the Firefly will cost you, let's say...2500 gold."

"How much?" I thought I must have heard wrong.

"Why that cheap? Well, you're a good person, even if you are a landlubber."

"Cheap? I thought we'd agree to 500!"

"You're no bastard of mine! Seventy-five percent is a huge discount."

"No, it isn't!"

"Watch your mouth," Neils said soberly and quietly. "That's as cheap as it goes."

I realized that there was no bargaining with him. Fine. I had enough gold for a few days, and then I'd see. On the other hand, maybe I wouldn't go at all. The game was fun and all, but I didn't really have much left to play for. My articles were written, and nothing else was keeping me there.

"Fine, you can be greedy if you want," I said, deciding to throw a parting shot at Holgerrson. "And I even took out the pirates for you!"

"You did?" The port master shouted for joy. "Well done yet again!"

You completed a quest: Get Rid of the Land Pirates.

Reward:

1100 experience

800 gold

An item from Neils Holgerrson's storehouse

+10% to your reputation in Mettan

"You're incredible. Fine—2000 gold a day. And here, I'm happy to give you this."

Ice Helmet

Protection: 210

+11 to strength

+14% protection from cold

+7% to dodge ability

Durability: 220/220

Minimum level for use: 32

"Thanks, Neils. I'm out then."

"Drop by when you're around these parts." The sailor waved. "Maybe you'll stay for a bit of ale after all?"

I declined and went outside. It was almost completely dark. The first of the dwarves' watercraft had reached the other bank, and their first ranks were already fighting. It was about time for me to head back to reality, but I didn't want to leave with all the hustle and bustle around me. Instead, I decided to go about 300 meters outside the city and log out somewhere nice on the bank of the river.

I left the city and was shocked by a notification:

Attention. Euiikh, a player you blacklisted, is nearby.

Well, that was the last person I expected to see, but see him I did. To be honest, the only feeling I could muster up for Euiikh and his henchmen was pity. They looked something like how I imagined the French in 1812 and the Germans in 1941 must have looked when they got to Moscow: miserable, impoverished, and pathetic. They had each dropped maybe three or four levels.

Each of the henchmen had one piece of equipment, while Euiikh himself had all of three. He even had a sword, though it wasn't much to look at. The other two were armed with sticks.

"You killed someone and split their stuff between the three of you?" I asked them.

One of the orcs nodded, though Euiikh had a question of his own.

"You turned all of us in to the Hounds?"

"No, not all of you; just you, Euiikh. I didn't say anything about your boys."

The orcs exchanged a quick glance behind Euiikh's back.

"How did you get here? It's quite a ways from where I last killed you."

One of the orcs took the time to explain. "We got a port scroll from someone. Lucky find. Everyone was after us back there, so we figured there might be fewer people here. And now you..."

"What are you talking to him for? You two surround him," hissed Euiikh as he advanced toward me.

320

"You really want to do this?" I asked. "I'll take all three of you out in a minute flat with those rags and sticks. Maybe not earlier, but now it'll be a piece of cake. What do you get out of this?"

"I'll make sure everything's fair." A voice wafted in out of the darkness. "I don't like when it's three on one."

A player in a cloak and hood walked out of the forest onto the road.

Euiikh howled in frustration. "This again? Who are you? What do you care? It's not fair!"

"I'm nobody, just a passerby," said the player, whose name was Wanderer. "And I told you, I don't like when it's three against one. What don't you understand about that?"

"Hey," said Gryk, one of Euiikh's friends, to me. "So the Hounds only care about him?"

"Yep," I said. "You should have just surrendered to them."

"Come on, man, let's get out of here," Gryk said to the second orc, who nodded in reply.

"We're cool with you?" asked Gryk, this time talking to me.

"What's done is done. We're even already."

"Where are you going, you swine?" roared Euiikh. "You rats!"

"Screw you!" Gryk yelled back at him. "All we got with you was one problem after another. And don't come after us, or we'll kill you, too."

The orcs turned and sprinted down the road in the direction of the forest.

"You should leave, too," I said to Euiikh. "You've been getting on my nerves these past two weeks. Why should I waste any more time on you?"

He looked at me, glanced at Wanderer, thought for a second, and disgustedly walked off in the opposite direction as his former companions. I could tell he meant to give Mettan a wide berth.

"I was going to go watch the river in the moonlight," I told Wanderer. "Want to come sit with me?"

"Why not?" he answered. "The Great River at night is a thing of beauty."

"We walked to the river bank and sat down on a log a few paces from the water. It was completely dark, though the sky was littered with stars. Fires burned on the far shore, and the sound of battle and dwarf curses drifted toward us.

"If this were real life, we'd have mosquitos eating us alive," I said thoughtfully.

"What's going on over there?" asked Wanderer with a glance across the water.

"Dwarves going for the sword."

"How many?"

"A hundred and fifty or so."

"They won't make it to the palace," said Wanderer placidly. "Three hundred or three hundred and fifty might, but a hundred and fifty definitely won't."

"They're tenacious," I said dubiously.

"Not tenacious enough." Wanderer obviously knew what he was talking about.

"Why were you looking for me?" I asked him.

"You have a crown belonging to the dead landlord, and I really need it." His explanation made it sound like it was the most natural thing in the world.

"Why couldn't you get it yourself? I mean, I'm not being rude; I'm just asking. The quest isn't hard."

"No, it isn't, but the chances of getting the crown are really low. It's just random, really. I've killed him a hundred times already and still haven't gotten it. He just doesn't want to give it to me."

Well, wouldn't you know? I'd gotten lucky! Isn't that how it happens... "I figured it was something like that."

"How did you guess?" asked Wanderer.

"It was strange how Marion responded when I said the word 'wanderer,' and she was also weird about the crown. When you came out on the road, I figured it out."

"Yes, she's helping me. So what about the crown?"

"Open your exchange."

I waited for the exchange window and gave Wanderer the crown.

"What do you want in return?" he asked. "Money, items?"

"Nothing," I said with a laugh.

I couldn't always be looking out for myself. Some things I needed to just do for other people.

"Oh, come on. I don't believe in people like that."

"And rightly so, but I like nonconformists. Okay, let's do this. I'll reserve the right to ask you one question and request help one time. You have to answer truthfully, and you have to help me. How does that sound?"

"Deal."

I thought I could tell that Wanderer was smiling under his hood.

"I ask Mesmerta, the Radiant Goddess, to bear witness to this agreement," I said quickly.

Besides a shooting star falling from the sky, nothing happened.

"That's one way of doing it," grunted Wanderer. "Look at you go."

Wanderer wants to add you as a friend. Accept?"

I accepted.

"You know, Wanderer, this isn't any of my business, but I want you to know." I decided to do one more and maybe my last good deed in Fayroll. "They're looking for you."

"I know. The Hounds."

"Not just them. All the clans they're friends with are, too, so be careful."

"You don't want to ask why?" Wanderer's voice was tinged with irony.

"Nope. I'll hang onto my question. And you hang onto your head."

"I'll do my best. Where are you off to?"

"Real life. I have a plane to catch."

"Where are you going?"

"Spain. Catalonia."

"A fine country. Have a good flight."

"Thanks. And you try to stay alive."

I looked back over the surface of the water one more time, glanced up at the starry sky, and gazed at the lights flickering on the other side of the river. We could hear the faint sound of swords clashing, not to mention voices coming from the city.

"You're terrible at the game, and you're just as bad at sports. Not like me!"

"Who cares about sports?" The two dwarves were still trying to figure out which of them was the most dwarfish.

"Life goes on," I said.

"Yep," said Wanderer with a nod.

I hit the button to log out.

As soon as I clambered out of the capsule, I checked the clock. It was 9:20.

"I made it," I said with a sigh of relief before starting my packing.

By the time Elvira burst into the apartment ready to shred anyone she found, I was sitting in the hallway next to my packed suitcase.

She barked an order and marched out into the stairwell. "Why are you still sitting there? Let's go!"

I walked around the apartment one more time to make sure I hadn't left any lights on, stopping to linger by the capsule. There, in that capsule, Wanderer was sitting on the bank of the river thinking about something. Somewhere else, in the same capsule, were Sir Gunther von Richter; Krolina, the carefree lady of his heart; shrewd Gerv; prudent Reineke Lis; Elmilora, who was waiting for me; and everyone else I'd met over the course of those two weeks. For a second I wanted to send Elvira off onto the steppes or somewhere in the mountains to the far north and head back to Fayroll.

"Kif, are you coming? We have to go!" Elvira's voice pulled me back, and the fleeting desire disappeared.

I closed the door to the apartment, turned the key in the lock, and pressed the elevator button.

End of book one

If you enjoyed this book, please consider leaving a review. That will help us promote the LitRPG genre and translate the rest of the series as quickly as possible.

Thanks so much!
    A. Vasilyev and the LitWorld team

Visit our website at http://litworld.info and subscribe to our newsletter to hear about all our upcoming releases for Fayroll and other great fantasy series!

Book recommendations

If you enjoyed this story then please look at the rest of the other Fayroll stories and some other books by great authors.

An ordinary young boy finds himself in a life and death struggle as he must adapt to his new environment. In order to survive after accidentally falling through a portal to another world, Andy must undergo an ancient ritual to become a Dragon. Read this exciting adventure now by the best-selling author Alex Sapegin. Becoming the Dragon is available now.

I want to recommend Realm of Arkon, a great series written by a friend of mine: G. Akella (Georgy Smorodinsky). He is one of the most popular and best-selling LitRPG authors in Russia. Book one is currently available for free on Amazon.

I would also like to recommend D.Rus who is another of the best-selling LitRPG Fantasy authors in Russia. His work is fantastic and very well received in Russia.

Don't forget if you enjoyed this book to join our Facebook group for Fayroll. You can find lots of competitions and information relating to the series and the advenutres of Kif.

About the Author

Andrey Vasilyev

At times, he feels he was meant to be an innkeeper someplace on the outskirts of Bree in J. R. R. Tolkien's Middle-earth. However, in real life, Andrey Vasilyev is a much-celebrated Moscow-based author, as well as one of the originators of the relatively new, yet insanely popular, LitRPG genre that blends cyberpunk, classic sci-fi, and fantasy.

By his own admission, he started writing in his late 30's and only *"because there was nothing handy to read,"* but after his first two books gained nearly instant acclaim, he had to give serious thought to changing his current banking career to that of a professional writer. Fortunately for his readers, who had voted his debut novel *More Than a Game* the "Best Book of the Year 2014," he never looked back.

Over the next few years, he continued work on his now-bestselling *Fayroll* series, maintained a blog, and participated in variouscollaborative projects. Andrey is also the author of *The Raven's Flock* and *The Arch* series, which will soon be available in English.

When he is not writing his intricately crafted, action-packed stories, he enjoys playing online games with his son or rummaging through second-hand bookshops and bookstalls in search of rare editions or personal favorites.

Endnotes

[1] An elite, upper-class region outside of Moscow.

[2] A Russian term referring to the high season.

[3] "Club of the Funny and Inventive People," an incredibly popular youth movement in Russia that combined team games with theatrical elements.

[4] A kind of beggar.

[5] A working-class neighborhood in Moscow.

[6] A prestigious suburb of Moscow.

[7] Imperial imposters in Russian history.

[8] A city car produced by Daewoo, a Korean car manufacturer.

[9] A street in Moscow.

[10] Russian parliament.

[11] A famous False Dmitry.

[12] A short German sword from the 14th—16th centuries.

[13] A small home in the countryside.

[14] A visa offered by a Schengen Area country that is good for travel throughout the entire area.

[15] A traditional Russian folk instrument similar to the banjo.

Made in the USA
Middletown, DE
01 June 2018